ADVANCE ACCLAIM FOR
WAKING HOURS

"This smart, spooky, high-stakes mystery engaged my mind and my spirit. Tommy and Dani's battle against the seen and unseen forces rising in East Salem has only just begun, but I'm fully invested in their journey."

—ERIN HEALY, BEST-SELLING AUTHOR OF
THE PROMISES SHE KEEPS AND *THE BAKER'S WIFE*

"A strong debut full of suspense, romance and supernatural mystery. A fine start to the series."

—ANDREW KLAVAN, BEST-SELLING AUTHOR OF
TRUE CRIME AND THE HOMELANDERS SERIES

"One word describes *Waking Hours* by Wiehl and Nelson—*WOW!* A gut wrenching ride of supernatural suspense that left me breathless and wanting more. The book was a reminder that the battle between God and Satan is not over. Highly recommended!"

—COLLEEN COBLE, BEST-SELLING AUTHOR OF
LONESTAR ANGEL AND THE ROCK HARBOR SERIES

"A gripping plot, intriguing characters, supernatural underpinnings, and a splash of romance make *Waking Hours* a fast-paced and thoroughly enjoyable read. I want the next book in the series now!"

—JAMES L. RUBART, AWARD-WINNING AUTHOR OF *ROOMS*

ACCLAIM FOR LIS WIEHL'S
TRIPLE THREAT SERIES

"Only a brilliant lawyer, prosecutor, and journalist like Lis Wiehl could put together a mystery this thrilling! The incredible characters and nonstop twists will leave you mesmerized. Open [*Face of Betrayal*] and find a comfortable seat because you won't want to put it down!"

—E. D. HILL, FOX NEWS ANCHOR

"Three smart women crack the big cases! Makes perfect sense to me. [*Face of Betrayal*] blew me away!"

— JEANINE PIRRO, FORMER DA; HOSTS
THE CW'S DAYTIME COURT TELEVISION
REALITY SHOW *JUDGE JEANINE PIRRO*

"Who killed loudmouth radio guy Jim Fate? The game is afoot! *Hand of Fate* is a fun thriller, taking you inside the media world and the justice system—scary places to be!"

—BILL O'REILLY, FOX TV AND RADIO ANCHOR

"As a television crime writer and producer, I expect novels to deliver pulsepounding tales with major twists. *Hand of Fate* delivers big time."

—PAM VEASEY, WRITER AND EXECUTIVE PRODUCER OF *CSI: NY*

"Book three in the wonderful Triple Threat Club series is a fast-paced thriller full of twists and turns that will keep you guessing until the end. What makes these books stand out for me is my ability to identify so easily with Allison, Nic and Cassidy. I truly care about what happens to each of them, and the challenges they face this time are heart-wrenching and realistic. I highly recommend!"

—DEBORAH SINCLAIRE, EDITOR-IN-CHIEF,
BOOK-OF-THE-MONTH CLUB AND THE STEPHEN KING LIBRARY

"Beautiful, successful and charismatic on the outside but underneath a twisted killer. She's brilliant and crazy and comes racing at the reader with knives and a smile. The most chilling villain you'll meet . . . because she could live next door to you."

—DR. DALE ARCHER, CLINICAL PSYCHIATRIST, REGARDING *HEART OF ICE*

WAKING HOURS

THE EAST SALEM TRILOGY
BOOK ONE

LIS WIEHL
WITH PETE NELSON

THOMAS NELSON
Since 1798

NASHVILLE   DALLAS   MEXICO CITY   RIO DE JANEIRO

Published in Nashville, Tennessee. Thomas Nelson is a registered trademark of Thomas Nelson, Inc.

Page design by Mandi Cofer.

Thomas Nelson, Inc., books may be purchased in bulk for educational, business, fund-raising, or sales promotional use. For information, please e-mail SpecialMarkets@ThomasNelson.com.

Scripture quotations are from:

The REVISED STANDARD VERSION of the Bible. Copyright © 1946, 1952, 1971, 1973 by the Division of Christian Education of the National Council of the Churches of Christ in the U.S.A. Used by permission.

HOLY BIBLE: NEW INTERNATIONAL VERSION®. © 1973, 1978, 1984 by International Bible Society. Used by permission of Zondervan Publishing House. All rights reserved.

The KING JAMES VERSION of the Holy Bible.

Publisher's Note: This novel is a work of fiction. Names, characters, places, and incidents are either products of the author's imagination or used fictitiously. All characters are fictional, and any similarity to people living or dead is purely coincidental.

ISBN 978-0-8499-4889-3 (IE)

Library of Congress Cataloging-in-Publication Data

Wiehl, Lis W.
  Waking hours / Lis Wiehl, with Pete Nelson.
    p. cm. -- (The East Salem trilogy ; bk. 1)
  ISBN 978-1-59554-940-2 (hardcover)
1. Supernatural--Fiction. 2. Murder--Fiction. 3. Forensic psychiatrists--Fiction. 4. High school students--Fiction. I. Nelson, Peter, 1953- II. Title.
  PS3623.I382W35 2011
  813'.6--dc22

2011021162

Printed in the United States of America

11 12 13 14 15 16 QGF 6 5 4

To Dani and Jacob,
with all my love,
from Mom

FRIDAY,
OCTOBER 15

1.

Tommy Gunderson woke in the middle of the night to the howling of the wind and the siren of his home's security system. *Probably an animal,* he thought, still half dreaming. But the system deployed a pattern recognition program calibrated to avoid false alarms from deer or raccoons. The alarm meant an intruder of the two-legged kind, intent unknown.

The swoop of the alarm seemed to deepen as Tommy threw the covers off and rolled out of bed. He pulled on a hooded black sweatshirt to match the black sweatpants he slept in and stepped sockless into a pair of running shoes. Fully awake now, he strode down the hallway to the kitchen, where he tapped on the space bar of his computer's keyboard and, when the machine lit up, clicked on the video feed to see what was going on. Thermal imaging revealed the orange heat signature of a human, crouched low by the edge of his fishpond.

Tommy moved quickly down the hallway again and threw open the door to his father's bedroom. Still sleeping, present and accounted for. He'd given the older man's caregiver the night off. Whoever was crouching by the pond was definitely uninvited.

Tommy didn't like uninvited guests.

He walked swiftly to the back door, grabbed the heavy black flashlight that hung from a hook by its strap, and hid it in the pouch of his sweatshirt. The moon was full, casting light on the yard, across the pond, and out toward the woods beyond.

He felt his heart rate quicken and was bracing himself for the cold when his cell phone rang from the kitchen counter where he'd left it to charge.

"Mr. Gunderson?" a woman's voice said.

"You got him."

"Sorry to wake you—this is the East Salem police. We have an automated alert from your system. Is everything all right?"

"You guys are fast," he said, keeping his voice low. In a community of wealthy estates like his, the police took special care to assist the residents whose taxes paid their salaries and funded their children's schools.

"Do you need assistance?" the dispatcher asked. "We already have a car in the area."

He quickly considered. "If it's no bother. I'll meet him at the gate."

Armed with his flashlight, Tommy went to the front door, tapped the security code on the keypad to disarm the system, then stepped out into the darkness. He walked briskly, keeping to the shadows, rounded the side of the house, and trotted up the driveway. Gold and rust-colored leaves had started to drop from the trees. He avoided stepping on them, lest he alert the intruder.

Tommy recognized the cop in the squad car waiting at the gate. Frank DeGidio, like most of the local cops, worked out at Tommy's gym. Frank was a burly bear of a man with a swarthy complexion, thick black eyebrows, a permanent five o'clock shadow, and bloodshot eyes.

"What's he doing by the pond?" DeGidio asked, staring in the direction of the intruder. Tommy's house sat on ten landscaped acres, with another twelve acres of woods beyond the cleared lot. The half-acre pond was at the edge of the woods, about a hundred yards from the house.

"I stocked it with rainbow," Tommy replied. "Maybe he's fishing?"

"Without a license," DeGidio rasped, "at three in the morning? That's gotta be illegal."

"Probably a kid," Tommy guessed. "Just give him a warning and a ride home."

DeGidio opened the trunk of the squad car and handed Tommy a Kevlar vest. Tommy hesitated.

"Probably a kid, but you never know," the cop said.

"Does this make me look fat?" Tommy asked.

"Donuts make you look fat," DeGidio said. "I speak from experience."

The vest fit tightly over Tommy's muscular physique. The cop adjusted his jacket to make sure he could reach both the Glock 9 on his right hip and the Taser on his left.

They moved quietly, Tommy leading the way. As they neared the water's edge, Tommy saw that whoever was there was dressed in white.

Ten feet away, their presence still undetected, he saw that the intruder was a woman. Stepping closer, he heard a low animal-like sound.

"Can I help you?" he asked, exchanging glances with DeGidio.

She turned. She was elderly, probably well into her nineties, her pale face a desiccated mask of leathery wrinkles. Coarse black whiskers protruded from her chin. Her thin, cracked lips curled inward, her hair a wild snarl of unruly white wisps, so thin that in spots the moonlight shone off her age-spotted scalp. Her eyes were dark and watery, darting about. She was barefoot. Her nightgown was muddy. A strand of spittle hung from the corner of her mouth.

Tommy knelt down beside her and spoke softly. "It must be past your bedtime," he said. "I think we need to find out where you live."

She paid no attention to him but shook her head violently back and forth, speaking to herself in a low mutter. "No, no, no . . ."

He leaned in closer.

"Luck's fairy tale can go the real diamond."

"Ma'am?" Tommy said, louder now.

No response.

DeGidio made a circular motion around his ear. "Alzheimer's," he said. "That or rabies."

Tommy tried again. "Can we give you a ride home?"

This time she looked at him. *"Lux ferre,"* she said, her eyes widening. *"Le ali congoleare di mondo."*

"Somebody's off her meds," the cop said. "What's she saying?"

"Something about luck's fairy," Tommy said. "Hang on."

He found his cell phone, tapped the camcorder icon, and held the phone a few inches from the woman's face. It was too dark to get a video image, but at least he could record her words.

"Good idea," DeGidio said. "I'm guessing she left her ID in her other nightgown."

The old woman turned to Tommy. "Do you know what I've got?" she asked, suddenly sounding quite lucid.

"What, dear?" he said. "Do you have something you want to show me?"

She extended her bony fingers toward him, cupped together the way a child might hold her hands in prayer. She opened them.

"A dead frog?" Tommy said.

"Take it."

"Thank you." He let her place the frog in his hands. It was cold and slimy and reeked.

"Do you believe in extispicium?" she asked.

"I'm sorry?"

The frog's entrails spilled from its belly. It had been ripped open, probably by an owl or a hawk. Unless she'd ripped it open herself.

"Extispicium," she repeated. "Do you see?"

"Do I see what?" he asked her. "What is it you want me to see?"

"This," she said. *"Ecce haruspices."*

DeGidio shone his flashlight on the disemboweled frog in Tommy's hands. The old woman poked through the frog's innards with her index finger, as if looking for a lost penny. She was shaking her head even more ferociously now, and muttering intently. She looked up.

"These are only the first to go," she whispered. "You'll be the last." She looked at Tommy again and seemed to recognize him. "You play football," she said.

"Not anymore."

"Ecce extispicium!" she said, now growling and looking Tommy in the eye. *"Ecce haruspices!"*

"That sounds like Latin," DeGidio said.

Tommy shifted the dead frog to his left hand, wiped his right hand on the back of his sweatpants, and touched the old woman lightly on the arm.

"Let's go back to the house and get you some warm clothes," he said.

"Lux ferre!" she screamed, rising suddenly from where she crouched

6

by the water, springing toward Tommy and locking her thin web of fingers around his throat.

She bowled him over, driving him into the weeds.

Her nails pressed in against his windpipe as he grabbed her thin wrists. Tommy bench-pressed 350 pounds easily, but somehow he found it impossible to break the old woman's grip. He pulled as hard as he could, trying to throw her off of him.

He needed oxygen. Blood to the brain. His head was about to explode. *Where is her strength coming from? I'm losing consciousness. I'm dying . . .*

Suddenly Tommy felt a sharp electric buzzing. His vision sizzled, and he felt pain in his fingertips, his toes, and his hair. Something screeched in his ears. He smelled burnt rubber. Then the old woman went limp and fell on top of him, still holding him by the throat.

He pulled her hands from around his neck and rolled onto his stomach.

Tommy gasped for air and coughed violently, turning on his side now to see Frank DeGidio removing the Taser darts from where he'd fired them into the old woman's back.

"You all right?" he asked.

Tommy nodded, still unable to speak.

"Sorry about that," the cop said. "I couldn't get her without getting you too, as long as her hands completed the circuit."

"That's all right," Tommy said, rubbing his throat where her nails had scratched him and coughing again. He glanced over his shoulder to see an ambulance flashing its lights at the gate. "What was that? How . . . ?" He got to his feet while the cop bound the old woman's hands behind her back with orange plastic flex cuffs.

"Adrenaline," DeGidio said.

Two EMTs took charge of his intruder. As they got her sedated and resting comfortably in the back of the ambulance, a third person examined Tommy's throat and advised him to wash his scratches with a disinfectant.

"You're lucky her fingernails weren't longer, dude," the man said with a gravel voice and an accent that sounded like he was from Texas or Oklahoma.

He looked more like a biker than a doctor, in black boots and jeans and a tattered jean jacket with the sleeves cut off. His arms and chest were tattooed and he wore silver chains around his neck. But after all the other strange happenings tonight, why not a biker-doctor too?

"You hold fast," he said, and headed back toward the ambulance.

DeGidio reappeared then and told Tommy they were already making calls to all the nearby nursing homes.

"We'll figure out where she belongs," he said. "My cousin works in a nursing home—she says this stuff happens all the time. A lot of old people get mellow, but some just turn violent. They don't know what they're doing anymore. It's like all the anger they've suppressed their whole lives comes out at the end."

"That's one explanation," Tommy said.

"We'll take care of her," DeGidio said. "Just for the record, you pressing charges? Trespassing? Assault?"

"Nope," Tommy said, watching as the ambulance pulled away. "Just let me know who she is when you figure it out."

"Will do."

Tommy walked him to his car.

"You'd be shocked at how much ground folks with Alzheimer's can cover when they get the notion," the cop said. "You ever see her before tonight?"

"Not to my knowledge," Tommy said. "She seemed to know who I was."

"Everybody knows who you are." DeGidio opened the door to his car. "I'm guessing you probably don't want the boys at the gym knowing a hundred-pound old lady beat you like a redheaded stepchild . . ."

Tommy offered a friendly smile, but something about the woman deeply disturbed him . . . a feeling that she hadn't arrived in his backyard by chance. He could have been killed tonight, yet somehow he knew she hadn't come to kill him.

"Fuggedaboutit," DeGidio said. "What happens in Tommy Gunderson's backyard *stays* in Tommy Gunderson's backyard."

"Thanks for stopping by," Tommy said, feeling his throat again.

"Anytime."

The officer drove away, and Tommy walked back to the edge of the pond. He saw the frog the old woman had given him, floating belly up, torn open, guts exposed.

He crouched low to examine it again. Why had she wanted him to see it? Her words, if they were Latin as DeGidio suspected, might have been the genus or species. What was she looking for?

It made no sense to him, but he supposed it might make sense to somebody else. She'd been clear about one thing—the message she wanted him to understand had something to do with the disemboweled frog.

He reached down to pick it up, thinking he could throw it in the freezer and send it to a biologist or laboratory. But when his fingers touched the amphibian, they passed right through it, and the animal that minutes earlier had been solid in his hand simply dissolved like bath salts, a murky gray cloud that dissipated in the dark water. He pulled his hand back reflexively. He found a stick and stirred the water, then threw the stick into the pond when there was nothing more to see.

These were the first to go, she'd said. *"You'll be the last."*

He was nearly back in bed when his cell phone rang.

"Tommy, it's Frank—you're still up, right? I didn't wake you?"

"Still up," Tommy told the cop.

"You said to call when we found out who she is. We got a missing persons from High Ridge Manor. Her name's Abigail Gardener. You know her?"

"Not personally," Tommy said. "She used to be the town historian."

"You okay?"

"A little shaken, to tell the truth," Tommy said. "The doctor said I was lucky her fingernails weren't longer."

"You already saw a doctor?" DeGidio asked.

"The one on the ambulance," Tommy said. "Blue jean vest and tattoos? Looked sort of like a biker?"

"What are you talking about?" the cop said. "There wasn't any doctor there—just the two EMTs, Jose and Martin. And nobody who looked like a biker."

Tommy thanked Frank and said good night. Then he went to his computer, hoping his surveillance system might solve the mystery. His property was covered by both high-definition video and infrared cameras capable of registering the heat signatures of warm-bodied visitors. The video feed showed only darkness at first, and then, once the ambulance arrived with its headlights pointed directly at the camera and its lights flashing brightly in the night, he saw only silhouettes crossing back and forth, making it impossible to count the number of people present, even in slow motion.

The infrared imaging was slightly more useful but still inconclusive. It clearly showed his own silhouette, and Frank's, and the old woman's, but once the ambulance arrived, the bright red heat signatures from the engine and the headlights again made it hard to sort out what he was seeing. Sometimes it looked like there were five images, sometimes six. He even saw some sort of digital shadow or negative ghost image in blue, flickering in and out of view.

He was tired and he'd given it too much thought already.

He knew what he knew—he'd spoken to a man who looked like a biker. Frank just must have missed him.

2.

Dani Harris was still in bed when her phone rang. The journal article she'd been reading, "Genetic Markers for Gender-Specific Disorders on the Autism/Asperger's Scale Among the Huli Tribesmen of Papua, New Guinea," by a team of researchers from Australia, lay open on her stomach. Her reading light was still on and her comforter, which she'd taken from the linen chest for the first time since the previous spring, had slid to the floor, where she found her cat, Arlo, curled up in the middle of it. She'd awakened from a bad dream sometime after two and read herself back to sleep.

The phone rang a second time. Her caller ID read "John Foley." Her boss.

"I didn't wake you, did I?" he asked.

"I was up," she lied. She tried to remember her dream, but she could retain only a vague image. Her father had been holding a stone in his hands, as if he wanted to show it to her.

"Sorry to call so early," John apologized. "Listen—I got a call from Irene. They want you at the Mt. Kisco office."

Irene Scotto was the district attorney for New York's Westchester County.

"What's it about?"

"Homicide," John said. "The victim appears to have been a juvenile. The only suspect is too. You turned on your TV yet?"

"Not yet," Dani said.

"It's a weird one," John said. "You can do this, Dani."

11

"Okay," Dani said, mystified by his encouragement. Not that he wasn't normally encouraging, but this sounded like a farewell. "See you there?"

"Uh, yeah," John said. "Maybe." He hung up.

Maybe?

Once she cleared her head and felt slightly more awake, she realized she needed to rethink her wardrobe. If she was going to spend the day at the DA's office, she needed to wear something other than the blue jeans and sweater she'd had in mind.

She showered quickly, dried her hair on high and ironed out the frizzies, applied her makeup minimally, and told herself it would have to do. She took a pair of lightweight wool dress slacks from the closet and a black cashmere turtleneck from a drawer.

As she dressed, she paused to look at the framed photograph on her dresser, a group picture of sixteen African boys lined up in order of height, with Dani in the middle. The smaller boys were smiling naturally. The older boys' smiles looked forced. It had been three years since she'd seen them.

She looked at another photograph, one she'd taken of her parents on the runway of a small airport in the African bush, the two of them squinting into the sun and grinning, palm and towering Kakum trees in the background. It was the last time she'd seen them as well.

She found a pair of black boots in the closet and stepped into them, then zipped up the sides. A thin gold chain and a pair of gold earrings, shaped like leaves, and she was finished dressing.

In the kitchen Dani put on a pot of coffee, threw a cup of milk, a banana, a handful of organic blueberries, and a measuring spoon of whey powder into the blender along with a half cup of Greek yogurt, then hit Liquefy.

"No-ooo!"

Too late. She'd forgotten to put the lid on the blender jar, and before she could turn the switch off, a few ounces of smoothie splattered the counter, the backsplash, and, unfortunately, her clothes.

The day was off to a great start.

She ran upstairs to change. By the time she returned to the kitchen, the coffee was done, so she filled a cup and dumped it in with the rest of her smoothie to kill two birds with one stone.

Dani admitted to being an indifferent cook. Her sister, Beth, who was far more accomplished at the girlie arts, suggested that in*ept* or in*edible* was more to the point.

She turned on her kitchen television as she sipped, clicking to the Westchester News channel. She read the crawl at the bottom of the screen: Gruesome murder on Bull's Rock Hill in East Salem, Northern Westchester.

Bull's Rock Hill was only four miles from her house.

On the TV screen, she watched a live shot from a helicopter of police activity below, cop car and ambulance lights flashing. Then a montage of the northern Westchester County landscape, elegant horse farms with split-rail fences, opulent mansions with slate roofs and circular driveways, wooded hillsides resplendent in the jacquard weave of peak autumn colors.

It was the shot TV news programs always used when there was a story in East Salem, the rolling woodlands and tree-lined dirt roads, all within fifty miles of New York City. The stock images depicted farm stands, waterfalls, polo matches, reservoirs with pairs of swans swimming, discreet pubs and trattorias where loving and attractive couples dined by candlelight. Sometimes it seemed to Dani as if the TV news producers never bothered to send camera crews to the actual locations but used images from travel brochures instead. They never showed the houses where people of modest means lived. Whenever something terrible happened in Westchester, the headlines were large font and bold, followed by exclamation marks, as if it were inconceivable that something heinous could happen in homes so large and well furnished.

She reached for the remote control to turn up the sound, but before she could, her phone rang again. Was the whole day going to go like this?

"Dani, it's Claire."

She'd known Claire Dorsett since she'd babysat for Claire's son back when Dani was in high school, Liam was a toddler, and Claire was a young mother. Now the two women were in the same book club . . . but from the distress she could hear in Claire's voice, Dani knew her friend wasn't calling about *Moby Dick*.

13

"What's up, Claire?"

"I know I shouldn't be calling you," Claire said. "But Jeffrey's out of the country, and I just couldn't think of anyone else. This is unbelievable."

"Claire, slow down," Dani said. "Tell me what's happening."

"It's Liam," she said. "They said they just want to ask him questions. It's too horrible . . ."

"What's horrible?" Dani asked. "Who's *they*?"

On her television she saw a picture of a crime scene, followed by a picture of East Salem High School, a large modern brick building that Dani thought looked more like a technology company's corporate headquarters than a public school.

"The police," Claire said. "They took Liam to the district attorney's office. I'm headed there now."

On the TV Dani saw a wooded crime scene, police cars, and a strand of yellow DO NOT CROSS police tape flapping in the wind. The crawl read GIRL'S BODY FOUND.

"This is about Bull's Rock Hill?" she asked.

"Apparently," Claire said, sobbing now. "I don't know. I don't know anything."

"Take a deep breath," Dani said. "I honestly haven't heard anything. Was Liam home last night?"

"I don't know," Claire said. "I thought so, but I have trouble sleeping when Jeffrey's out of town, so I took a sleeping pill."

It wasn't hard for Dani to imagine the scene at the high school. The police probably had a squad car in the high school parking lot with the flashers on to generate as much wireless conversation among the students as possible . . . evidence they could potentially use later.

Dani tried to think of what to say. Claire was a friend, but Dani was a forensic psychiatrist whose firm consulted with the DA's office. Her boss, John Foley, and his senior partner, Sam Ralston, both psychologists, had hired her because she was young and female and a psychiatrist.

"Claire, before you say anything else," Dani said, "I have to remind you, I'm an officer of the court. If there's anything you want to say to me that you don't want included as evidence, don't say it. I want to help you, but be really clear about who I work for. Do you understand what I'm saying?"

"I do," Claire said. "I do. Of course. I just don't know where else to turn. Why did they take him to the DA's office?"

"They may just want to talk to him where things are a little less crazy," Dani advised her friend. "What did Liam say when he called you?"

"He didn't call me," Claire said, and began to cry again. "He called his *coach*. His coach called me."

"Who's his coach?"

"His trainer or whatever. Tommy Gunderson."

"He called Tommy Gunderson?"

"Tommy called me and said he was meeting Liam at the district attorney's office. I'm going there as soon as . . . Why? Do you know him?"

Dani's pulse quickened.

Probably just the caffeine kicking in.

"We went to high school together," she said. "Let me see what I can find out."

She heard a beep.

"I have another call," she told her friend. "I have to take it. I'll be in touch, Claire. Be strong."

Dani turned off the television, donned her Tory Burch trench coat, pulled the kitchen door closed behind her, and return-dialed the number for the call she'd missed as she headed for her car.

Stuart Metz answered. He was the assistant prosecutor for Northern Westchester, and when Irene Scotto needed something, Stuart was usually the one who asked for it. He was lean and wiry and surprisingly awkward for someone who'd graduated from Harvard Law.

"Good morning, Stuart," Dani said.

"*Good* isn't the word I'd use," Stuart said. "You heard about Bull's Rock Hill?"

"Just what was on television," Dani said. "What do we know?"

"More than we want to," Stuart said. "Are you on your laptop?"

"I'm in the car," she said, turning the key in the ignition of the black BMW 335i coupe she'd inherited from her father.

"So am I. Don't log in on a full stomach," he said. "This one's hideous. Probably bled out between one and two o'clock this morning. Almost beheaded. Banerjee just got the body."

Baldev Banerjee was the county medical examiner, a soft-spoken English expat whose quiet efficiency Dani always appreciated.

"They're still going over the scene, but it looks like the killer cleaned up," Stuart continued. "The body was discovered by a yoga instructor leading her class to greet the morning sun. Some greeting. We also got a new investigator on the case. Detective Phillip Casey. Just transferred in. Haven't met him yet."

"Transferred from where?" Dani asked.

"Providence," Stuart said. "He got into some sort of hot water. They say he's good. Old school."

"What time did they find the body?"

"Just before six," Stuart said. "It looks ritualistic."

"In what way?"

Dani turned onto the blacktop and headed into town on Main Street. None of the roads in East Salem were flat or straight for more than a hundred yards, and over half the time they were lined by stone walls or split-rail fences, and the hills were heavily wooded, which meant you could never see for more than a quarter mile in any direction unless you were looking across a lake or reservoir. Some people found the topology closed in and suffocating. She found it cozy.

The sky was blue, the air clear and clean-smelling, a brilliant fall day. The night before had witnessed one of the brightest full moons she'd ever seen. She recalled the theory held by a criminology professor she knew, about why so many crimes happen during the full moon: it's easier to see what you're doing.

"How the body was displayed," Stuart said. "Method. I don't know what else."

Dani swallowed hard. It was at times like these that she questioned the path she'd chosen—she wanted to do work that was important, that made a difference, and she was good at what she did, but she was still shocked and disheartened by the evil things people did to each other. When she'd interviewed for the job, she'd told Sam Ralston that if she could use her education and her gifts to stop a single crime from happening, she'd know she'd made the right choice. He'd smiled and said, "Well, I hope that happens for you."

About 90 percent of the work the firm did was with the judicial system, determining whether defendants were sane enough to assist in their own defenses or evaluating defendants or witnesses who were usually involuntary and often hostile participants. The other 10 percent was corporate, when the firm was hired to help businesses that wanted to settle issues in-house. Dani had a fantasy of opening a part-time clinical practice on the weekends to help kids, but so far she was so busy with the rest of her job that the notion remained a dream.

"Why did they bring in Liam Dorsett?" she asked.

"I thought you hadn't logged in."

"His mother called me. She's a friend."

"Is there anybody in Westchester you don't know?" Stuart said. "He's the only lead we've got. Found his cell phone in the weeds. Get this—we're standing there, and the thing *rings*. ID blocked. I got people doing the phone records. Irene is waiting for you before she talks to the boy."

"Is John there yet?"

"Foley?" Stuart asked.

"I'm meeting him there."

"He said that?"

"He called me," Dani said. "He asked me to come in."

"He said he'd meet you there?" Stuart asked again. "You haven't heard?"

"Apparently not."

"John got popped for DWI last night on the Cross-County Expressway," Stuart said. "Blood alcohol one point eight."

Double the legal limit. He didn't have to spell out the implications.

Dani's boss was frequently called upon as an expert witness for the state in prosecutions. With a Driving While Intoxicated arrest on his record, the DA couldn't possibly put him on the stand, because anything he might say would be permanently impugned. That was what Foley had meant by *maybe*.

"That's awful," Dani said. Her boss was in the middle of a nasty divorce, with two teenage daughters caught in the crossfire. It was no excuse, but she felt sorry for him. "He's been under a lot of stress lately."

"Who hasn't? Life goes on. I'm stopping at Starbucks," Stuart said. "The usual?"

"Venti vanilla soy latte," she said. "Full strength."

"You got it."

As she spoke, she drove past her office at Ralston-Foley Behavioral Consulting, a large old Victorian house on East Salem's Main Street, on the square opposite a row of boutiques and antique stores. The town always felt more like New England than New York to her, with its broad green commons with a gazebo in the middle, a white steepled church on one side of the square, a row of shops and stores including a hardware store where the wooden floor still squeaked, and a quaint old brick library opposite the church. From her desk she could look out the window and see children playing on the green, young moms with babies in strollers, and sometimes nannies from Germany or France chatting on park benches by the swing sets while their charges played.

Sam was too arthritic to sit in court but maintained his practice from the Main Street offices—he'd be available to give Dani advice, but to a great extent, she was on her own, sink or swim. So far she had assisted John with evaluations and competencies, but he was still grooming her to testify. An experienced defense attorney could make mincemeat out of an inexperienced forensic psychiatrist if she didn't know what she was doing. She hoped she wasn't in over her head.

She flashed to the image from her dream, her father in his cheesy multi-pocketed safari vest, holding a stone. Why a stone? She wished she could call him up and tell him about her self-doubts and hear him say, "You're gonna knock it out of the park, kiddo."

Dani drove south on the Sawmill Parkway, a road built in the thirties to handle a third of the traffic it handled today. When she hit a traffic jam, she threw up her hands in dismay. Today of all days to be late. She was a mile north of the Chappaqua exit and knew all the back roads, but first she had to get to the exit, and the cars weren't moving.

While she waited, she used her phone to log onto the Internet. She went to Google and typed in "Tommy Gunderson."

There were hundreds of thousands of references to the famous ex-football player. He'd been homecoming king their senior year of high school, and she, much to her own surprise, had been voted queen. She clicked on a link to a YouTube video, tagged as "FATAL HIT." While she waited for the video to download, she remembered what she could of his career, a path that had taken him from East Salem High School to All-American at Stanford to the heights of stardom, a Super Bowl ring with MVP honors and a contract that was the highest ever paid to a linebacker.

She clicked Play and saw Tommy, positioned twenty yards behind the line of scrimmage, deep for a linebacker, protecting against the long pass just before the two-minute warning in the conference championship game. Tommy pointing, calling out defensive signals, reading the offensive formation. A long count, hoping to draw the defense off side, then the snap. A gifted young receiver named Dwight Sykes slicing across the field at full speed, looking to his quarterback for the ball. Tommy reading the quarterback's eyes. Tommy launching himself over a blocker to hit Sykes a split second after the ball reaches his fingertips, one of the most spectacular collisions in NFL history, the announcer says. Tommy getting to his feet after the play. His chest-thumping warrior strut.

But Dwight Sykes doesn't get up. Trainers and team doctors rush onto the field. The collision in slow motion shows Tommy turning his head to avoid helmet-to-helmet contact, but simultaneously, Sykes turns his head in the same direction. Sykes's neck snapping back. Medical personnel working on Sykes where he's fallen. Tommy on the sidelines, helmet off, waiting, concerned, then praying on one knee, head bowed. Tommy praying with his teammates circled around him, holding hands. Sykes loaded onto a stretcher, then onto a golf cart, moving slowly off the field, the crowd silent. Faces in the stands. Girls crying. Everyone waiting to see Dwight Sykes give a short wave or a thumbs-up to tell the fans he's going to be okay.

But Dwight Sykes doesn't move.

The video clip ended with a caption: "Dwight Sykes died half an hour later in an ambulance on the way to a hospital."

19

Dani was startled when a horn honked behind her. The cars ahead of her had moved thirty feet. Whoever was behind her apparently wanted to move thirty feet too.

She logged off, put the car in first gear, and inched forward.

She wondered what it would be like to see Tommy again. The last time she'd seen him, she'd freaked out, panicked, been overwhelmed by cognitive dissonance—a doctorate in psychiatry and she still couldn't figure out what to call it. It wasn't anything he'd done.

It was who he was.

Which had seemed, at the time, too good to be true.

Which meant she was fooling herself.

Hence the panic.

3.

The morning following Abbie Gardener's strange visit, Tommy had gone to the fitness center at his usual time. He'd built All-Fit (the full name was All-Fit Sports, Health, and Fitness Center of Northern Westchester) when he'd retired from football, five buildings and 90,000 square feet of the latest in indoor tennis courts, turf fields, running tracks, batting cages, weight rooms, aerobic rooms, and all the newest training equipment.

He was reading through Nordic Track catalogs, evaluating the latest gear, when the front desk told him he had an urgent call from Liam Dorsett.

Liam was in tears. He'd been arrested, he said, or he was going to be arrested if he wasn't already. The police had taken him out of school and were bringing him in for questioning. His dad was in South America fishing and Liam was too embarrassed to call his mother and would Tommy call her for him?

"Slow down," Tommy said. "Take a knee. What do they want to talk to you about?"

The kid was six foot two and gangly, not yet grown into his body, with close-cropped hair and freckles across his face that made him look several years younger than he really was. Tommy had a hard time imagining him in police custody.

"I don't know," Liam said. "It's on the news."

Tommy turned on the TV in his office and saw a report on a murder at Bull's Rock Hill.

Liam was a nice kid, a decent athlete, but not somebody who was likely to participate in varsity sports beyond high school. He was lanky and wanted to bulk up, and Tommy had put him on a weight program and a high protein diet. In the five months that they'd been working together, Tommy had gotten to know Liam well enough to know one thing—the boy didn't have an aggressive bone in his body.

"Sit tight," Tommy said. "I'll make some calls."

"Is it going to be all right?" Liam asked.

"Absolutely," Tommy said. "Don't say anything right now if you can avoid it, but if you have to say something, tell the truth. You got it?"

"Got it."

Tommy called Claire Dorsett first to give her the information he had, then called Frank DeGidio. When he'd opened the center three years ago, Tommy had offered free memberships to law enforcement—partly because he was a local and knew a lot of the guys, and partly because it was never a bad idea to make the cops your friends.

"Twice in one day," Frank said. "We gotta stop meeting like this."

"I got a call from the kid you popped from ESH," Tommy said. "Liam Dorsett. He's one of my guys. Can you help me out?"

"I wish I could, Tommy," Frank said, "but they're really clamping down on this one. It's all need-to-know, and apparently I don't need to know."

"Is that to keep it out of the papers?"

"That'd be my guess," the cop told him. "All I got is that they put his cell phone on the scene."

"Liam's?"

"Yeah."

"Where are they taking him?"

"Kisco," Frank said. "DA's office. Across from the hospital. You know where that is?"

"I do. Thanks," Tommy said. "Next round of hot wings is on me."

"So was the last one," Frank reminded him.

Tommy had taken the Harley that morning because he knew there weren't going to be many days left when it would be warm enough to ride it. He decided to swing by Bull's Rock Hill on his way to the district attorney's office.

22

He rode over the hill and down the blacktop to the turn for Bull's Rock Hill where he saw, parked at the end of the gravel road that led to the scenic overlook, a police car surrounded by TV news trucks. The land surrounding and including Bull's Rock Hill belonged to East Salem's only country club, known simply as The Pastures, but it was too hilly to use as part of the golf course. The name came from a natural granite formation at the top of the cliff that resembled a sleeping bull.

Tommy parked the bike and traded his helmet for his watch cap and sunglasses, hoping no one would recognize him. He walked the final thirty yards until he stood next to one of two police officers. The other, positioned in front of a strand of yellow police tape closing off the road, was telling a handful of cameramen and reporters they would have to wait.

"Hey," Tommy said casually.

"Nobody past the tape," the cop said, and then he did a double take. Tommy had seen the look a thousand times before.

"You're Tommy Gunderson," the cop said.

"You're Peterson," Tommy said.

The cop looked stunned.

"Your name is on your badge. I live nearby."

"I know," the cop said. "I mean, I'd heard you did, but I didn't know where."

"What's all the commotion?" Tommy asked. "This where they found the girl?"

"Up there. Flat out on the rock," the cop said. "Not a stitch on. Weird one."

"When did they find her?"

"A couple hours ago," the cop said. "You know the area?"

"Like the back of my hand," Tommy said. "They know what time she died?"

The cop shrugged. "I'm just traffic control."

Tommy took a few steps to the side but not forward—he had no wish to aggravate the cop, who was only doing his job. He stood, hands in his jacket pockets, trying to get a sense of things. Despite the commotion, the woods seemed oddly empty, not a bird in the sky or a squirrel rustling in the leaves. Nothing stirred, nothing moved in the wind, nothing cried out from the distance. Perhaps because of the stillness, he had a distinct sense that someone was standing behind him. When he played football and covered pass receivers on their routes, he'd always had a gift for knowing where his man was, even with his back turned, some sort of sixth sense, sportscasters had commented more than once. He felt it now.

Yet when he turned, he was still alone. Indeed, the cop he'd been speaking with had moved off.

You're losing your touch, he told himself. *Either that, or you're letting yourself get spooked.*

The shiver he felt was as real as the feeling had been. It was not the sense that something had been there. It was the sense that something was still there, palpable but not visible. A sense (and now he thought he really was losing his mind) that the forest was grieving, or that something in it was dying.

Tommy looked around. There didn't seem to be anybody else to talk to. Suddenly he wanted to leave; he had a sense that staying would make him sick somehow, as if the place itself had been poisoned, or the air was toxic and he had to stop breathing it. It was an odd feeling, the way a worker in a nuclear power plant might feel after learning he'd just given himself a fatal dose of radiation.

He was walking back to his motorcycle when he heard a voice behind him.

"Gunner! Tommy Gunderson!"

He wanted to keep walking, but the man called his name again, now from only a few yards back. He turned.

As soon as he did, he wished he hadn't. The out-of-breath reporter running to catch up to him was from the *New York Star*, a tabloid that sensationalized everything it covered and specialized in headlines that made terrible and often off-color puns. The reporter's name was Vito Cipriano, and he looked like a rat with a hat on. He had the charm of a rat as well. Vito was pushing fifty and was at least that many pounds overweight, with hair dyed black and black-rimmed eyeglasses to match. Tommy had never seen him wearing anything except an athletic warm-up suit. Perhaps it was Vito's presence he'd sensed, though usually that was more like getting sprayed by a skunk.

He'd dealt with Cipriano in the past, including an incident when the man had tried to take Tommy's picture. When Tommy raised his hand to block the lens, Cipriano had stepped forward to make it look like Tommy had punched him. The reporter tried to sue, but fortunately another member of the paparazzi had caught the entire incident on video. The fact was, Tommy had wanted to punch Cipriano countless times, just not that once.

"Hey, man—good to see you again," Vito said. "What brings you here?"

"I live down the road," Tommy said. "As you know, because you used to camp out at the end of my driveway."

"That's near here?" Vito said. "I didn't realize. I get outta Manhattan and I'm hopeless. You hear what went on up there?" He gestured over his shoulder.

"No," Tommy said. "You?"

"I got nothin'," Vito said. "I'm trying to get my editor to pony for a helicopter. So why'd you stop if you didn't know what happened up there?"

"Like I said," Tommy told him, moving toward his motorcycle. "I live nearby. I was just wondering what the commotion was all about."

"You still in touch with Cassandra?" Vito asked.

Tommy didn't bother to reply.

"How the mighty have fallen," Vito called out.

Following the Sykes accident, Tommy had started the next game, the Super Bowl, but outraged his fans when he removed himself from the lineup after the second series of downs. He never went back. The papers talked about all the money he'd walked away from. At the time he was engaged to twenty-five-year-old Cassandra Morton, an actress who'd appeared in a number of hit romantic comedies. The celebrity bloggers, fanzine Twitterers, and talk show ne'er-do-wells tried to tie the accident to the breakup with "America's sweetheart." It was Cipriano who had first reported the story that they'd been engaged and that Tommy had left Cassandra at the altar.

Tommy waved good-bye over his shoulder.

He raced west on Route 35 and then headed south on the Sawmill. He was forced to slow when he came to a traffic jam a few miles north of the

Chappaqua exit. When he considered how scared Liam probably was, he decided to risk getting a ticket. He pulled the motorcycle onto the shoulder and sped past all the stalled cars until he reached the exit, and then took the back road into Mt. Kisco.

The receptionist in the DA's second-floor office told him the boy they'd brought in was downstairs, level B. In the elevator he reminded himself to stay as cheerful and as positive as he could. He knew he couldn't tell Liam, or anyone else, at least not now, that when he'd visited the scene of the crime, he'd sensed something he'd never felt before. He couldn't explain it. He'd been kidding himself when he thought it was Vito Cipriano he'd worried about—it was more than that, and it was not a joke.

It was a feeling, if he had to name it, that evil had been there. Close to him. Watching him. A sickness, like cancer, but with volition and intent, looking for a host.

4.

The district attorney's branch office for Northern Westchester was in Mt. Kisco, on a residential street across from Northern Westchester Hospital. The building was utterly without charm, a two-story yellow brick box shared with the Department of Parks and Recreation and the Department of Conservation.

Dani rode the small claustrophobic elevator up to the second floor. As the door opened, she greeted the receptionist. *"Buenos días, Luisa. ¿Cómo va tu día? ¿Ya llegó Irene?"*

"No, llamó para decir que iba a llegar tarde," Luisa said. "Your Spanish is getting better."

"Is the boy they brought in downstairs?" Dani asked. The basement had a processing office, a holding facility, and a pair of interrogation rooms where suspects or witnesses could be questioned by the DA or by any of her investigators. A parking garage beneath the building afforded an area where prisoners could be brought in away from prying eyes or cameras.

Luisa shrugged.

"Was there a man here?" Dani asked. "Asking about the boy?"

"¿Es muy guapo?" Luisa smirked when she saw Dani's reaction. "I told him to ask downstairs."

Once the elevator door closed behind her, Dani couldn't help glancing in the small mirror on the elevator wall. It was normal to want to look good, she defended herself, when greeting a friend you hadn't seen in years. In her senior yearbook picture, taken before she'd gotten contact lenses, she looked like a bookish nerd trying hard not to look like a bookish nerd, with eyeglasses too big for her face and hair that really wasn't working for her.

Her cell phone rang just as the doors opened on the first floor, and she stepped out into the ground floor lobby to take the call.

"Got a sec?" Beth asked.

"Maybe that. What's up?"

"Grandpa Howard wants to come out for the Christmas holidays," her sister said. Their Grandfather Howard lived in Libby, Montana, where he'd retired as a district court judge and spent most of his time fly fishing. "I'd like to tell him you have room, but I wanted to check with you first."

"Oh, Beth." Dani tried to switch gears. "I mean, sure, if he wants to stay in a room that has no wallpaper."

"He can stay in my old room," Beth said.

"I stripped that one too." She'd been trying to rehabilitate the house she'd inherited from their parents one room at a time, to get it ready to sell, though she wasn't sure she really wanted to let it go. It was certainly more house than she needed, a four-bedroom French colonial with a gambrel roof, the clapboard siding painted a smoky mustard with sage green shutters. "I suppose, if he doesn't mind."

"He won't. Why don't you just paint?" Beth said. "Or hire somebody. No offense, but the idea of you trying to hang wallpaper in a straight line isn't working for me."

"I gotta go," Dani said. "Tell Grandpa he can stay as long as he wants. By the way—guess who I might run into?"

"Who?"

"Guess."

"Dani . . . ," Beth said impatiently.

"Tommy Gunderson."

"Get out of town! Wow. You think you might fall in love with him again?"

"I didn't fall in love with him the first time," Dani protested. "I freaked out."

"Yeah," her sister said, "because you fell in love with him."

"I *so* did not."

"That's your story and you're sticking to it," Beth mocked. "You know what I think? I think he dumped Cassandra Morton because he was still in love with the high school homecoming queen."

Dani should have known better than to tell Beth about it. As shocked and overwhelmed as Dani had been, first being nominated for homecoming queen and then actually winning the title, she'd been even more overwhelmed the night she was actually crowned. She'd pretended she thought it was all a big joke, but she wasn't immune to the teenage need for peer approval and the craving for popularity. She'd been flattered to the point of blushing when she heard her name called, but that wasn't it either. She'd held herself together as she took the stage, stood next to Tommy, and leaned forward, nodding her head so that the assistant principal could fasten the tiara to Dani's prom-do. She'd taken the floor to dance the traditional Homecoming King and Queen dance with Tommy when, thrilled and embarrassed, she'd let him take her in his arms, and she'd looked him in the eyes, and seen him smiling at her from ear to ear, and she could have sworn that something . . .

Passed between them.

Something physical and tangible. It was as if she'd been suddenly filled with a certain knowledge that this boy, this man, who held her in his arms, who all the other girls thought was so perfect, was, in fact . . . perfect . . . but only for her and no one else. Even odder than that was the sense, the surety, there was no denying it, that Tommy Gunderson felt the same way about her.

And then she'd panicked, broken away from his embrace, waved to the crowd, and told her dates—she'd come with two of her girlfriends—that she wanted to go home because she was feeling hypoglycemic. She didn't even know what hypoglycemic meant, but she needed an excuse to leave, because it was all too much too soon and the future she had in mind for herself was only going to happen if she got as far away as possible from Tommy Gunderson immediately.

The only person she'd ever told was her sister, who then, of course, was able to torment her about it for the rest of her life.

"Oh, shut up," Dani said. "What are you doing today?"

"Well," Beth said, "first I spent the morning very carefully combing the girls' hair because we got an e-mail blast from school saying they had a kid with head lice. Now I'm on my way to a barn call. Red Gate Farm."

Beth had been a full-time large animal veterinarian before giving birth to her girls. Now she worked part-time, trying to maintain her client list and be a mom at the same time.

"Mad cow?" Dani asked.

"Mad horse," Beth said. "Except they're not mad—just slightly annoyed. The owner thinks they're allergic to hay. They can't stop sneezing."

"Horses allergic to hay?" Dani stepped back into the elevator. "That can't be good."

"Better than fish being allergic to water, I suppose," Beth said. "Say hi to Tommy for me."

Dani pressed the down button and rode the elevator to the basement. She recognized Tommy immediately, even with his back to her—partly because he was dressed in the same basic outfit he'd worn in high school. A pair of black sweatpants and a black-and-gold hooded East Salem High sweatshirt with the sleeves cut off and curling at the elbows, with a black down vest over the sweatshirt. Broad shoulders, muscled calves and thighs, powerful arms, a bodybuilder's build.

Why are you looking at his thighs? Be professional.

It had been awhile since she had read any stories about Tommy Gunderson in the tabloids. She preferred to remember the Tommy she'd known in high school, the golden boy, All-State as a wrestler in the 198-pound division and a high school All-American in football. He was the boy no girl could resist. His hair then had been a kind of Bon Jovi shag/mullet. It was more sensible now, still long enough to hang over his ears and the same light brown it had been back when her own hair was not exactly the expertly highlighted light auburn it was now.

The police officer talking to Tommy cocked his fist behind his ear, opened his hand, and made a throwing motion. Of course they were talking football. A second cop laughed, both cops clearly awed by the famous athlete, a man the newspapers had once called the most feared linebacker in the NFL. Dani was aware of his other reputation, that of the unrepentant cad who'd left his bride at the altar. The tabloid fodder had never sounded like the Tommy from high school, but people could change. How much Tommy Gunderson had changed remained to be seen.

The cops barely noticed her as she approached.

"Hi, Tommy," she said, standing a few feet behind him.

He turned and smiled to see her.

"You still go by Tommy?"

She knew he had a lot of nicknames. T.G., Mister T, Teej, T-Bone, Tommy Gun, Gunner. She felt like she might be sick, or perhaps those were just butterflies in her stomach.

"Hey, Danielle," he said.

"Dani," she corrected him.

"Dani," he agreed. "Claire told me I might run into you."

"Small world," she said. For some reason, she didn't want him to know this was her first day flying solo.

"I apologize if I smell bad," he said. "When Liam called, I rushed here without grabbing a shower."

"You smell fine," she said.

Why were they talking about how he smelled? When had she ever talked to anybody about how they smelled?

"I have a cold," Tommy said, sniffing. "You look like you probably smell good."

Now what was she supposed to say?

Dani had been to Tommy's fitness center only a few times—for a niece's birthday party and once for an aerobics class. Each time she was glad she hadn't run into him, because the fact was that she wanted to run into him. Beth had pointed out that that made no sense. Beth had an irritating habit of doing that.

"How's your family?" she inquired.

"My aunt's still full-time at the library," he told her. "My dad's had a bit of a decline."

"I'm sorry to hear that."

"It's not Alzheimer's," Tommy clarified. "It's called Lewy body dementia. LBD. Some days he's got the attention span of a housefly, but not every day. I was really sorry to hear about your mom and dad."

31

"Time heals all wounds," she said, her usual lame response.

"Claire told me you used to babysit for Liam," he said. "He asked me to meet him here. We're pretty close. Guys talk to each other when they're working out. He's a good kid."

"Do you think he'd do drugs?" she asked. She recalled a case study she'd read about a high school wrestler who'd raged out of control. "Steroids, maybe?"

"Absolutely not," Tommy said. "He's a straight arrow. Plus, he'd be out of the gym in a heartbeat if I caught him taking anything more than aspirin."

"There was a murder last night up on Bull's Rock Hill," Dani said. "I don't have the details."

"I know. They found the victim on the rock with some markings on her body, written in blood," Tommy said. "That's what the cops just told me five minutes ago."

It annoyed her that Tommy already knew more about the crime than she did. She remembered the way his celebrity, even in high school as the Big Man on Campus, had opened doors for him that other people had to work hard to open. It wasn't that he had a big head about it. He still seemed self-effacing and ego-less. After their big moment on the dance floor, or whatever it was, she'd been worried that he might call her, and then she'd have to explain her behavior, to herself if not to him. She'd been standoff-ish when she passed him in the hall and even a bit rude. She focused on her goals, to go to college and then medical school, and nothing was going to distract her from that. And Tommy was nothing if not distracting.

"It's good to see you," she began, when she was interrupted by the uniformed officer monitoring the door to the parking garage, calling out, "Look busy, people!"

Irene Scotto strode through the door the way a bull enters a bullring, alert and ready for a fight. Stuart Metz walked behind her, carrying a cardboard tray from Starbucks in both hands. Irene, in a double-breasted navy suit with white piping and white buttons, smiled at Dani as she passed. Stuart handed Dani her coffee as he hurried to catch up to his boss, for whom the elevator door opened as if it knew she was coming.

"Time for me to get to work," Dani told Tommy.

"Can I tell you something?" Tommy said. "Whatever it was that happened up there on Bull's Rock Hill, Liam didn't do it. Not in a million years. I'd bet my life on it."

"Well," Dani said, "I hope you're right. See you around, maybe."

"I'm not going anywhere," he said. "I'm waiting for Liam's mom."

"Oh yeah, you said that," Dani said, feeling awkward now and anything but professional. "So then . . ."

She got on the elevator before she said anything stupid.

5.

"You look like you probably smell good."

Tommy wanted to kick himself. He hadn't really said that, had he?

Back in high school, he'd spent an hour staring at the telephone, summoning the courage to ask the formidable Danielle Harris out before realizing it was a losing battle. The East Salem High newspaper had called the homecoming pair "Beauty and the Beast," but he'd gotten a report from a reliable source that others were calling them "the Princess and the Pea-brain." Given how she'd fled from him on the dance floor, she must have agreed. She was even prettier than she'd been in high school, but how was that possible? Her eyes seemed bigger, maybe just because she wore makeup now. Some girls peaked in high school. Dani wasn't one of them, even though she'd been more interesting in high school than the girls who were peaking.

He took a seat on the bench by the water fountain. He refreshed the screen on his phone and Googled "Danielle Harris." He clicked on a link to the home page for Ralston-Foley Behavioral Consulting, then on the bio for Dani. She'd graduated from East Salem High School the same year he did— that much he already knew. She'd completed her undergraduate degree at Brown two years before he'd taken his BA from Stanford. It didn't surprise him to learn she'd finished four years' worth of college classes in two—from what he remembered of her, he wondered what took her so long. She'd made a similar rush through Harvard Medical School and had spent two years as a psychiatric intern in Senegal, West Africa, with Doctors Without Borders, where she'd helped child soldiers reintegrate with society. She'd interned at

Maclean Hospital in Belmont, Massachusetts, outside of Boston, and she'd worked with troubled youths at the Blair-Hudson School in Stockbridge, Massachusetts. Her bio listed scholarly papers she'd written or coauthored—several, Tommy noted, on the uses and misuses of selective serotonin reuptake inhibitors and other psychotropic medications for the adolescent or developing brain.

"A lifelong resident of East Salem and Westchester County, Dr. Harris brings a welcome medical component to the practice and an expertise experientially comparable to physicians twice her age."

Her bio added that she also taught part-time at the John Jay College of Criminal Justice.

She's still out of your league, Gunderson. But knowing you're doing something stupid never stopped you before . . . Why let it stop you now?

He returned to Google and typed in "Abigail Gardener" + "East Salem, NY."

A link brought him to the book pages of Amazon, where he found four titles attributed to Abigail Gardener: *The History of East Salem*, *The Ghosts of East Salem*, *The Witches of East Salem*, and *The Natives of East Salem*. None was still in print. Used copies of the first three could be purchased for $1.97 each.

Hard to imagine how a person's lifework could be had for $5.91.

He recalled the time she'd visited his class, her energy and the enthusiasm she had for her subjects. He'd driven past the Gardener Farm countless times, a property described by some magazines as the most valuable undeveloped land in Westchester, 150 acres on the southern shore of Lake Atticus.

With Abbie in a nursing home, the old house would now be occupied by her son, "Crazy George." Tommy's house was on a direct line from High Ridge Manor to the Gardener Farm. Had Abbie been trying to get home?

Bull's Rock Hill was on the line too.

Was she a suspect? Nobody would guess a woman her age was capable of such a crime, but then, no one would expect her to have the superhuman strength he'd experienced when she'd attacked him. Almost as if she'd been possessed.

By what?

It was something he intended to look into.

6.

The DA's office was the only one in the suite with windows, albeit bullet-proof ones, with a view of the hospital across the street and what was surely the biggest elm tree in the state of New York.

"Dani Harris," Irene said, "this is Detective Phillip Casey. He'll be my lead investigator on the case. Detective Casey, Dani Harris."

Phillip Casey gave her a smile so weak it would have been taken for a frown in any country outside of Scandinavia, accompanied by a grunt that may have been the detective clearing his throat but seemed more like an expression of disgust.

"The detective was just telling us that in his years of experience with Providence law enforcement, forensic psychiatrists did nothing but let bad guys off the hook by saying they were crazy," Stuart said. "We told him you and Sam and John have been invaluable to us."

Dani appreciated Stuart trying to break the ice on her behalf.

"How old are you?" the detective asked her.

Dani tried not to bristle outright. She'd had an instructor in medical school, a man who was ex-military by-the-book and a bit of a bully, but he'd liked Dani because she stood up to him. Dani guessed Casey might be of a similar ilk.

"Twenty-nine," she said. "What do you weigh?"

Stuart smiled, then wiped the smile from his face before Casey noticed. The senior detective was of medium height but had clearly spent more time at the pasta bowl than the salad bar. He had a gray brush cut that reminded Dani of pictures she'd seen of mystery writer Mickey Spillane. He was clean-shaven, pushing sixty, and wore a plaid sport coat that made him look like a sportscaster at a local affiliate in rural Canada.

"I can't resist my wife's risotto," he told her flatly. "You look twenty."

"Thanks," Dani said, though she wasn't sure he'd meant it as a compliment. She decided she liked him, and she suspected he liked her too, though it would probably take both of them awhile to admit it. "Can somebody tell me what happened last night?"

Stuart dimmed the lights. There was a 50-inch flat-screen monitor mounted on the wall to the right of the district attorney's desk. Detective Casey stared a few moments at the screen, then at the computer used to generate the PowerPoint presentation. Dani watched the cursor move tentatively from field to field as he manipulated the mouse, unsure how to operate the program.

"Allow me," Stuart offered, taking a seat at the laptop.

Casey turned his attention to the picture on the screen, an image of a wooded uphill path. "This is Bull's Rock Hill," he said. His delivery was dry and matter-of-fact. "I gather you people know where this is."

"It's about four miles from my house," Dani said.

"Is it?" Casey said. "I actually wasn't wondering where you live. The body was found this morning by a yoga instructor, a little before sunrise, which was . . ."

"7:01," Stuart said, adding, "AM."

"Thank you," Casey said. "AM? You're sure? So she gets about forty feet away when she sees this . . ."

Dani had seen plenty of crime scene photographs before, twenty-megapixel images that could be enlarged to show the smallest details, but she'd never seen anything as brutal as this. Casey let the picture speak for itself before gesturing to Stuart to click through a series of similar photos taken from different angles.

"Your ME is working on the details, but we think the victim is a girl between fourteen and twenty. Blond or light brown hair. No way to tell eye color, obviously."

Stuart zoomed in on the victim's eyes, now just blackened sockets, burn holes in a ghoulish Halloween mask.

"We don't know what the killer used for fire. Preliminary indications suggest possibly a blowtorch. We had a guy in Providence once, friend of mine's informant, who got caught ratting out the boys on Federal Hill—we found him in a pizza oven. Apparently they put him in it alive and then turned on the flames. I used to think nothing could top that, but now I ain't so sure."

Stuart zoomed out again, clicking to a slightly more distant view of the next slide, then zoomed back in. Dani noted the position of the body, the victim's head and neck. Her training in anatomy gave her the names of the exposed tissues, ligaments, and bones, but she was more interested in the mind of the killer than the body of the victim. Considerable trauma had been done to the body, but for some reason Dani didn't think she was looking at mindless violent actions. Rather, this seemed to be the work of a killer who was brutal, deliberate, and methodical. The things they'd said about Jack the Ripper.

"No clothing at the scene, but no preliminary indications of sexual assault either," Casey continued. "The ME can tell us more."

"Signs of struggle?" Irene asked.

"Nothing so far," Casey said. "Nothing under the fingernails, but again, we'll know more after we get the labs. The body appears to have been repositioned postmortem."

"Moved?" Irene said. "Hard to imagine somebody carrying a body up that hill."

"We don't know."

Dani tried to put herself in the mind of the victim. The absence of resistance, John Foley had told her once, indicated that either the victim was unconscious when she was killed, was surprised by a stranger, or was killed suddenly by someone she knew and trusted. The blood of violent crime victims often showed elevated stress hormones secreted to produce a fight/flight response. Banerjee could test for that.

What would it feel like, she wondered, to know you were about to die? More specifically, what did the girl on Bull's Rock Hill experience? Had she gone willingly, or was she forced? Tricked?

Casey turned to Stuart Metz. "What do we have next?"

Stuart clicked to a picture of the victim's toes, the nails painted a bright red, then to a picture of the victim's hands, the nails done in the same color. She wore a red-and-black braided friendship bracelet around her right ankle.

"If that's a pedicure, it's not a very good one," Irene said.

"Uneven application on the right hand," Detective Casey said. "I'm thinking she's right-handed and did it herself. What's a pedicure go for around here?"

Dani blurted out, "Thirty-five dollars," at the same time that Irene Scotto said, "Seventy-five." It was no surprise that they didn't go to the same salon.

"Harris, is it safe to say that up where you live there are plenty of girls who wouldn't think twice about paying seventy-five dollars for a pedicure?" Casey asked.

"Safe to say, yes," Dani agreed.

"So this girl does it herself. To save money?"

"Maybe she did it to cheer herself up?" Irene said.

"Maybe she was going to a party?" Dani said. "Or on a date?"

"Ah," Casey said, pointing his finger at Dani. "I'm with Harris on this one."

Stuart clicked to the next photograph, a picture of the victim's upper body. There was a burned-out cavity in the center of the chest, but it was hard to tell from the photo how deep the burn had gone.

More intriguing to Dani was a marking on the victim's stomach, and she asked Stuart to zoom in. It appeared to be a symbol, something like the letter G, and then its mirrored image, abutting at the vertical ascenders: ᛒ

The four of them stared at it a moment.

"Anybody?" Casey said. "We found this on the girl's stomach, written in blood. How long will it take serology to turn this around?"

"Depends on the backlog," Irene said. "The FBI office is in Federal Plaza, Manhattan. If they can't do it, we send it to Quantico."

"So how long?" he asked again.

"A week," Irene said. "Maybe less."

"How many people do we think were involved?" Stuart asked.

"The crime scene guys tell me between four and ten," Casey said. "Based on multiple partial footprints in the dirt where the grass was worn away. Whoever it was cleaned up after themselves. No cigarette butts or beer bottles or swords with the killer's fingerprints and DNA on the handle. We should be so lucky."

"Swords don't have handles," Stuart said. "They have grips, quillons, counterguards, or ricassos. I fenced in college."

"What are your thoughts, Dani?" Irene asked. "How would between four and ten people do something like this?"

Dani paused. John Foley would normally be the one to provide analysis, but Foley wasn't here. How she answered the question could determine the course her career would take. No pressure.

"Well," she said, "I'd like to think there aren't ten people in the entire country who could do something like this. And if there are, I doubt they'd ever be in one place at the same time."

"Four to ten," Casey reminded her.

"Even four. I wouldn't look for four psychopaths, or ten. I'd look for one leader and nine followers. One person with some kind of power over the others. Whether that's charisma or fear or mind control is hard to say, but I think the kind of person who could actually do something like this is fairly rare."

"No offense, Harris," Casey said, "but when you've had as many years in this job as I have, you see everything. Including guys who've been baked in a pizza oven."

Now Dani felt the hairs rising on the back of her neck. She saw Stuart and Irene exchange a glance.

"Detective Casey," she said, keeping her tone measured and in control, "during my internship in Africa with Doctors Without Borders, I worked with child soldiers who'd been forced or psychologically coerced into committing atrocities far worse than anything you could possibly have experienced. My job was to help put their shattered psyches back together, but to do that, they needed to talk to me about what they'd done. With all due respect, don't tell me what I've seen in my twenty-nine years."

The room was silent.

To Dani's surprise, Detective Casey looked embarrassed.

"I apologize for my thoughtless comment, Dr. Harris," he said. "I was 100 percent out of line. I hope you can forgive me."

Dani was impressed. He understood that when an apology was in order, one didn't say, "I'm sorry, but . . ."

"I can do that," she said. "And I do appreciate your sense of humor, Detective, but I think it's better if we can all work as a team."

Casey gave her a nod and gestured for her to continue.

"I was saying that it's very difficult for a normal human being to take responsibility for this kind of behavior—to initiate it. It's not so hard to say, 'I was just following orders,' or 'So-and-so made me do it, and I was afraid he'd kill me if I didn't.'"

"You seem certain the killer is male?" Irene said.

"*Certain* isn't the word I'd use," Dani said, "but in order to do something like this to another human being, you have to depersonalize the other. Most of us have the capacity for empathy, but it's not necessarily something we're born with. A child has to learn it. It's pretty well established that girls can identify and understand emotions much sooner than boys can."

"Some of us are still working on it," Stuart said.

"That's why little girls are so much sneakier than little boys," Dani said. "They're playing sophisticated head games while little boys are still firing imaginary laser beams from their fingers. Developing empathy is essential to creating the attachment bonds we need to survive, but when the faculty is damaged, you get disorders on the autism spectrum—Asperger's, autism, and a variety of other cognitive developmental impairments. And about 80 percent of all the children who have disorders on the spectrum are male."

"What about the markings?" Casey asked, shifting the discussion. "And why fire? If it's ritual, what kind? Does this guy get some sort of kick out of it?"

"I agree that it seems ritualistic," Dani said. "What somebody might get out of it varies. Psychologically, people with OCD, for example, use ritual to control the chaos that threatens them. Sociologically, human beings have always needed rituals. Some mark the passage of time or some special event, like putting candles on a birthday cake. Some designate a group identity, 'We-are-the-people-who-always-do-this.' Some mark an initiation or rite of passage—like a bachelor party where the groom goes out with his buddies to a strip club where he's supposedly tempted, and then in front of all his friends he resists the temptation and says, 'Sorry, guys, I'm getting married tomorrow.' He shows the world he's willing and ready to become a husband."

"I can think of two guys off the top of my head who didn't get that," Stuart said.

"So what kind of ritual do you think this one is?" Casey asked.

"I can't be specific," Dani said, "but I think it might mean the killer had some sort of fantasy he wanted to act out, and the ritual has meaning within the context of the fantasy. I can make some generalizations. The person who did this probably has a history of mutilating animals as a child. It starts with squishing bugs and then it moves up to frogs or fish, then bigger animals. They're testing themselves to see how big an animal they can destroy before they start to feel anything. In a way it's like the rest of us, trying to figure out what life means, but a psychopath is missing something normal people have."

"A conscience?" Casey said.

"Basically," Dani said. "He's missing the voice that says, 'Don't hurt that animal—it has feelings too.' The Bull's Rock killer clearly had no regard for what his victim might have been feeling. That said, I don't think he was angry at her. This wasn't a crime of sudden impulse; this was planned. The way the body is displayed also speaks to acting out some kind of fantasy. Serial killers often arrange their victims' bodies to conform to some prewritten script."

"You think this is a serial killer?" Irene asked.

"I can't say that," Dani said. "I'm just saying that one indicator of a serial-killer mentality is ritualistic body display."

"What about the symbol on her stomach?" Casey asked.

"No idea. Another indication of ritualistic fantasy, but what it means specifically, who knows? It might mean something only to the killer. It could be something he saw in a comic book."

There was a knock at the door, and a uniformed officer told the district attorney that Liam Dorsett's mother had arrived, along with her lawyer.

"More to come," Irene said, turning to Casey. "Let's talk to the boy and see what he can tell us. Interrogation Room 1. Good work, Dani. Could you write up a one-page brief summarizing what you just said?"

"No problem," Dani said, feeling like she'd passed the test. "But, Irene? I know Liam. I babysat him until he was four. It might be useful if I sat in."

The DA looked at Casey, who thought a moment, then nodded.

"Detective Casey is the lead," Irene reminded her, "but I think you're right. The boy might feel more comfortable if you were there. He's the only witness we have."

"Other than Lady Woo-Woo," Stuart added, pointing at his head and making a circular gesture.

"Who?" Dani asked.

"They found an old woman wandering around in the vicinity, lost in space," Stuart said. "Apparently she saw little green men landing in the woods. We're sending a man to Mars to see if her story checks out."

"I thought little green men came from Ireland," Dani said.

"This one's so weird, it wouldn't shock me if leprechauns *were* involved," Casey said. "I'm not ruling them out."

7.

Tommy recognized the lawyer who arrived with Claire Dorsett only because he knew him as a local real estate attorney who'd helped one of Tommy's friends close on a house. Claire's mascara was smeared from crying. The waiting room was stark and featureless, without magazines to read or art on the walls to look at, and the bare linoleum floor gave it the feel of a veterinarian's clinic.

When a policewoman led Liam in, Tommy stepped aside as the boy rushed to hug his mother, burying his face in her chest and sobbing. At the same time, Dani stepped out of the elevator with three people Tommy didn't recognize.

"Is there anything I can do to help?" he asked her. "Liam would probably be more comfortable if he had someone there with him. Either me or his mom."

"He probably would, but no friends or family present during questioning," Dani said. "Just his lawyer. Did Claire find a good one?"

"She did if you're trying to sell your house," Tommy said.

Don't try to be clever. Just be yourself.

"This is the preliminary investigation, not the trial," Dani said. "Still informal. Liam's not yet a person of interest. I'll look out for him. What you could do is be with Claire. You can watch in Room 2 on closed circuit if you want."

The interrogation room was windowless, with a plain desk, chairs, a TV camera mounted in the corner, and a television monitor on a stand. As Dani showed Tommy and Claire where to sit, the monitor showed Liam taking a seat in Room 1, his lawyer beside him.

"I don't know how long we'll be," Dani said. "Liam's not a suspect. He's a good kid, Claire—don't lose sight of that. He needs to know you believe in him."

Claire sniffed and nodded. When they were alone, she turned to Tommy. "Thank you for being here," she said. "I'm sure you have better things to do with your time."

"Can't think of one," he said.

"My husband's in Patagonia, on a fishing trip."

"I know," Tommy said. "Liam told me. He was a little hurt because his dad didn't want to take him along."

Claire looked surprised. "Liam hates fishing."

"Not the point," Tommy said.

On the monitor, he saw the district attorney look to Dani and then gesture toward Liam, asking Dani to begin. Impressive. She'd apparently done well for herself.

"Hi, Liam," Dani said. "How you doing?"

"Okay," Liam said, drying his eyes with a tissue and then dabbing at his nose. "I mean, not really. But I'm okay. I guess."

"Do you know why you're here?"

"No."

"Did they tell you what your rights are?"

"Uh-huh."

"Kind of weird, huh?" she said. "Being read your rights. Just like you've seen on TV a thousand times."

"Yeah."

"It's important that you understand them. You do, don't you?"

He nodded.

"Do you have any questions?"

"Am I under arrest?"

Dani looked at Irene, who shook her head.

"No," Dani said. "We're just trying to clear things up and figure out what happened."

"Okay," he said. "I don't know if I know anything, but I'll try."

"This is Detective Casey," Dani said. "He has some questions for you. If you have any questions about how to respond, you can ask your lawyer what the right thing to do is. Right now, we're just trying to collect information so we can sort it out later."

Claire took her eyes from the monitor in Room 2 and turned toward Tommy. "Do you know this man Casey?" she asked.

"Never saw him before now."

Liam told the detective that he'd been to a party the night before. He knew his mom wouldn't wake up when he got home because she'd taken one of her sleeping pills and had two glasses of sherry, which you weren't supposed to mix.

"She always has trouble sleeping when my dad's out of town," he said.

"I did not have two glasses of sherry," Claire said.

"You don't have to convince me," Tommy said.

Liam told the detective it was just a party. Yes, there was alcohol at the party, and marijuana too, but he didn't smoke any pot because he was an athlete, and he'd heard high schools were talking about implementing drug testing for sports and he didn't want to be kicked off the team.

"It wasn't just that I didn't want to be caught," Liam said. "I don't like pot. It makes me hyper."

"You've tried it?" Casey asked.

"Sure," Liam said. "Once. But I hated it. Really. You can ask anybody."

"Can I ask the other kids who were at the party?" Casey said. "Who else was there?"

Liam hesitated.

Tommy saw Claire lean forward in her chair, silently urging her son to tell the truth.

"I understand that you want to protect your friends," the detective said. "They probably want to protect you too, but if we don't know who they are, we don't know who to talk to. You know how this works, don't you? If only one guy says he didn't do it, we don't take him at his word, but if six guys, independent of each other, tell me Liam Dorsett had nothing to do with it, then we pay attention. But if we don't have those other names, all we have to go on is what you tell us." He paused. "I'm sure they'd like to get all of this cleared away, just like you do. You want to go home again, don't you?"

"They can't hold him overnight, can they?" Claire asked.

"They can hold him for twenty-four hours as a material witness," Tommy said. "After that, they have to either charge him or let him go. Or take him into protective custody."

Claire looked doubtful.

"I took a criminal procedures class," he explained, hoping to reassure her.

"Dani told me you went to high school together," she said.

"Middle school too. And part of grade school. But we ran in different circles. Correction—I ran in circles and she ran in a straight line."

Liam looked like he was going to cry again. It appeared to be dawning on the boy, Tommy guessed, that he was in bigger trouble than he'd thought.

"You know, Liam," Dani interjected, "we're going to learn the names eventually, so it would be a lot better if you told them to us now."

"She told me she used to babysit Liam," Tommy said to Claire.

"She was our favorite," Claire said. "I think she was the only babysitter we ever had who did the dishes once Liam was asleep. Never had any boyfriends over either. Never had any boyfriends, period, as far as we could tell."

Tommy had always assumed Dani must be dating somebody older and smarter who didn't go to East Salem High.

Liam hesitated, then rattled off a list of names: "Logan Gansevoort, Terence Walker, Parker Bowen, Amos Kasden, Julie Leonard, Rayne Kepplinger, Khetzel Ross, Blair Weeks."

Tommy recognized three of the last names from reading the *New York Times* financial pages. And Khetzel was the daughter of Vivian Ross, actress of stage and screen. Tommy had met Vivian several times, though he doubted she'd remember.

Liam told the detective the party had been at Logan Gansevoort's house because his parents were out of town.

"And you guys were just getting drunk or high?" Casey said. "Nothing more than that?"

"That's all," Liam said.

"What was it? Beer? Wine? Hard liquor?"

"Liquor," Liam answered, running his hand across the top of his close-cropped head and scratching behind one of his large ears.

"You ever drink hard liquor before?" Casey asked.

Liam shook his head.

"Did you drink hard liquor at the party?"

Liam nodded. "But I had too much," he said. "I thought I was going to throw up."

"That's not why we're here," Casey said. "You understand that, don't you? I don't care if you did or didn't drink alcohol as a minor. That's nothing anybody has to worry about."

"I understand," Liam said.

"So what happened after you all got drunk?" Casey continued.

"I don't remember," Liam said. "Honest to God, I don't remember. I passed out."

"You don't remember anything getting a little crazy?" Casey said. "A little out of hand? Somebody got mad at somebody? Or somebody wanted to go do something stupid? That's part of the fun of being drunk, isn't it?"

"I don't know. I guess," Liam agreed, scratching his ear again.

"So what happened?" Casey said. "What aren't you telling me?"

"I don't know," Liam said. "I don't remember anything."

"I don't think you're telling me the truth," Casey persisted.

Liam said nothing.

"Okay," Casey said. "In that case, I'm going to show you some pictures. I'll show you what happened, and then maybe you can tell me what the pictures mean."

Dani rose from her chair, crossed to where the detective was standing, and whispered in his ear. Casey looked annoyed, and then the two of them left the room.

"What do you suppose that's about?" Claire asked Tommy.

"No idea."

A moment later Dani returned to the conference room alone. Tommy had seen the good-cop/bad-cop gimmick played out a thousand times on television. This bore a resemblance, but he assumed Danielle Harris was more sophisticated than any stock TV character.

"Detective Casey had to make a phone call," she told Liam. "He'll be back in a minute."

"Okay," Liam said.

"You don't much care for Detective Casey, do you?"

"He's scaring me."

"Maybe we can get this over with before he gets back," Dani said. "Here's the deal, buddy. There was a terrible crime committed last night. A girl was murdered. And the only clue the police have is that they found your cell phone near the body."

In Room 2, Claire gasped.

Liam said, "They did?"

Dani nodded. "Do you remember what you did with your cell phone?"

"I lost it," Liam said.

"That's true," Claire told Tommy. "I asked him this morning if he had it, and he said it was lost."

"When was the last time you used it?" Dani asked.

"Before the party," Liam said. "To call Terence to come pick me up."

"What time did you get home last night?"

"About three, I guess. I walked home."

"You got drunk at Logan's house and passed out, and then you woke up at Logan's house?"

"Uh-huh."

"Was anybody else there when you woke up?"

"I don't know. I was on a lounge chair by the swimming pool," Liam said.

"What woke you up?"

"I was cold. It got windy. I didn't go back inside. I just went home."

"When did you notice your phone was missing?"

"This morning," he said, "when my mom asked me if I had it. I called it from the landline so I could find it, but I didn't hear it ringing."

"Okay," Dani said. "Let me see if I can go find Detective Casey to see if he has any other questions."

"Danielle," Liam said, and she paused. "Are you going to tell the others that I gave you their names?"

"We won't," Dani said. "But you did the right thing. Now we know where to go next. That's going to work in your favor."

She disappeared off camera, and a moment later Tommy heard a knock on the door.

Dani stuck her head into Room 2. "Why don't you go in and sit with him for a second?" she said to Claire. "I think we're finished, but I have to check."

Tommy stepped out into the hall, where he heard the district attorney tell Dani she wanted to coordinate their schedules. A large portrait of the current governor of New York hung at the end of the hall.

Tommy waited until Dani was alone, and then he had his chance. "That was impressive," he said. "I think you passed the audition."

"What do you mean, *audition*? How did you know it was my first time?"

"I didn't know it was your first time," he said. "I just thought you looked nervous. You kept touching your hair. That's a tell. According to the guys I play poker with."

"I was doing that?" Dani said. "Gosh. I'm so hungry, I can't think straight."

She asked him not to talk to the media.

"We want to keep the kids' names out of the papers for as long as possible. The reputable media know not to publish the names of minors, but there's no way to control the digital media or the blogosphere," she said.

"Gotcha," Tommy said. "What was the deal when Casey left the room?"

"I asked him not to show Liam pictures from the crime scene. He wanted to see how Liam would react, but if he's innocent, it would scar him for life. I asked him to let me try to talk to him."

"Looks like it worked," Tommy said. He worked up his courage. "You wanna get something to eat? It's lunchtime."

"No thanks," she said. "I'm not really hungry. I still have work to do here. They found an old woman wandering in the woods who might have seen something."

"Abbie Gardener," Tommy said. "Don't get your hopes up. She's mad as a hatter."

"Abbie Gardener?"

"Crazy George's mom," Tommy said. "Author of all those scary books."

"I know who Abbie Gardener is," Dani said. "How did you know she's the one they picked up?"

"They found her at my house," Tommy said. "In my yard. Talking to a frog. But I didn't recognize her. I remember when she came to our fourth-grade class. She must have been a hundred years old then."

"So she would have been a hundred and three by the time you finished fourth grade," Dani said.

Tommy laughed. "Good one."

"Why do they call him Crazy George?"

"Probably because when we were kids, he'd go crazy if you stepped on his property."

As he drove back to the gym, Tommy reviewed their closing conversation. He had no idea what it was he said, but apparently he'd put his foot in his mouth. When he asked her out to lunch, she'd said she wasn't hungry. A minute earlier, she'd told him she was so hungry she couldn't think straight.

Maybe it just wasn't meant to be. Yet some part of him believed she'd come back into his life for a reason. Seeing her again, he realized the one word that described how he had felt about his friendship with Danielle Harris all those years before: unfinished.

8.

"No thanks, I'm not really hungry."

She hadn't really said that, had she?

Right after telling him she was so hungry she couldn't think straight. How a mature, sensible, educated, professional woman could become so tongue-tied was beyond her—and for what? A guy she knew half a lifetime ago?

"He must think I'm an idiot," she said out loud.

Dani spent the afternoon in her office researching Alzheimer's to prepare to interview Abbie Gardener and certify whether or not the old woman was competent to give reliable testimony or speak in her own defense. She'd read Abbie Gardener's books as a girl, particularly *The Witches of East Salem*, which told hard-to-believe stories about some of the very houses and places Dani rode past on the bus on her way to elementary school. Kids called her "the witch lady." No one dared go near the Gardener Farm on Halloween where, according to local kid lore, three trick-or-treaters had once rung the doorbell and been so frightened by what they saw next that their hair turned white. Parents knew better, but they still steered clear of the farm on Halloween.

Like everyone else in East Salem, Dani had driven past the hundred and fifty acres of Gardener Farm, demarked by ancient stone walls, and fantasized about someday buying the place and renovating the big Queen Anne–style house. Visible from the road only in winter, the house, with its detailed turrets and gables, pitched slate roof, and elaborate gingerbread trim, might make a friendly "painted lady" if coated in brighter colors and if, perhaps, there were children's toys scattered across the front lawn. But with its reddish brown siding and black trim and wild ivy crawling from the ground all the way to the widow's walk at the top, covering the windows with dirt and leaves, the house seemed to forbid any guests or visitors. In all the times that she'd driven past it, she'd never seen a light on. Rumors had circulated for years about any number of billionaires and celebrities who'd stopped by to make Abbie or Crazy George an offer, only to be chased off. It was hard not to imagine that the house was hiding something.

She was nearly home for the day when her phone rang.

"Just letting you know," Detective Casey said, "we ran down all the names that Liam gave us of the kids who were at the party. The only one who didn't show up to school today is Julie Leonard. Seventeen. We're bringing the mother down to the ME's to make the ID. Like that's something a mother should ever have to see. Hopefully there's a birthmark on a hand or foot, and we won't have to show Mrs. Leonard any more than that."

"The girl had a red-and-black friendship bracelet around her right ankle, didn't she?" Dani recalled gently. "The kind kids tie on at camp and wear until they fall off."

"I forgot about that," Casey said. "Maybe that will be enough."

"Do you need me there?"

"No," Casey said. "But I'm gonna tell the mother we're gonna catch whoever did this. I'm gonna need you to help me keep my promise."

Dani hung up, pulled over to the side of the road, then typed the name "Julie Leonard" into the search box on her Google screen. She was about to hit enter, but changed her mind.

Tomorrow, she decided, and logged off.

Just before getting home, she stopped by the A&P Plaza where she bought a new HD radio/alarm at RadioShack for her bed stand. The radio also featured digital samples of various soothing sounds to help the listener fall asleep . . . a summer thunderstorm, a spring meadow full of birds, waves crashing on the beach, crickets chirping on a warm summer night. She was looking forward to getting a good night's sleep.

Three miles from her house, she saw flashing red, blue, and yellow lights ahead and slowed her car. Her first thought was a car accident, but as she drew closer she saw a police car, a fire truck with its ladder partially extended, and an electric company utility truck with a bucket lift. She parked and got out of the car to see if she could be of any medical assistance. As she rounded the rear of the fire truck, she saw that a fireman and two electrical workers were working on something above the road. She took a few steps farther and gasped.

Somehow a deer had become entangled in the wires fifteen feet above the asphalt, snagged and bleeding and hanging by the antlers. To her further horror, she saw the deer suddenly kick its hind legs, trying to free itself.

She watched an electrical worker, unable to free the animal, shake his head. The bucket lift was lowered to the ground. The electrical worker opened the bucket gate, and a cop climbed in. He unholstered his service pistol as the bucket rose. Dani wanted to look away but couldn't. She watched and listened as the officer fired two bullets into the deer's brain from point-blank range and put the poor animal out of its misery.

When a second cop advised her to step back, she asked him what happened.

"I work for the DA's office," she told him, as if that had anything to do with it.

The cop said he'd seen deer get hit by cars and thrown a hundred feet. This was probably a truck, moving at high speed, hitting the deer just as it was trying to jump from harm's way, causing the animal to fly up into the wires.

"The driver didn't stop?" Dani asked.

"He might not have noticed. Coulda walked back and not found what he hit. Who'd think to look up?"

She watched again as a fireman, using a small power saw, cut through the dead deer's antlers, and then the carcass fell to the ground.

"Fresh one for the wolf sanctuary," the cop said, referring to a nearby wildlife rescue operation where all the local roadkill went.

Once the fire truck blocking the road moved, Dani was allowed to proceed. When she got home, she opened a can of chicken and rice soup and heated it in a pan—her mother's "recipe." She missed her parents. They belonged in this big old house where she now lived without them.

She changed into her pajamas, brushed her teeth, washed her face, drank a glass of warm milk, and went to bed. When she tried to read the instructions to program her new clock radio, she concluded that the manual had been written by someone for whom the English language was a second if not a third tongue. What happened to the good old days, when a radio was just a radio and a clock was just a clock?

Finally she set the alarm for seven and instructed the clock, she hoped, to wake her to the sound of a spring thunderstorm.

As she closed her eyes, she thought of the deer hanging from the power lines. It was the sort of thing that might give a person nightmares, but she knew from a lecture on dream analysis in med school that it was uncommon to dream of something you saw the same day you saw it. Usually it took about a week.

She fell asleep, but instead of waking at seven, she sat up in the middle of the night, thinking she'd left the water running somewhere. The clock read 2:13.

Rising slowly to a fuller state of consciousness, Dani remembered her dream. She'd seen her mother standing under a tropical waterfall . . . then the water had turned to blood.

She remembered the dream from the night before, her father holding a stone.

It occurred to her that she'd woken the night before at the very same time: 2:13. Weird.

She sat up in bed, found the remote, turned on the television, and channel-surfed, watching as many different shows as she could to drive the disturbing image from her consciousness. The news channels told of oil spills and environmental catastrophes, local crimes and tragic car accidents. She turned the television off and picked up *Moby Dick*.

"Is it that by its indefiniteness it shadows forth the heartless voids and immensities of the universe," Melville wrote of the whiteness of the whale, *"and thus stabs us from behind with the thought of annihilation, when beholding the white depth of the milky way? Or is it, that as in essence whiteness is not*

so much a color as the visible absence of color; and at the same time the concrete of all colors; is it for these reasons that there is such a dumb blankness, full of meaning . . . ?"

But it wasn't the color white or the lack of all color that kept Dani awake. It was the vivid red of the blood that fell on her mother's head, and the feeling she had that she was the cause of it.

9.

Tommy had two reasons to go see his friend Carl. One was because he wanted to do anything he could to help Liam. The other was that he saw helping to solve the mystery as a way to score points with Dani. He wasn't sure exactly why he wanted to do that. Perhaps just to dig himself out of the hole he was in and get back to zero.

Carl Thorstein was one of the most learned men Tommy knew. They'd met at the local gas station, where they'd both stopped to fill the tanks of their motorcycles. Talking about Harleys and Indian Aces and 1952 Black Vincents had quickly led to friendship and talk of deeper things. Carl was a theologian and a scholar, and he had helped Tommy at a time when the younger man needed sage advice. Tommy came to believe he'd met Carl at the gas station that day for a reason. It was Carl who told Tommy it would be all right to walk away from football—much to the consternation of Ham Jeffers, the multibillionaire team owner. Carl had encouraged Tommy to do what he needed to do, which was not play a sport where he could kill a fellow human being.

Before the accident, Tommy had taken the sport he played seriously. Afterward, it seemed meaningless. How could he say, *"A man is dead, but we scored two more touchdowns than the other team, so it was worth it"*?

Ham Jeffers thought Tommy should be able to shake it off. "Get it through your thick skull," he shouted at Tommy. "It was an accident!"

Carl told Tommy it was indeed an accident, but it was also a turning point, a crossroads. There was a reason it happened, or at least a way to *give* it a reason. Carl didn't try to soothe him with pat answers.

"You may never know why God allowed it," he told Tommy, "but maybe God wants you to ask that question. If life has meaning, then death has meaning, even if it seems senseless to you at the moment."

Tommy was still asking. In the meantime, to make sure it would never happen again, he took the necessary steps. On a personal level, he'd walked off the field in the first quarter of the next game he played before he hurt somebody else, and because he knew he didn't belong there anymore. He'd always played with an equation in mind: *(mass x velocity) = force*, and the greater force prevailed. Some players hit the brakes in the split second before impact. Tommy accelerated. After the accident, he found himself shying away from hits and decelerating. His heart was no longer in it.

The other thing he knew he had to do was open a fitness center to train athletes and teach them how to be strong. He took full responsibility for the consequences of his actions, but he also knew that Dwight Sykes, although a gifted natural athlete with blinding speed, had also been lazy. He rarely used the weight room and spent his off-seasons pursuing television acting opportunities and chasing girls. If Sykes had been stronger, he might have been able to take the hit Tommy delivered.

The fitness center was a way to make everybody who used it stronger. It wasn't something Tommy wanted to do with the rest of his life, but it was what he needed to set in place before transitioning to the next thing.

—⁂—

The morning sun was still rising in the east when Tommy pulled up to Carl's home and found his friend working in his garden, ripping out his withered tomato plants. Carl had lived alone ever since losing his wife to breast cancer. Tommy tried to set him up on dates whenever he met single women of an appropriate age, but Carl never called the numbers Tommy gave him.

Carl got to his feet when he saw Tommy and held his muddy hands out to his sides in a gesture that said, *To what do I owe the pleasure?* He had a salt-and-pepper beard, full-faced but closely trimmed, and was bald on top.

"What are you doing?" Tommy asked him. "Planting season is spring."

"A friend from Holland brought me some bulbs," Carl said. "Can I offer you a cup of coffee?"

They moved to the porch, where Tommy took a seat in an Adirondack chair while Carl went inside. He came back a little later with two steaming mugs.

Carl sat down heavily in the chair next to Tommy. "Wow," he said, rubbing his back. "I can't bend over like I used to. Or more accurately, I can't stand up again like I used to. What brings you to this neck of the woods?"

"Research, actually," Tommy said. "Did you hear about Bull's Rock Hill?"

"Just a little bit on the radio," Carl said.

"I'm sort of involved," Tommy said. "I told you about my buddy Liam, right?"

"The skinny kid?" Carl said.

Tommy nodded. "They found his cell phone at the scene. He has no idea how it got there."

"Is he the only suspect?"

"I don't know," Tommy said. "He gave the police the names of the other kids at the party. I believe they're thinking one of them did it, but maybe someone unrelated to the party found her on her way home. Have you ever heard the name Abbie Gardener?"

"I know Abbie," Carl said. "As much as anyone can, given her condition. I've seen her at High Ridge when I visited some other residents there. What's Abbie have to do with this?"

"Probably nothing," Tommy said, "except that last night she got out of the nursing home and ended up in my backyard. My alarm went off at three in the morning. The police think she might have seen something."

"It won't be easy to talk to her," Carl said. "I understand she's in the final stages of Alzheimer's."

"Can I show you something?" Tommy asked, digging his phone from the pocket of his jacket. He flipped screens until he'd queued up the video

59

he'd taken the night before. "She was saying something when I found her, but it wasn't anything I could understand. I thought maybe if I played it for you—you speak like a hundred languages, right?"

"Not quite a hundred," Carl said. "Before you do—are you working on this as a case?"

Carl was one of the few people Tommy had told of his new career path.

"Sort of. I'm just an interested party. Did I ever tell you about Dani Harris?"

"Is that the party you're interested in?"

"She's a forensic psychiatrist with the DA's office."

"Did you tell her you're studying for your PI's license?"

"Not yet," Tommy said. "I didn't want to seem pushy. Anyway, she's working on the case and she asked me to help her. Okay, she didn't exactly ask me." He handed Carl his phone. "Can you translate this?"

"I can try." He pressed the screen's Play arrow and listened.

Tommy watched the expression on his friend's face change from curiosity to concern. "It's crazy stuff, isn't it? What's 'luck's fairy'?"

"The first part's in Italian," Carl said. "Do you mind if I take this inside? I just want to check something on my computer. I'll be right back."

While he waited, Tommy watched a flight of geese fly overhead in chevron formation, headed in a northerly direction. He'd always had a remarkably good sense of direction, even on a cloudy day or night when the sun or the stars were hidden. It was the wrong time of year for geese to fly north, but he assumed they knew what they were doing. Circling back, perhaps, to pick up stragglers.

Carl returned to the porch carrying a book. When Tommy opened it, he saw it was written in Italian. He turned back to the cover and read the title, *La Divina Commedia, di Dante Alighieri.*

"It's a nineteenth-century translation of the Ferrari original," Carl said. "I thought I remembered the passage from the *Purgatorio*, but I was wrong. It's from the *Inferno*. Haven't read this since I was in seminary."

He reached over and opened the book to the page he'd bookmarked and pointed with his finger to the exact line.

"*Le ali congoleare di mondo.* My Italian's not as good as it should be,"

Carl said, "but I would translate it as 'His wings freeze the world.' In context, 'God's most splendid being, who beats his wings and freezes everything that surrounds him.'"

He handed Tommy a printout he'd made of his translation.

"What about 'luck's fairy'?" Tommy asked.

"Well, it's not l-u-c-k-apostrophe-s. It's l-u-x. *Lux*, that means 'light.' In Latin, not Italian. And *ferre*, spelled f-e-r-r-e, means 'to bring.' 'Bringer of light' would be the translation. 'Whose wings freeze the world.' *Lux ferre* is from the Bible. It refers to a person."

"And who would that be?" Tommy asked.

"*Lux ferre*," Carl said. "Combined to make 'Lucifer, whose wings freeze the world.' At least according to Dante. But what's he written lately?"

"So Abbie Gardener was ranting about Satan?"

"I would say yes," Carl said. "Which would be consistent with her lifelong fixation on all things ghoulish and dark. I've done a lot of work with old people. Most find peace and have no problem getting old, but for some . . . the demons come out. It may have something to do with atrophy of the frontal lobes that govern impulse control and morality. Sometimes old people lose their self-control and start whacking each other with their canes. It sounds silly, but it's not funny when you see it."

"Saw it firsthand," Tommy said, pulling down the turtleneck to show Carl the scratches on his throat. "She jumped me. Out of the blue. Unbelievably strong."

Carl leaned in to have a look.

"One more question," Tommy said. "She asked me if I believe in something I'd never heard of—I couldn't even find it in the dictionary. Ecstaspizium?"

"Extispicium," Carl corrected him. "E-x-t-i-s-p-i-c-i-u-m."

"You know what it means?"

"It refers to the practice of sacrificing an animal so that you can predict the future by interpreting the entrails," Carl said. "A form of soothsaying practiced by the Roman haruspices."

"Haruspices?"

"Fortune-tellers," Carl said. "Or maybe prophets."

"That explains what she was doing with the frog," Tommy said. "'These are the first to go, you'll be the last,' she said."

"Last to what?"

"Dissolve," Tommy said. "And let me tell you about the doctor who looked at my throat."

He told Carl the whole story as best he could. When he was done speaking, Carl leaned back in his chair, thinking.

"What do you make of it?" Tommy said. "Figment of my imagination?"

"Maybe," Carl said. "Or maybe you were visited by someone."

"By whom?"

"By an angel," Carl said. "Just a guess, but I'm biased in that direction."

"An angel dressed as a biker?" Tommy said. "As in Hell's Angels?"

"If you think about it," Carl said, "if you're an angel trying to be incognito, you could hardly pick a better disguise. Did he say anything?"

"Anything angelic?" Tommy said. "He told me to put something on the scratches."

"So he was helpful. Are you going to tell Dani?" Carl asked.

"She'd say I'm losing my mind," Tommy said. "Which may very well be the case. My aunt used to know Abbie pretty well. I was thinking I might try to talk to her at High Ridge Manor."

"Good luck," Carl said. "Let me know if you want me to go with you. As a bodyguard."

"Thanks," Tommy said.

"And, Tommy?"

"Yeah?"

"Just . . ." Carl paused. "Be careful. We can make jokes about a crazy old lady in the woods, but . . ."

"But what?"

"Satan is nothing to joke about. Allow for the possibility that evil is real."

"I know it's real," Tommy said. "I'll be careful."

SATURDAY,
OCTOBER 16

10.

"It's so amazing," said the woman standing next to Dani on the platform for the Metro North to Grand Central, fifty miles away. "I can't believe there are all these woods and lakes so close to New York City."

Dani placed her accent as Midwestern. "They're not all lakes," she told her. "Most of them are reservoirs. This is where New York City gets its drinking water. They built the dams and aqueducts in the 1800s."

"What a good idea!" the woman exclaimed. "I'm from Minnesota. We have ten thousand lakes. Have you ever been there?"

"No," Dani said.

"You probably wouldn't like it," the woman said, a comment that left Dani perplexed, but the woman moved down the platform before Dani could ask her to elaborate. Perhaps she'd mistaken Dani for a city girl, even though East Salem was a place where, for as long as anyone could remember, New York City captains of industry and robber barons and Wall Street tycoons built their castles and gentlemen's farms specifically to get *away* from the urban din and clamor.

As the train pulled out of the station, Dani recalled riding into Manhattan with her parents to visit the Museum of Natural History or the MoMA or to see the Ringling Brothers Barnum and Bailey Circus at Madison Square Garden. She'd been fascinated as a child by how rapidly the landscape beyond the window changed from rural to suburban to city to inner city, how it started with trees and fields and ponds full of ducks and geese, then houses, then the ugly hindmost parts of warehouses and storage sheds, more and more decay, old tires, broken glass, graffiti, and occasionally homeless people sleeping under cardboard boxes. Then the train would be swallowed up in darkness as the rails led underground, until it stopped and her mother or father led her by the hand into Grand Central Station and the world turned magic again.

She remembered looking at the businessmen and women on the train and wondering what she would do with her life. She'd gone into medicine because her father was a doctor. She'd turned to psychiatry because she'd found illnesses of the brain to be the most complex, challenging, and endlessly fascinating. But there were days when she wished she'd stuck to her original childhood plan of going out west and feeding wild horses by dropping bales of hay from a hot air balloon.

"I don't think wild horses need to be fed from a hot air balloon," her father had told her. "They already have lots of grass to eat where they live."

So much for that dream.

At Grand Central she took the shuttle to Times Square and the uptown local to 56th Street, where she walked the short distance to John Jay College of Criminal Justice, a collection of buildings between 10th and 11th on Manhattan's West Side. John Jay was a unique school where the athletic department included men's and women's rifle teams, and undergraduates took all the usual liberal arts requirements in literature, philosophy, and the social sciences before pursuing law enforcement specialties as graduate students. The previous semester Dani had taught Psych 716, Assessment and Counseling of the Juvenile Offender. This semester she was teaching Psych 701, Psychology of Criminal Behavior.

The morning passed quickly, the Bull's Rock Hill murder never far from her thoughts. She delivered her lecture on crime and birth order (last-borns were generally more trouble than firstborns), met with an advisee, spent a few minutes chatting with a colleague, and was about to collect her mail when she saw a familiar figure browsing the employment notices on the bulletin board outside the graduate studies office. He was wearing Skechers, jeans, and a black leather jacket over a white dress shirt.

"Tommy, I think this is a little much," she said. "If you want to talk to me, just call my office—don't follow me around."

He smiled at her. She had to admit he had a nice smile.

"I'm sorry?" he said.

"What are you doing here?" she asked him. "How did you know I'd be here?"

"I had no idea you'd be here," he said. "I mean, I knew you taught here, but I didn't know when. It said you taught here on your bio."

It was then that she noticed a leather strap over his broad shoulder, connected to a briefcase. He seemed to be trying to hide it.

She waited.

"I'm taking a class," he said. "And honest, I didn't know you'd be here. But I'm glad to see you."

"What are you taking?" she asked.

"CJ 727."

"Cybercriminology?"

"Yup," he replied. "It's really interesting. Do you have any idea how many bot-networks there are out there? I'm never going Wi-Fi in an airport again."

"So . . . why are you taking this class?" she asked. "What does it have to do with running a fitness center?"

"Nothing," he said.

"So?"

"Maybe running a fitness center isn't what I want to do with the rest of my life," he told her. "Maybe I'm trying to broaden my horizons."

"Doing what?"

"You have to promise not to laugh," he said.

"I promise not to laugh." She couldn't help noticing how nine out of ten college women going by gave Tommy more than a passing glance, and probably not because they recognized him from his playing days. He had to know how good-looking he was. If he didn't, she certainly wasn't going to tell him.

"Well," he said, leaning his head back as if bracing himself, "actually, I'm studying to be a PI."

"What?" she said, laughing, then catching herself. "Why? From watching reruns of *Magnum, P.I.*?"

"Don't knock *Magnum*," he said. "That was a great show."

"Why?"

"Well, first of all, there was the Hawaiian locale . . ."

"Not why was it a great show—why a PI?"

"There's actually an answer to that," Tommy said. He smiled briefly. "Tell you later. But if you don't mind my asking, why not? Why does it seem so ridiculous to you?"

"It's not ridiculous," Dani said. "I'm sorry. It's not ridiculous at all. I just thought you already had something you were doing."

"I have something that makes money," Tommy said. "And I like working with kids. But the rest of it's pretty boring."

Clearly Tommy was not one of those retired sports celebrities who wanted to spend his days attending memorabilia shows or writing tell-all books . . . though of all the retired athletes with stories to tell, his might be the most interesting.

"It's something I always wanted to do," he explained, leaning back against the wall with his briefcase as a cushion, hands in his coat pockets. "Ever since I was little. I wanted to either play professional football or be a private investigator. I used to think I could do both. Fight offensive linemen during the season and crime in the off-season. They're actually kind of similar."

"How are they similar?"

"Puzzle solving," Tommy said. "Middle linebacker is the most cerebral position in football. Most people think quarterback, but the defense doesn't get to know the play beforehand. You have to read and react in a split second."

"And then you smash into people."

"Yup," Tommy agreed. "At which point you shut your brain off and let your body do the work. You zone in."

"Zone in?"

"The zone," Tommy explained. "And I don't mean the diet. A guy interviewed hundreds of athletes who'd broken world records, and nine out of ten said, 'Actually, I've done better.' And the guy said, 'Actually, you haven't—we've been keeping track,' but the athletes all said they didn't feel at their peak when they broke the record. They weren't focused, or they hadn't slept the night before."

"How is that being in the zone?" Dani asked.

"It means you do your best when you try without trying. You can't get in the zone by saying, 'Now I'm going to get in the zone.' If you overthink it, you mess up. You train and train and think and visualize and focus and do your mental reps, and then you let go and trust your body to do the right thing."

"So how many cases have you had?" she said. "As a PI?"

"Yours is the first," he told her, straightening and adjusting the strap to his briefcase higher up his thick shoulder. "Look, I have to get back to the gym, but it was great running into you. Oh—I have something for you. Got it this morning."

He fished in his briefcase and handed her a printout.

"I had a friend translate," he told her. "This is what Abbie Gardener said when I caught her stealing dead frogs from my pond. She's out there where the buses don't run, but I thought you might be interested."

Dani took the printout but didn't look at it. "Wait a minute," she said, following him down the hall and out into the sunshine. "What do you mean, mine is the first?"

"I misspoke," he said. "Liam's case is the first. He asked if I could help him."

"Claire hired you?" Dani asked. She walked beside him, the October sky above them clear and blue.

"Nobody hired me," Tommy said, tossing his head back to throw his hair from his eyes. "I have more money than I know what to do with. I'm doing this because Liam is my friend, and he needs help. And you're my friend too, I hope, and if you need my help, you've got it. If you ask me for it."

Dani didn't know quite what to make of his offer. On the one hand, the last thing she needed was a blundering amateur muddying up the waters and trampling on the evidence. On the other hand, she needed all the help she could get. She'd been John Foley's gofer. Now she was the lead consultant, and she didn't have a gofer. Tommy was clearly a lot brighter than she'd given him credit for, and the fact of his celebrity could open doors for her that might otherwise be closed.

They'd reached the curb, where Tommy had parked his motorcycle, a matte-black Harley Davidson Iron 883 Sportster with matching black saddlebags. He unlocked his helmet from the handlebar and put it on.

"You get one of these," he told her, patting the seat of his bike, "and you never have to worry about parking in the city." He mounted the bike, turned the key in the ignition, and revved the throttle. The engine growled.

For a moment Dani pictured herself riding behind him cross-country, camping along the way . . .

"So what do you think?" he asked her, throttling down. "We could make it official, and you could hire me. That way you could fire me if it doesn't work out."

"Not sure it's in the budget," she said.

"One dollar," Tommy said. "And that comes with a money-back guarantee." He offered her his hand.

She considered. "But I'm the boss," she said.

"You're totally the boss. You say jump, I say on whom. So what do you think?"

She hesitated, still weighing the pros and cons. His hand hung in the air.

"Sure," she said finally, taking his hand and shaking it. "But you can't tell anybody you're working for the district attorney. That didn't come out right. I work for the DA. You work for me. You're not—"

"Official. I know," Tommy said. "For the third time, I'm not doing this because anybody hired me. I just want to help. Do you have the dollar?"

"I don't think so," she said. "I'd have to find an ATM."

"You're good for it," he said, revving the throttle. "You going to the candlelight vigil for Julie Leonard tonight? Eight o'clock at the high school."

The vigil had come together with remarkable speed, Dani thought, but with Twitter and Facebook and texting and instant messaging, such things were possible these days. Kids were frightened. There was strength, and comfort, in numbers.

"I'll be there," she said. "It will be interesting to see who shows up. We're questioning the kids who were at the party tomorrow. Call me on my cell."

"What's the number?"

He entered her numbers into his phone as she spoke them.

"This looks like the start of a beautiful friendship," he said. "That's from *Casablanca*."

"I know where it's from," she said.

As he rode off, she wondered what he'd look like in a white tuxedo jacket.

When he was gone, she read the printout he'd given her. The old woman's words were consistent with the research Dani had done into Alzheimer's the day before. A confusion of fact and fantasy; an inability to find the words needed to communicate, hence the Italian and Latin; the inability to locate temporally, hence the confusion of present and future tenses. A person with Alzheimer's sometimes substitutes words for what they really mean, she had read. They are trying to say something that's important to them, though it's often difficult to interpret what they're trying to say.

When Dani read the reference to *lux ferre*, she flashed on her memory of the deer hanging from the telephone wires. The image was that of a tortured soul waiting for release. She recalled the terror she'd seen in the poor animal's eye and the explanation the cop had given her. Collisions with deer were everyday occurrences in Westchester. Surely that was what had happened. The idea that someone, or something, had left the deer hanging from the wires on the route Dani took home as a warning to her was simply preposterous. Superstitious. Absurd.

Why, then, had she felt such a peculiar sense of . . . foreboding? She felt it again, a sense that the beast had, for lack of a better way to understand it, looked at her . . .

And more precisely, recognized her.

Silly girl.

She stopped at a newsstand in Grand Central before catching her train back to Katonah. When she saw the cover of the *New York Star*, she stopped in her tracks. The headline read WESTCHESTER RIPPER, and below it was a photograph of the victim's body. Somebody had leaked the photograph. The firewalls and security codes that encrypted and protected police files and the district attorney's office computers were supposedly hacker-proof, but it didn't mean somebody from a newspaper as notoriously unscrupulous as the *Star* couldn't bribe somebody for a story. They'd done it before.

Irene would be livid.

When she got off the train in Katonah, Dani paused a moment to open an e-mail she'd received from the DA.

Dani—hate to impose and sorry for the short notice, but I need you. Special town meeting called (by citizens) today, 4:00 PM at the Grange Hall, East Salem. Do you know where that is? Sending Casey and Stuart too. They'll fill you in. People are scared, re. "Ripper" etc. Expect a lot of "Why aren't you doing anything?" And prepare to say, "We cannot comment at this time." Along evidentiary guidelines, obviously. Hoping you'll know how to assuage and reassure. Also go to FB and search Friends of Julie Leonard. Ten minutes ago, 174 members. Now up to 398. Ugly mob forming. All that's missing are torches and pitchforks. Call me if you have any questions. Courage. Irene.

The Grange Hall was on the square in East Salem, across the parking lot from the library. Dani arrived early enough to get online using the library's Wi-Fi. When she found the "Friends of Julie Leonard" page on Facebook, she saw what Irene was talking about—a virtual lynch mob of people who were angry and frightened and looking for support, though the "information" being shared was entirely rumor and speculation.

I saw a white light over Lake Atticus that night but when I told the police, they blew me off, one person wrote.

My dog was pacing back and forth all night—animals have extrasensory perception where these things are concerned, wrote another.

If you need to buy a gun, there's a gun show in Rhode Island—that's what I'm doing.

Don't buy a gun—don't be a hater!

If someone broke into my house and threatened to kill my kids, I don't think I'd call a tree-hugger. I think I'd rather invite my two best friends, Smith & Wesson.

The same thing happened on the exact same spot in 1831.

You people are all forgetting something. Julie wouldn't have wanted any of this. Remember Julie!

Dani encountered a similar hysteria at the town meeting, where she had to shoulder her way past several television news crews to get through the front door of the Grange Hall. The building was over two hundred years old, with rows of folding chairs on the wooden floor and permanent chairs in the U-shaped balcony, and windows in the clerestory that could be opened to vent the summer heat.

Stuart opened the meeting with a statement from the podium on the stage. Dani and Casey sat on folding chairs behind him. He told the crowd that he and Detective Casey and consulting psychiatrist Dr. Danielle Harris were there to answer as many questions as they could. The investigation was ongoing, which he hoped everyone would understand meant that there were going to be a lot of questions they simply couldn't answer, either because they didn't know the answer or because giving an answer could compromise the investigation.

"Have you been able to identify the victim?" someone asked.

Casey stepped to the podium and confirmed that the victim was one Julie Leonard, seventeen, a senior at East Salem High.

"How was she killed?"

"I can't really go into that at this time," Casey said.

"Was the photograph in the paper from the crime scene?"

"We don't release crime scene photographs to the press."

"That's not answering the question," a woman holding her baby said.

"I haven't seen the papers," Stuart said.

Dani suspected that wasn't the truth.

"You can't even look at the papers?" a man in a Red Sox cap asked. "Even *we* can do that."

"I stopped reading the *Star* when they said Abraham Lincoln was really a woman," Stuart quipped. Some in the room laughed.

"Do you have any suspects?"

"We are currently pursuing a number of lines of inquiry," Casey said. "We have a lot of people on this, and we're making good progress."

"Have you made any arrests?"

"We have not made any arrests at this time."

"Do you expect to?"

"Do we expect to?" Casey said. "Yes. We expect to solve this crime."

"When?"

"When?" Casey said, suppressing a laugh.

"I have a friend who explores caves"—Stuart leaned in to interrupt—"and he's often asked, 'How many miles of unexplored cave are there?' You can't answer questions like that before you've finished investigating."

"Who's talking about caves?" an older man asked.

Dani didn't know his name but recognized him as one of the owners of the hardware store.

"We want to know who did this and why you haven't arrested them yet."

"Once we have a suspect, it's our intention to arrest them and bring them in for questioning," Casey said.

Dani admired his patience and his grace under fire.

"You said 'them,'" said a middle-aged woman whom Dani recognized from the meat department at the supermarket. "Does that mean you think there's more than one killer?"

A murmur spread across the room.

"I apologize," Casey said. "My grammar isn't as good as it should be. We don't have a suspect or group of suspects. We're still gathering information. We just want to reassure you that we're doing everything we can to solve this thing."

"What are you doing that will allow us to leave here knowing we're safe?" a woman asked.

Dani had seen her before with her kids at the playground, across from her office at Ralston-Foley.

"We're doubling our patrols in the area," Casey said, "and we've added personnel to the night shift until this thing is in the can."

"Does that mean my taxes are going to go up?" asked a man in a suit.

"No, sir," Stuart said. "This will have no impact on your taxes."

"We've got people transferring over from the state police," Casey added. "We believe our manpower numbers are adequate."

"Just adequate?" a bearded man called out. "I'd think you could do better than that."

"We're doing the absolute best we can," Casey said.

"We already have a voluntary fire department," the bearded man said. "What we need is a *mandatory* police department."

A woman in the front row raised her hand. Dani recognized her as a waitress at The Pub.

"Can you tell us, then," she asked, "what we can do to feel safer?"

Casey looked at Dani for help. She moved to the podium.

"What you can do to feel safe," Dani said, "is to remember that this is a tightly knit community. The fact that you're all here is proof of that. This isn't one of those suburbs where all the houses look alike and nobody knows who lives in them. We know each other. I think I recognize half the people here. If somebody's garage door is left open when it shouldn't be, we know it. So we can take our cell phones when we walk the dogs and report anything unusual or suspicious to the police. We can check in with each other. Beyond just locking our doors and windows and leaving the porch lights on, we can help each other. You might want to put together a neighborhood watch."

"That's good in theory," a blind man said, rising from his seat and using his white cane for support. "I'm concerned for the elderly and the disabled. Some of us can't take as good care of ourselves as we used to."

Dani recognized him, a local piano tuner who'd been part of her parents' dinner group. His name was Willis Danes, and as long as Dani had known him, he'd been active at town meetings and engaged in local politics. He was in his seventies but still full of positive energy.

"So if your neighbors are disabled or elderly, take special care of them," Casey said. "Check in on 'em. That's all good. Vigilantism is not. But by all means, be careful and care for each other."

"Does that mean you think the Ripper is going to kill again?" an older woman asked. "Are we talking about a serial killer?"

Casey shook his head. "Nobody is talking about that," he said. "This headline, calling him the Ripper—let me tell you, people, I can sit in my house with my remote control and find more serial killers on television in one night than the FBI deals with in ten years. I'm not trying to minimize anything, but you have to be realistic. And it doesn't really help anything when ignorant newspapers print uninformed stories."

"So you can definitely rule out that it's a serial killer?" a man asked.

Dani recognized him. It was Vito Cipriano, the reporter from the *New York Star*. She wondered how he'd gotten in. Reporters were supposed to have been barred from the meeting.

When she heard a cell phone ring, she reached in her purse and checked her BlackBerry. Not hers. Casey looked at his phone, held up one finger to the audience, took the call, and listened for five seconds, then hung up and gave the crowd a parting smile.

"Thank you all for coming," he said.

Cipriano repeated his question, shouting above the others who clamored for further information.

Casey touched Dani gently on the arm and spoke in her ear. "Let's use the back door," he said. "I think there're going to be reporters out front."

"Was that a strategically timed call to end the meeting?" she asked.

"I wish," he said. "We've got a fire on West Ridge Road. I gotta go, but no need for you to come along. But I'm glad the phone rang when it did anyway. I was about done."

She said good-bye to Casey and then moved through the crowd to where the blind man stood, as if he were waiting for someone. When she saw that he was alone, she touched him on the arm.

"Mr. Danes, it's Danielle Harris," she said. "Fred and Amelia's youngest. I haven't seen you in a long time—how are you?"

"Dani," he said, smiling and turning his head slightly toward her. "Yes, it's been a long time. I was enormously saddened when I heard about your folks. That was a great tragedy."

"Thank you," she said. "And how are you?"

"Things are looking up," he told her with a smile. "Would you mind helping me to the parking lot? Much appreciated."

Dani remembered what a great spirit Willis Danes had, ever the optimist. When she was very little, he did magic tricks for her, sleight of hand with coins and pencils. She recalled how he would ask, "Did it disappear?

Because I sure can't see it," before pulling the object from behind her ear. His wife, Bette, was a potter and a knitter. She was always at his side, driving him to his piano tuning jobs and picking him up when he'd finished. Dani didn't see her.

"Can I give you a ride home?" she asked.

Willis thanked her but told her he had a personal caregiver now who drove him.

"Bette didn't pass the test when she went to renew her driver's license," he said. "She'll get it next time, but they make you wait six months before you can take it again. You can walk me to my car though."

They made small talk as she helped him down the steps and across the parking lot. When they got to his car, where his caregiver waited for him, he said, "So you're a psychiatrist. Do you have an office here in town?"

"I do," she said. "Right on Main Street. But my clinical practice is on hold. I've been working with the courts . . ." She stopped when she noticed his expression. Something was bothering him. "Are you okay? Do you need somebody to talk to?"

He took a deep breath. "I'm having a little trouble sleeping. My gerontologist thought I should talk to someone like you, but I don't know any therapists."

She had the feeling he wasn't telling her the whole truth.

"If you're worried about what happened on Bull's Rock Hill—"

"No, no," he said. "This started some time ago. Before that."

"I can see you if you'd like," she said. "I'll have to check when I have time."

"If it's a bother . . ."

"It's not," Dani said. "I just need to find an opening in my schedule. I'll call you."

"Thank you," he said, his lower lip trembling. "Thank you. I came here tonight hoping to have a word with you. Just let me know when it's convenient for you."

She watched him drive away, his caregiver behind the wheel.

Then it occurred to her—how could Willis Danes have come to the Grange Hall hoping to speak with her? Her attendance hadn't been announced. She hadn't known herself that she'd be at the town meeting until shortly before the event.

It was probably just one of those things people said when they were making casual conversation. Yet it reminded her, improbably, of the deer hanging from the wires, not in the content as much as the sense that strange things were happening for a reason. It was one sign of mental disturbance, she knew, to see patterns where none existed.

Don't let the job get to you, Dani, she told herself. John Foley had given her the same advice.

Easier said than done.

11.

There wasn't a square inch of the football field at East Salem High that Tommy didn't know intimately. He'd probably spat half of it back out after having his face planted in the turf, making a tackle. He'd run up and down the bleachers when he was in training for football or track, and he'd scrambled beneath them as a boy, chasing or hiding from his friends. But he'd never seen it like this, somber and solemn and dedicated to a higher purpose. Three girls in school hoodies handed out small white candles at the gates by the scoreboard, newcomers lighting theirs from candles already lit. Some kids had apps on their smart phones that displayed pictures of candles.

Tommy paused by the gates where people who knew Julie Leonard had erected a kind of memorial to her, signs and notes and photographs taped to the fence. There were pictures of her marching in the Memorial Day parade in her Brownies uniform and pictures of her at Girl Scout camp. From her art class, examples of her artwork. She was a gifted painter and an even better drawer. Handwritten notes on the fence said, *We miss you, Julie!* and *We'll never forget you*. Someone had even mounted an iPad displaying a video clip of Julie playing the tuba in the school pep band and laughing at herself, her eyes bulging to match her cheeks. What kind of girl played the tuba, Tommy wondered. One who didn't take herself too seriously, he guessed, or who didn't care what people thought of her—or wanted people to think she didn't care.

Kids gathered in small groups, holding hands or leaning against the landing pad by the pole vault pit or sitting on tackling dummies, but the largest group had gathered at midfield between the thirty-yard lines, more than five hundred kids but fewer than a thousand, Tommy guessed. On the first riser of the bleachers, a few feet above field level, a microphone had been set up, connected to a portable PA system. Tommy stood to the rear of the crowd and listened. The first speaker was the school principal, who cautioned students against spreading unsubstantiated rumors, urged them to support each other, and told them the school guidance counselors would be available after school every day until five thirty for any students who needed someone to talk to.

When she said the microphone was open for anyone who had anything to say or share, no one came forward at first, a silence that grew more awkward with each passing second. Then a girl stepped up and said she just wanted to say what a good friend Julie was to everybody, how she watched other people's pets for free when the owners went on vacation, and how she cheerfully shared her food when other kids forgot to bring their lunch money. Another girl remembered how Julie had organized a campaign to send letters and Girl Scout cookies to soldiers. A boy said Julie was the kind of person who always remembered the names of new students. Her younger sister, Kara, spoke of how her big sister taught her how to read and let her sleep in her bed when there were thunderstorms and never ate the last brownie in the pan.

Tommy listened, trying to hear any reason why someone might want to hurt Julie or take advantage of her. From the sound of it, Julie Leonard had led a sheltered life. There were no stories of Julie traveling in Europe with friends or trekking in the Himalayas. She was a nice kid who just wanted to have as many friends as possible.

Vulnerable, Tommy thought. *Victim* began with the same letter.

Tommy felt his phone vibrate in his pocket. He reached to shut it off, but when he glanced at it, he saw he had a text message from Dani.

Are you here? Where are you?

He texted back: I'll meet you where they do the coin toss.

Where is that?

You're kidding, right?

Of course I'm kidding.

MIDFIELD.

THANK YOU. BY THE WAY, KEEP YOUR EYES OPEN. WE THINK THE KILLER IS PROBABLY HERE.

It made sense, Tommy thought, if they were dealing with a killer who was trying to make a statement of some kind. What good was making a statement if you missed the reaction?

He surveyed the crowd, seeing mostly the backs of people's heads and silhouettes in the darkness. There should be some sort of scientific device that could pick up someone's evil aura, he thought, maybe an infrared camera that could discern between normal human beings and the cold-blooded variety. But the truth was that killers looked just like everybody else, had mothers and fathers, ate when they were hungry, felt hot in the summer and cold in the winter. What made them different? Dani could probably answer that. It was odd to think he could be within a few feet of a murderer and not know it.

Dani was dressed in a black turtleneck sweater, jeans, and black boots that came to just below the knee.

"Let's not keep meeting like this," he said. "How you holding up?"

"Long day," she said, smiling weakly. "I went through something like this earlier at the Grange Hall. Town meeting. People are scared."

"Then count me as 'people,'" Tommy said.

"I didn't think of you as someone who was easily scared," Dani said.

"Define 'easily,'" Tommy said. "Maybe *shocked* is a better word. Things are happening in this town that aren't supposed to happen in this town. Or anywhere. It's hard to put into words."

"You don't have to. I know what you mean."

"If you had to guess," Tommy said, "off the record, would you say whoever did it is likely to do it again?"

"If I had to guess?" Dani replied. "Yes. Likely. But not right away. Meanwhile, everything seems suspicious. We had a garage fire out on West Ridge Road. I didn't go. They think it was a nine-year-old kid who was trying to help his mom clean up after his birthday party, and he accidentally threw away one of those birthday candles that keeps relighting itself after you blow it out."

"I hate those things. But I'm pyrophobic. I lit my bangs on fire when

I was six, blowing out the candles on my cake. And those were just the regular kind."

"So how was your day?" she said.

"Unproductive. I asked some of the high school jocks who work out at the gym if they knew anything. They're pretty freaked out. Talking about what they'd do to the killer if they got their hands on him. Just macho bluster. You see anything here of interest?"

"If I have, I won't know until later," she said. "We have people taking pictures. Discreetly."

"I was thinking somebody should do that," Tommy said. "By the way, the mother's name is Connie Leonard. The father is unaccounted for and skipped out on his child support payments ten years ago. Kara and the mom live on Lake Kendell."

"And you know all this how?" Dani asked.

"Gerald Whitney told me," Tommy said. "The funeral director. I called him. He was my scoutmaster. What have you got going on tomorrow?"

"I'm impressed. Casey is questioning the other kids at the party," Dani said. "He wants me there."

"What time?"

Dani took a moment to choose her words. "Tommy," she said, "you're not allowed. Even as my paid assistant."

"I prefer the term *flunky*."

"I'm sorry," she said.

"I can get you coffee," he offered.

"If I need something, I'll text you," Dani said. "You're more than a flunky, Tommy. I'm glad you're part of the team."

"How about Executive Director of Investigative Services?"

"Don't push it," she said, smiling. She checked her BlackBerry to make sure she hadn't accidentally deleted his contact information.

"I hope your phone number is unlisted," he said.

"I unlisted my phone numbers and deleted my address from as many databases as I could two years ago," Dani said. "When your job involves meeting face-to-face with insane psychopaths, you want to keep a low profile."

"Tell me about it," he said. "I used to date cheerleaders."

Tommy realized that the crowd had begun to sing, led by the school glee club, as beautiful a rendition of "Amazing Grace" as any he'd ever heard. As he and Dani listened, Julie Leonard's mother walked past them, supported by her daughter Kara, who hugged her as they walked.

"If the killer is here," Tommy asked Dani, "what do you think he'd feel if he saw what we just saw? If he knew how much pain he's caused Julie's family?"

"He wouldn't feel anything," Dani said. "That's the difference. So be glad you feel something."

"I know what you mean," he said. "But I can't say I'm glad."

When Dani said she'd check in with him tomorrow, he offered to walk her to her car, but she declined. He watched her go and then, as the glee club began an a cappella version of the Beatles' "In My Life," he backed away from the crowd and walked to a large oak tree beyond the end zone at the end of the field opposite the scoreboard. He took a seat on a bench beneath the tree. The leaves above him were brown but had yet to fall—oak leaves were always the last to drop, he recalled. He sat in the darkness as the waning moon struggled to emerge from behind the clouds.

It had been his habit to sit on the bench, alone, before every game, his "moment of solitude" according to the caption beneath the photograph of him in the high school yearbook. He'd never told anybody why he needed such a moment before every game. Some speculated that it was where he performed some secret ritual to psych himself up, but in fact it was simply where he prayed. He took issue with coaches of any team sports who believed God favored one team over any other, but in his private and personal conversation before each game, he kept it simple and asked the Lord only to give him—and everybody else on the field—the full capacity of his gifts and talents, so that everyone would play to his personal best, and nobody would get hurt.

Tonight, he had a different prayer in mind.

Lord, he prayed silently, *I know I don't have to tell you how much pain Julie's mom is in. If it's part of your plan, make me . . . make us, everybody who's working on this, your instruments in solving this thing. Help us use the gifts you gave us, and help us bring this woman some sort of closure. She doesn't deserve any of this. I mean, who does? But she needs peace. Amen.*

When he got to his car, he turned the key in the ignition and paused a moment to let the engine warm up. While he waited, he used his phone to check his e-mail. He scrolled through a half-dozen requests from freelance writers and literary agents who wanted to help him write his memoirs, and another request forwarded to him by his talent agent from a new television show on ESPN that wanted to have him on as a guest.

Keep forwarding these, but for now my answer remains the same—no thanks, he typed. Sooner or later, to keep all his business ventures going, he'd have to do publicity, but for now he picked his spots. He'd been there, done that.

He paused when he came to an e-mail from Liam:

Tommy—I don't know what to do w/ attached video but I trust you'll know. Girl in vid is Rayne Kepplinger. She used a pixilation filter but it's her. My mom's lawyer thought it would be a bad idea if we came to the memorial service. I don't know what to do.

Liam

Tommy texted a reply. Pray for her. I will pray for you.

After he hit Send, he returned to Liam's e-mail and opened the video file the boy had attached. It was short and to the point, a pixilated image of a girl's face speaking into a webcam in a voice that was measured but intense. "If you tell anybody about what we did, Liam, we will kill you," the girl in the video said.

Tommy thought a moment, then forwarded the video to Dani, adding:

Liam sent this and said he hoped I would know what to do with it. I am sending it to you for the same reason. Not sure what the rules are re. evidence/confidentiality. He identified the girl as Rayne Kepplinger. The filter she used is a standard feature with all HP Media Smart webcams and a lot of others. Your tech people should have no problem removing the filter to see exactly who the speaker is. If they don't know how, have them call me because we covered this in my cyber-criminology class two weeks ago. Good luck tomorrow.

Magnum

SUNDAY, OCTOBER 17

12.

She woke up in the middle of the night when she heard her alarm go off. She'd gone straight to bed, exhausted. The sky beyond the window was dark, the leaves on the trees motionless.

She looked at her clock.

It was 2:13.

This time she was certain she'd set the alarm properly.

She pulled the radio's plug from the wall outlet and sat in the dark, watching the moonlight pour through her bedroom window. She remembered the dream she'd been having. Her parents were sitting side by side on the limb of a large tree, looking down at her. She was not particularly Freudian when it came to dream interpretation, but it made a certain kind of sense, given that her parents' plane had gone down somewhere in the northern reaches of the Congolese jungle. She'd pictured them before, in her waking thoughts, hung up high in the canopy, upside down and lifeless. Like the deer.

The dream's message was loud and clear, a representation of the guilt she felt, the unbearable guilt, hanging over her head.

In the morning she checked her e-mail. She opened one from Beth, who informed her that the head lice problem at school continued and the horses were sneezing uncontrollably. Cause still unclear, lab results pending, but the immediate problem was equine insomnia. And how was seeing Tommy?

Dani checked her voice mail next and saw a message from an "unknown caller."

"This is the Westchester Ripper," the caller said. "I'm going to kill you next, Dani."

She shuddered involuntarily, then felt a dull pain in her stomach.

Breathe, she told herself.

The caller was either a male with a high voice or a female trying to sound like a man. She guessed the former. The tone was measured, the affect flat, the volume just above a whisper.

"If it was sent from a cell phone, it could be tough," Casey told her later, after she let him listen to the message. "I'll get someone on it, but it could take awhile. Any wacko who reads the *New York Star* could think it would be a funny prank. Was your name in the papers?"

"No," Dani said. "But anybody at the town meeting would know about my involvement."

"How'd they get your cell number? You don't give it out."

"Not if I can help it," Dani said. "But someone who has it could have given it out."

"If we ID the cell tower that made the initial relay, that'll narrow it down," Casey said. "You want me to post an officer outside your house?"

"No," Dani said. "Just let me know if you learn anything."

Her day continued with a meeting in Irene's office, where the DA shared an e-mail from Dr. Baldev Banerjee, displayed on the flat-screen monitor on the wall. Stuart looked like he hadn't slept much the night before. Detective Casey looked like he'd slept, but in his clothes.

Re. Bull's Rock Hill b.#A847TS

1. Serology reports complications. Only result for now: blood on Liam Dorsett shirt [E#18.76et] is match to blood of victim. T cell DNA molecules indicate blood on victim (not hers) is 17 years (+/-9).

2. Burn wounds consistent with exit vector, not entry. No external tracheal/ naso-sinal scorching.

3. COD still unknown. Exsanguination likely. Tissue damage likely postmortem.

4. Victim @ t.d. [0200 hours e.s.t. +/- <.50 hours]. No signs of struggle.

"Thoughts?" Irene said to open the discussion. "Reactions?"

"Cause of death unknown?" Casey said. "Call me old-fashioned, but I saw the pictures. 'Exsanguination *likely*'? Does he mean she was dead before she bled out?"

"He's saying he needs to be certain. Dani?"

"I'd like to know what the complications are," Dani said, "but given that she didn't struggle, I'm thinking she might have been drugged. Ketamine is strong enough to cancel out any pain she may have been feeling. Army field medics use it to stabilize combatants with wound trauma."

"We're still waiting on toxicology. What about 'exit wounds'?" Irene said. "How does somebody have fire shooting out of their body?"

Dani had no answer.

"Blowtorch?" Casey said.

"It's a stretch. I want to bring Liam in," Irene said. "The blood and the phone put him at the scene. I don't want him going anywhere."

"If I may?" Dani asked, and the DA nodded permission. "There's no flight risk—"

"You told me, Dani," Irene said. "You babysat him."

"I'm not speaking as his babysitter," Dani said. "He knows he's in trouble, and he's scared out of his mind. He wants to help. Stuart—did they finish working on the video I sent you?"

"Got it right here," he said, clicking until the Windows Media Center screen appeared on the monitor. "They were able to wipe the filter, just like you said."

"It wasn't me," Dani said. "My . . . assistant came up with that."

Stuart clicked the Play icon, and they watched the message Rayne Kepplinger had sent to Liam.

"If you tell anybody about what we did, Liam, we will kill you . . ."

Stuart played it again, and then again.

"Does he need protective custody?" Irene asked. "What's she saying?"

"I think we should hear what she says when we talk to her," Dani said.

"Is this a literal threat?" Casey asked. "People say 'kill the ump,' but they don't mean *kill* the ump."

"She says *we*," Irene said. "Who's we? She and Liam? Everybody at the party? She's talking about the murder?"

"Not necessarily," Dani said. "We can't infer that."

"They always say they don't know," Irene said. "She's obviously telling him not to talk about it."

"But we don't know what *it* is. It could be something else. Liam said he didn't know what happened on Bull's Rock Hill. I believe him," Dani said. "He wouldn't have sent me—sent my *assistant* the clip if he knew what it was he wasn't supposed to say. I mean, he doesn't feel guilty, because he doesn't know what happened. She's warning him not to talk, but he sent us the clip anyway. He's trying to help. You don't need more leverage. You need him to feel safe. He'll feel safe at home."

Irene considered Dani's words.

"I appreciate your input," she said. "I'm going to agree with you. But if any witnesses make him a person of interest, I'm going to have to pull him in."

"Liam's a follower," Dani said. "He's not a leader."

"Okay," Irene said. "Let's see if we can figure out who the leader was. We have one hour before we meet at the Peter Keeler Inn. Stuart, have the techies finished setting up?"

"Not quite," he answered, "but they'll be ready when we get there."

"All right then. One hour. Check to see if you're being followed. And, Dani," she said, taking her aside and lowering her voice, "Detective Casey played me the threat you received. I'm assigning an officer to protect you until we figure this out. You just do what you do, but if you see someone in your rearview mirror, it's him, so don't worry about it."

"Irene—" Dani began.

"This killer doesn't like women," the DA said. "Don't argue with me."

13.

Tommy called All-Fit and told his day manager he wouldn't be in, then donned his barn coat and headed out to gather breakfast. His property had come with a horse barn, which he'd converted to a six-car garage where he kept his cars and other boy toys. Attached to the barn was a chicken coop, which he'd left intact when he'd decided on a whim to keep exotic chickens. He'd stocked it with white tufted Sultans and green-black Sumatras, but his best layers were the French Marans, lustrous black with copper hackles and bright red combs. Their eggs, with their dark-chocolate colored shells, sold for as much as $200 a dozen. They made nice gifts for friends, but the best thing they made was an omelet. He'd recently added a rooster, a giant twelve-pounder named Elvis, hoping to increase the size of his flock.

Usually Elvis came running out of the henhouse at the first sign of Tommy's approach, doing battle before allowing Tommy to get near the hens and their tasty eggs. Today, the coop was strangely quiet.

Inside the henhouse Tommy braced himself, expecting the rooster to rush him. Instead, he found only hens, some nesting, others rooting placidly in the feed bin.

"Elvis . . . ," he called out.

He went outside to the fenced-in chicken yard, but the rooster was nowhere to be found. He'd had the coop professionally reinforced against predators, including an expanse of chicken wire overhead to keep out the owls and the red-tailed hawks. The wire at ground level was of a small enough gauge to keep out snakes and weasels and wood rats and obviously anything larger, like foxes or raccoons. The henhouse floor was an impenetrable slab of poured concrete. He examined the fence and gates for holes, the ground for invasive burrows, but found none. His rooster was simply gone. The only explanation he could think of was that a raccoon, with its near-humanlike hands, had figured out how to undo the gate latch.

He took the Jeep to Katonah and sat with his father at Grace Lutheran, where the local descendants of the Scandinavians who'd resisted the temptation of cheap farmland in Wisconsin and Minnesota worshipped. It was at an after-church coffee hour that Tommy first noticed his dad was failing, unable to recognize faces or remember the names of friends he'd known all his life. Now when Tommy brought him, those friends understood and introduced themselves by name and shook Arnie's hand and let him know he was still loved, even if the people who loved him were strangers.

After church Tommy dropped his father off at the senior center, where Lucius Mills would pick him up. Lucius (pronounced "Luscious") was Arnie's visiting personal caregiver, a gentle black man who was bigger than many of the offensive linemen Tommy had battled when he played football. He was also a combat veteran. Tommy initially hired him as security when he'd received bags of hate mail and threats after quitting the game.

Tommy then drove to Clark's Hardware in East Salem to purchase a padlock for the gate. Clark's had been there since 1874, and so had some of the stock on the shelves. A clerk told him that padlocks were in the basement.

"Ideally padlocks with combinations raccoons can't figure out," Tommy said.

"They're all thieves," the hardware man said. "That's why they wear those masks."

The treads squeaked as Tommy descended the wooden stairs. He found what he was looking for in aisle 5, but when he turned to go upstairs and pay at the cash register, he recognized the man in aisle 4. Crazy George Gardener.

George was eighty-one years old, his white hair close-cropped and thin on top, his face tanned from the hours he spent cutting hay for the local horse farms. Tommy had driven past the Gardener Farm any number of times and seen the old man working in his fields. He was still robust enough to lift the bales and handle heavy machinery, and his posture was erect and stiff. He had large ears with tufts of black hair extruding from them like coils of barbed wire, and one of the more spectacular strawberry noses Tommy had ever seen. He was wearing dark green pants and a matching green shirt that made him look like a custodian in a public school.

He was examining furnace ducts when Tommy approached him.

"George Gardener?" Tommy said.

The old man turned, and Tommy offered his hand.

"Tommy Gunderson. I live up the road, past the country club. My dad owns the nursery. I think we've sold you some plants from time to time."

Crazy George was suspicious.

"I know," Gardener muttered, lowering his head and gazing at Tommy sideways through his overgrown eyebrows.

"Have you got a second?" Tommy said. "I was hoping maybe you knew something about chickens."

"Strange thing to hope."

"It's just that yours is the only farm around here that does something other than raise pretty horses to look at," Tommy said. "So I thought you might know."

"What's your question?"

"Well," Tommy said, "I lost a rooster. A French Maran. I checked the coop, but I couldn't find any tears in the wire or burrow holes or anything. I was thinking maybe raccoons figured out how to open the gate. They're pretty smart."

"Smarter than some people," Gardener said.

Tommy laughed. "Anyway, that's the only explanation I can think of."

"Maybe the hens got him," Gardener said. "Pecked him to death and ate him."

"That can happen?"

"Anything can happen."

"Well," Tommy said, "anyway, I'm hoping the raccoons aren't smart enough to pick a padlock."

Gardener said nothing.

"Your family's been on that farm how long?" Tommy asked.

The old man's expression remained cautious, wary. "Since snakes walked," he replied.

"Well, thanks for your help," Tommy said. "Hope your mother's okay—I was the one who called the police the other night when she got away from the nursing home. I found her in my backyard. I don't think she knew where she was."

"You found her?"

"Uh-huh," Tommy said. "Middle of the night. I thought maybe she was trying to get home. My house is more or less between the nursing home and your place. Have you talked to her?"

The old man's expression softened. "Thank you for taking care of her," he said. "I wouldn't call it 'talking to her.' She do that?" He was looking at the marks on Tommy's throat, nearly faded now.

"No," Tommy said. "This was a rosebush that got the best of me. Is she okay?"

"They gave her something for sleep," Gardener said. "But she won't take it."

"That can't be good," Tommy said. "I read if you don't get enough sleep, you start dreaming while you're still awake."

"One way to look at it," Gardener agreed.

"Same night that poor girl was killed up on Bull's Rock Hill," Tommy said. He left the statement hanging, but the old man didn't take the bait.

"Has she ever done that before?" Tommy asked. "Tried to come home? I gather she isn't as clearheaded as she used to be."

"Even salmon can find their way home," George said. "And pigeons."

"Maybe that's what happened to my rooster," Tommy said. "Maybe he went back to France."

"Doubt it," the old man said. "You know what I'd do?"

"What?" Tommy asked.

"Look a little harder. It's easy to miss something right under your nose."

When Tommy got home, he gathered the tools he needed to reinforce the gate and walked to the chicken coop where, as soon as he pressed on the latch, he heard a raucous noise from the henhouse. Elvis charged him, crowing with all his might, wings flapping in a cloud of noise and dust.

Tommy left the gate closed and considered.

He'd looked everywhere he could think of for a hole in the wire, a way a predator might have gotten in, or a way his rooster might have gotten out. He hadn't considered that his rooster might have been hiding from him . . . maybe sitting in a nest, where a hen might sit. In his search for one thing, he had missed another thing that was right under his nose. He could have looked right at it but not seen it, because it wasn't what he expected.

There was an important lesson in that.

George Gardener had called it.

He'd known.

He'd known about the marks on Tommy's throat too, though Tommy hadn't told anyone but Carl and Frank . . . and the doctor who wasn't real.

14.

"Well, that's forty minutes of my life I'm never going to get back," Detective Casey said. "Let's hope the next one is a bit more cooperative. Thoughts?"

"Very unlikely to be a killer," Dani said. "Terence is just a kid who wishes he knew more than he does."

"Lying? Hiding anything? Protecting someone?" Casey asked.

"Maybe protecting someone," Dani said. "Let's see what the others have to say, and we'll know better."

Part of Dani's role was to help investigators determine the order in which witnesses were questioned. She'd done as much research as she could into the lives of the participants, checked their academic records, scanned their Facebook pages, read their Twitter tweets, talked to their friends. On her recommendation, they'd spoken first with Terence Walker, a tall, fair-haired young man who showed up wearing dress slacks, loafers, a clean white dress shirt, and a blue-and-red-striped tie.

He struck her as easily manipulated and likely to cooperate, and if he seemed so to Dani, he would have seemed so to the other witnesses, who waited together in nervous anticipation. The others would wonder how much Terence said if he went first.

A good interviewer played witnesses or suspects against each other. "X said you did this, but Y said you did that, so which one is lying?" Casey agreed that they wanted to speak to Rayne Kepplinger last and use the threatening video she'd sent Liam for leverage.

96

Unfortunately, Terence's answers were as unilluminating as Liam's. He'd been to a party at Logan Gansevoort's house. Logan had invited him. He'd gotten wasted at the party and passed out. He didn't remember what happened next and woke up several hours later in the entertainment room in Logan's basement. He thought he remembered hearing music. He walked home around four in the morning. Nobody heard him come in. It was all a blur.

"What can you tell me about Julie Leonard?" Detective Casey asked. "Did you know her from school?"

"I knew who she was, but that night was the first time I ever talked to her."

"What'd you say to her?"

"Just stuff like, 'Where do you live?'"

"What'd you think of her? Did you like her? She like you?"

"I didn't really form an opinion."

"What kind of mood was she in? Good mood? Bad mood?"

"She was having a good time. She was dancing."

"Who with?"

"By herself."

"Did you have a conversation with her?"

"No."

"Why not?"

"I don't know. She didn't seem to have a lot to say."

Today, because it was Sunday and the DA's office was closed, but also in deference to the families and to keep the names of the teenage suspects out of the newspapers, Irene had decided to use a safe house away from prying media eyes and telescopic camera lenses. She'd chosen the Peter Keeler Inn, just off the East Salem town square. It was a large slate-roofed multigabled building with white clapboard siding covered in ivy, black shutters, and a wraparound porch. Inside were a four-star restaurant and, upstairs, a dozen elegant rooms and suites.

The Empire Suite was comprised of a master bedroom and a sitting room, separated by double doors. Each room had its own hall entrance. In the sitting room, a pair of video cameras on tripods pointed at a pair of easy chairs and a sofa. Cables snaked from the cameras through the double doors to recording equipment and monitors in the bedroom. The witnesses were made to wait in a room across the hall, which was also under surveillance. Their parents and their lawyers waited downstairs in the lobby; the lawyers were summoned when it was their client's turn to answer questions.

Dani had learned to recognize the signs of guilt, the body language where crossed arms served as protective armor and a backward slouch was an effort to gain distance. She'd seen how guilty people waived their right to counsel with surprising frequency and were willing to talk to investigators simply because they wanted to learn how much the cops already knew. She'd seen how exhausting it was to lie, to carry the burden of guilt. Criminals who tried to remember everything and keep their stories straight and out think the cops sometimes actually fell asleep during breaks in questioning. It was one reason the cops often made the interview sessions last as long as possible.

"If you tell the truth," Mark Twain said, "you don't have to remember anything." The corollary was if you lie you have to keep track of everything.

Detective Casey had requested a lie detector in the room, not to actually use, just to scare people into telling the truth. Sometimes implied threats were more effective than explicit ones.

Dani and Casey questioned the witnesses, accompanied by their lawyers. The law required that a uniformed officer be present as well to provide corroborating testimony as to what went on during the interrogation. Stuart, assisted by a technician, watched on the monitors in the bedroom, which also provided a secure video feed over the Internet to Irene in her office twenty-five miles away.

"When we're done, walk the kid all the way back to the parents and chat him up," Casey advised Stuart. "One time I was questioning a guy we thought was breaking into apartments. Three hours, I get nothing. We tell him he can go, I'm riding down in the elevator with him, and he laughs and says, 'Actually, I broke into all five of those apartments.' Like now that we're in the elevator, he's free to confess."

The people Liam named had been invited to come in voluntarily. Two, Logan Gansevoort and Amos Kasden, had failed to respond to the invitation. Blair Weeks had a soccer game and would be late.

Dani's early impression was that Julie Leonard was a sweet girl who wanted to be something more. She'd been invited to a party with the "cool kids" and she was trying hard to simply fit in and not make any mistakes or social faux pas. She was lonely, and desperate not to be. Dani hoped to have a full picture of the victim by the end of the day.

Dani and Detective Casey next questioned Parker Bowen, who'd arrived accompanied by a pair of lawyers in expensive suits and by his father. Parker Bowen Sr. was a lean man in his late forties with hair a bit too black and a tan a bit too orange for either to be natural.

Parker Bowen Jr.'s story differed little from the one they'd just heard. He'd been to a party, got wasted, passed out, couldn't remember anything. Yes, he'd passed out at parties before. No, he didn't think he had a drinking problem. No, he didn't remember what he'd been drinking, a little of this, a little of that. No, he didn't know Julie Leonard before the party, though he'd heard she had a reputation.

"A reputation for what?"

"You know."

"No, I don't know. Why don't you tell me?"

"For hooking up."

"Based on what?"

"It's just what some people said."

"What people? I have to tell you, this does not fit with what we know about Julie Leonard. It doesn't sound like her."

"I didn't say it was true. It was just what people said."

"That why you went to the party? Hoping maybe she'd have too much to drink and then you'd hook up with her?"

"No."

"What else do you remember?"

"Nothing."

They paused when they were finished with Parker to consult with Stuart. Blair Weeks had arrived and was waiting across the hall with Rayne Kepplinger and Khetzel Ross, though Rayne and Khetzel sat together while Blair kept herself apart.

"Something's going on between them," Stuart said. "Also, we got early labs back from serology. Now we know what the delay was all about. Guess what the blood type was for the blood used to draw the symbol on the body? O, A, B, negative, positive—guess."

"None of the above?" Dani said.

"Try all of the above," Stuart said. "They think they have DNA from at least five people. Banerjee wants STRs and SNIs. We're getting swabs from the kids. Once they've isolated the sample, they can run them through CODIS, but I'd be shocked if anybody here is in an FBI database."

"At least it gets us warrants to search the houses," Casey said. "Irene's gonna like that."

"Also," the assistant DA said, "while you were talking to Mr. Bowen, I met in the lobby with Davis Fish." He paused to see who recognized the name. "Logan Gansevoort's lawyer. The one who's on TV all the time, commenting on prominent cases. Apparently Logan has a medical emergency"—Stuart made quotation marks in the air with his fingers—"and won't be joining us."

"They sent his lawyer to tell us that in person?" Casey asked.

"No," Stuart said. "They sent Davis Fish to tell us Logan is being advised by the one and only Davis Fish. We can still get Logan to talk to us, but not by sending a polite request to stop by the office for a chat."

"What about the other kid?" Casey asked, looking at his notes. "Amos Kasden. Did we send somebody to his house?"

"Doesn't have a house," Stuart said. "He's a student at St. Adrian's Academy. Which has *en loco parentis* grandfathered into their charter. Since Detective Casey was in diapers. We need a writ."

"I didn't wear diapers," Casey said. "Went straight to boxer shorts. When you get the warrants for the kids' houses, make sure to get the shoes they were wearing. We got wholes and partials in the mud at the crime scene."

Dani watched the three teenage girls yet to be questioned on the monitor. Rayne had beautiful black hair that shone like a crow's feathers. Khetzel had short blond hair and severe bangs that made her look like the art director at a fashion magazine. Blair had long blond hair and was both the prettiest and the least adorned of the three.

According to what Dani had found out from perusing their Facebook pages, Rayne was the leader of the cool clique at East Salem High, and Khetzel was her consigliore. They'd skied on the ski team together, swam at the same swim club, boarded their horses together at Red Gate Farm, and formed the East Salem High School Girls Equestrian Club. More significantly, they'd both dated Logan Gansevoort, Rayne in sixth grade and Khetzel in ninth.

Dani wondered how exactly you "dated" someone in sixth grade. It was her recollection that in sixth grade boys were still covered head to toe in cooties and boy germs. When did that change?

At Dani's suggestion, Stuart asked Khetzel Ross to step into the sitting room of the Empire Suite. If Rayne was the alpha female in the pack, they might get Khetzel to flip on her. Her mother, the actress Vivian Ross, had called the front desk of the inn to ask them to tell the police she'd been held up and to please wait for her before getting started.

"Who does she think she is?" Casey had asked.

To which Dani answered, "She thinks she's Vivian Ross."

Khetzel, proving herself to be every inch the diva her mother was, announced that she wanted to fire her lawyer and represent herself. As her lawyer objected, Dani explained that as a minor, Khetzel was required by law to have representation. Khetzel countered by saying she'd been held back a year before starting kindergarten and was eighteen.

"You can make that decision," Dani said, "but I would advise against it."

"Fine," Khetzel said. "It's made." She turned to her lawyer. "You can go."

"But . . ."

"Please. I'm sure Mother will pay you your retainer or whatever it is."

When the lawyer was gone, she dropped a second bombshell.

"Rayne and I want to talk to you," she said, looking at Dani. Then, turning to Detective Casey, she added, "Alone. And I can't tell you the reason why until we're alone."

"Khetzel," Dani said, "I'm an officer of the court. Anything you tell me, I'm going to relay to Detective Casey and the district attorney anyway—you understand that, don't you?"

"I understand that," Khetzel said. "But you're a psychiatrist, and you went to East Salem High. We Googled you."

"I can't talk to Rayne without a lawyer," Dani said, "for the same rea—"

"She's eighteen too," Khetzel interrupted. "Our moms held us back together. We've already agreed. We want to talk to you."

"Why?"

"I can't say."

"If you can't tell me why—"

"People could die," Khetzel said. "That's why—okay?"

15.

During the six years that Tommy played professional football, his aunt Ruth, who worked at the town library, had kept him apprised of the local news. She wasn't a gossip, but as the coordinator of so many town activities, she usually had an inside track on the village scuttlebutt. Tommy found her in the children's room at the end of story hour, reading to a small group of preschoolers.

She smiled when she saw him waiting for her. "You really should get one of those," she told him when she'd finished, nodding over her shoulder at the room full of children. "They're a lot more fun than motorcycles."

"Someday," he said. "I need to get a learner's permit first."

That his aunt had never married and was childless had always seemed to Tommy to be one of life's greatest injustices. He couldn't think of anybody who'd be a better mom. Her hair, which she wore in a dignified braided ponytail, was partly gray and mostly blond. Her face was round, with a bright smile and sparkling blue eyes. So far she'd resisted his efforts to set her up with his friend Carl, but he was still working on it.

"Oh beans," she said. "You'd be a natural. What brings you here?"

"Research," he said.

"All yours." She gestured to the computer room, filled with computers and monitors and servers purchased with money Tommy had donated.

"You're the only resource I need," he told her. "What do you know about Abbie Gardener?"

His aunt sighed. She explained that Abbie had once been a vital life force in the town, active in the church, an avid letter writer to the local paper, a favorite dinner guest, and as the town historian a tireless chronicler of the town's narrative and chairman of the East Salem Historical Society. She'd been outgoing and extroverted until her health began to fail.

"What do you want to know?"

"Who'd she marry?" Tommy asked.

"Who says she did?" Ruth replied. The identity of George's father had long been the subject of speculation, most of it pointing to a hired man who'd lived on the farm before the war and left shortly before George was born. The rumor was that he had died in World War II, killed on D-day. "I couldn't say one way or the other. But she was always such an independent spirit. She might have planned to be a single mother from the start. It used to be looked down upon, you know. But Abbie always went her own way."

Ruth knew little of the Gardener family ancestral history, even though the farm had been held by the Gardener family since the town first started keeping records.

"Abbie seemed to think it wasn't fitting to talk about herself," Ruth said. "She never wanted people to think she was in any way different or special. Which is part of what made her so special.

"Over the years, a lot of people have used the library's archives to research the property itself," she added. "One hopes the Gardeners have done a bit of estate planning, but if they haven't and George passes on without naming an heir, it's going to be a free-for-all. I shudder to think."

"What's the deal with her obsession with ghosts and witches?" Tommy asked.

"Folklore," Aunt Ruth said. "That's all I ever made of it. She collected stories. Perhaps not what an academic historian might collect, but Abbie was never an academic. If I may ask, why are you interested?"

Tommy explained that he'd found Abbie lost in his backyard the night of the Bull's Rock Hill murder. "The police wonder if she saw anything. I'm helping Dani Harris look into it. You remember Dani?"

"I do," Ruth said, looking sadder than before. "She's part of our book club. So terrible, what happened to her parents."

"What was that all about anyway?" he asked. "I never heard the details."

"Dani's parents went to visit her before she finished her term of service with Doctors Without Borders. They wanted to fly home with her, but she wanted to stay an extra week to be with her boyfriend."

"Who was her boyfriend?"

"Some brilliant research scientist," Ruth said. "According to her sister, Beth. Beth brings her girls in from time to time."

Tommy's spirits sank.

"The boyfriend didn't work out, by the way," his aunt added.

"Why are you looking at me like that?"

"As I understand it," she said, "the pilot was unable to obtain fuel for his plane, so Fred and Amelia had to book the only other flight they could get, with another pilot who smuggled guns and such. According to Beth, Dani has never stopped blaming herself for not being more careful. Can you imagine? The plane was never found. Dani spent every last penny she had to keep searching, but it was no use."

Tommy could only imagine how awful Dani must have felt.

"You know what they say," Ruth said. "Everything happens for a reason, but sometimes it's for God to know and us to find out."

In which case, he wondered, what was the reason Abbie Gardener had found her way to his house the night of the murder? There were plenty of other houses along the way where she might have stopped. Why his? Who or what had made Abbie choose him?

16.

Khetzel Ross and Rayne Kepplinger were willing to tell Dani what she wanted to know, but stipulated that they didn't want the interview recorded. Dani and Detective Casey stepped into the hall to discuss it. From somewhere down the hall, Dani heard the muffled sounds of a television broadcast of a football game, and for a brief moment thought of Tommy before returning to the business at hand.

"For what it's worth," Dani told Casey, "I know girls like this. I think I may have actually been one once. Women talk to women."

"This one of those women's intuition things?" Casey asked.

"That's sexist," Dani said. "Or so my woman's intuition tells me. At the very least, you can use what they tell me if you want to question them yourself."

"They understand they're not immunized, right?" Casey said. "They know we can use whatever they tell us?"

"I'll make sure they do," Dani said. "I'll be careful."

She returned to the sitting room, where she told Rayne and Khetzel that Detective Casey had agreed to let her talk to them in private.

"So what's going on? How's that Rogaine thing working out for Mr. Forbes, by the way?" Dani began, referring to the veteran East Salem High science teacher who, in her day, had covered his encroaching baldness with increasingly conspicuous toupees. She'd seen a recent picture of him when she'd visited the school website.

"He looks like a nectarine with mold," Khetzel said.

Dani laughed.

"Is what we're about to tell you protected by doctor-client privilege?" Rayne asked. "What someone says to a psychiatrist is just as private as what you say to a priest in confession, right?"

"I'm a doctor, but you're not my clients," Dani said. "As I said, I advise the district attorney."

The girls eyed one another and signaled their agreement.

"We just really have to tell somebody," Khetzel said, "but we know if we told our lawyers, they'd tell our parents."

"I can't promise that what you tell me won't get out," Dani said. "I know you know your rights, but I have to remind you that whatever you say can and may be used against you in court. That's just the way it is."

"We know," Khetzel said. "We trust you."

"I'm glad you feel you can," Dani said, then looked at Rayne directly. "Particularly after the video clip you sent to Liam, threatening to kill him."

Dani could tell by the way the girl blushed that she knew better than to pretend she was innocent.

"I am so sorry I did that," Rayne said. "I wanted to take it back as soon as I hit Send."

"It sounded pretty angry," Dani said.

"It was just an expression," Rayne said. "You know, like saying 'Get outta town.' You don't really want somebody to move. I wasn't really going to kill him."

"Unfortunately, you sound very much like you want to, in the video," Dani said. "If a jury hears that, they're going to reach their own conclusions."

"A jury?" Rayne said. "No. I just—I wasn't angry."

"If you weren't angry, what were you?"

"Scared," Rayne said.

Her statement confirmed the conclusion Dani had reached after viewing the video clip with the pixilation filter removed. She'd asked the technician to make absolutely certain that the colors were as true as possible. A person expressing fear could look very much like a person expressing anger, with one exception. An angry person's face is generally red. The face of a person filled with fear is generally pale, and that's what Dani saw on the video clip. She was seeing it now, in person.

"I know you're scared," she told the two girls. "Personally, I don't think you hurt Julie Leonard, but we need to find out who did. Anything you tell me could help. Were you both at the party at Logan Gansevoort's house?"

The pair nodded. Khetzel reached inside her boot to scratch her leg.

"Did you know Julie?" Dani asked. "Was she a friend? The boys didn't seem to know much about her."

"We knew her in grade school," Rayne said. "Some years she was in my class and some years she was in Khetzel's."

"What was she like in grade school?"

"She was so funny," Khetzel said. "She wrote these skits that were so goofy. That's what I remember."

"She was always the peacemaker on the playground," Rayne said. "And she liked playing wall ball with the boys."

"Did you stay friends with her in middle school?" Dani asked. "High school?"

"We tried to," Rayne said. "I mean, we weren't *not* friends. We weren't, like, mean to her or anything. She was a good kid."

"So what happened?" Dani asked. "Why weren't you close friends anymore?"

"Well," Rayne said, "you know how in elementary school everybody is pretty much equal, but then in middle school things kind of move apart sometimes?"

"We *wanted* to invite her to do stuff," Khetzel said. "But she couldn't afford it. It's not like we held it against her or anything, but we'd ask her to do stuff with us, and she never could because she didn't have any money."

"After a while," Rayne said, "you can't keep inviting somebody like that to go with you when they can't afford it because it just makes them feel bad. It's better to just let it go."

"I get it," Dani said. She remembered too well the pain of not being invited to the parties of friends who'd invited her all her life. "So who asked her to the party?"

"We don't know," Khetzel said. "We were a little surprised to see her there, actually. And dressed like that . . ."

"Like how? What was she wearing?" Dani asked.

"Showing a little skin," Rayne said.

"She had on a party dress," Khetzel explained. "I think it was from JCPenney. The rest of us were just dressed normal."

"I think Blair might have invited her," Rayne said. "Or else put Logan up to it. Blair has a huge crush on Logan and thinks we don't know, but she's acting really weird. She won't talk to us."

"Did Julie come alone?" Dani asked.

"I think she came with that other boy," Khetzel said, scratching her leg again.

"Liam?"

"No," Rayne said. "Liam was with Blair. I think his name was Amos."

"I thought Blair had a crush on Logan," Dani said.

"She does, but she was trying to make him jealous by flirting with Liam," Khetzel said.

"You're not sure who Amos was?" Dani said. "You don't know him from school?"

"He doesn't go to ESH," Rayne said. "He goes to St. Adrian's. He went to ESE for a while."

"Did it look to you like they were a couple?" Dani asked. "Julie and Amos?"

"I don't think so," Khetzel said.

"How about the other boys?" Dani asked. "Were any of them interested in Julie? I get the sense Logan's had a lot of girlfriends. Do you think Julie had been with Logan?"

Khetzel made a face.

"Not his type?" Dani asked.

"Logan doesn't have a type," Rayne said. "If it walks and breathes, it's his type. I don't think Julie had ever hooked up with anybody."

"No?" Dani said. "What makes you say that?"

Rayne shrugged. Dani noticed that Rayne had a large Band-Aid on her ankle, visible beneath her dark tights.

"It's just something you know about somebody," Khetzel said.

"So you got to the party when?" Dani asked. "What time?"

"Around midnight," Rayne said. "Logan said not before."

"He texted," Khetzel said. "He just said we should be ready."

"Ready for what?" Dani asked. She waited.

"It was more than just a party," Rayne said. "It was a passage party."

"You'll have to explain that one to me."

"We'd heard about passage parties," Khetzel said, "but it's supposed to be secret. You're not supposed to talk about it."

"It's where you cross over," Rayne said.

Dani waited again.

"You die," Khetzel said. "For seven minutes."

"How do you die?"

"You drink zombie juice," Khetzel said. "That's what Logan called it. It's supposed to be some ancient secret formula."

"You drank something, but you didn't ask what was in it?" Dani said.

"You have to believe in it," Khetzel said. "It only works if you believe it's going to work."

"What happens if you don't believe in it?"

Rayne looked at Khetzel.

"You don't come back," Khetzel said.

"And what happens if you do?"

"First you see a white light," Rayne said. "And then if you move toward the light you feel . . . ecstasy. Like a spiritual insight. And the closer you get to the light, the more you feel. But if you keep going, you pass the point of no return and you don't come back. The zombie juice makes it possible to come back. It's supposed to change your life forever."

"We heard that sometimes people who see the light get to talk to their dead relatives," Khetzel said. "I wanted to see my dog, Rufus. He was hit by a car."

"What did you want?" Dani asked Rayne.

"I guess I just wanted to see for myself if heaven was real," she said. "We don't go to church. My parents . . . Anyway, I thought if I could just see it . . ."

Rayne was close to tears.

"So what did you experience?" Dani asked. "You drank the zombie juice. Then what happened?"

"We don't remember," Rayne said. "Honestly, we don't. We've tried, but we can't remember. Khetzel thinks she saw the white light, but she isn't sure."

"Khetzel?"

"You can't talk about it," Khetzel said. "That's why we didn't want you to record us."

"Why?" Dani asked. "What happens if you talk about it?"

"You die," Khetzel said.

Dani knew the girl was serious. She looked pale, her breathing shallow.

"And I'm sorry, but I really don't feel good. I think I'm going to throw up. Oh God. It's happening . . ."

"Khetzel . . ."

"Oh no . . ."

"Khetzel, listen to me," Dani said, moving directly in front of the terrified girl and grasping her by the shoulders. "Look me right in the eyes. Okay? Nothing is going to happen to you. I won't let anything happen to you. Look at me and keep looking at me. Khetzel, I need you to listen. You're having a panic attack."

"I feel so strange," Khetzel said. "Everything is . . ."

"Tingling . . . ," Dani said. "It feels like your hand is falling asleep, right? Just hold on."

Quickly Dani found a plastic laundry bag in the closet and handed it to Khetzel.

"Breathe into this," she said. "You're hyperventilating. You're exhaling too much CO_2, and it's elevating the pH levels in your blood. It's called hyperalkalosis. That's why things are tingling. If you rebreathe your own exhalations, you're going to feel better."

She watched as the bag inflated and deflated.

"Okay? You're feeling better already, aren't you?"

Khetzel nodded, breathing into the bag.

"Good," Dani said. "Just breathe slowly. Good. Now take the bag away. Okay?"

Dani leaned back and smiled. *"Never underestimate the power of a thera-peutic smile,"* her clinical psychology professor had been fond of saying.

"That was scary," Rayne said.

"Listen to me," Dani told Khetzel, who grew calmer with each deep breath she took. "The power of the mind to heal the body, or do the reverse and harm the body, is profound. It's something science doesn't really understand. You've heard of the placebo effect."

"You mean sugar pills?"

"Exactly," Dani said. "Sometimes half of the patients given the placebo show improvement. They think they're going to get better, so they do. Or you can make yourself sick. But it's you, making yourself sick. Because you're suggestible."

"Like those hypnotists in night clubs who make people cluck like chick-ens," Khetzel said.

"Something like that," Dani agreed. "Nothing is going to kill you if you talk about what happened at the passage party. Magic works because you believe magic works. Every time a magician pulls someone from the audience to help with a trick and asks, 'Have we ever met before?' and the person says, 'No'—the person is lying. Magicians put plants in the audi-ence all the time. That's how it works. The only trick is making you believe they're not plants."

"That is so disappointing," Rayne said.

"I might add," Dani said, "psychoactive drugs called hypnotics can make you even more suggestible. Sodium-penthathol, for one. Did Julie drink the zombie juice?"

"Everybody did. It was sort of like truth or dare," Khetzel said. "Nobody wanted to look like they were afraid to drink it. Except Liam."

"Did Logan supply the zombie juice?"

"I don't know. It was just sort of there," Rayne said.

"Okay," Dani said. "One more question—have you ever seen this symbol?"

She showed them a drawing she'd made of the symbol the crime scene guys had found written on Julie Leonard's body in blood. Each girl looked closely at the drawing.

"I haven't," Rayne said.

"Me neither," Khetzel said.

"One more question and I'll let you go. Do you have any idea who might have wanted to hurt Julie Leonard?"

"We have no idea," Rayne said.

"Okay then," Dani said, standing up. "I think we're done, but let me ask Detective Casey."

"Can I just ask you something?" Khetzel asked before Dani opened the door. "What would have happened if you hadn't given me that bag to breathe into?"

"Nothing too serious," Dani said. "You would have felt increasingly light-headed until you fainted, and then your breathing would slow down and your pH levels would return to normal and you'd feel fine. The worst that could happen would be if you fainted and hit your head on something."

"Or if I was driving and passed out," Khetzel said. "Or if I was hiking and fell off a cliff."

"Sure," Dani said. "I suppose."

"So talking about it really could have killed me," Khetzel said. "Right?"

"In that sense, I guess you're right," Dani said.

"Can I ask you another question?"

Dani nodded.

"Would it be possible for somebody to hypnotize you into killing somebody?"

Dani's first thought was to say no, it wasn't possible, but she hesitated. She recalled the famous Stanford Prison Scandal, a 1971 experiment where a Stanford University psychology professor had twenty-five student volunteers act as prisoners in a mock jail while twenty-five other volunteers—good, educated kids from stable homes—were told to act as guards. The experiment was designed to last thirty days but had to be called off after six when the guards displayed levels of sadism and cruelty the professor hadn't expected, simply because they'd been given permission.

She also thought of the notorious Milgram experiment, where Yale psychologist Stanley Milgram asked volunteer "teachers" to inflict electric shocks on "learners" in the next room. The shocks weren't real, but the "teachers" didn't know that; they were told that the shocks increased in voltage each time the learner answered a question wrong. The "teachers" continued to administer shocks even after hearing (faked) screams of pain from the adjacent room, simply because Milgram, the authority figure, said in a very calm and measured voice, "Please continue."

Good "normal" people could, under the right conditions, slip the bonds of morality and conscience.

"No, Khetzel, that's not possible," Dani said.

Nevertheless, she wondered . . . Had somebody drugged and hypnotized the kids at the party, then persuaded them to kill Julie? Was it possible to turn a normal person, against his or her will, into a monster?

In her opinion, it was.

17.

Tommy listened again to the voice mail Dani had forwarded to him—"This is the Westchester Ripper—I'm going to kill you next, Dani"—accompanied by a note: *My day is going just swell—how's yers? Dani*

When he texted her back, telling her he had information and asking her where she was, she said she was at the Peter Keeler Inn, about to conduct the last interview of the day, and invited him to join her.

Ten minutes later he knocked on the door to the Empire Suite. Stuart let him in.

Dani was bent over a laptop but looked up when Tommy entered. When Casey, standing next to her, cleared his throat to get her attention, Dani made the introductions.

"Detective Phillip Casey," she said, "I'd like you to meet my . . . assistant, Tommy Gunderson. Tommy, Detective Casey. He's been dying to meet you."

"Dani and I go way back," Tommy told Casey. "She says all good things about you."

"Tommy Gunderson," Casey said, shaking Tommy's hand. "I was actually at the game in Green Bay when you intercepted three passes for touchdowns. My in-laws have a place near Sturgeon Bay. I was so cold I half expected to see polar bears chasing penguins across the field."

"Polar bears don't chase penguins," Tommy said.

"They don't?" Casey said.

"They probably would if they could," Tommy said, "but penguins live at the South Pole. Polar bears live at the North."

"Learn something new every day," Casey said, nodding in the direction of the sitting room adjacent. "One more to go."

"That's not exactly new," Tommy said to Dani, once Casey was out of earshot. "What's Vivian Ross doing in the lobby? And did you figure out what Rayne didn't want Liam to talk about?"

"We did. It's not her," Dani said. "I'll fill you in. We just finished talking to Vivian's daughter. I didn't expect you here so soon. Can you wait until we're done, and then maybe we can get some coffee and compare notes?"

"Whatever you need," Tommy told her. "Anything you want me to do in the meantime?"

Casey stuck his head back in the room and gestured to Dani that he was ready.

"Just observe," Dani said. "And give me your impressions later."

As they watched on the monitor while Detective Casey laid out the ground rules to Blair Weeks and her attorney, Stuart explained to Tommy the gist of what they'd learned so far, including the confusing serology reports. Blair was, in Tommy's opinion, an extraordinarily pretty girl, with straight silky blond hair down to the middle of her back, smooth skin, blue eyes, and full lips.

"Why do pretty girls travel in packs?" Stuart asked. "I could never figure that out."

"You probably never will, either," Tommy said.

Detective Casey told Blair that Dr. Harris would be asking the questions.

Tommy listened. No, Blair didn't know what she was drinking. Yes, she agreed it's a bad idea to drink something if you don't know what's in it. She couldn't remember much about what happened. She barely knew Julie. She'd woken up around the time Rayne and Khetzel had, but she wasn't sure of the hour. She'd gotten a ride home from them. No one said anything on the ride home.

When Dani asked her what she was hoping to get out of attending a passage party, Blair looked startled.

"Rayne and Khetzel told me all about it," Dani said. "And I'm quite certain nothing bad has happened to them. Just as I'm certain nothing bad is going to happen to you. Rayne said you wanted to talk to your grandfather. When did he die?"

"Two years ago."

"Were you close to him?"

"Really close. Closer than I am to my parents."

"You live with your mom?"

"I do, but I'm moving in with my dad next week."

"Do they get along with each other? Your parents?"

Blair laughed. "She blamed him for everything that was wrong when they were married," she said, "and now that he's moved out, she blames him for everything that's wrong now. She was the one who wanted the divorce."

"Love is complicated," Dani said. "Your grandfather is your mom's dad?"

"My dad's."

"What did you want to say to him?"

"I'm not sure. I just wanted to talk to him."

"Did you see him? After you drank the zombie juice?"

"I don't know. I think so. It's kind of blurry."

"What do you remember?"

"He was mad at me. For wanting to join him."

"What do you mean by 'join him'?"

"I wanted to make sure he was there waiting for me," Blair said. "In heaven. Because if he was, I was going to join him."

"Do you mean take your own life?"

Blair nodded, fighting back tears. Dani handed her a box of tissues and waited for the girl to regain her composure.

"People look at me and they think everything must be so perfect," Blair said.

"Are you seeing somebody about these suicidal thoughts?" Dani asked.

Blair nodded. "Please don't tell my mom or dad. I just . . . I can't do this anymore. I can't stand having to choose between them. It's not my job to be their go-between."

"It's not. Definitely," Dani said. "It gets better, Blair. It really does. You'll come out of it stronger, but right now it hurts."

"My grandpa understood," Blair said. "Without him to talk to . . ."

"So he was angry with you for wanting to join him?"

Blair nodded.

"Do you have any idea why Julie was at the party? What she wanted to get out of it?"

"I think she wanted to find out if her father was on the other side," Blair said.

"If he was in heaven?"

"I guess. She told me she didn't know where he was or if he was alive or dead, but if he wasn't on the other side, then she'd know he was still alive. He left when she was really little."

"When did she tell you this?"

"Before we drank the punch."

"How did she seem at the party?" Dani asked.

"Happy. Really optimistic."

"And you can't think of anybody who might have wanted to hurt her?"

"Logan didn't think much of her," Blair said. "He said she was a slut. But he's an idiot."

"Rayne and Khetzel thought you had a crush on him."

"They don't know what they're talking about."

"Is that why you're mad at them?"

"I'm not mad at them. I'm just sad. When I get sad, I just want people to leave me alone."

"What about Amos? What can you tell me about him?"

"I didn't know why he was there," Blair said. "I'd never seen him before. He just sat there and didn't say anything. Like he was just there to watch. I tried to make conversation because I try to be nice to everybody, but he didn't say anything so I left him alone."

"Maybe he was already high on something?"

"Maybe."

"So you were mostly hanging out with Liam at the party?"

"Liam is a friend," Blair said, her posture straightening in defiance.

"With benefits?" Dani said.

"No," Blair said. "He's a *friend*. We talk. He's really smart. We just talk. He's actually really shy around girls."

"Thank you, Blair," Dani said. She turned to Casey, who leaned closer to the girl.

"I don't have too much to add," he told Blair. "What do you think happened? I know you can't remember, but you must have been thinking about it. Who do you think could have killed Julie Leonard?"

"If I had to guess," she said, "Logan Gansevoort."

"Why Logan?"

"Because he's evil," Blair said. "In my opinion."

"She totally had a crush on Logan," Tommy, in the other room, said to Stuart. "That's what girls say when boys won't call them back."

Stuart nodded in agreement.

The interview was over. Tommy watched the monitor as Casey, Dani, Blair, and her attorney all rose from where they were sitting.

"Why doesn't Casey ask them how their blood ended up on Julie's body?" Tommy said.

"Not this round," Stuart said. "So far, it sounds like none of them is even aware of it. We'll know more after we talk to Logan and Amos. I gotta walk her down to the lobby. Look busy."

Dani and Casey reentered the bedroom. Tommy waited while they spoke about what was on the schedule for tomorrow. Finally she smiled at him.

"Sorry to keep you waiting," she said. She looked exhausted.

"Where do you want to get coffee?"

"Coffee?" Dani said, looking around. "How about over there?"

She pointed to the table by the windows where Tommy saw a large coffeemaker, a stack of Styrofoam cups, and a box of Dunkin Donuts.

"I'm too tired to go anywhere," she said. "If you don't mind, I need to go to the ladies' room and splash water on my face. But help yourself. I'll be right with you."

Tommy crossed to the table, where Detective Casey had staked out the half-dozen remaining Munchkins and begun to refuel.

"Is it true what they say about cops and donuts?" Tommy asked him, eyeing the gut protruding from between the panels of the detective's unbuttoned sport coat.

"Is what true?" Casey replied with a straight face while stuffing a powdered sugar Munchkin into his mouth and licking his fingers.

Tommy was fairly certain Casey was joking with him. He just wasn't certain enough.

"Never mind," he said.

Dani came back and set up her laptop on the desk, telling Tommy she wanted to show him something. She logged onto the East Salem High Web site, where she opened the link to the previous year's online yearbook.

She clicked to a photograph of Logan, then another, and another. In several of the pictures Liam was standing next to him. The two boys were obviously friends.

"And you're showing me this . . . why?" Tommy asked.

"He reminds me of you," Dani said.

"Thanks a lot."

"I just mean he's a jock," Dani said. "You know more about jocks than I do."

"I certainly hope so."

"Could you talk to Liam again and ask him about Logan?" she said. "We're looking for someone who has sway over the others."

She turned her computer so Tommy could better see the screen and brought up a different photograph, a jpeg of a boy and a girl. The girl was Julie Leonard. The boy was no one Tommy recognized.

"We got this off Liam's cell phone. That doesn't mean Liam took it, but we think it might be from the party. This has to be Amos. Which also makes it the last image we have of Julie alive."

In the photograph, Julie was looking at Amos, but Amos was looking at the camera. Tommy didn't know why, but just from the photograph, he took a disliking to the boy. Maybe it was the kid's posture, or his expression, or the way he was ignoring the girl he was supposed to have been with.

"Speaking of witnesses, I talked to Crazy George," Tommy told her.

"He wasn't terribly helpful, but I got the impression his mother had escaped the nursing home before."

"You talked to George Gardener?" Dani said. "Tommy—you're not supposed to be interrogating witnesses before the police can talk to them. Do I have to explain that?"

"I ran into him at the hardware store," Tommy said. "We were talking about chickens."

"Chickens?"

"It's a long story," Tommy said. "Actually, it's a short story, but it's beside the point. So what are you thinking, now that you've talked to everybody?"

"Almost everybody," Dani reminded him. "As far as guilt, I couldn't say. But something happened that changed these kids. They don't remember what it is, and I can't explain why they don't, but I think it's in there. Hypnosis might help, but they'd have to volunteer. You can't hypnotize someone against their will." She began packing up and put her laptop into her briefcase.

"I'll walk you to your car," Tommy said, and held out his hand toward her second bag, filled with books and folders. "That looks heavy—may I?"

Dani seemed surprised.

"I didn't get a chance to work out today," he said.

She handed him the bag, slung her purse over her shoulder, and took a firm grip on her briefcase. "Thanks," she told him.

Tommy almost made it out of the lobby of the inn without being recognized, but then he heard someone call out his name. His policy was always to sign autographs except when the person seeking it was a professional collector who turned around and sold his autographs on eBay. "Just a second," he said to Dani.

"Tommy Gunderson," Vivian Ross sang, throwing her arms out dramatically and hugging him, air kissing him on each cheek. She beamed at him. "How *are* you? They told me you were here. Do you remember when we met on the red carpet in Los Angeles? I believe you were escorting one of Hollywood's latest young . . . things." She lingered on the word *things*. "Not poor Cassandra—the one after that. I love your bag."

"Hi, Vivian," Tommy said. "It's not mine. Good to see you again."

"Listen, Thomas, dear—could I have a word with you?" She hooked her arm around his and pulled him aside. Tommy wondered how it was some Americans ended up with British accents, like Orson Welles, or William F. Buckley, or Vivian Ross.

"I was hoping," she said, lowering her voice to a range somewhere between confidential and top secret, "if you could do me a big huge favor and tell me what went on up there? Apparently my daughter had the bone-headed idea to dismiss her lawyer, and she won't tell me a thing. I swear, Thomas, if there was the world's most complicated way to peel an orange, that girl would find a way to make it even harder and wait for a bad day to do it."

"I can't tell you, Vivian," Tommy said. "Even if I wanted to. I got here after they'd finished."

"Well, who can, then?" she asked, arching an eyebrow.

"I believe the conversation was private."

The actress dropped all pretense of cordiality. "Nice to see you again," she said, giving him the most theatrically insincere smile he'd ever seen.

Tommy waited in the parking lot while Dani scrounged in her handbag, searching for her car keys. He thought to offer her the use of his metal detector, but he'd left it at home.

"Have you ever heard of a passage party?" she asked him. "Liam never mentioned anything, did he?"

"He didn't," Tommy said. "What's a passage party?"

Dani told him what she knew.

"It sounds crazy-dangerous. Liam's not a big risk taker."

"This is going to sound naïve," Dani told him, "but sometimes, even after all the work I've done with juveniles, I still don't understand why they want to get high. I never did. I think I had one sip of crème de menthe at a slumber party in eighth grade and I felt like I'd swallowed toothpaste. I wanted to throw up."

"You're asking the wrong guy," Tommy said. "Your one sip is one more than I've ever had."

"Seriously?" Dani said.

"You sound surprised," Tommy said.

"I am," she said. "I could have sworn I saw a picture of you with a bottle of something in your hand."

"If you did," he said, "it would have been champagne when we won the Super Bowl. But I was squirting it down my friend's pants, not drinking it."

"I guess the tabloids tried to make you out to be a party lizard," she said.

"The tabloids say a lot of things," Tommy said. "If you try to correct them, it only makes it worse."

"You never drank even in high school?"

Tommy shook his head. "I just always knew what I wanted," he said as she found her keys and unlocked the car. "Drinking or doing drugs wasn't going to help me get to where I wanted to go. It seemed obvious. If you want a healthy body, don't put stuff in it that's bad for you. I don't even like to take Tylenol."

"Kids give in to peer pressure," Dani said.

"I guess. Depends on who you consider your peers. Do you think it's strong enough to make somebody kill someone?"

"Excellent question. I've been asking myself that. I worked with a juvenile once who wanted to join a gang. They told him that as an initiation he had to shoot a homeless person. And he did. There were other factors, but that was peer pressure." She sighed. "I feel like I could sleep for three days straight. But I'll settle for three hours. Do you ever have trouble sleeping?"

"Only when the burglar alarm goes off," Tommy said. "Or if my dad's having problems. I actually have a baby monitor in his room. How's that for irony?"

"You're a good son," she said.

"Did you know that the animal that has the most dreams is the platypus?" he told her.

"How do you know that?"

"How do you *not* know that?" he said. "It's common knowledge. I read it somewhere."

"What do platypuses dream of?"

"Probably about being anything other than a platypus." He'd also read somewhere that trying to impress a girl with random facts was something only morons did.

Then he saw a flash of light reflecting off a telescopic lens. "Get down!"

He grabbed Dani by the shoulders and spun her around, shielding her with his body. She heard automobile tires screeching and broke free of his embrace in time to see a black sports car speed away.

"Who was that?"

"I don't know," Tommy said. "Paparazzi. Using a 1200 millimeter tele-photo lens. I used to see a lot of those. Prepare to see your picture in the papers tomorrow."

"Why would they want a picture of me?"

"No offense, but they don't," he said. "You'll probably be described as the mystery woman on the arm of ex-footballer Tommy Gunderson. Sorry about that. My reflexes aren't what they used to be."

"Do you know the name Vito Cipriano?" she asked him. "Gossip col-umnist for the *Star*?"

"Know him?" Tommy said. "I punched him in the face once . . . Aren't you going to ask why?"

"Do I need to?" she replied. "He was at the town meeting at the Grange Hall. He called my office four times today asking for a comment. We don't release the names of juveniles. Why is a gossip columnist covering a murder?"

"Because the parents are in the Who's Who of East Salem," Tommy said, zipping up his jacket and lifting the collar to cover the back of his neck.

"Except the victim's," Dani replied. "I apologize for my tone earlier, by the way. It's really good to have you on my side."

"No worries," Tommy said. "You haven't mentioned the voice mail you sent me. You okay?"

"It's just some nut job."

"What do you mean, just some nut job? The murderer is a nut job too."

"I'll be careful," she promised.

"Be more than careful," he told her. "Be totally paranoid. Err on the side of caution."

18.

When Dani called her office to check her voice mail, she was surprised to hear the receptionist pick up.

"What are you doing there?" Dani said. "Why aren't you home raking leaves?"

"I had some things I needed to finish," Kelly said. "Sam said I could have tomorrow afternoon off. There's a sale at the mall."

Kelly was twenty-four but could pass for eighteen. Hearing her voice gave Dani an idea.

"Could you do something for me, Kell?" she asked. "How'd you like to get paid to go to the mall?"

"Ooh," Kelly said. "My dream job gets even dreamier. What's up?"

"I need you to go to places where local kids hang out, like Starbucks or the Miss Salem Diner or the mall," Dani said. "Just blend in and see what they're talking about. Can you do that?"

"You mean go undercover?"

"No . . . ," Dani began. "I mean, yeah, I guess. Go undercover."

Dani was close to starving by the time she got home. She found a Tupperware container in her refrigerator, but when she opened it, the smell that escaped nearly made her lose her appetite. She put the lid back on and threw the whole thing into the garbage.

She cracked a pair of eggs into a cereal bowl, added a little milk (smelling it first to make sure it hadn't turned sour), blended it with a hand blender, grated some cheddar cheese, and made an omelet, though when she lifted the lid from the frying pan to see if the eggs had fluffed up, the cheese stuck to the lid. She couldn't start over because now she was out of both cheese and eggs, so she set the lid upside down on the cereal bowl and scraped a little melted cheese off it with each bite of egg.

She stared into space as she ate, daydreaming, which made her think of platypuses, which made her think of all the things she was learning about Tommy Gunderson, most of which were proving wrong the old things she'd thought about him. She wondered how many girls he'd dated, how many Hollywood starlets or models, and what they'd meant to him. She wanted to ask him about Cassandra Morton. Had he ever fallen truly, deeply in love?

Her reverie was interrupted when Arlo meowed loudly and wrapped himself around her legs. His dish was empty.

"Sorry, pal," she said. "My bad."

She refilled it, then noticed the light blinking on her answering machine. She hesitated, unsure what she'd do if she received another threat. Gary, Beth's husband, had argued that as a single woman living alone, she'd be smart to keep a gun in the house. Better to have it and not use it than need it and not have it, was his philosophy. She'd decided against it simply because she was a klutz with mechanical things. The cheese-covered frying-pan lid was a good example. If she owned a gun, she'd probably shoot herself in the foot.

The message on her answering machine was from Willis Danes, asking her if she'd had a chance to look at her calendar. She felt bad for forgetting him. It was too late to call him now, but she wrote a note reminding herself to call him in the morning and taped it to the bathroom mirror.

As she waited for the bathtub to fill, she drew the symbol found on the body of Julie Leonard on the steamed mirror with her finger. What did it mean? She believed that if they could answer that one question, the other answers would fall into place. She remembered what her Grandfather Howard had told her. *"Kids are easy to figure out because no matter how tough they think they are, they still have a little bit of innocence left inside, and if you can find it, it opens them up like a key in a lock."*

She thought of the young people she'd interviewed, trying so hard to be sophisticated and adult, when only three or four years ago they were probably still sleeping with stuffed animals tucked under their arms. Even though she hadn't met him yet, her prime suspect, based on what she knew so far, was Logan Gansevoort. She wondered what small piece of innocence was left in him.

Then a thought occurred to her. Her father had been a pediatrician, a good one, and practically the only one between Ridgefield and Mt. Kisco. It was possible that he'd been Logan Gansevoort's pediatrician too.

She turned off the water in the bathtub and then, on a hunch, went to the basement. In the far corner on a shelf, wedged between boxes of files she'd moved from her father's office after his death, she found his computer, an old Compaq that had been state-of-the-art the day she'd helped him buy it. Today there was more computing power in the toys they put in children's breakfast cereals.

She brought the computer upstairs and set it on the kitchen counter, then returned to the basement. It took her a few minutes to find all the proper cables and wires. In the kitchen she dusted off the CPU and wiped the dust from the monitor. When everything was connected properly, she plugged the cord into the wall, closed her eyes, and turned her head in case anything exploded, then turned on the computer by pressing the button in the back.

Nothing exploded. That was a good sign.

She crossed her fingers, waiting for the screen to light up.

The familiar partly cloudy sky that once served as the default wallpaper for Windows 95 appeared, along with a window asking her to input a password. This was unexpected, but when she typed in her mother's name, Amelia, the program opened with a friendly, "Welcome, Fred Harris." Her father, fearful that his paper files could be lost in a flood or fire, had been converting to digital and inputting all his medical data by hand. She'd helped him with some of it and was familiar with the software.

She found his patient files, went to the G section, and found what she was looking for. She skipped over the parts covering Logan's standard vaccinations and BMI growth percentiles and went straight to the Physician's Notes section, where her father had jotted down personal thoughts and impressions. The first note that caught her attention was one saying that Logan was still wetting his bed at the age of eleven. Late bed-wetting, Dani understood, was a predictor of adolescent emotional dysfunction.

Logan also suffered from nocturnal hydrosis, or night sweats. What would give a kid night sweats, a condition more common to older people and to women of menopausal age? Her father's note said he suspected Logan was taking his parents' prescription medications. That would do it. She wasn't surprised to read that when her father apprised Logan's parents of his suspicion, they'd terminated his services.

The bathwater wasn't nearly warm enough anymore, so she drained it, took a shower instead, brushed her teeth, and then checked her BlackBerry one last time before bed. She read an e-mail forwarded to her by Stuart, a note from Davis Fish. He was telling the district attorney's office that he had advised Logan not to speak with the police unless compelled by law. That meant Logan had to be either subpoenaed to testify before a grand jury or arrested outright.

Dani sat on the edge of her bed, staring at her new clock. 10:00 PM. She wanted to set it to wake her at eight, but she was too tired to figure out how it worked, so she put the clock on the floor and threw a pillow over it just in case it went off on its own.

She fell asleep quickly but awoke suddenly in the middle of the night. When she removed the pillow covering her clock radio, she read the time. 2:13 AM. Again.

She sat up. It took a second for the fog to clear, but as it did, she recalled her dream.

It was her first day of kindergarten. She was wearing a yellow dress. Both her parents were holding her hands as they walked to school. Her mother was wearing a matching yellow dress. Dani was scared of going to school, but she trusted her parents. When they got to school, she came to a very tall building where she was told she had to climb an endless ladder to get to class.

Jacob's ladder? Jung considered a ladder to represent the soul. He said that the angels Jacob saw in his dream were the words of God, lifting souls in distress or descending to earth to rescue souls in trouble.

Dani had climbed the dream ladder, but when she was high above the ground, a rung broke. She lost her grip and began to fall. As she fell, she saw down below that her father was going to try to catch her, and then she panicked because she knew that she was going too fast, and if she landed on him as he tried to catch her, she'd kill him.

She screamed for him to get out of the way and let her die, but he couldn't hear her.

Suddenly she blinked, looked around her, and only then realized she was standing in her kitchen.

The water was running in the sink.

She knew she was awake . . . before, she'd only *dreamed* she was awake. She'd walked in her sleep, dreaming that she was awake but still dreaming. She looked at the digital clock display on her oven.

It was 2:13.

She turned off the water and ran upstairs to her bedroom, where she saw her clock radio on the floor beside her bed with a pillow over it. She removed the pillow and watched as the numbers changed from 2:13 to 2:14.

Dani picked up her phone and dialed the first six digits of Tommy's home number before hanging up. *Don't be such a baby*, she told herself. *Calm down. Take a deep breath. Take another. You sleepwalked. It's not unusual.*

Before she went back to sleep, she checked her voice mail. Her call log showed she had two messages, one from Detective Casey and the other from an exchange in Fishkill, New York, a town on the Hudson River forty miles to the west. She listened to Casey's message first.

"Hey, Dani, it's Phil Casey. Listen, don't be concerned, but we traced the voice mail you got to the state hospital up in Fishkill. The relay tower matches. We're looking into it, but I thought you should know. I'll have a car keep an eye on your house."

She looked out the window and saw a police car parked at the end of her driveway.

She listened to the second message.

"This message is for Dr. Danielle Harris," a woman's voice said. "Dani,

I don't know if you remember me, but this is Ellen O'Reagan from the Fishkill Corrections Facility. I do meds here. We consulted about a year ago when you were helping evaluate one of my patients, a man named Jalen Simmons. Well, I have to apologize because apparently two days ago when I left the room, he grabbed my phone and found your cell number in it and called you. I'm sorry if it caused you concern, but don't worry because he's still here under lock and key. I called the DA's office and left a message, but again, I apologize. Call me if you have any questions."

Dani remembered the patient, a psychopath who'd killed three kids but had nevertheless managed to pass a polygraph test. Dani observed him wiping his hands on his pants and correctly diagnosed him with obsessive-compulsive disorder. She suggested that to get him to talk, they needed only to take away his soap and shut off the water to his sink. Within a few hours he was telling the police everything they needed to know.

She went back to her bedroom, stopping first in the bathroom to get a drink of water. She glanced at the mirror and remembered the note she had taped to remind herself to call Willis. She looked on the floor, in the wastebasket, everywhere. The note was definitely on the mirror when she'd brushed her teeth, just before 10:00 PM.

Now she couldn't find it anywhere.

MONDAY,
OCTOBER 18

19.

Tommy Gunderson had a weakness for gadgets.

He didn't just like them a little. He liked them a lot, and he had enough money to buy anything that caught his fancy, from the latest iPhone or digital e-book reader to an ice-fishing reel that had a built-in GPS to help locate the exact spot on the frozen lake where you drilled a hole and caught fish the last time you went ice fishing. He owned one of those, and he didn't even ice fish. He couldn't pass a Brookstone or a Sharper Image without picking up something, and the SkyMall catalogs he read on airplanes were the best part of any flight. When he'd decided to act on his childhood dream to become a private investigator, his first step was to take classes at John Jay College of Criminal Justice, but his second step was to go shopping.

He went to bed early but set his alarm to wake him shortly before moon-set, 3:53 AM, knowing the task he had in mind was best accomplished in absolute darkness. He dressed quickly, donning black sweats and boots, a black hooded sweatshirt, and his Barbour raincoat with the multiple pockets he'd need to carry the gear he'd laid out on the kitchen table. His ATN PVS7 Generation 3 military-grade night vision goggles went in one pocket. His SureFire 10X Dominator flashlight, which emitted 60 lumens for normal purposes but switched to 500 lumens, like a Star Trek phaser set to stun if you needed to temporarily blind someone, went in another. His Iridium 9555 satellite phone, which gave him reception anywhere on earth, went in the vest pocket. His Garmin Nuvi 680 GPS transponder, to bookmark his path, went in a side pouch.

In a matte black canvas backpack he stowed away three spray bottles of aminophthalhydrazide, commercially known as Luminol, a chemical that could reveal, by a chemo-luminescent reaction visible to NVGs, the presence of blood in solutions as dilute as one part per million, even if it had been exposed to the elements for up to three years.

He threw the backpack over one shoulder and his White's Spectra V3i metal detector, the best money could buy, over the other. He was about to leave when he thought twice and went to his top dresser drawer, where he kept his .45 Taurus 1911SS automatic. He moved the gun aside and found what he was looking for, the Boy Scout knife his father had given him when he'd become a Webelo. He put the knife in his pocket.

He checked his cell phone to see if he'd missed any calls from Dani. He'd been doing that a lot lately. She hadn't called. He hoped she was sound asleep. He armed his security system and checked himself one more time in the mirror and grabbed the keys to the Jeep.

The night was pitch black, but he didn't need light to see where he was going. He'd rambled and explored the woods of Bull's Rock Hill and the shores of Lake Atticus since he was a boy. He never got lost. Maybe that was where he'd gotten his sense of direction. It was where he'd played hide-and-seek or flashlight tag, and where he'd hiked with his dad, bug jar in one hand and butterfly net in the other. It was where he'd learned to ride a bike and where, beginning in seventh grade, he had run the trails and bridle paths before and after school to get in shape for sports. His triumphant moment came when he ran all the way to the top of Bull's Rock Hill without stopping. Eventually he ran the hill with ankle weights, then with ankle weights and a full weight vest, and finally, on a bet, he ran it carrying one of his teammates on his back, though by the time he reached the top, he was more staggering than running. He knew the way by daylight, and he knew it by moonlight, and he knew it when there was no moon at all and the path was difficult to find.

There were three routes to the top of the hill. The easiest was the southwestern approach along a gravel road and then a well-trodden path to the top. Next easiest was a footpath from the northwest that wound for about two miles through the woods. The most difficult route was a trail from the northeast that ultimately zigzagged up a steep incline via a series of switchbacks. The southern and southeastern faces of the hill, overlooking Lake Atticus, were too steep to be scaled except by rock climbers.

When Tommy tried to imagine somebody going to Bull's Rock Hill to commit a crime, any crime, but in particular the gruesome murder he was hoping to help solve, he couldn't imagine the perpetrator taking the first approach, where he'd be visible for much of the way. Nor could he imagine anyone taking the third, because it was too steep. So he parked his car on Keeler Street, at the gravel pull-off where the middle path began. The fact that the land was private property had never deterred the joggers and hikers and picnickers who used it, nor had The Pastures ever made a point of asking trespassers to stay away as long as they respected the lower reaches of the golf course itself.

At the head of the trail Tommy saw a trash can, and above it a sign that, in the beam of his flashlight, read No Littering. Someone with a black Magic Marker had altered the sign to read No Lettering. On a tree, another sign said All Dogs Must Be Leashed, beneath which someone had tacked a printout of a scruffy-looking brownish grinning mutt named Molly and the words LOST DOG / MUCH LOVED—13 YEARS OLD—PART TERRIER AND PART ??? IF FOUND, CALL 917-555-8746. A third sign said "Prevent Lyme Disease / These Woods Are Home to Deer Ticks."

He worked slowly, sweeping the trail with his metal detector and spraying with Luminol, using his NVGs to search the grounds. According to Frank DeGidio, the police had already searched the trail in daylight but found nothing. Tommy had about three hours until sunup.

In the first mile he found an earring, forty-five cents, a man's watch, and a silver filling from a tooth.

Halfway to the peak, he stopped.

To one side of the path, where he sprayed the Luminol, he found a drop of blood, then smaller secondary drops in a splash pattern. He'd read about splatter paths in a few scholarly criminology papers and a chapter in a textbook, but he was no expert. He used his GPS to bookmark and cache the location. If he had to guess, it looked as if the blood had dropped from a height of perhaps two or three feet, ruling out—also only a guess—a kill by some bird of prey, a hawk or an owl swooping down on some unsuspecting vole or wood rat.

Taken alone, there was no way to give the blood droplets any meaning. He moved in a circle, spraying with Luminol and using the NVGs, looking for indications of any larger configurations.

Don't be in a hurry, he reminded himself. *Maybe Sherlock Holmes saw the whole story in an instant, but for the rest of us it takes time.*

He was thinking the first configuration of droplets was an isolated incident, when he found a second set showing splatter paths similar to the first.

He marked the spot again with his GPS, visualized a line from the first drop to the second, then projected where the line might lead, from the first to the second to a possible third. He walked the line and had gone another thirty yards when he came to the stump of a mountain ash, sawn off years ago during a forest service timber cull. As a kid he'd learned that ash stumps made great places to hide things because they tended to rot and turn hollow from the inside out. Usually they held stagnant water where mosquitoes bred. Expecting nothing, he sprayed the inside of the hollow stump.

It was full of blood.

Oddly, he found no splash or splatter paths on the surrounding ground. Instead, he noted a saturation along one side of the stump's inner wall, from the top to the pool below. It was as if somebody had very carefully poured blood into the stump, making sure not to spill.

Why? Were they disposing of it? Trying to hide it?

He switched off his NVGs and used the flashlight at low illumination. The reservoir inside the stump was probably part rainwater by now. He took an eyedropper from the evidence collection kit he'd bought online from a police supply website and drew a sample, then marked the stump with both a cached GPS reading and a white evidence flag.

He returned to the trail. Sweeping and spraying as he went, he moved slowly up the hill to the crime scene and the bare granite promontory overlooking the lake. He could get no closer than fifty feet before he came to the area marked off with yellow police tape. He half expected to find a police officer there keeping watch, but he was alone. He considered stepping over the tape but remembered how Dani had cautioned him against contaminating witnesses. That probably went for crime scenes too. He respected the perimeter and stayed outside the circle.

Even so, there might be something the others had missed. In the movies it was always the most dogged detectives who solved the crimes. He moved slowly, working mainly with the metal detector. He found a rusted bolt, a penny, a BB from a BB gun, and a foil wrapper from a piece of gum.

As he circled, he looked back to the scene of the murder. He tried to picture two people, or three, four, eight, ten. What were they doing? Standing in a circle? In a line? In a random pattern? How were they killing her? Taking turns? Stabbing? Worse? One kid? Two? All of them? Were some looking away, afraid? Were some holding themselves at a distance? Was anyone hiding, perhaps, or even watching from the bushes, trying not to be seen?

Liam's cell phone had been found in the weeds beneath a tree, Dani had said. Tommy found the closest tree and scanned the weeds around it.

Nothing.

He kept moving, measuring, trying to imagine what had happened and why. They were saying it was some kind of ritualistic killing. What did rituals do? What rituals were there? Weddings. Birthdays. Funerals. Rites of passage. Offerings. Transitions from one state to another.

Which was this?

He could probably rule out weddings and birthdays.

He stood beneath a maple tree, gazing toward the bare rock, the image of a sleeping bull lit by the beam of his flashlight. Had someone stood in this spot the night of the crime, with a view of the killing and the darkened countryside beyond?

He put the metal detector over his shoulder because it was getting heavy and turned toward the lake, then the woods. When he got a momentary false positive from the detector, he turned it off. Then he turned it on again. It wasn't going to give him false positives, suspended in the air, resting on his shoulder. The dish had been pointing toward the trunk of the tree. He scanned the tree and heard another positive. There was something metal about six feet above the ground on the trunk.

He turned on his flashlight.

Felt with his hand.

Something.

He found a small nail, the kind used to hang lightweight picture frames, pounded into the rough bark of the tree at an angle. It appeared to be made of blued steel, not brass or aluminum. It was not rusted. It was new. It had been driven into the bark at an angle. Why at an angle? To hang something from it. Hang what?

A picture?

No.

A mirror?

A hammock?

A hammock for gerbils maybe. Why would gerbils want hammocks?

Concentrate, Tommy.

Something had hung from it. Something on a strap. Something small enough not to pull the nail out.

Something electronic.

A camera.

Why?

To record the ritual.

Why?

To show it to somebody.

Who? Why?

Then he heard something behind him . . .

Tommy shut the flashlight off and turned. Nothing. He crouched down and moved from where he'd been standing, just in case someone had him in the sights of a rifle.

He waited.

He flipped the night vision goggles down. The electronically amplified starlight revealed an odd array of shadows and shapes. He was certain that he'd heard something.

Then he saw what appeared to be the outline of a man standing opposite him in the woods, in the shadows between two large trees, but unmistakable. The goggles gave him nothing more than the silhouette. He flipped them up, then found his flashlight and adjusted the setting from sixty to five hundred lumens. He aimed the flashlight at the place where the man was standing and pressed the button, the woods filling with light nearly as bright as a night baseball game.

There was no one there.

He searched the area to make sure. Nothing.

He remembered a story from his days as a Boy Scout, just one of those campfire tales intended to scare, purportedly from ancient Indian lore, a legend about a shape-shifter who resided in these very woods, a demon who was there one minute and gone the next. The Paykak, Old Whitney had called it. Probably scarier because his scoutmaster was also a funeral director, though he never talked about his profession during scout meetings.

Tommy had bought the premise hook, line, and sinker as a Webelo and had been scared half to death and stayed up until dawn in his tent with the pocketknife his father had given him open in his hand.

But of course, now that he was older and wiser, he knew the story as just that . . . a story and nothing more.

He felt in his pocket for the jackknife all the same. He was older and he was wiser, but he was still human. Something had been there, and then it was gone.

Tommy drove home and considered going back to sleep, but he had too much on his mind. So he went to the gym instead, thinking he might work off some of his excess energy. He arrived at five and disarmed the security system, turned on the lights, dropped three mesh bags of towels down the chute to the laundry, checked to make sure the snack bar was stocked, and then walked the facility to see if there was anything else he needed to attend to.

At the batting cages he saw that someone had left a helmet on home plate in the pros cage. The machines were set to various speeds, ranging from 30 mph in the kiddie cage all the way to 105 mph in the pros.

Tommy entered the cage and bent down to pick up the batting helmet.

As he rose, a reflexive sensation he could only describe as a kind of instinct, a faculty honed on the football field to protect himself from blindside hits, told him something was coming.

He turned his head, reacted in a microsecond, and hit the deck just before a hundred-mile-an-hour fastball zipped past his ear and clanged into the wire backstop. Had the pitch been another inch lower or a few miles an hour faster, he would have been beaned and, at that speed, possibly killed.

He stayed low and crept out of the line of fire, but the pitching machine at the other end of the cage was now still, a red light showing instead of green. He listened. He was alone in the building. He approached the far end of the cage carefully along the side wall, opened the door to the maintenance area, and felt the pitching machine. It was warm. Someone had left it on all night.

He shut it off, grabbed an Out of Order sign from where it hung from a peg on the wall, reentered the batting cage, and hung the sign from the front of the machine. He picked up the ball, which had rolled back down the gutter to the reloading chute. Nothing about it seemed at all unusual, except that it had just tried to kill him.

"What did I ever do to you?" he asked the ball.

Then he heard something, distant and impossible to locate. He'd turned up the heat in the building. It could have been a radiator making the sound of someone laughing.

He was fooling himself.

"Allow for the possibility that evil is real," Carl had said.

Allowing for that possibility in as open-minded a way as he could, Tommy concluded that something evil was trying to kill him, possibly the same person who killed Julie Leonard. But it was also possible that it wasn't a person. The thing in the woods. The batting machine. He'd been fearless on the football field, but he couldn't fight what he couldn't see or understand.

Suddenly, he wasn't feeling fearless anymore.

20.

Dani checked her calendar, then called Willis Dane's home number and told his caregiver she'd have time to see him Wednesday afternoon.

She made toast for breakfast and then called Tommy. She'd wanted to tell him what she'd learned regarding Jalen Simmons and his copycat voice mail as soon as she'd learned about it, but of course it was the middle of the night. She told him that Logan Gansevoort's lawyer, Davis Fish, was still being uncooperative, as was St. Adrian's Academy.

"I've gotta run—have an appointment with the guidance counselor at ESH," she told him. Later she intended to talk with Julie Leonard's mom and sister and with Amos Kasden's parents, and she hoped Tommy would come along and provide a second point of view.

"Great," she said when he agreed. "I'll pick you up at All-Fit in an hour."

⁂

East Salem High consistently ranked in the top-ten high schools in New York, despite chronic budget wrangling and school board politics and hirings and firings. Fed by four elementary schools and two middle schools, the school had a predominantly white upper-middle-class student body and had developed a reputation for excellent athletics and strong programs in the creative arts, theater, music, and writing.

To Dani, the hallways seemed weirdly unchanged. The display case in the lobby outside the main office had been decorated in Halloween themes by the Debate Club, black cats and pumpkins and black construction paper silhouettes of owls saying *whom* instead of *who*. On the wall beside it, a map of the world showed the places where senior class projects had helped build affordable housing or schools or clinics. Dani often found herself defending her hometown where, yes, outsiders correctly observed, there was a great deal of wealth and self-interest, but there were also a lot of good people who gave of their time and money and wanted to make the world a better place.

When she made an appointment with the office, she'd been happily surprised to learn the guidance counselor was a former classmate, Jill Ji-Sung. She'd been a popular cheerleader when Dani was a bookish dweeb.

Jill remembered Dani too and filled her in on the current social scene at East Salem, which was in many ways not so different from when they had attended, but in other ways was unrecognizable. Cell phones. Text messages. Twitter. Facebook, IM chats, Formspring. The same social dynamics prevailed, the rivalries and petty jealousies and mean kids who picked on weak kids, though now there was cyber-bullying to add to all the traditional ways the strong harassed the meek. Julie Leonard was probably among the latter group, according to Jill.

"A bit invisible," the guidance counselor said, "maybe as a survival strategy. We had an incident last year when somebody wrote an anonymous comment about Julie in one of the girls' bathrooms. Something about the outfit she was wearing. I called her in and asked her if her feelings were hurt. She said it was just somebody who didn't know her trying to be funny, and everybody had a right to an opinion. She really tried to see the good in everybody. Not as a goody-two-shoes. Just because that was how she wanted to live."

That had been Jill's only contact with Julie Leonard. On the other hand, she had spoken to Logan Gansevoort on numerous occasions, once when drugs were found in his locker and again when a younger boy complained that Logan had snapped him with a wet towel in the locker room.

"I have to say," Jill confided, "it seemed pretty clear to a lot of us at the time that Logan's father applied some sort of pressure on the principal or the school superintendent. He got probation where other kids would have been suspended."

"Do you think he's capable of violence?" Dani asked.

"He certainly has a sense of entitlement," Jill said. "And maybe impunity too. I'm no psychologist, but it seems to me he keeps pushing the limits precisely because his parents never set any. It's not that he wants to get caught, but he wants them to set boundaries. Kids who grow up without any think their parents don't care."

"Unfortunately, sometimes they're right."

"He's definitely the G-Money around here," Jill said.

"Speaking of which . . . ," Dani said, then described how she'd come into contact with Tommy Gunderson after not seeing him for nearly a dozen years. He seemed the same, Dani said, then corrected herself. "Actually, he seems better. More mature. 'Course, most of us are more mature at thirty than we were at eighteen . . . one hopes."

"He had such a crush on you," Jill said. "When he told everybody he knew they had to vote for you but that you'd kill him if you ever found out, I was sure you guys were going to end up in a big house on Willow Pond with lots of little homecoming princes and princesses."

Dani thanked the guidance counselor and left before she blushed red enough to set off the smoke alarms. Outside, she took a moment to recover. It had never dawned on her that Tommy Gunderson had felt anything but sorry for her in high school, if she ever crossed his mind at all. He'd asked people to vote for her? Really?

～～

Today Tommy was wearing hiking boots, khaki cargo pants, and a leather bomber-style jacket over a white shirt. She wondered if he even owned a tie, and suppressed a fleeting desire to take him shopping.

He was sitting on the curb outside the gym, but jumped to his feet when Dani pulled up. He ran a hand along the hood of her car as he walked to the passenger side.

"Where we going first?" he asked, getting in her car.

143

"To see the Kasdens. Amos's parents. Then Julie's mom," she told him. "Phil Casey talked to her, but he thought it would be a good idea if we did too. The Kasdens live right in town."

"I know," Tommy said. "Mitchell Kasden is my dad's dentist. Dad was having a good night last night, memory-wise. He said he remembered once when Mitchell came into the nursery. He had a kid with him who kept pulling the heads off the flowers. That was Amos."

"Interesting."

"How so?" Tommy asked, pausing to shut off his cell phone.

It occurred to Dani that none of the men she'd ever seen socially did that. She had Tommy's undivided attention.

"Kids who torture animals often turn into very troubled adults," Dani said. "I'm not sure if decapitating flowers counts. It's not dissimilar."

"She hates me, she hates me not," Tommy said. "I was actually at the library looking up stories about people who tortured dogs. Did I tell you I walked the back trail up Bull's Rock Hill last night and found a tree stump full of blood?"

"Excuse me? No, you didn't tell me."

He explained his findings of the previous night, the blood and the nail in the tree, drawing an imaginary map on the dashboard to show her approximately where each event took place.

"I called my cop friend Frank and told him what I'd found out," Tommy said. "He said he'd make sure Detective Casey got it. Frank thought the blood was probably from some animal, which made me think. Where I parked the car, there was a sign for a lost dog. I heard George Gardener once shot a dog that wandered onto his property, but maybe that was just one of those local legends kids make up. I asked my Aunt Ruth to look through the archives of the East Salem *Courier*. No luck. I thought of George because of the double G."

"What double G?"

"The symbol," Tommy said. "The one they found on Julie's stomach."

"This?" Dani said, reaching into the backseat as she drove and fishing in the side pouch of her briefcase to show Tommy the drawing of the ⑺ she'd shown the girls the day before.

Tommy took it and stared at it. He turned it upside down once, then right side up again.

"Never mind," he said, putting it back in her briefcase. "I thought maybe if George was a suspect, he was signing his name. That's all."

"You thought it was a double G?"

"Never mind," Tommy repeated.

Suddenly she had a reasonable diagnosis. "Tommy," she said. "Are you dyslexic?"

He didn't answer at first. "Maybe a little," he said. "I spent a year at a special needs school relearning how to learn. That's why fourth grade took me two years. Not three. As per your earlier comment."

"I'm so sorry," she said, remembering the joke she'd made. She took her eyes off the road to look at him. "Tommy, I had no idea . . ."

That explained why he was so observant. People with dyslexia had to look harder at the details surrounding them and overcome a dysfunction of the visual pathways, decoding what information was meaningful and what wasn't. It was like trying to hear what someone was saying at a really loud party. For dyslexics, the world was full of visual noise.

"It's all right," Tommy said. "I'm not ashamed of it. I just don't talk about it much because people look at you funny. Or they feel sorry for you."

"I admire anybody who overcomes it," Dani said. "For the record." She changed the subject. "Do you remember Jill Ji-Sung?"

"Of course," he said. "Who wouldn't remember her?"

Dani couldn't deny that Jill had been cute as a button, but Tommy's words stung slightly. "What do you mean by that?"

"We only had one Korean cheerleader," Tommy said. "Right? Did I miss one?"

Dani had to laugh. "Well, she's now the guidance counselor at East Salem."

She related what Jill had told her about Logan Gansevoort. He was finishing his education at a public high school because he'd been thrown out of two private schools. He had a variety of problems, most of them involving substance abuse. He'd been arrested once for getting into a fight in a bar during a winter vacation his family had sent him on to Nevis/St. Kitts.

"Sent him?" Tommy said. "They didn't go with him?"

"They figured he was old enough," Dani said.

"How old was he?"

"Fifteen."

"Sheesh," Tommy said. "Seems a little young to be getting into bar fights. Can you put people in jail for bad parenting?"

"Not until somebody actually gets hurt."

She wondered what kind of parenting she'd find as she drove to the Kasden home. The neighborhood was one of the newer developments, if you could call it a neighborhood when no house was visible from any of the other houses. The Kasden home was a large colonial, set back from the road behind a wall of shrubs and a gated driveway.

Dani used her cell phone to call the house, and the gate opened. She usually assumed gates at the ends of driveways were there to keep people out. When she saw a yard filled with skateboards and bicycles, pitch-backs and soccer balls, discarded sweatshirts and stray footballs and baseballs and basketballs, she decided that the Kasdens' gate was probably there to keep the wildness in.

Jane Kasden apologized for the mess before letting them in. Dani estimated, by the quantity of detritus strewn about, that the Kasdens had either twenty girls or four boys. The latter turned out to be correct. In addition to Amos, they had sons twelve, eight, and four. The oldest child was African-American, the middle child was Asian, and the youngest had Down syndrome.

The mother escorted Dani and Tommy into the study, which was as orderly as the rest of the house was messy. Mitchell Kasden was at his desk, paying bills. He rose from his chair and invited Dani and Tommy to sit on a large leather couch.

"I like your man-cave," Tommy said.

"The boys aren't allowed in," the father said, "and yet I regularly find Lego blocks and Pokemon cards in my files. How could that be?"

When Dani asked them to give her a little background on their unusual family, they explained how they'd learned, after losing their first child to Tay-Sachs disease, that they were both carriers of the recessive gene that caused it. The chance of losing a second child to Tay-Sachs was too high. They decided they could afford to adopt a family.

Amos was the first child they'd taken in, adopted at age six through an accredited agency in the former Soviet Union. He'd attended East Salem Elementary despite not speaking a word of English on his first day, did well academically but began developing behavioral problems. Mitchell Kasden thought it started the day he taught Amos to play chess.

"We knew he was extremely bright," he said. "Within a few months he was beating me regularly, and I'm pretty good. But then he couldn't stop thinking about chess. We had to take the board away from him, but he kept playing games in his head. We wondered if it had something to do with his coming from Russia. Chess is almost the national game there."

"And then he started speaking Russian again," Jane said. "It was the strangest thing. You're not supposed to be able to retain your native tongue if you don't have anybody to speak it with." She looked nervously at her husband.

"Sometimes we'd find him in his room, speaking Russian," Mitchell said. "Frankly, it frightened Jane. And me. As if he were having conversations with someone who wasn't there."

"Did you ever get a Russian-speaking person to tell you what he was saying?" Dani asked.

"Once," the father said. "But Amos refused to talk."

"He knew someone was listening?" Tommy asked.

"We don't see how he could have," the father said. "We didn't tell him the man we brought in was fluent in Russian. Anyway, we did some research and learned that St. Adrian's is one of the most highly regarded schools in the world for boys with emotional or developmental impairments. And here it was, right in our own hometown."

"They've done wonderful things for him, I have to say," Jane said. "He has tutors for every class. He has friends. He was home for two weeks last summer and he played so nicely with his brothers. We really couldn't be happier."

"It's not cheap," Mitchell said. "But it doesn't matter if it helps him."

When Dani asked about the night that Amos had gone to the party, they said they didn't know much. The Kasdens had talked to the dean of students and the assistant headmaster. The school had a policy of strictly controlling contact between students and family, "since so often it's the family relationships that are causing the behavioral problems," Jane explained.

"Amos had off-campus privileges that night," she continued. "He'd gone into town. He told us he'd known a few of the kids at the party from elementary school but he'd lost touch with them."

"He found them again on Facebook," Mitchell said. "He ran into Logan and Terence downtown the night of the party. That Gansevoort boy is just a bad kid—" He stopped himself and apologized, then added, "Rayne Kepplinger is a piece of work too. I did her retainers. I've never had a patient complain as much as she did."

"The point is," Jane said, "yes, Amos went with them to Logan's house, but when he realized there was going to be drinking, he left. He walked back to campus. The surveillance video shows him brushing his teeth in the bathroom in his dorm. We saw it."

"What time was that?" Dani asked. "I haven't heard of any surveillance video."

"The school told us they just sent it over to the police this morning," Jane said. "It was taken a little after one in the morning. The police said it would have taken Amos at least half an hour to walk from Logan's house."

Meaning, Dani realized, that Amos would have been in his room at the time of the murder. The look Tommy gave her told her he'd done the same math.

"We heard they were drinking," Mitchell said. "Amos knows he can't combine alcohol with his medications."

"What are his medications?" Dani asked.

"His doctor could tell you exactly," Jane said. "It's a combination, but it's strictly monitored."

"The school won't release his medical records without your permission," Dani said. "In writing."

"You've got it," Mitchell said. "I'll send it today. You understand why they're so concerned with security, don't you? There are children of nine world leaders enrolled there. And six from royal families. They have to be careful."

Dani thanked them and said they'd been very helpful. On their way out, she and Tommy were stopped by the three other Kasden boys, all carrying magazine covers and footballs they wanted Tommy to autograph with a black marker. One had a poster for the New York Giants. Tommy explained that he'd never played for the Giants, but the boys wanted him to sign it anyway.

"What'd you think?" Dani asked once they were in the car again.

"I think they're good people," Tommy said. "I'm liking Logan Gansevoort less and less."

"I'm liking him more and more," Dani said. "As a suspect."

From the Kasdens' house it was a ten-minute drive to the Lake Kendell community, a cluster of small Craftsman homes and three-season cottages on the southern shore of the lake where Westchester County abutted Putnam County. This was East Salem's response to the New York State Housing Reform Act, which required every town to develop a percentage of housing for low-income families. In the rest of East Salem, the minimum lot size was four acres. At Lake Kendell there was no minimum. Some cottages were built as little as ten feet apart. Some dwellings, on waterfront lots, were well-kept and afforded a pleasant if not luxurious lifestyle with boating and water-skiing and fishing opportunities. The houses farther back from the lake were less well kept and had gardens that needed weeding, siding in need of painting, rusted gutters, fences with missing slats.

The wealthy considered Lake Kendell an eyesore. Those who lived there considered it home, a place to drink beer on their porches and put pink plastic lawn flamingos in their gardens if they had a mind to.

The house where Julie Leonard had lived was at the end of Sunset Lane, set back from the lake without a view of either the lake or the setting sun, as best Dani could tell. It was painted a muted periwinkle blue with off-white trim. She saw three pumpkins at the end of the porch, uncarved, and a bird feeder hanging above the railing. There were home-crafted dream catchers and stained-glass sun catchers hanging inside the picture window. The brass door knocker was in the shape of a horse's head, and Dani decided to give it a try.

Connie Leonard let them in and, after they'd introduced themselves, immediately offered them coffee. "I'm sorry about the mess," she said, referring to the basket of unwashed clothes on the kitchen counter and the dishes in the sink. "I'm still not quite myself."

Connie was in her forties, her thin light brown hair teased and brushed back. She was wearing a beige cardigan over a light blue cotton turtleneck and gray sweatpants, with sheepskin slippers on her feet. She wore no makeup and looked tired, defeated, spent.

"That's all right," Dani said. She noticed a framed portrait of a girl on the mantel and recognized the face and the signature as Julie's. The portrait was neither self-flattering nor self-deprecating. It was honest, and it was good. The eyes were particularly well done and seemed to be looking straight at the viewer.

"That's my Jules," Connie said, noticing where Dani was looking.

"Pretty," Dani said. "If this is a bad time . . ."

"No, no," Connie said. "I mean, the last few days have been one non-stop bad time. I'm not sure I have anything more to say than what I already told the detectives."

"The lead detective asked me to follow up," Dani said, handing Connie her card.

Connie looked at it, gesturing for Dani and Tommy to sit in a pair of armchairs opposite the couch, where she then sat.

"I was wondering what you could tell us about Julie," Dani began. "She sounds like a great kid."

"She was the best," Connie said. She sounded hoarse.

"Was she popular at school?"

"She had friends," Connie said. "I imagine she could have wanted more. All kids want more friends. You know how kids are."

"Enemies?" Dani asked.

Connie shook her head. "That's the weirdest part. There's just no . . . nothing logical about it. There's just no reason anybody would want to do something like this. I can't make any sense of it."

Dani wondered if she'd ever heard a voice so lost.

"Maybe the police can make sense of it," she said. "The kind of person who could do something like this doesn't see the world the same way we do. We can't understand it because we can't see through their eyes."

"I suppose you're right," Connie said, grabbing a fresh tissue and drying her eyes.

"Do you know if Julie was friends with Rayne Kepplinger or Khetzel Ross or Blair Weeks?" Dani said.

Connie grimaced.

"Were they ever over here to visit? Did she ever go to their houses?"

"They were never here," Connie said, looking around sadly, staring at a spot on the rug before looking up. "Julie would have been too embarrassed to ask any of them over. But I know she was in the Kepplingers' and the Weekses' homes because I have service contracts with them. Julie started helping out after I had to let two of my girls go. I just couldn't afford to pay them anymore. Since the recession."

"Julie helped you clean the houses of her friends?" Dani asked.

"Kara too," Connie said. "I know how that must have felt to her. She never complained. We tried to do it during hours when they weren't home, but that wasn't always possible. You know, the newspaper quoted me saying I think the rich kids are going to get away with murder, but I didn't say that. I said if you've got money, you can do whatever you want, but I was half out of my mind. I'm sure they get special favors sometimes . . ." She let the thought go.

"Actually," Tommy said, "it's sort of the opposite. I know most of the East Salem cops, and they're all townies. They pop the preppies every chance they get."

Dani looked up when Julie's sister, Kara, came down the stairs and sat on the couch next to her mother, hugging a decorative pillow to her chest. She was fourteen or fifteen, Dani guessed, wearing an oversized East Salem High sweatshirt. Dani wondered if it belonged to Julie. Where Connie seemed lost and forlorn, Kara looked angry.

"Is it all right if Kara joins us?" Connie said. "We've decided there aren't ever going to be any secrets between us anymore."

"Were there secrets between you and Julie?" Dani asked.

"I'm sure there were," Connie said. "Girls always hide things. But nothing important. Smoking in the garage. Just normal stuff."

"Did she ever talk about the supernatural?" Dani asked. "Was she into vampires like the rest of the kids are these days?"

Connie looked at Kara.

"She liked 'em," Kara said. "But there's nothing wrong with that."

"What did she like about them?"

"She just liked how the people in the books were totally in love with each other spiritually but they could never consummate their love physically because one was a vampire and the other wasn't," Kara said. "She didn't believe in vampires, but she believed you could love people who weren't necessarily lovable."

"Did she have a boyfriend?" Dani asked.

Connie again looked at Kara.

"I don't know if you could call him a boyfriend," Kara said, "but about a year ago she had a huge crush on one boy. I don't know if they ever went out."

"Do you remember his name?"

"Liam Dorsett," Kara said.

Dani looked at Tommy, who gave no indication that he knew anything about a relationship between Liam and the victim. She knew he would have said something if he'd known.

"She was upset because he dumped her," Kara said. "Why? Is he involved in this?"

"Kara," her mother said, "Dr. Harris is trying to help us. Please dial it down."

"Had Julie ever sneaked out of the house before?" Dani asked.

Kara nodded.

"Do you know what she did or who she was with? Did she ever sneak out to see Liam Dorsett?"

Kara shook her head. "I think Julie was embarrassed," she said. "I don't know what he did to her. She wouldn't talk about it."

Dani asked questions to reconstruct Julie's last night. Connie had fallen asleep on the couch. Someone had thrown a blanket over her, presumably Julie. The police found the clothes Julie had changed out of in the garage. She'd changed into a party dress.

"It sounds like she was really looking forward to the party at Logan's house," Dani said.

"You wouldn't believe how excited she was," Kara said. "She made me promise not to tell."

"Did she know who was going to be there?"

"She mentioned some girls from school."

"How did she get there?" Dani asked. "It's pretty far from here. Did she have a car?"

"I think someone picked her up. I was asleep," Kara said.

"Did you know what kind of party she was going to?" Dani asked.

Kara hesitated. Then she said, "It was a passage party. They're—"

"I know what they are," Dani said. "Did she know? Did she think she'd be safe?"

"It's only dangerous if you don't believe," Kara said, taking her mother's hand and squeezing it. "I told her not to go. I told her it was stupid. I was worried."

"Why were you worried?" Dani asked.

"Because you're not supposed to mess with stuff you don't understand."

"Do you mean the drugs?"

"Any of it," Kara said. "But I never saw Julie drink anything. Or smoke pot. I swear."

"Do you know why she went?"

Kara gave her mother an apologetic glance, then said, "She was hoping she could talk to our dad."

Dani was aware that Tommy was resting his hand on the back of her chair, but now she felt him touch her reassuringly.

"We don't know what happened to him," Connie apologized. "Julie was convinced her father was dead, because otherwise she was sure he would have tried to find her. Kara thinks she just wanted to know for sure, one way or the other."

"She tried to track him down online," Kara said, again glancing at her mother. "We both did. We Googled him and used the different websites, but we never got a hit."

As the conversation continued, Tommy asked if he could use the bathroom. While he was gone, Dani showed Kara the picture taken of Julie and Amos the night of the murder. Kara didn't recognize Amos, but that didn't mean anything. Julie sometimes chatted with people online, she said, or went to the Facebook pages of other people from school and fished their listed friends to invite kids to become her friend too.

Dani recalled what Casey had told her they'd learned after his team had gone over Julie's laptop. Julie had eighty-seven Facebook friends. Only one kid from the party was on her friends list, Rayne Kepplinger, who had over three thousand friends. Most of the messages posted on Julie's wall were prosaic exchanges like *I'm really worried about today's test*, or *Does anybody know what pages we're supposed to read tonight from Hamlet?* Only one seemed relevant to the crime, a brief exchange with Liam, almost a year old.

Julie Leonard: One question. Why?

Liam Dorsett: It just wasn't going to work out.

Casey had also discovered that Julie had deleted her browsing history. All her stored e-mails had been deleted as well, and her recycle bin was empty.

Dani asked Kara if clearing her caches was something Julie did on a regular basis. "Do you think she wanted to hide something?" Dani asked.

"She would have told me," Kara said. "We talked about everything."

"Can I ask you one last question? I hear a lot of anger in your voice. You said you didn't want her to go to the party, that you were worried, and yet you also said you were asleep when she left. How was it that you fell asleep? If I'm worried about something, it keeps me awake."

"She promised me she wasn't going," Kara said. "She lied to me . . ."

Now Kara's anger gave way to tears. Her mother went to her and hugged her.

"A penny for your thoughts," Dani said as she turned the car back onto the main road away from the lake.

"I was thinking that was hard," Tommy said.

"It was," she agreed.

"And I think Julie Leonard was a very lonely girl," Tommy said.

"It's such a hard age," Dani said. "There's nothing more important than having friends."

"Or a father," Tommy added.

"I'd never say single mothers can't raise happy children," Dani said, "but it's twice as hard when someone has to be both mother and father. Kids without fathers are significantly more prone to violence and under-achievement than kids with active dads in their lives."

"I see it at the gym all the time," Tommy said. "Speaking anecdotally. I've had trouble over the years with six kids, and all six of them came from households without dads. I'm batting a thousand."

"But not all kids with single moms give you trouble," Dani said.

"No," Tommy said. "But all six who did were."

"The one thing I know," Dani said, "is that kids without dads look for them. Or seek them in someone else."

"I think I might have found something interesting in the bathroom," Tommy told her. "I looked in their medicine cabinet."

"You can't go looking in other people's medicine cabinets."

"What planet do you live on?" he said. "Everybody looks in medicine cabinets. Besides—I'm a professional private detective."

She gave him a look.

"In training," he corrected himself.

"Without a search warrant," she reminded him. "Nothing you found is anything we can use in court."

"Which is fine," he said, "because I didn't find anything."

"I thought you said you found something interesting."

"I did," he said. "What was interesting was that I didn't find anything."

"Do you want to help me understand that?"

"Who do you know who doesn't have medicine in the medicine cabinet?" he said. "They had nothing. No little orange bottles. Nothing for allergies. No over-the-counter painkillers. Just toothpaste and soaps and moisturizers."

"Maybe they keep the medicine somewhere else?"

"Why would they do that?"

"Because . . . ," Dani said.

But he was right. Why would they do that?

⁂

When she got home, she put a potato in the microwave, made a mental note to go to the grocery store because the potato was all she had to eat, then booted up her father's old computer.

"I've seen the bare bottoms of over half the people in this town, kiddo," he'd once said. *"It gives me a whole new perspective whenever I vote."*

Both Julie and Kara Leonard had been patients, according to his medical records. Dani found the recorded dates for all the standard vaccinations but no record for any office visits. No earaches, sore throats, fevers of causes unknown, rashes, bruises, insect bites—nothing. It wasn't a matter of keeping a sick kid home because she couldn't afford the co-pay; Connie Leonard had maintained full health coverage.

Dani opened her laptop in the kitchen and logged into her work files. She reexamined the crime scene photographs of Julie's body, enlarging the images to the maximum before they pixilated. She could find no blemishes on Julie's skin, no acne on her face. Julie's dental files had been included as part of the information Baldev Banerjee had used to confirm the body identification. The dental files showed that Julie had perfect teeth as well.

What were the odds of that?

Dani desperately needed to sleep. She tried one more time to figure out how to set the alarm on her new clock radio. Then she had a better idea. She found her parents' old alarm, the kind with a dial face with hands on it and a knob on the back that pulled out to set the alarm and pushed in to shut it off. She moved the hands to the correct time and set the alarm for seven, pulled the knob on the back, set the clock atop her dresser so she'd have to cross the room to shut it off, and plugged the cord into the wall. Satisfied, she turned off the light and fell asleep.

She awoke when she heard the phone ring. The morning light pouring in through the window told her she'd slept through the night. According to the clock radio, it was 6:41. The phone rang again, and then she heard her assistant Kelly's voice, leaving her a message:

"Hi, Dani, it's Kelly. I hung out where you asked me to and I couldn't come up with anything, but I guess somebody figured out I was snooping because they drew the symbol they found on Julie Leonard's body on my windshield. Sam said I could take my vacation, so I'm going to spend a week with my brother in Philadelphia because I'm really freaked out."

At first Dani thought it was a copycat, but how could it be? The police hadn't released any information about the symbol. The only one who would know about the symbol was the killer. Or, she suddenly realized, Rayne or Khetzel—Dani had shown it to them. A rookie mistake, but she should have known better.

Dani laid her head back down and pulled the covers over her face. When she did, she remembered the dream she'd had.

It had been an apocalyptic dream. A flood had washed out New York City. Millions of people were fleeing the city in white vans, white trucks, white cars, while she sat on a hillside watching helplessly. People were jumping from the windows of tall buildings.

"You can't dream of something you've never perceived consciously," her med school professor had once said. *"Dreams recombine data, but they do not import data. It's more than sorting and moving data from temporary to permanent storage—the unconscious is writing the scripts that give our lives meaning."*

In the dream it made no sense for people to jump from tall buildings. They were safe. The water could never reach that high, and yet they jumped anyway, like lemmings hurling themselves off a cliff. The people in the dream were gripped by a compulsion for self-destruction. Millions of people dying. And then she'd gotten into a boat. She'd raced upstream to the headwaters of the flood, hoping to stop it.

Dani found her BlackBerry and Googled the words "flood" + "Noah's ark." She read:

The LORD saw that the wickedness of man was great in the earth, and that every imagination of the thoughts of his heart was only evil continually. And the LORD was sorry that he had made man on the earth, and it grieved him to his heart. So the LORD said, "I will blot out man whom I have created from the face of the ground, man and beast and creeping things and birds of the air, for I am sorry that I have made them." But Noah found favor in the eyes of the LORD.

"Why did God want to blot out the birds, Daddy?" she recalled asking her father after he'd read her the story when she was young. She could understand why God might have been angry at man, but why would he be angry at birds?

"I think he wanted to wash the whole world clean," her father had answered, but it still didn't make sense, because the ducks and the seagulls wouldn't need an ark to survive. Nor, for that matter, would the fish.

In the dream she'd seen her father, standing like Noah, wearing a physician's white lab coat, though in life he'd treated patients wearing only a blue oxford dress shirt with his necktie tucked between the second and third buttons. She'd raced upstream in her white speedboat until she'd reached a waterfall. Her parents were standing beneath it, her mother in a white dress. Then, as Dani watched, they began to dissolve. Her father was holding a stone, offering it to her. Then he and her mother disappeared, washed away by the water.

Suddenly she was standing atop a tall building, looking down at the roiling waters of the sea. A voice said, "It's your turn."

Whose voice? Her turn for what?

Her turn to jump.

And then she jumped. She was flying.

Dani sat up in bed, trying to clear her head. It was not unusual for her to have unpleasant or frightening dreams, but they'd never been as intense as they'd been since the murder, or as frequent or as hard to delete from memory once recalled.

She felt a breeze, a soft movement of air across her cheek. She remembered closing the windows before going to bed because of the wind. She thought she'd closed the French doors, too, that led from her bedroom to the second-floor deck, but they were opened a crack. When she went to close them, she saw a puddle of water on the deck, just beyond the French doors, and a set of human footprints leading from the puddle to the edge of the deck. When she stepped outside in her bare feet and walked to the edge of the deck, Dani was able to confirm her suspicion.

The footprints were her own.

She'd sleepwalked again.

"This is too strange," she said, returning to her bedroom and closing the doors behind her.

She went to turn off the alarm she'd set atop her dresser, but when she reached for it, she saw that the red second hand wasn't moving. When she looked down, she saw that in her sleep she must have unplugged the clock. And when she looked at its face, she saw that she'd unplugged it at exactly 2:13.

But if she had been walking about at 2:13, how was it that the footprints on the deck were still wet? They should have evaporated. Either she'd sleep-walked twice, or she'd been somnambulant for hours.

She quickly found a piece of paper and wrote down her dream and her interpretation of the night's events. She didn't want to wonder later how accurate her memory was.

In the kitchen, she turned on her father's old computer and went to his medical records. Turning on his computer was as close as she could get to having a conversation with him. As a doctor's daughter, she'd grown up believing her father could fix anything. Maybe all little girls think that about their fathers.

In the box labeled *Search Medical Records*, she typed "2:13 AM."

Her search produced three hits. One was a reference to an article in the *Journal of American Pediatrics*, volume 2, issue 13. The second was a note about a patient who'd been hospitalized on February 13 in Amherst, Massachusetts. The third was a citation in her own medical file, where she learned she'd been born in Northern Westchester Hospital.

At 2:13 in the morning.

Which was crazier, she wondered, seeing patterns when they weren't there, or ignoring patterns when they obviously were?

How was it possible, and more to the point, what did it mean?

Think, Dani. Think harder.

21.

Tommy made pasta e fagioli with homegrown tomatoes and herbs and a smidgen of Naga Jolokia peppers for zest, with a mushroom risotto and a garden salad. As the son of a nursery owner, he'd been spoiled with fresh produce all his life and had been delighted when he learned the house he wanted to buy came with a greenhouse. He made enough food to serve four because he was cooking for himself, his father, and Lucius, who had the appetite of two.

After dinner Tommy drove to George Gardener's house. He brought along, as a housewarming gift, presuming George would let him in the house, a dozen dark brown eggs from his henhouse. He wasn't sure what he was going to say, but he was certain George knew more than he'd let on in the basement of the hardware store.

It was dark when Tommy reached the Gardener farm. A light shone in an upstairs window, the only indication that the house wasn't abandoned. Weeds grew in front of the porch nearly as high as the railings. A chest of drawers sat next to the front door with the top drawer half open, where Tommy saw three grease-stained plastic quart containers of motor oil. The mailbox held two leather work gloves and a pair of hedge clippers. A cat's litter box at the far end of the porch divided a stack of collapsed cardboard boxes from bundles of old newspapers tied with twine. There were two lantern-style porch lights to either side of the door, but neither of them contained a lightbulb.

The doorbell appeared to be out of order as well.

He knocked.

Nothing.

He waited, then knocked again.

Nothing.

He knocked a third time and waited another minute before concluding that either no one was home or he wasn't welcome. In anticipation of either event, he'd written a note that said, *I'm Tommy Gunderson. We spoke at the hardware store about chickens. I was hoping to have a word with you. Please call me. And enjoy the eggs—they're fresh.* He'd included the numbers for both his cell phone and his landline, as well as his e-mail address, though the chances that George Gardener was online were slim. He left the eggs in front of the door, where George was sure to see them, then thought better and moved them to the mailbox, where George wouldn't step on them.

As Tommy walked back down the long gravel drive to his car, a distance of perhaps a quarter mile, he became aware of a presence. He was certain that someone was watching him. He turned to look back toward the house. He saw nothing moving, no window curtains pulled aside, no window shades lifted higher than they'd been before. Whoever—or whatever—was watching him was not in the house.

He kept walking without changing his pace, glancing about in the darkness but trying not to let on that he knew someone was there.

Then he saw it, the dark silhouette of a man at the edge of the field to his right, moving parallel along the tree line. Tommy slowed as he considered his options. He calculated that if someone were stalking him, the person probably believed he had the advantage. The last thing he'd expect would be for Tommy to turn and attack, which meant it was probably both the smartest thing he could do and the stupidest.

He bolted, leaping over the stone wall at the edge of the field and running at top speed, sprinting to the rise midway across the field and veering left where he saw the figure disappear into the woods.

He picked up his pace. The highlight reel of his career, compiled by his former coach in hopes of persuading Tommy to return to the team, showed

Tommy catching speedy wide receivers from behind on a regular basis. *Sports Illustrated* called him "the fastest white man in the game."

Whoever he was chasing into the woods was faster.

Tommy penetrated the tree line, veered toward the road, then stopped running. Whoever it was had gotten away, perhaps more by stealth than by speed, but there was no one to chase.

He sat on a rock to catch his breath.

———※———

Driving home, Tommy wondered who'd been watching him from the edge of the woods, whether he'd try again, and how he'd found him in the first place. He'd told no one where he was going. He hadn't been followed. Tommy could think of only one person who knew he was there—George Gardener himself, though it clearly wasn't George running through the woods. Was someone else living on the farm?

As he drove, he smelled something burning. He first thought someone was burning leaves, but at this hour? Then he detected an electrical smell, like the pungent odor that came from the transformer of the model railroad his father used to set up under the tree each Christmas. He looked at the temperature gauge on the dash. The needle was buried past the red.

Then flames shot from the air scoop.

Tommy slammed on the brakes, the car pivoting 180 degrees before it screeched to a stop in the middle of the road. He opened the door and ran from the car, jumped a stockade fence in a bound, and kept running up a hill until he felt he was far enough away to stop and catch his breath.

He turned.

His car was burning, smoke pouring from under the hood.

He felt foolish for running.

Then it exploded, a colossal fireball rising to scorch the limbs and leaves of the overhanging trees.

He no longer felt foolish for running.

He used his cell phone to call the fire department. A few minutes later a police car arrived, and soon a fire truck and an ambulance. While the hook and ladder company put out what was left of the fire, Tommy sat in the back of the ambulance and allowed himself to be examined. The EMT bandaged a cut Tommy had received on his left calf, apparently when he'd jumped the fence, though he hadn't noticed the cut or felt any pain.

"You ever make any calls accompanied by a tattooed doctor who wears chains and a jean jacket?" Tommy asked the paramedic.

"Nope," the younger man said, "but I'm new on the job."

When the paramedic pronounced him good to go, Tommy jumped down to the ground and answered questions for the responding officer, a state trooper he didn't recognize.

"You said you saw somebody in the woods as you were leaving the Gardener house?" the cop asked.

"Just a shape," Tommy said. "Like a human."

"*Like* a human, or human?" the cop asked. "Sasquatch is *like* a human."

"Too dark to tell," Tommy said.

"Maybe it was George," the cop said, folding his notebook. "You see the No Trespassing signs he's got all over the place? He don't like unexpected guests."

"Has he ever called you to report them?" Tommy asked.

"Not to my knowledge," the cop said. "Given how spooked this town is, George might be the only resident who hasn't called us. Phone's ringing off the hook. One woman said she had a suspicious car in her driveway. It was her husband. Same car he'd been driving for ten years."

The trooper finished making notes just as the tow truck arrived. The driver was Raymond DeGidio, Frank's brother. Ray had worked on the car for Tommy and helped restore it. He knew the engine inside out, literally, Tommy thought.

"I read a service report that said sometimes a float in the carburetor gets stuck in the old Mustangs," Ray said. "Fuel overflows and ignites when it hits the manifold."

"Any way to be sure?" Tommy asked. "Like an autopsy or something?"

"On a car? You want me to comb through the pieces?"

"Don't bother."

"She was a beauty," Ray said.

"She was," Tommy agreed. "Why do they call cars *she*?"

"Because they blow up?" Ray guessed. "Not that I would personally know anything about that."

"Sorry to hear you're having problems at home, Ray," Tommy said.

"I'd rather not talk about it," Ray said. "You know your marriage is in trouble when you realize the best way to get the love you need is to fake a stroke. You need a ride?"

Before Tommy could answer he heard a sound in the distance, deep in the woods and muffled but nevertheless piercing, shrill and metallic, like a steel saw blade grinding hard against a cast iron frying pan. It lasted five seconds and then stopped, but the aftertones seemed to reverberate in the darkness.

Ray DeGidio heard it too. The two men looked at each other.

"Did you hear that?" Tommy asked.

Ray nodded.

"Wolf sanctuary?"

"That's six miles from here," Ray said. "Maybe a wolf could hear another wolf from six miles, but I don't think we could. I've heard female foxes make a sound like that when they're in season."

"That's probably what it was," Tommy said.

"Yeah. Probably."

When he got home, still a bit rattled and shaken, Tommy logged onto the Internet and navigated to the East Salem High online yearbook, clicking on the sports links, then the track team. His hunch was correct. Logan Gansevoort was on the track team. He was a sprinter. He'd run the 400-meter race in 49.53 seconds. Not bad, Tommy thought, clicking down to the all-time school records where he found his own name, clocking in at 47.01. In a moment of vanity he was happy to see he still held the school records for the 100- and the 200-meter sprints as well.

Yet whoever he'd chased was faster.

"Have I lost *that* much speed?" he said out loud.

All the same, he couldn't believe Logan Gansevoort could have outsprinted him.

He returned to his search engine. When Old Whitney, his scoutmaster, had told scary stories around the campfire about monsters in the woods, he'd described one that had a piercing scream, sounding like nothing else. He tried several possible spellings before successfully finding what he was looking for:

Paykak (pakàk in the Algonquin language), also Baykok (or pau'guk, paguk, baguck; bakaak in Ojibwe) a demon described in the Anishinaabe aadizookaan ("Death" in *The Song of Hiawatha*); an emaciated skeleton-like figure with thin translucent skin and glowing red eyes like coals, said to fly though the forests to prey on warriors using invisible arrows or beating its prey to death with a club. After paralyzing or killing its prey, the Paykak then rips open the victim's chest, splintering the bones, and devours the liver.

Tommy locked his doors, armed his security system, replaced all the 9-volt batteries in his smoke detectors, made sure the gun in his dresser drawer was loaded, and went to bed where, before falling asleep, he recited a psalm from memory, with an emphasis on one line in particular: "Yea, though I walk through the valley of the shadow of death, I will fear no evil; for thou art with me . . ."

When he awoke in the morning, he recalled an odd dream. In the dream, New York City was being wiped out by a flood. Panicked people were seeking higher ground in white trucks and vans. Other people were jumping from tall buildings into the water. The dream ended when, in the distance, he saw someone racing upstream in a speedboat.

He told himself to remember the dream and tell Dani about it.

TUESDAY,
OCTOBER 19

22.

Dani received a letter, printed on St. Adrian's Academy stationery.

Dear Dr. Danielle Harris (the psychiatrist),

My name is Amos Kasden, and I am a student here at St. Adrian's Academy. I have been talking to the headmaster here at the school, Dr. Wharton, and he suggested that I send you a letter to tell you, in my own words, what happened on the night that Julie Leonard was killed. I am so sorry that I was there at the party at Logan Gansevoort's house that night in question, and for what happened, but I don't know how I could be of any use to you in your investigation because I left the party about twelve fifteen and walked back to my dorm. I did not want to have anything that people were drinking at the party because I am taking medications for a few things and I am not allowed to mix them with anything else. I was also afraid because of something Logan said to me in an e-mail. I have known Logan since we were in Cub Scouts and did the Pinewood Derby together and we won. I lost touch with him but then when I got on Facebook we became friends again, but then I was not so sure that he was the same person I used to know. I sort of tried not to be such good friends with him, so when he said to me in an e-mail, "This is going to be awesome. No one suspects anything," it made me scared, even though I did not know what "this" was. That was another reason I left early, because at this school, we are told that boys become men only when they are good men, and I have been trying to be good about many things. I did not see anything or hear anything at the party that might make me think I know who would have hurt Julie or help somebody else hurt her. I had never met her before that night, and the last time I saw her, it looked like she was having fun.

Sincerely,

Amos Kasden

Senior at St. Adrian's Academy

Dani read the letter, then scanned it into her computer and forwarded copies of it to Detective Casey, Stuart Metz, Irene Scotto, and Tommy. Tommy e-mailed her back thirty minutes later:

Dani,

Spoke with Liam this morning, like you asked. Had a good talk. I think he was being quite honest with me. Three things.

1. He says he's not close friends with Logan, nobody is, but that if you want to be where things are happening (party with the cool kids, etc.), Logan is inevitably there. Liam remembers a time he and Logan took M80 firecrackers and blew up a dead fish. Not sure that counts as cruelty to animals.

2. Told him about how we'd found the exchange of messages on Julie's Facebook page and how Kara told us Julie had a crush on him and he broke her heart. As for the crush part, he said he didn't have any idea what Kara was talking about, and I do not believe he was lying. I'm guessing she was throwing herself at him and he was oblivious, and she went home crying.

3. As for the Facebook notes, it's not what we thought. Liam had a band and Julie wanted to try out to be the singer after she saw a notice he put up on the bulletin board at school. She tried out for the band, and according to Liam, she was terrible. Liam was trying not to hurt Julie's feelings so he

didn't tell her the reason they picked someone else. That was why she asked him on Facebook, "Why?"

See you later today.
Tommy

p.s. my car blew up.
p.p.s. remind me to tell you something else

"What do you mean, 'P.S. my car blew up'?" Dani said, trying to keep her voice to a whisper. "You can't just say to somebody, 'P.S. my car blew up'! How did your car blow up?"

She'd asked Tommy to meet her for lunch at the Miss Salem Diner, an old-fashioned railroad-style eatery on Main Street at the southwest corner of the town square. While she'd waited for him, Dani noticed a change. Eating at the Miss Salem had always been a special treat when she was little, on the rare occasion when her mother was away or busy and it was up to her father to supply the nourishment. Later, the diner became the teen hangout where she'd meet her girlfriends for burgers and gossip. One summer she'd even worked there as a waitress.

It was ordinarily a place of lively discussion, energy, cheer. Today people looked different. They spoke low so as not to be overheard, glanced nervously whenever someone entered, or fidgeted anxiously, rolling their napkins into balls. There was tension in the air, as unmistakable as the aroma of onions frying on the grill. Dani wondered if her sweet little town would ever get back to normal.

"My mechanic friend thinks it was a stuck float in the carburetor," Tommy said. "That's the chance you take when you restore a car with after-market parts. It was only a Mustang."

"The one you drove in high school?" Dani said.

"Not the exact same car, but same year," Tommy said. "The one I had in high school was a Boss. This was a Mach 1."

"What happened to the one you had in high school?"

"Senior year I bet Gerry Roebling that I could beat him in a race around Lake Atticus. The loser had to sign over the title to the winner."

"What?" Dani asked. "There's no road that goes all the way around Lake Atticus."

"You don't need one in January," he told her. "The lake was frozen. Just not frozen enough."

"You went through the ice?"

"Uh-huh," Tommy said. "But at least I wasn't the owner of a car at the bottom of a lake."

"Why didn't he go through the ice?"

"He was on a motorcycle," Tommy said. "Good thing too, or I wouldn't have had a ride home. As I was saying about teenage boys doing stupid things . . . it's more than a theory. It's the hormones."

"No, it's not," Dani said. "Boys are just stupid. Don't argue. I'm a doctor."

"Anyway," Tommy continued, "Liam said Blair thought it was Julie who supplied the zombie juice, not Logan. When are we going to get to talk to Logan? Or Amos? By the way—the letter Amos sent you doesn't sound like him."

"How would you know what he sounds like?"

"I don't," Tommy said, "but I thought Amos was supposed to be smart. The letter sounds like a nine-year-old wrote it. You remember Arkady Dimitrikos from East Salem Elementary?"

"The kid who came from Greece?"

"Yeah," Tommy said. "Didn't speak a word of English. Everybody thought he was stupid. And you remember how he turned out."

"He won the Scripps National Spelling Bee," Dani said.

"He learned English with a vengeance. Plus, Julie was maybe five one or two," Tommy said. "And in the photograph from Liam's phone that you showed me, Amos is standing next to her, and he's about the same height. So say he comes here from Russia without speaking any English, and he's small, and really smart, and he gets thrown into a public school where kids think he's stupid because he can't speak English and they pick on him because he's smaller than everybody else. How is he *not* going to learn English? That letter sounds like somebody else wrote it. Or coached him. In my humble opinion."

Tommy's humble opinions were worth more than he realized, Dani thought.

"Also," Tommy added, "Liam said they made audition videos of everybody who tried out for his band, and Julie's was so bad that one of the guys wanted to post it to YouTube as a joke. Liam deleted it before he could. Just to show you how Liam meant her no harm. And guess who was in the band? Parker Bowen and Terence Walker."

"Not Logan?"

"Doesn't play an instrument and can't sing."

"That describes half the people on MTV."

"How was your day?" he asked. "How's your sister doing with the horses allergic to hay?"

"Oy," Dani said. "It's not allergies. Somehow they got infested with botflies. They lay their eggs on the horses' legs, and then the horses bite their legs where they itch and the larvae get in the horses' noses and they sneeze."

She recalled a boy in Africa who'd been horribly infested by *Dermatobia hominis*, a botfly that used humans, in addition to a variety of other animals, as hosts. The larvae grew under the boy's skin until it looked like he was covered in boils.

"You hungry?" Tommy asked, setting the menu aside.

Most townies ignored the menu, Dani recalled from her time as a waitress, because it hadn't changed in twenty years.

"I was a minute ago," she said, setting her own menu down. "Caesar salad with grilled chicken on the side."

She felt a comfortable familiarity talking to Tommy. She no longer felt like she needed to impress him, or keep him at arm's length. It helped to be sitting in the old town diner where she'd spent so many hours talking to friends or reading in a corner booth.

He slid the menu away from him, then smiled at her. "Why are you looking at me like that? Do I have something on my face?"

"Your face is fine."

"So's yours. Except for the weird expression on it."

"Jill Ji-Sung said you told people to vote for me for homecoming queen."

Tommy looked caught, guilty. "Well," he protested, "it's not like I thought you couldn't win it on your own . . ."

"That's not what I mean," Dani said. "And you're wrong. Lindsay Cameron would have won easily. I'm not mad at you. I was just wondering why you did it."

"Because I thought you were the best person in the school," he said. "And the prettiest. From the eyes up at least."

"Excuse me?" Dani said.

"That's all I ever saw," Tommy said. "Your face was always buried in a book." He held a hand horizontal and flat in front of his face to illustrate. "This was you," he said, raising his hand to cover his nose. "Book, eyebrows, top of head. I was scared of you."

"Maybe I was hiding. Why in the world were you scared of me?"

"Because you were so awesome," Tommy said. "I felt totally out of my league around you."

Dani wanted to ask him if he'd had a crush on her—if he'd felt the same thing on the dance floor that she'd felt, or if she'd been deluding herself—but she couldn't decide what would be more awkward, if he said yes or if he said no. She was about to change the subject when the waitress came to take their orders.

"Okay," she said once the waitress was gone. "Another question. You said there was a reason you wanted to be a private eye, but that you'd tell me later. It's later."

She immediately saw that her question made him uncomfortable. "Unless you'd rather not."

"No, it's okay," Tommy said. "Do you remember when my mom died when we were in eighth grade? The car accident on the Taconic?"

"I remember," Dani said. "We were all shocked. Didn't she hit a deer?"

"She wasn't driving, but her boss did," Tommy said, tracing the grain of the wooden tabletop with his finger. "They were at a Housing and Urban Development conference in Mahopec. She was in administration."

"If this is too painful . . ."

"No, it's fine," Tommy said. "Like you said about time healing things. I was fourteen. That's a long time ago."

The waitress brought their drinks. Tommy added cream to his coffee and tore open two packets of sweetener, shaking them first in a gesture that reminded Dani of how her father shook the mercury thermometer before taking her temperature.

"So I went to the funeral," Tommy said, "and it was pretty terrible. But afterward something just wasn't sitting right with me. The way people were looking at me, like there was something they weren't telling me. I don't know. Something felt wrong. So I started doing some investigating, like I'm a big TV show private eye . . . like I'm Magnum, I guess. And I learned the accident happened on the northbound lane, up near Chatham. Where her boss had a vacation house. At ten minutes before midnight. Chatham is about fifty miles north of Mahopec. So why were they going to Chatham, to his country house, at midnight?"

"Oh, Tommy," Dani said.

"I found some e-mails she'd written him on her computer," Tommy said. "Part of me didn't want to know, but the rest of me had to. It was pretty obvious they were having an affair. My dad didn't know anything about it."

"Did you ever tell him?"

"What would be the point?" Tommy said. "I deleted the e-mails. Actually, I trashed the whole CPU with a sledgehammer so he'd never find them. Or maybe he knew all about it but never let on because he didn't want me to know. He loved her the way he knew how, but that wasn't the way she needed to be loved. That's the best I can do."

"How did it hit you when you figured it out?" Dani asked.

"Hard," Tommy said. "I used to picture her boss's face on the chests of the running backs I'd tackle. I had all this anger, and it was like I had a switch I could flip, on/off, and when I needed to hit somebody, I'd just flip it on and go."

"Is it still there?" Dani asked. "The switch?"

What she really wanted to know was, had he flipped the switch the night he tackled Dwight Sykes?

"Do I have to answer that?" he said. "It is. But I haven't flipped it in a while. The guy had actually been to our house for dinner. He and my dad were friends. But you know, his wife and kids didn't deserve to be hurt either. The worst part, for me anyway, is remembering all those happy moments together as a family, the three of us, and wondering if it was all a lie."

"She loved you," Dani said. "That couldn't have been a lie."

"I know," Tommy said. "Can I ask you a personal question? How often do you think about your folks?"

"All the time," Dani said. "Every day."

She told him the story of how she'd lost them, the great last day they had together, and being awakened in the middle of the night by her team leader, who began, *"Dani, I have some terrible, terrible news . . ."*

Tommy reached across the tabletop and held her hand, nothing more. She didn't want to look at him right away. Finally she wiped her nose with her napkin and sniffed.

"Sometimes I forget to remember them, but they always come back. And lately I've been having these weird dreams about them."

"Such as?" He leaned back to make room for the waitress to set down their plates.

Dani told him, in as much detail as she could recall, about her dreams, all but the last one, when she'd nearly sleepwalked off the deck. Tommy listened closely, without interrupting.

When she finished, she laughed and said, "I don't think Sigmund Freud would be scratching at his beard over what they mean. I'm obviously trying to deal with my guilt. You know, a hundred years ago dream analysis was a huge part of any psychotherapist's training. Now it's barely mentioned. It makes you wonder what's going to be considered out of date a hundred years from now."

"So you're pretty sure you understand them?" Tommy asked.

"Why?" Dani said. "What do *you* think they mean?"

"Well," Tommy said, "you're the doctor, but I think they're trying to tell you something."

"Okay," she said. "What?"

"Well, the image of them sitting in a tree . . ."

"*Looking down* on me," she said. "As in *disapproving*."

"*Looking down* is your choice of words," Tommy said.

"What words would you choose?"

"Watching over?"

His insight took her aback. She'd never thought of that.

"You could be right," she allowed. "It's not uncommon for people to think their ancestors are watching over them as protectors."

"No," Tommy said. "I don't mean in a general sense. I mean specifically. The night you dreamt your father was showing you the stone was the same night Julie was killed, right?"

"It was."

"And it woke you up at 2:13. And Julie was killed on a bare rock. Was the stone in the dream a bare rock?"

"Tommy," she said. "I had the dream *before* I knew about the murder. Dreams can only reconfigure. You can't dream about something you don't already know."

"But you did."

"Tommy—a stone could mean . . . just about anything."

"It could," he agreed. "But a dream about a stone that wakes you up at 2:13, on a night when a girl is killed on a stone at exactly the same time, doesn't mean 'just about anything.' It probably means just what you think it means. Ockham's razor. The simplest theory is the one most likely to apply. Your father was trying to warn you."

"About what?"

"About a psychopathic killer on the loose, for starters."

"Tommy . . ."

"What time did the ME say she died?"

"He can't be that precise."

"What did he estimate?"

"Around two," Dani said. "What about the dream where my parents were walking me to school and I climbed a ladder and then fell on top of my father?"

"You tell me," Tommy said.

177

"Well," Dani said, "the school is symbolic of my education. And the high tower is the proverbial ivory tower. Meaning with all my education, I still wasn't smart enough, and my poor decision killed them."

"Or," Tommy said, "the problem isn't that your education let you down. The problem was that you let go. There was nothing wrong with the tower. Or the ladder. One faulty rung and you let go. Your parents led you there, and they encouraged you to keep climbing. And your father was there to catch you if you slipped up. Literally, if your hand slipped. Maybe they want you to keep going."

"Keep going where?" Dani said. "Back to school? What about the water? The waterfall turning to blood?"

"I'm not sure," Tommy said, wiping his mouth with his napkin and pushing his plate away. "I had a doozy water dream the other night."

He told her the dream he'd had of sitting high on a hillside, watching as New York City was flooded with water, and of people fleeing the city in white trucks and vans and cars, and people committing suicide by jumping from tall buildings, and finally he told her how he'd dreamed of someone racing up a river in a speedboat.

"I'm thinking Noah's ark," Tommy said. "Did you know the Bible says Noah was five hundred years old when he fathered three kids? I wonder how old his wife was."

"Probably twenty-two," Dani said. Without a word, she reached into her briefcase and took out the piece of paper upon which she'd written down the details of the dream she'd had . . . the exact same dream as his.

Tommy read, then looked up. "What are the odds of two people having the same dream?" he said. "And I don't mean three kids and a big house in Connecticut."

Dani didn't know what to say. "I've never put a lot of stock in coincidence," she finally said. "Or premonitions."

"What does that have to do with having the same dream? At the risk of seeming too . . . forward, I don't know how you can write this off as a coincidence."

"What do you mean by 'forward'?"

"I mean there's a reason why you and I met again. We were meant to meet again. It wasn't accidental. There's a reason why you and I are right here, at this moment."

"Which is?"

"We're supposed to do this together," he said. "Someone wants us to do this together."

"Someone?"

"God," he said. "That's how I would understand it, but put it any way you want. Fate. Destiny. Just don't write it off as coincidence."

She didn't say anything right away. Then, "So you're saying God wants us to be together?"

"Maybe *forward* isn't the right word," Tommy allowed.

"You let me know when you think of what the right word is. And I'm not writing it off as coincidence. I'm just not writing it in as something else. Not until I've had more time to think about it. Do you know what a false positive is?"

"Do you mean like when your doctor performs a test that says you have something, but actually you don't?"

"Exactly. They're just as dangerous as false negatives. Some say more because it's human to want to think you can rely on the test. A negative means you still don't know the answer, but a positive means you do, and it's really easy to settle for that, even when there's a chance that the problem is with the test and not the result."

"In other words, you don't trust your own intuition."

"It's not . . ."

"What?"

"You're right. It's exactly that. I haven't been sleeping too well. The chief characteristic of self-deprivation is the inability to tell you're sleep-deprived. You go two or three weeks on three or four hours a night and you think you're doing fine, maybe a little tired, and then you open your refrigerator and find your bowling ball and you can't remember why you put it there, but you know you had a good reason at the time. In other words," Dani said, "this is really freaking me out."

"Is that your professional diagnosis? Because it's freaking me out too."

"It's not in the DSM-IV," Dani said. "I don't understand how this is possible."

"I don't either," Tommy said. "Not rationally, anyway. Maybe when we weren't paying attention, we both drove past a billboard for a movie, or . . . we saw something on TV . . ."

"You're reaching," Dani said. She looked around the diner, at the faces of the people there. "I'm scared," she said. "To be honest."

"Then you probably don't want to hear what else I have to say," Tommy said.

"I probably don't," Dani said. "What is it?"

"You said there was a puddle on the deck, and that you saw wet footprints that matched yours leading to the edge of the deck. Except that it didn't rain that night. So where did the water come from?"

Dani saw Tommy look up as if someone were standing behind her. Someone was.

Phil Casey smiled and gestured to an unoccupied chair. "Mind if I join you? Stuart told me I could find you here."

Dani nodded, and he sat down. She exchanged glances with Tommy and did not feel the need to tell him that what they'd been talking about was just between them. For now. To be continued.

"I've been meaning to check this place out," Phil said. "What's the *soup d' jour*?"

"That's the soup of the day," Tommy said.

Phil turned to Dani without cracking a smile. "They say when he played, he was the king of trash talk," he told her.

"Still got it," Tommy said.

Phil handed Dani a folded piece of paper from his inside pocket and told her they'd been searching Facebook and found a photograph of Logan Gansevoort, taken years earlier at a Cub Scouts Pinewood Derby event.

"Logan was a Cub Scout?" Tommy said.

"Kicked out for smoking. Guess who the other kid in the photograph is?"

"Amos Kasden," Dani said.

Phil nodded, then told the waitress all he wanted was coffee.

"Did you read the letter I forwarded to you?"

"I did," Phil said.

"Tommy thinks somebody coached him when he wrote it," Dani said. Phil turned to Tommy.

"It seems dumbed down," Tommy said. "To us."

Dani appreciated being included, even though it was Tommy's idea, not hers.

"Have we made any progress bringing Logan in?" she asked Phil.

"We're being stonewalled. The wheels are turning, but slowly."

"I might have better luck," Dani said. "The family lawyer asked me to meet with him tonight at the country club."

"I made an appointment to go to the nursing home to talk to Abbie Gardener," Tommy said, looking to Dani for what she assumed was permission.

She shrugged to say, *Why not?*

"Good luck. We got nothing from her," Phil told him. "Maybe you can win her over. You have more charm than I do."

"I'm lowering my expectations even as we speak."

"I also left a message with a friend of my grandfather's," Dani said. "A man named Ed Stanley. He retired to Montana, where he met Grandpa Howard, but before that he worked for the State Department and lived in Moscow for over twenty years. My grandfather said if anybody could get information about the orphanage that Amos came from, Ed Stanley could."

"To what end?" Phil asked. "I'm not saying you shouldn't, but what difference does it make?"

"Maybe none," Dani said, "except that to understand a fellow human being in full, you need to start at the beginning. If you can't get a good picture of the first formative years, you can't get a clear picture of the grown-up."

"I think you're right about the letter," Phil said to Tommy. "It's a little too perfect." He finished his coffee, stood, and threw a five-dollar bill on the table.

"Coffee's only a dollar," Dani said.

"I know," Phil said. "This seems like the kind of place where sooner or later everything that goes on in this town gets talked about. I want the waitress to think well of me the next time I need to ask her a few questions. It's an old cop trick. Plus it's deductible." He turned to Tommy. "Works for PIs too."

"You told him?" Tommy said once Phil was gone.

"He's all for it," Dani said. "He said he'd teach you everything he knows."

"Yes!"

Dani fished in her bag for her wallet, only to have Tommy tell her it was his treat. When she insisted, he said he'd already had the cashier run his credit card before he sat down.

"Let me know what the lawyer says," he told her. "Maybe you'd learn more if you just went home and took a nap and dreamed."

Dani smiled. "Is this case freaking you out too?" she asked. "Maybe a little?"

"You mean they aren't all like this?"

"For now," she told him, "I'm writing off the similarity of our dreams as coincidence. Pending further study."

"Call it what you want," Tommy said, "but I think somebody is trying to tell us something."

23.

Tommy rode his motorcycle to High Ridge Manor, a single-story assisted living community where he'd delivered flowers from time to time when he'd worked for his dad in high school. He was pleased to see Carl Thorstein's unmistakable gray Volvo in the parking lot, the rear bumper and trunk plastered with stickers that said WAR IS NOT THE ANSWER and A MIND IS LIKE A PARACHUTE—IT ONLY FUNCTIONS WHEN IT'S OPEN and HATE IS NOT OKAY and simply WWJD?

Tommy asked at the front desk and tracked Carl down in the cafeteria, where he was talking to an old man bent over in a wheelchair. Tommy waited until Carl saw him and waved him over.

"Robert?" Carl said, leaning in to speak directly into the old man's ear in a voice that could have been heard from across the room. "I'd like you to meet somebody—this is my friend Tommy Gunderson. He used to play professional football. He's very famous."

"Who?" the man in the wheelchair asked, looking up without straightening.

"This is Tommy," Carl repeated. "He used to play football."

Tommy took the man's hand and shook it but didn't squeeze for fear of breaking the old man's bones. "It's a pleasure to meet you, Robert," he said, leaning closer. "Do you know who I am?"

"What?" the old man asked.

"Do you know who I am?" Tommy said louder.

"No," the old man said, "but if you ask down at the front desk, they'll tell you."

When a nurse said it was time for Robert to take a nap, Carl rose to his feet and let the nurse wheel the old man down the hall. Then he turned to Tommy.

"What brings you here?" Carl asked.

"I was going to ask you the same thing," Tommy said.

"Just visiting an old friend," Carl said. "You?"

"I was hoping to talk to Abbie Gardener," Tommy said. "Her doctor said I was welcome to give it a shot. Care to join me?"

"If you don't think I'd be in the way."

They found the old woman in a rocking chair, watching television in the solarium. She was dressed in a white nightgown and pink terry-cloth bathrobe, her hair a faint halo of blue fuzz. The television was tuned to *Jeopardy*. Her eyes seemed clear and focused, her cracked lips mouthing the answers the contestants were giving.

Tommy clicked on his phone's camcorder icon and then handed the phone to Carl. "See if you can record this," Tommy said. "Just press the button that looks like a roll of film."

Tommy pulled up a chair and sat next to Abbie while Carl sat on a chair nearby. Tommy moved his chair closer to the old woman and waited for her to glance his way, but she didn't take her eyes from the television, an old floor model in a mahogany cabinet with the cable box on top.

"Abigail?" Tommy said over the sound of the television. "Would you mind if I talked to you for a few minutes?"

She turned to look at him when she heard her name.

"I'll take Potpourri for six hundred, Alex," she said.

"My name is Thomas," Tommy said, hoping not to hurt her feelings by correcting her. "Thomas Gunderson. My aunt is Ruth Gunderson. Your friend from the East Salem Library. She said to say hello and to give you her love. I'm her nephew."

"Who is Ruth's nephew?" the old woman asked.

"Correct," Tommy said enthusiastically. "Six hundred for Abbie. You have the board."

"I'll take Presidents for two hundred, Alex," she said.

"Okay," Tommy said, trying to think. "This president helped his father out in the *garden* by chopping down a cherry tree—Abbie!"

"George!" she said with glee.

"Yes," Tommy said, looking at Carl, who gave him a look that said, *Whatever works.*

"That's right, Abbie—George the gardener. Do you have a son named George Gardener, Abbie?"

"Yes yes yes," she said, watching the screen.

"Were you going to see him the other night?" Tommy asked. "Abbie? Abigail? Were you going to see your son?"

She didn't answer. Tommy worried that he might be pressing too hard. "You have the board, Abbie," he said.

"World Religions for four hundred."

Tommy looked at Carl for reassurance. "This name, translated from the Latin, ironically means 'bringer of light.'"

He waited. There was something about her that seemed entirely present and mentally accounted for, a method to her madness, as the saying went.

"Lucifer!" she said, snarling as she spat the word out. "Whose wings freeze the *world*."

"Well done," Tommy said, sensing that Abbie was on edge and wary now. He exchanged a quick glance with Carl. "You have the board."

"World Religions for six hundred," Abbie said, her voice rising in volume.

"The Book of Revelation prophesies—"

"The Beast!" Abbie said. "The Beast and the antichrist. The false prophet and the false teacher. You'd better be on your toes, Alex. They stand on their heads by the crossroads at the foot of Mt. Maggedo with the 999 and think they're fooling us! They think we don't know the war has already started! That the Tribulation is just the school of hard knocks! Ha!"

Tommy wasn't sure what to make of her answer.

"We're going to have to go to the judges," he said, pointing at Carl.

"Aramaic for Mt. Maggedo is Har-Maggedon," Carl said. "Armageddon.

The location of the final battle. And if you stand 999 upside down, you get—"

"666," Tommy said. "The mark of the Beast."

He turned back to the old woman. "The board is still yours, Abbie."

"World Religions for eight hundred, Alex," she said.

Tommy thought. He exchanged glances with Carl, hoping his friend could guide him, but Carl just shrugged.

"This son of Abraham was sacrificed . . ." Tommy began.

"Not a son!" Abbie said. "A daughter! A virgin girl. You'd think we would have done away with human sacrifice by now. After all, we're not Aztecs. We don't eat the hearts of those we capture—though we might poison them just a little bit."

"Are you talking about the girl on Bull's Rock Hill?" Tommy asked her.

"World Religions for a thousand, Alex."

"Abbie, tell me what you mean by—"

"World Religions for a thousand, Alex!" she repeated. "Anyone for a little game of dodgeball? Dodge one, Dajjal."

"Please remember to put your answers in the form of a question," he said softly, hoping his quiet tone might soothe her. He leaned back from her on the chance that his proximity was adding to her distress.

"World Religions for a thousand, Alex!" Abbie shouted. "It's both the question and the answer, Alex. The beginning and the end—what more do you need to know?"

Abbie had become agitated. Tommy tried to take her hand, but she pulled it away. She seemed suddenly terrified of him. "Get away from me!"

He pushed his chair back.

"Don't you dare," she said.

Two male nurses came to hold her down; yet somehow the old woman was able to break free of both of them and rise to her feet before being wrestled back into the rocker. A third male nurse arrived with a wheelchair, and together they lifted Abbie into it and wheeled her to her room while she muttered incoherently under her breath.

"Potpourri for one hundred, Alex—this common element is something you pass, but that's asking a lot . . . Make your way with all haste and look not behind you, 'cause you never know what's sneaking up on you, Satchel Paige! Baseball for two hundred, Alex—this Sultan of Swat is the boy's best chance! Native Americans for five hundred, Alex—this Native American sorcerer's black magic killed the daughters of Hiawatha . . ."

When she was out of earshot, Tommy looked at Carl. "How crazy is she?" he asked. "In your opinion."

"I believe the medical term for it is *bonkers*," Carl said. "But I'm not a doctor."

"Ruth said she was a brilliant woman, back when she had all her marbles."

"Smart doesn't help," Carl said. "Some of the smartest people in history were also the craziest. It's like the crazy part has more to work with. More fuel. But cut her some slack. What is she, 102?"

"My aunt said William Howard Taft kissed her when she was a baby during the 1908 presidential campaign," Tommy said, zipping up his motorcycle jacket. "You gotta be really old if you were kissed by William Howard Taft."

The two men walked to the parking lot. It had gotten colder, a temperature drop of at least ten degrees. When Carl asked Tommy why he was riding the Harley, Tommy said only that he'd had a problem with the Mustang's carburetor. He didn't want his friend to worry.

"I'm thinking maybe me and vintage Mustangs don't mix," Tommy said.

"I'm thinking I need to wash my car," Carl said, drawing a line in the dirt on his windshield.

Seeing the dirt gave Tommy an idea. "Let me ask you something," he said, drawing the symbol they'd found on the body of Julie Leonard in the dirt with his finger. "Does this mean anything to you?"

Carl looked at the symbol, tilting his head at first one way, then the other. "You're sure that's it?" he asked.

"When I saw it, I thought it was a double *G*," Tommy said. "Do you know what it is?"

"Well," Carl said, thinking. "Maybe." The older man took his phone from his pocket, opened a word processing document, and typed the letter

Z in a 72-point font. "Now watch," Carl said as he opened his font menu and converted the letter Z from the Latin alphabet into the Cyrillic.

Z became Ѿ.

"Cyrillic is what?" Tommy asked. "Russian?"

Carl nodded.

"It means *Z*? As in Zorro?"

"Not quite," Carl said. "More like omega. The end."

"The end of what?"

"Who knows?" Carl said. "Maybe the end of Julie Leonard?"

24.

Dani arrived at the East Salem Country Club early and decided to wait in her car rather than feel conspicuous waiting in the lounge. The clubhouse was a sprawling white Greek revival mansion with columns and gables, something like a massive rectangular wedding cake sitting on a green velvet tablecloth. She'd been to the clubhouse for a variety of fund-raisers and events and a few weddings, but she'd never gotten past the lounge or the dining room. Neither her father nor her grandfather golfed, and she had no affinity for the game.

While she waited, she used her phone to check her office voice mail. Willis Danes had called to reschedule their appointment. Tommy left a message asking her to call him. The cleaning service she'd contacted had finally called back to say the price had doubled now that they'd had a look inside. She recalled how her mother used to look at Dani's room and say, *"Dani, if I wanted a pigsty, I would have built one behind the garage."* The word *pigsty* triggered a sudden recognition.

She sent a text to her sister.

U TALK?

She waited for Beth's response.

NOT NOW. AT SCHOOL. GIRLS' VIOLIN CONCERT.

HOW IS IT?

LOVELY. AT TIMES. U?

HAVE YOU IDENTIFIED SPECIES OF BOTFLY INFESTATION?

THIS HAS BEEN BOTHERING YOU? NO. WHY?

LOOK FOR DERMATOBIA HOMINIS. JUST A HUNCH.

DON'T YOU HAVE BETTER THINGS TO HUNCH ABOUT?

I WISH. DERMATOBIA HOMINIS INFECTS HUMANS AS WELL AS HORSES, CATTLE, GOATS, ETC. SAW MULTIPLE INSTANCES IN AFRICA. LAYS EGGS UNDER SKIN. LARVAE GROW, BUMP IS RED, LOOKS LIKE BOIL. I INTERVIEWED TWO GIRLS WHO BOARD THEIR HORSES AT RED GATE FARM. BOTH HAD LARGE RED WENS ON LEGS, SCRATCHING.

I HATE TO ASK. WHAT HAPPENS WHEN LARVAE HATCH?

DON'T ASK. EMERGE FROM SKIN. IF I'M RIGHT, YOU'LL WANT TO CONTACT EVERYBODY WHO RIDES/WORKS AT FARM. LET ME KNOW RE. RAYNE KEPPLINGER AND KHETZEL ROSS.

WILL DO. BELIEVE IT OR NOT, THIS SOUNDS PREFERABLE TO LISTENING TO 20 4TH GRADERS PLAY THE VIOLIN. ONE QUESTION—VECTOR? HOW DO AFRICAN BOTFLIES END UP IN WESTCHESTER?

BEATS ME. GOTTA GO.

L8R

Her appointment was for five o'clock. She pressed the button to lock her car, walked to the front entrance, and stood by the portico. She waited a minute, and then a black Mercedes pulled up. The driver was a nice-looking young man in a white shirt and black tie, not the lawyerly type Dani was expecting. Then the lawyerly type Dani was expecting got out of the backseat.

"Miss Harris," the man said, extending his hand. "Davis Fish. Nice to meet you. I'm glad you could make it."

He was about forty, lean, clean-shaven, and wore stylish horn-rimmed eyeglasses that stopped just short of too much. He took off his black cashmere coat to reveal a black Armani suit, blue shirt, and red power tie. He was not a handsome man, had a nose that bent slightly to the left, thin lips, and a weak chin. His hairline had begun to recede, but to compensate he wore his hair long and swept back over his ears. Dani followed him to the dining room, where the maître d' seated them. A waiter brought menus.

"Please order dinner if you'd like," Fish said. "I tend to eat early. The chef here used to work at the Four Seasons. Do you like food, Dr. Harris?"

"Do I like food?" Dani said.

The fact was, she was quite hungry, but her better judgment told her not to order. She saw the meeting as adversarial, if not confrontational. One party provisioning food for the other gave the provisioner an advantage, a social custom that went back thousands of years. It could be meant as a legitimate peace offering, the breaking of bread together, or it could be a tool for negotiation.

"I like food just fine," she said, "but only when I'm hungry."

"Good for you," Fish said. "I applaud your discipline. Do you golf?"

"No," Dani said. "Never did."

"Neither do I," Davis Fish said. "I think when I was born, the Sports Fairy skipped me and gave all the athletic talent in the family to my brother. What was it Mark Twain said? 'Golf is a good walk spoiled'?"

"That's what he said," Dani told him.

The lawyer smiled and ordered a glass of Chateau Mouton-Rothschild 1982, asking Dani if she'd join him. She again declined.

"Are you sure?" he said. "It's $700 a bottle but worth twice that, in my opinion."

"That's the thing about oenophiles," Dani said. "To you, it's worth that. To someone who prefers the taste of chocolate milk, it isn't worth a nickel. But don't let me stop you." She ordered iced tea.

So much for small talk.

"I have to ask you why you wanted to meet with me," Dani said. "I presume if you have business with the DA's office, you'd speak to Irene Scotto or to one of her assistants."

Fish set his briefcase on the table, reached into it, and pulled out a folder, which he handed to Dani. When she opened the folder, she saw her résumé.

"My business is with you," he said.

He smiled, insincerely, Dani thought, like a used-car salesman trying to sell a lemon.

"Where did you get this?" she asked.

"It is your résumé, is it not?" Fish asked. "I was hoping you'd look it over to make sure there aren't any mistakes or corrections you think we need."

"Who's *we*?" she said. "And why do you need it? Who gave it to you?"

"A headhunter I know had it on file." Fish smiled. "It's their job to be aware of people like you. I'd like to talk to you about a possible position."

"I thought we were here to talk about Logan Gansevoort," Dani said.

"But we are," Fish said, sipping his wine. "That's the position I'm talking about. Mr. Gansevoort—Andrew Gansevoort—has made himself thoroughly acquainted with your talents and your résumé, and we've called a few references—"

"What references?" Dani asked.

Andrew Gansevoort was beyond wealthy. He'd made headlines the previous year when, during the worst economic downturn the country had seen since the Great Depression, he'd given himself a $65 million year-end bonus at the hedge fund he managed.

"I believe the references asked for anonymity," the attorney said, "but they all spoke quite favorably of you, which is why Mr. Gansevoort wants to hire you."

"To do what?"

"To work with his son," Fish said.

"I can't work with his son," Dani said. "I work for the district attorney."

"Yes, of course," Fish said. "You would have to leave your current position, but Mr. Gansevoort intends to make it worth your while. What do you bill now? $150 an hour? $200?"

Dani didn't answer. It wouldn't be hard for anyone to guess.

"Mr. Gansevoort is willing to pay you $750 an hour as a retainer."

She understood what they were asking for, but not why.

"All right," Fish said. "I'm authorized to go to $1,000 an hour. Equal to my own rate. I think your quality of life would improve immensely, whatever level you may think it's at now. Did I say we were thinking of a full-time retainer?"

"Full-time?" Dani said. "Forty hours a week at $1,000 an hour?"

"It could be more than full-time," Fish said. "If, for example, the family travels and takes you with them. Mr. Gansevoort thinks there may be occasions when Logan might need help around the clock."

"And what is it you want me to do, exactly?" Dani said.

"Serve as his counselor," Fish said. "His life coach. Guardian angel. What I'm telling you now is protected information—"

"Nothing we say is protected or privileged, Mr. Fish," Dani reminded him. "I work for the DA."

"I understand," Fish said.

Dani wondered if he was wearing a recording device. He'd just tried to trap her by giving her information that, if she used it against them later, could be thrown out because she hadn't clarified her authority.

"Then let's just say Logan is a troubled soul. With a troubled past. A history of getting kicked out of schools, and a failure to govern his impulses. Mr. Gansevoort thinks Logan needs someone to stand at his side, for a therapeutic length of time, and guide him. Someone with your history of working with adolescents with personality disorders."

"You want a babysitter," Dani said.

Fish smiled. "At $160,000 a month, you can call it what you will, but that's a lot to pay a babysitter."

"He'd have to rent me a DVD of my choice too," she said. "Plus snacks."

Davis Fish was not amused. "Mr. Gansevoort is also, obviously, concerned with possible future legal problems. He'd like you to evaluate the sanity and competence of certain potential witnesses. And it goes without saying that he wants you to evaluate Logan to determine whether he has mental problems severe enough to render him not responsible for his actions."

"So you want to buy me off and then hire me to turn the tables on the prosecution," Dani said. "I'll give your boss credit. He has a strong sense of . . . entitlement. Like the child who kills his parents and then throws himself on the mercy of the court because he's an orphan."

"That's an inappropriate analogy," Fish said.

"That's an inappropriate offer," Dani said. "And unethical, if not actionable."

She was about to go when she saw an elegant man approaching, mid-forties, fit, tanned, and familiar—she knew Andrew Gansevoort from the pictures she'd seen of him in the paper, though she'd never seen him around town. He rarely left his property, and sent other people to do things for him like buy groceries or shuttle children. His hair was light brown and full and swept back. He wore a pink shirt, with a silver cashmere sweater draped over his shoulders. He smiled at Dani, showing her his whitened and veneered teeth, and offered her his hand.

"Miss Harris," he said, smiling. "I was hoping I could catch you and meet you in person. Please tell me you and Mr. Fish have come to an understanding."

"Oh, I think we have," Dani said, rising without shaking the man's hand and pushing her chair in. "Haven't we, Mr. Fish?"

25.

"Am I catching you at a bad time?" Dani said.

"One word," Tommy told her. "*Borassus aethiopium.*"

"I think that was two words . . . but excuse me?"

"African fan palms. A woman out in Willow Pond Estates imported African fan palms for her solarium," Tommy said. "They're very decorative, but I think she got them on the black market because the root balls were infested and now her house is full of grasshoppers. Technically, desert locusts. She wants us to come in and spray. You're on your cell—where are you?"

"Why doesn't she call an exterminator?"

"She's done business with my dad for years," Tommy said. "I think she feels bad because she didn't order the palms from us. I got a call in to a guy we use."

"Tell your guy to spray for botflies too," Dani said. "There's a bug going around. Literally."

"What's up?"

"I need help," she said. "I'm at the country club. In the parking lot. I locked my keys in the car."

The nursery was ten minutes from the country club. When Tommy arrived on his motorcycle, he found Dani on a bench by the driving range.

"They wouldn't let you wait inside?" he asked.

"I walked out of my meeting to make a point," she told him. "It would have been too embarrassing to slouch back in and say, 'Excuse me, um . . . I'm locked out of my car.'"

He walked to where she'd parked, bent over, and cupped his hands to the passenger side window to look inside the car, where he saw the keys, still in the ignition.

"At least they're right where you need 'em," he said. "If you rode a motor-cycle, this wouldn't happen. You want me to call my friend Ray?"

"I just want a ride home," Dani said. "I have a spare set of keys. I can get my sister to give me a ride to my car in the morning."

It occurred to Tommy that she could have called her sister now. Maybe she had and her sister wasn't home . . . or maybe he'd been the first person she thought of. That had to be good. He handed her his helmet.

"Put this on," he said. "I only have one."

"You want me to ride on that?" she said, pointing at the motorcycle.

"Unless you want me to go to my house and get a car," he said.

"No," she said. "This will be . . . fine."

"Good thing you're wearing pants," he said.

"No wheelies," she said, pulling the helmet on and climbing onto the back of the bike. He showed her where to put her feet.

"Hold on tight," he shouted above the engine noise. "If your hands get cold, just put them in my jacket pockets. I promise I'll take it easy."

Her hands were cold in a matter of seconds. He knew they would be. When she put her hands into his jacket pockets and held on as they leaned gently into a turn, he went with the illusion that she had her arms around him for other reasons. They'd gone less than a mile when he felt something cold sting his face, and then again. It was raining.

"Hold on," Tommy shouted, speeding up to outrun the rain, but it was no use. It seemed as if the sky opened up all at once. He slowed to a stop beneath an overpass.

Dani dismounted and stepped back as Tommy turned the engine off and lifted the motorcycle back onto the kickstand. He helped her remove the helmet. Her hair was dripping. His was too.

"Well, that was refreshing," he said. "You all right?"

"Am I all right?" she said. "Do I look all right?"

"You look wet and cold," he said, taking his jacket off and wrapping it around her shoulders. "Take it. I'm good. Hang on." He opened a saddlebag and found his Gore-Tex rain shell.

"There," he said as he put it on. "I think we're going to be here for a while."

"Looks like," she said. The rain was hard and steady, but they were dry beneath the bridge.

"Let's get out of the wind," he said. "Come on."

He spied a rock ledge, higher up beneath the overpass. She followed and took his hand when he turned to give her a pull. They sat side by side. When she shivered, he put his arm around her and moved closer to share his body warmth.

"These boots are ruined," she said.

"I'm sorry," he said. "This rain will probably stop."

"Ya think?"

"That was stupid," he admitted, realizing that something had changed. He could still say idiotic things to her, but he no longer feared losing her good opinion. She might even be starting to like him.

"I'm also starving," she said. "I didn't eat anything at the country club because it would have given Davis Fish the upper hand."

"Wait here," he said. He ran to the motorcycle, opened a saddlebag and reached inside it, then ran back, clambering up the incline.

"Here," he said. She held out her hands. He gave her a ProteinPlus PowerBar, a Rice Krispy Treat, half a bag of Pepperidge Farm Goldfish Crackers, a box of Mike and Ike candies, and a bottle of Gatorade. "Sorry if the menu is a bit limited. I just throw stuff in there when I'm traveling and empty it out every few years."

"This," she pronounced, ripping open the PowerBar, "is a feast." She chased the power bar with the Rice Krispy Treat, followed by the Goldfish, then washed it all down with the Gatorade. She split the Mike and Ikes with Tommy.

"I can't believe I just ate the contents of a motorcycle saddlebag," she said. "Which one's Mike and which one's Ike?"

"It's a mystery," Tommy said.

"An ambiguity you can live with?"

"Yup."

"What's another?"

"What's another?" Tommy thought a moment. "Why you love some-body."

"I beg your pardon?"

"Not why in general, but why one particular person and not some other person."

"They've done studies—" Dani began.

"Stop," Tommy said. "It doesn't matter what the studies say. You mentioned you're reading *Moby Dick*—did you get to the part where they slice the whale up and boil it down in the try-works?"

"I didn't know you'd read it," Dani said. "Parts of it are hard to get through."

"Three times," Tommy said. "You can chop a whale up into a million wafer-thin slices and boil it down to the purest essence, and you still don't understand the mystery of what makes it a whale. So don't slice love down into a million pieces and reduce it to science. It's bigger than that."

"Point taken," Dani said. "Can I ask you something?"

"Anything," Tommy said. "You're my boss. Remember?"

She shivered.

"Are you cold?" he asked her. Another stupid question.

She couldn't stop shivering.

He crab-walked up the embankment to move behind her, then slid down so that she was sitting between his legs. He put his arms around her and squeezed her with his legs. She nestled in. The rain fell even harder than before.

"That better?" he asked.

"Much."

"What did you want to ask me?"

"Well," she said. "It's none of my business, but I wondered if you were in love with Cassandra Morton."

"You heard about that, huh?"

"Heard about it?" she said. "It was in all the trashy celebrity magazines for months. Not that I read trashy celebrity magazines."

"I was kidding."

"Never mind," she said. "I know you don't talk about that. Which I admire. I'm not big on men who kiss and tell. Or women, for that matter."

"Can I hire you as my therapist?" he asked. "For one dollar? Which you already owe me as your assistant, so let's just call it even."

"I normally charge twice that," she said, leaning her head back to look at him, "but sure. Though usually when I see a patient, I'm not sitting under a bridge in the rain with the client's arms around me."

"This isn't how Freud did it?"

"Not usually."

"Okay," Tommy said. "So what I'm telling you is confidential, patient to doctor. The answer is yes, I was in love with her. At first. It's pretty heady to be with a woman the whole world thinks is glamorous and wonderful and perfect, and everywhere you go people take your picture and stare at you. It's annoying too, but it's heady. You think of who you're with and realize she loves you and she chose you out of the literally millions of guys she has to choose from. But it's also confusing, because you can't be sure what's making you feel what. Cass is a really loving person."

"But . . . ?"

"But nothing. She was all those things. That part was real."

"But . . . ?"

"You wanna hear something really weird?" he said. "I went fishing with some buddies, up in Canada, in lieu of a bachelor party, and I was sitting in the boat and I thought, *If she's the one for me, show me a sign.* It's not like I was praying. I just thought those words. *If she's the one for me, show me a sign.* Split second later, I caught the biggest northern pike I've ever seen. I thought at first it was a muskie. Twenty-one pounds. Big as my leg. And I'm thinking, *Is this a sign, or is this just a fish?*"

"Which was it?"

"It was just a fish," Tommy said. "I'm thinking you don't believe in signs."

"In premonitions?" Dani said. "No. Or put it this way—I think I probably have a thousand premonitions a day, projecting my thoughts into a variety of possible futures. When one comes true, I don't slap my forehead and say, 'Oh my gosh—I had a premonition about that!' What about the other 999 that didn't come true? Don't those deserve equal weight? Were you superstitious when you played football? They say a lot of athletes are."

"I never sat down during a game, but that wasn't a superstition."

"What was it?"

"If you sit down on the bench without looking, the guy next to you might set his Gatorade cup on the bench and make you sit on it. Football humor."

"You had no superstitions? None whatsoever?"

"Maybe a couple," Tommy allowed. Not washing his socks during the season, keeping a raw egg in his locker, never eating anything red before a game, never leaving a hat on the bed in his hotel room . . . Just a few. "And you don't have any?"

"I try not to," Dani said. "Which isn't to say there aren't a lot of things in the universe that are beyond our understanding. I guess I just think, if there isn't an explanation, don't make one up just because the ambiguity makes you uncomfortable. Just embrace the ambiguity. And wait. Then again . . ."

"What?"

"You were saying," she reminded him. "The fish was just a fish?"

"There's more to Cassandra Morton than anybody knows. Don't get me wrong—the whole America's sweetheart thing wasn't just because of the roles she played. They suited her. She could be a total sweetheart."

"But . . . ?"

"But," Tommy said, "there were some ugly parts behind the public persona. *Ugly* isn't the right word. *Damaged*, maybe. You can use your imagination to fill in the blanks, but this was a girl who looked like a grown woman when she was twelve years old, with a stepfather who was an alcoholic who had his alcoholic friends over . . ."

"I get it," Dani said.

"In public she was America's sweetheart," Tommy said. "On film she was America's sweetheart. In person the whole America's sweetheart thing was a house of cards. She could turn violent and abusive . . . It was like she couldn't stop herself. No one would have ever believed me if I told them. I thought I could help her. You tell yourself, 'I'll be the one who can help her get past the demons.' But eventually you realize you can't. Only she can do that. Finally she called off the wedding—"

"*She* called off the wedding?"

Tommy nodded. "I wasn't exactly surprised. But we made a deal," he said. "She needed to maintain the image. I told her I'd make it look like I called it off and be the bad guy. She'd get her picture taken being publicly heartbroken and bravely carrying on with her head held high, and I'd get myself photographed dating Playboy bunnies or whatever, and then she could go on being America's sweetheart."

"What did you get out of it?"

"What did I get out of it?" Tommy said. "Nothing. I had nothing to lose, and she did. She still needed to be a public figure. I just wanted to disappear. It's tough when it's all so public. Things like that take on a momentum . . ."

A car passed in front of them beneath the bridge. He watched the headlights approaching and the taillights receding. He listened to the Doppler effect as the sibilance of the tires against the wet pavement turned from a hiss to a fading sizzle. She'd felt tense in his arms, but now her body relaxed as she leaned back into him. They were safe and out of the rain where they were, even when the wind picked up, strong gusts driving the rain almost horizontal.

"Are you still in touch with her?" she asked, resting her head against his chest.

"Once in a while," he said. "On the phone. You can imagine what would happen if we had lunch and somebody took a picture."

"I see why you never said anything," she said.

"The *New York Star* offered me a lot of money for the story," Tommy said. "That's also confidential."

"My lips are seals, as my niece is fond of saying."

"Can I tell you something else?" Tommy asked.

"Okay."

He realized that for the first time in as long as he could remember, he trusted someone completely. The feeling that he'd known Dani his entire life wasn't quite true—he'd been aware of her for most of his life, but he was only getting to really know her now. Everything she told him made him want to know more. She got all his jokes. She didn't necessarily like all of them, but she *got* them. Mostly he knew that with Dani, what you saw was what you got, and he really liked what he saw. She wasn't hiding anything. She was such a decent person.

"I swore I wouldn't tell anybody, but given the circumstances, you'll understand. I can't swear you to secrecy because it's relevant to the case, but I know you'll do the right thing."

"Okay," Dani said.

"It's about Liam," Tommy said. "He told me in confidence, and I told him I wouldn't tell anybody. Summer before last, he had sex with a girl. They were both lifeguards at Lake Kendell. The point is, Liam didn't turn sixteen until the end of August, and the girl had just turned eighteen. So he was a minor and she wasn't."

"And he felt weird about it?" Dani asked. "According to the law, he's not considered capable of giving consent at fifteen."

"I know," Tommy said. "All he knew at the time was that this girl who was older and cool liked him, and he liked her. He was . . . let's just say he was consenting. But she was extremely aggressive. So much that it really scared him. And afterward she got weird. She started calling him, but he wouldn't go out with her again. He thought she was crazy. Eventually, she said she was going to go to the police."

"That makes no sense," Dani said. "She was the one who—"

"I know," Tommy said. "That's how little he knew about what was going on, but she said she was going to claim he'd been the aggressor."

"What did Liam do about it?"

"He told me," Tommy said. "He couldn't tell his parents. The girl was the daughter of his parents' best friends. I handled it."

"How?"

"I talked to her. Privately, but in a public place where I had witnesses."

"What did you say?"

"I told her she was being unreasonable," Tommy said. "I'm telling you this because there's a possibility someone is going to say Liam had trouble with a girl before. He sent her a letter that said, 'Leave me alone or else.' He was trying to sound tough, but a prosecutor could turn that around and use it against him. That's why he called me instead of his mother when the police brought him in for the Bull's Rock Hill murder. He knew I knew all this, and Claire didn't."

"How did you explain to the girl that she was being unreasonable?"

"Something about people fitting each other like pieces of puzzles, or not fitting, I don't recall exactly, but it's one of the stranger benefits of being famous," Tommy said. "People give you a *lot* more credit than you deserve. I told her she needed to get help. She was just really messed up."

Dani turned around to face him, their faces six inches apart. He was 99 percent certain that she wanted to kiss him, and 100 percent sure he wanted to kiss her.

"Can I just say—" she began.

They were interrupted by the sudden blare of a police siren, then by the white light of a squad car's spotlight, its flashers flashing blue and red.

"Everything all right?" said a voice over the loudspeaker.

Tommy shielded his eyes with his hand.

"That you, Tommy?" the amplified voice called out.

Tommy told Dani to wait where she was and approached the squad car. Frank DeGidio was in the passenger seat. The cop behind the wheel was another local Tommy knew from the gym.

"Sorry, Tommy," Frank said. "I didn't know it was you. Is that that lawyer from the DA's office?"

"Forensic psychiatrist," Tommy said.

The cop in the driver's seat turned off the flashers.

"She don't look like any shrink I know. Sorry to bother you—we got a call from the neighborhood watch," DeGidio said. "Somebody said they saw a suspicious motorcycle abandoned under a bridge."

"It's a Harley, Frank," Tommy said. "What's suspicious about a Harley?"

"Vigilance is one thing," the cop said, "but I swear, somebody is going to hear a squeak on the front porch and shoot the paperboy. Crazy night. The wind blew a tree down on the lines and knocked the power out north of here, which happens like four or five times a year around here with all these old trees, and people are acting like it's a sign of the apocalypse. Sorry to bother you."

Dani met Tommy at the bike and offered him his jacket back.

"I should get home," she told him. "It looks like the rain has stopped."

"Keep it until we get to your place," he told her. The moment had passed, but he felt confident there would be another. *But in case there's any doubt*, he thought, *show me a sign.*

He put the bike in gear, let out the clutch, and accelerated slowly, then slammed on the brakes. The motorcycle skidded sideways and slid to a stop just as two dark shapes charged from the woods. He saw a pair of horses, one black, the other gray, eyes wild with fear, running without direction. The black horse slipped on the wet road, hooves clattering and screeching like fingernails on a blackboard. Then the big stallion righted himself, regarded the two humans with a snort, ears laid back, threw his head up and whinnied, kicked his front hooves out, and followed the gray across the road. The animals jumped the ditch and leapt over the stone wall, disappearing into the trees opposite as if they were being chased by something unseen.

"You okay?" Tommy asked Dani.

"Give me a second," she said.

He felt her hands, inside the pockets of his rain shell, squeezing him and trembling.

"What was that?"

"A sign," Tommy said. "But not the one I was waiting for."

"Should we call somebody?" Dani asked.

"I'll let the police know after I drop you off," Tommy said. "This whole town is going crazy."

26.

When she got home, Dani checked her BlackBerry and read an e-mail from Irene, who'd been busy obtaining subpoenas for Logan Gansevoort and Amos Kasden. Dani called Kelly to make sure she'd gotten to Philadelphia safely. She called Ed Stanley, her grandfather's friend from the State Department, and left a message to make sure he had both her phone numbers and all three of the e-mail addresses where he could reach her.

When she checked the Friends of Julie Leonard Facebook page, the posts confirmed what Tommy had said about the town going crazy, a collective paranoia that fed on itself. Three women proposed forming a drum circle to perform a healing ceremony, while several men proposed different solutions, variations on a theme of "If the person who killed Julie Leonard is reading this, we're going to find you and take the law into our own hands." There were dozens of reports of supposedly "suspicious activities." A girl said her dog wouldn't stop walking in circles. A woman said her tap water had turned brown. A man said he'd recently parked his Mercedes in the driveway, where it had been damaged in the night by hail, even though there were no hailstones on the ground when he discovered the damage.

Hysteria had more than a foothold in East Salem.

Dani started running the tub upstairs, then went to the kitchen to check and refill the cat's dishes. After she took a hot bath to chase the chill from her bones, she went back downstairs to turn off all the lights and only then noticed that her cat hadn't touched his food or water.

"Arlo?" she called out. "Here, kitty kitty kitty . . ."

She listened but heard no yowling in reply.

She opened the back door. Sometimes the cat sneaked past her in the morning and made his escape without her knowing it.

"Arlo!" she called out loudly. "Here, kitty kitty . . ."

Now she was worried. She reminded herself that there was no connection between a missing cat and a town gone mad, but that was how paranoia worked. If you looked for things to be afraid of, you could find them everywhere.

In the kitchen, she called again. She called upstairs. She called into the living room, came back to the kitchen, and opened the door to the basement.

She screamed as the cat darted past her, racing to his food.

"There you are!" she said, profoundly relieved. She picked him up and stroked his fur. "You scared the daylights out of me, you bad boy."

She set him down and left him to his meal, closing the door to the basement.

Then she remembered, clearly, that when she'd left the house in her usual hurry that morning, the basement door had been open. She was certain of it. She'd noticed the door, slightly ajar, and said, "Don't go into the basement, Arlo—there are scary things down there."

Arlo couldn't have locked himself in the basement, because he would have had to pull the door shut behind him.

So who locked the cat in the basement?

27.

"I need you to come over right away," Dani said. Tommy looked at the clock. It was almost midnight. Her voice held an urgency bordering on panic. "I think there might be someone in my basement."

"Hang on," he told her. "I'll be right there."

This time he went to his dresser, left his Boy Scout knife where it was, and took the .45 caliber automatic from its case, shoving the gun into the pocket of his leather jacket where Dani wouldn't see it.

She was waiting for him at the end of her driveway, wearing her bathrobe over her pajamas and a pair of men's Canadian Sorel winter boots. This time, Tommy had taken the Jeep. She climbed in, shivering. He turned up the heat.

"Love the outfit," Tommy told her. "You look like a spokesmodel for the Hudson Bay Company."

"My dad kept the boots in the garage for when he shoveled snow," she explained, then told him about the basement door. "Just to rule out the obvious, it could have been the wind, right?"

"You get a lot of wind inside your kitchen?" Tommy asked. "Who else has keys to your house?"

"My sister, Beth, but she wouldn't use them without telling me."

"Do you have a spare key outside the door, maybe hidden under a rock?"

"I wouldn't be so stupid as to hide a spare key under a rock."

Tommy parked away from the house. She'd left the lights on. They sat in the Jeep for a moment. In his pocket, he moved the safety on the gun from the on position to off, then on again, just to make sure he remembered how to do it.

"Are there any lights on now that weren't on when you ran to the garage?" he asked.

"Whisper!" she whispered.

"Dani, we're fifty yards from—"

"Whisper!" she commanded.

"No one can hear us," he whispered.

"Yeah—now," she said.

Tommy told her to wait by the car. She followed him anyway, her hand lightly touching his back, the way a blind person might.

"Wait by the car—no way!" he heard her muttering. "Everybody knows it's the girl who waits by the car who ends up hanging upside down from a meat hook. Wait by the car . . ."

As they approached the house, Tommy saw nothing suspicious. Walking softly, he mounted the back steps. When he tried the doorknob, it wouldn't turn.

"It's locked," he whispered to Dani.

"I locked it behind me accidentally. The key is under the rock," she admitted, pointing. "That one."

Tommy went first. Dani clutched her robe closed at the throat. He kept his hand on the gun in his coat pocket.

Dani pointed to the basement door. Tommy put a finger to his lips and gestured to her to stay put.

"You're not going to leave me here, are you?" she whispered.

"Do you want to come with me?"

"No."

"Well, it's got to be one or the other."

"I'll wait here," she said.

Tommy searched the basement. He found nothing out of the ordinary, other than that the glass fill indicator for her boiler was below that red line. He turned the valve and restored the water to the required level so that she wouldn't run out of heat in the middle of the night.

"Everything looks good," he called out. "Did you check upstairs?"

But when he got back to the kitchen, he could tell that she was not all right. She sat at the kitchen table holding a can of Raid in her lap.

"What's that for?" he asked her.

She set the can on the counter. "Self-defense."

"From bees?"

She smiled weakly. Arlo did a figure eight around Tommy's legs.

"He loves men," Dani said. "I hope you're not allergic to cats."

"Can I make you a cup of tea or something?" he offered.

"Why would I want a cup of tea?"

"Don't people always have tea at times like this?" he said.

"I wouldn't know. I've never had a time like this. This is . . ." She looked around the room, searching for something.

"This is what?"

"This is more than I can understand," she said, looking up to meet his gaze. "I didn't think I was the kind of person who got scared. It's not just Julie Leonard. It's your car, the water, my dreams—*our* dreams. I don't know how I'm supposed to think about it. I can't get a handle on it. I can't think of anything I could read to explain it."

"I know what you mean," Tommy said. He sat at the end of the table and slid his chair closer to her.

"You're not scared?" she asked him.

"Maybe a little," he said. He took the gun from his pocket and held it in the air to show it to her, then put it back in his pocket.

She opened her eyes wide, then stared out the window for a moment before returning to him. "I'm afraid of something that can't be shot at," she said. "Maybe I'm just scaring myself."

"Do you remember Darryl Dawkins? The basketball player?" Tommy said. "I met him at a celebrity golf tournament. He played center for the 76ers. An interviewer once asked him, 'Darryl, you're six eleven, 300 pounds—is there anything you're afraid of?' And he said, 'I'm only afraid of two things. The unknown, and ice skating.'"

Dani laughed. Tommy wished he had more than levity to offer her.

"What's that supposed to mean?" she asked.

"It means have faith," Tommy said. "Or as Vince Lombardi once said,

'It's good to have faith, but it's better to have faith and a gun.' I just made that up, but it sounds like something he would have said."

She laughed again, but the smile on her face soon disappeared. He waited.

"What do you make of it?" she asked him. "All these weird things going on. It's just . . ."

"Just what?"

"Inexplicable," she said. "I mean, any one thing, maybe, but add them all together and . . . Do you know what I mean?"

"I do," he said.

"There's no pattern," she said. "At least none that I can discern."

"Well . . . ," Tommy began, wondering if he should share with her a thought he'd had earlier.

"Well, what? Tell me. No matter how crazy. It can't get any crazier."

"It's just that I noticed . . ." He tried again to think how best to put his theory into words. "You remember me telling you about a call we got at the nursery from a woman in Willow Ponds about her solarium?"

"Grasshoppers?" Dani tried to recall.

"Locusts," Tommy corrected her. "Similar. My pest control guy said they have to burn the palms she put in and order new ones."

"Okay," Dani said. "And this is related . . . how?"

"Well," Tommy said, "when's the last time anybody in East Salem had trouble with locusts?"

"I don't know," Dani said.

"So," Tommy said, holding his hand out so that he could count on his fingers, "one, we've got locusts. Two, Abbie Gardener was holding a dead frog. Three, you told me your sister's school was having problems with head lice. Four, you said two of the girls who rode horses at Red Gate Farm had botfly bites, which looked like boils, right? You with me so far?"

"Not even a little," Dani said.

"Five," Tommy said, bending back his left thumb, "botflies are flies, so we've got not just boils, but flies."

He held out a finger on his right hand.

"Six," he said, "I read on the Julie Leonard Facebook page that a man thought his car got damaged by hail but he couldn't find any hailstones . . ."

"I read that too," Dani said.

"Seven, Frank told me when he stopped under the bridge that there'd been a power outage north of here," he continued. "That's another one. Plunged into darkness . . ."

"Tommy . . ."

"Just hear me out," he said, "because your sister said the horses at Red Gate Farm were sneezing, right?"

"Right," Dani said.

"And the two we saw tonight didn't look all that well. So that's sickness of livestock. Plus," Tommy said, holding up all ten fingers, "there's Julie Leonard, and frogs, lice, flies, diseased livestock, boils, hail, locusts, and darkness. Ring any bells?"

"Bells?" she said. "You're still losing me. This is related to the murder of Julie Leonard exactly how?"

"Death of the firstborn," Tommy said.

"Meaning?" she asked. "I get the reference—it's biblical."

"Exodusical, to be precise," Tommy said. "Is that a word? Exodusian? It's from Exodus."

Dani flashed on the word and recalled her dream, people fleeing a city. "What are you saying?" she asked. "You think God is sending us plagues?"

"Not necessarily," Tommy said. "I would think that if any three or four of those things happened at the same time, it wouldn't mean anything. But the odds against all ten happening at once is sixteen trillion to one, to quote a statistic I just made up."

"Tommy . . ."

"I don't know what it means," he repeated. "But that's not the same thing as saying I think it's meaningless. It's not disconnected—"

She held up a hand to stop him. "All I'm saying," Dani said, "is that sometimes if you look for something long enough or hard enough, you'll find it even if it isn't there. I had a patient once, an old woman who was convinced that there was a secret organization that was taking over the world."

"But—"

"She had rock-solid proof," Dani continued, "because according to her, and this is textbook paranoia, every time this sinister secret organization took over something, they put a circle around the logo. She had proof. The telephone company had a logo with a circle around the bell. At all the bus stops, there was a T with a circle around it. To everyone else, it stood for transit, but to her, it meant a secret cabal had taken over the bus company. There are circles everywhere, if you look for them. The consciousness sets up a screen or a filter, on the lookout for things that are threatening, so it screens out everything that isn't a threat and locates everything that is."

"So you're saying I'm paranoid?" Tommy asked.

"Not at all," Dani said. "I'm just saying that the perception of a pattern is not proof of design. Look at the constellations—the ancient astronomers saw hunters and swans and big dippers in the night sky. They saw patterns. To us, now, it's just a bunch of stars distributed at random."

"So you don't think there's anything strange about seeing ten biblical signs at one time?" Tommy asked her.

She considered what he'd said. "Yes," she agreed. "I'll give you strange. I just don't know what else we can say about it."

"Neither do I," Tommy said.

"What was the story from Exodus?" Dani asked. "Remind me?"

"The pharaoh told the Israelites, 'If your God is so powerful, prove it,'" Tommy explained. "So God sent the plagues, until the pharaoh finally said okey-dokey and let the Israelites go."

"Pharaoh said okey-dokey?"

"Words to that effect, in ancient Egyptian," Tommy said, joining the tips of his right thumb and index finger in a circle. "In hieroglyphics, it looks like this."

Dani smiled again.

And again, the smile faded quickly. Tommy knew where Dani, the scientist, was coming from. In his Introduction to Investigative Theory class at John Jay, he'd been told that the investigator's job was to look for patterns but to be wary of superimposing patterns on random facts, and to always remember that coincidence did not imply causality. He knew Dani understood that. Something else was bothering her.

"You seem a little shaky. Would you like me to stay?" he offered. "I can sleep on the couch. I just need to call Lucius and make sure he can stay with my dad."

She didn't answer right away.

"Thank you," she said. "I'm trying to figure out how I can stop myself from sleepwalking. The footprints on the deck . . . What if I'd climbed over the railing and kept on going? Feeling like you don't know what you're going to do after you fall asleep is a bit disconcerting."

"I'll sleep on the floor by the door," he said. "I actually sleep on the floor at my house when my back acts up. I took a hit against the Patriots that gave me a compressed disk."

Dani offered to inflate an air mattress for him. Tommy declined but accepted her offer of a foam rubber yoga mat. She found a sleeping bag for him in the basement. When she unrolled it, she found the Girl Scout sash she hadn't seen since eighth grade.

"Impressive," he said when he saw the sash and all her merit badges. It didn't surprise him. She'd been an overachiever from the first day he'd known her in elementary school, where the students pasted small book-shaped stickers on a chart to record all the books they'd read over the summer. Dani's count was literally off the chart and halfway to the guinea pig cage.

She led him to her bedroom and showed him where to put the sleeping bag. When she came out of the bathroom in her oversized flannel pajamas, he was already in the bag on the floor, blocking her from somnambulating out onto the deck again. She locked the bedroom door and left the night-light on in the bathroom.

She got in bed and pulled the blankets up to her chin.

"Would you mind taking the bullets out of the gun?" she asked him, eyeing his leather jacket, which hung heavily to the left.

"It's not going to go off by itself," he said.

"That's not what I'm afraid of," she said. "If I can walk in my sleep, I don't know what else I might do in my sleep."

"I think I'll just take the bullets out of the gun," he said, moving quickly to the jacket.

He'd locked all the downstairs doors and made sure the windows were secured. He tried to close his eyes and fall asleep, but within a matter of minutes he heard a whistle. He sat up. He heard it again. It soon became evident that the whistle was coming from Dani's nose. It was almost cute, but he soon realized that he was not going to get much sleep with the sound repeating in the darkness.

The only solution he could think of was to move his pad and sleeping bag out onto the deck. The rain had stopped, and the bag was warm, and the spot beyond the French doors was dry, and the cool air was refreshing. Sleeping inside or out, he was still blocking the door. Dani was just as safe.

He was awakened in the middle of the night by a blood-curdling scream and Dani shouting, "Tommy! Where are you? Tommy!"

He found her in her bedroom, backed into the far corner, clutching her bedspread to her chest and sobbing.

"Where were you? Where'd you go? Tommy . . ."

"Calm down, I'm right here," he told her, hugging her. She put her arms around him and buried her face in his chest, sobbing for a moment longer before pulling back.

"Where were you? I looked for you but you weren't here . . ."

"Slow down and take a few deep breaths," he told her. She did as he instructed. "I was sleeping outside, just on the other side of the doors."

"Why?" she said. "I thought . . . When did you go outside? Why did you sleep outside?"

"You were snoring."

"I don't snore. I was snoring?"

"Just a little. Sort of a nose whistle. It was kind of cute, actually, but it was keeping me awake."

"Tommy . . ."

"Shh, shh," he said softly. "Just tell me what scared you."

"I thought," Dani said, taking a few more deep breaths. "I thought . . . I was certain . . . Tommy, do you promise me you were outside the whole time? Do you swear you're telling the truth?"

"I swear. I wouldn't lie about something like this. What is it? What scared you?"

She seemed considerably calmer now, but no less perplexed.

"I thought . . ." She looked at him. "Tommy, you're going to think I'm losing my mind. There was someone in the bed with me."

"Dani . . ."

"At first I thought it was you, and then I just thought we had some boundary issues we needed to discuss, but I was still half asleep. And then . . ."

"Then what?"

"Then I sat up, wide-awake, and turned . . . and there was no one there. And then I screamed."

"Dani," Tommy said, wanting to tell her that she'd only had a bad dream.

"It was absolutely real," she said. "I could feel you—I could feel *him* . . . breathing on my neck."

"It was a bad dream," he reassured her. "Maybe a very realistic one, but that's all it was. You've been having a lot of them lately, right?"

"I have," she agreed. "You think that's all it was?"

"I do," he said.

For now.

But the truth was, he did not think that was all it was. He was of the conviction that it was more, but he didn't know how to put it, and he knew this was not the time to talk about it.

Nor was it the time to tell her that when he heard her scream, he'd jumped from his sleeping bag to push open the French doors to her bedroom and found them locked.

From the inside. He'd had to force the doors open with his shoulder.

Now was probably not the best time to tell her that. She was scared enough already, and so was he.

WEDNESDAY, OCTOBER 20

28.

Dani's mind whirled as she drove to work. The first thing she knew she could cross off her list was the possibility that Tommy was lying. She believed him completely, based on everything she'd learned about his character and integrity—and on everything she knew about how to tell when someone was lying. She never should have accused him of coming into her bed.

Yet the sensation that someone had been lying next to her, behind her, was utterly and undeniably real. She'd felt his breath on her neck. Definitely a *he*, a male presence. She'd felt a strange warmth, and a weight.

Dani knew herself as the kind of person who faced challenges rather than running away from them. She confronted things even if they made her uncomfortable, and kept thinking, kept trying, when other people quit. So, as she drove, she reviewed everything she knew about delusions, what produced them, how to understand them. She reviewed everything she knew about dreams, and everything she knew about sleep deprivation, for clearly she was sleep deprived. She went beyond what she'd learned from books or from teachers to what she believed about reality itself. She was a rational, logical woman. She'd been rational and logical since she was a little girl. She'd wised up about Santa Claus when she was three, and the Easter bunny when she was four, though she didn't let on until she was nine because she liked the jelly beans. She was a skeptic. She wanted solid proof. She didn't care to speculate. She was never fooled by magicians. She didn't believe in ghosts. She saw through how charismatic individuals could push buttons and twist suggestible minds.

She believed there were things that humans still didn't understand, things unknowable and beyond comprehension, but real all the same.

It seemed logical and rational to believe in God, in that the world itself, the universe, had a logic to it independent of anybody's perception or interpretation, immutable mathematical and physical laws that would exist even if human beings never existed, and the way to study and understand that logic was through reason and science and skeptical inquiry. Some people worried that science was going to somehow explain away the mystery or the wonder, or that there was something antitheological about it, but there wasn't a single scientific discovery she could think of that didn't create more wonder and open the door to greater mysteries. And to her way of thinking, God was that infinite wonder and boundless mystery. Tommy had tried to tell her she'd probably just had a very realistic dream. She tried to let that explain it. It didn't go far enough.

When she got to the DA's office fifteen minutes early, she parked on the street and paused in her car to use her BlackBerry to open her search engine. She'd tried to think it through rationally—and rationally, if there wasn't a rational explanation, the next thing to do was look for irrational explanations. What was it Sherlock said about eliminating the possible? Once you did, whatever was left was the best explanation.

She searched for: "demon" + "nocturnal visitor."

The Boolean logic of Google kicked back an answer in a microsecond.

Incubus.

She clicked on the link and read.

Incubus. A male demon first recorded in Sumerian legend around 2400 BC, a demon who preys upon women when they sleep, lies with them and impregnates them. St. Augustine believed in them, wrote that there was too much undeniable evidence, as did Thomas Aquinas. The half-human, half-demon offspring was called a *cambion*. There were stories about incubi, variations, all over the world and throughout history, the *Alp* of German folklore, the *Popo Bawa* of Zanzibar, the *Trauco* of Chile, the *Tintin* of Ecuador, the *Lidérc* of Hungary, all who came to women in the night while they slept, lay down with them . . .

Dani shrieked and dropped her phone when it suddenly buzzed in her hand.

"Are you okay? You don't sound good," Beth said when Dani answered.

"I'm fine," Dani said. "You scared me."

"How did I scare you?" Beth said. "I dialed your telephone number."

"I was holding it in my hand when you called."

"And I repeat—what's scary?"

"Rough night," Dani said. "Do you remember when I had nightmares when I was little?"

"You never had nightmares," Beth said. "I had them all the time. It was totally unfair."

"I think I'm catching up," Dani said. "Why did you call?"

"Just to check in and see how you were," Beth said. "Now I know. This thing is getting to you."

"Maybe a little," Dani lied, knowing her sister would worry if she told her the truth. "I gotta go or I'll be late for my meeting. Thanks for calling. You just interrupted a rather silly train of thought."

Irene had asked for a morning meeting. Dani decided the best thing she could do was throw herself into her work.

The district attorney was in a foul mood. She said at the meeting that she'd called for a press conference at eleven, and she didn't like press conferences. She was annoyed because somebody had released the image of the symbol found on Julie Leonard's body. It was in the morning papers.

"That was me," Dani confessed. "I asked the girls if they recognized the symbol. I showed it to them. They probably talked about it."

"Maybe," Irene said. "That's the thing. Maybe they leaked it, or maybe the killer did. Problem is, now we can't trace it back to the source because there's more than one source.

"I can't say I'm thrilled," she continued. "The more this gets talked about in the papers, the more likely a defense attorney is going to say the jury was influenced by media coverage. Now I have to go out there and face

Vito Cipriano and the rest of those weasels and give it a spin. And I hate it when I have to spin. It makes me dizzy."

For a moment Dani considered resigning her position. Maybe she wasn't cut out for it. Perhaps they could find someone who was.

"It's okay, kiddo," Irene told her as if reading her mind. "This is one little glitch. You're doing great. Everybody learns on the job. Right, Detective Casey?"

"My first day in uniform, I accidentally turned on the siren during a surveillance," Phil said dryly. "My partner was unenthusiastic about the prospect of our ongoing collaboration."

"What have you got, Dani?" Irene asked. "Let's put our notes on the table and see where we are."

Dani gave the DA the information she had, what she'd learned talking to Julie's mom and sister, what Tommy had learned from Liam about his band and how he'd rejected Julie because she couldn't sing. She related how Tommy had discovered that the symbol might just be the letter *Z* in Cyrillic. She decided not to say anything about the plagues of Egypt or the dreams she'd been having. The Kasdens had given Dani the name of the White Plains child psychologist Amos had first consulted before transferring to St. Adrian's.

"Anything there?" Irene asked.

"Possibly," Dani said. "Amos wet the bed until he was thirteen. They even had him see a urologist, who found nothing wrong physically. Amos also liked to start fires in trash cans. Taken separately, neither is reason for concern, but together they might be. Late bed-wetting, fire-starting, and cruelty to animals, in constellation, indicate serious psychopathologies."

"Any reason to believe the Kasdens might have been abusive?"

"None whatsoever," Dani said. "I've contacted a man who worked in Moscow for the State Department. He said he'd make some calls to find out what he can about the orphanage Amos came from. I hope to hear from him today. The Kasdens also said they'd give the school psychologist at St. Adrian's permission to talk to us."

"Good," Irene said. "The Friends of Julie Leonard page on Facebook is up to three thousand members. Lots of suspicions but nobody naming the names we have, so that's good. Phil, anything on Liam?"

"Just what we've got," Phil said. "The blood on the Dorsett kid's shirt is a match, along with the mud on his shoes. The mud on the other kids' shoes match too. They were all there."

"Nothing more from Logan or Amos?"

"They were served this morning," Phil said. "We got a meeting with Amos today, but they want the school psychologist present. I can work with that if we have to. I want to avoid any further delays."

"Dani," Irene said, "can you go with him?"

"Absolutely," Dani said.

"What about Logan?" Irene asked.

"Appearance is scheduled for four o'clock this afternoon," Stuart said.

"I'm not holding my breath on getting a look at his shoes or clothes," Phil said. "They've had enough time to take care of anything incriminating. Same with the other kid."

"The surveillance videos put Amos in the dorm anyway," Stuart said.

"Would it be all right if I brought Tommy when we talk to Amos?" Dani asked.

"Why?" Irene said. "St. Adrian's is skittish enough already. Do you really need an assistant?"

Dani wasn't sure how to frame her request.

"I'd like it too," Phil said. "The kid's a big football fan. He might talk to his hero if he won't talk to us."

Irene approved Dani's request.

Dani walked with Phil in the hallway. "Thanks," she said. "How did you know Amos is a big football fan?"

"Made it up," he said.

Dani got it. The detective had her back and would support her even if it meant putting himself on the line. She was in his debt.

~~~

The sky was dark gray, and it was raining again, a steady autumn rain that soaked the countryside under a mat of soggy leaves, when they arrived at All-Fit to pick up Tommy. He was wearing a green Barbour raincoat, Timberland boots, and a black baseball cap.

Dani had always hated the movies or TV shows where the females seemed helpless and in need of male protection or rescue, and she'd always thought of herself as someone who could take care of herself. But at the same time, she couldn't think of two men whose company could make her feel safer.

They turned at the sign for St. Adrian's Academy for Boys. The school property was enclosed by a high stone wall that made it feel more like a prison than a place of learning, a fortification, Dani had always thought, modeled after the walled colleges of Oxford and Cambridge.

At the gates, Detective Casey showed his badge to the video camera, and the wrought iron gates swung open. The camera swiveled to follow them as they drove through, and then the gates closed behind them. The school grounds were immaculately groomed. The drive wound up the hill to the Grand Commons, an imposing slate-roofed, ivy-covered brick mansion that was grand in every sense of the word, with leaded windows, a central bell tower, and towers at the end of either wing. The dormitories and academic buildings were similarly imposing, redbrick and ivy and slate except for the athletic facilities and the science building, which were modern and state of the art.

"It's a nice campus, but I'm glad I decided not to go here," Tommy said.

"You could have?" Dani asked, surprised.

"It's part of the original charter," Tommy said. "Every year they give full scholarships to two kids from town, and in exchange they don't have to pay taxes."

"They wanted you to play football?" Phil asked.

Tommy nodded.

"Why didn't you?" Dani said. "This school has probably the best academic reputation in the country. If not the world."

"I didn't because when they gave me a tour, everybody I met was a jerk," he said. "It was kind of weird. Not one person I wanted to spend any time with."

When they reached a circular at the end of the drive, Phil dropped

Dani and Tommy off beneath the covered front portico, out of the light rain. He parked the car in a space just beyond the portico and joined them.

The porter asked their names, then ushered them into the foyer, which opened into a larger hall lit from above by a massive domed skylight that reminded Dani, she told him, of the pictures she'd seen of the Crystal Palace from the Chicago World's Fair of 1893.

The porter smiled in condescension. "The glass is indeed from the Crystal Palace," he said. "Erected in 1851 in Hyde Park, London, during the Great Exhibition. Designed by Joseph Paxton, who had been a student here. I'll tell the headmaster you've arrived."

The walls of the great hall were decorated with murals depicting the history of mankind, which, Dani noted, had been reduced to a series of battles and wars, kings and thinkers, all male, with an occasional mechanical invention thrown into the mix, a railroad locomotive or a biplane. Closer to the floor, the walls were painted white, and paintings were hung every ten feet and lit with spotlights. She saw a Breughel and a Matisse and a sketch by Leonardo da Vinci. Above an arched door, carved into a marble shield, was a saying from Confucius: *The most beautiful sight in the world is a little child going confidently down the road after you have shown him the way.*

From an office off the hall, Dani heard someone tapping on a keyboard. Three students shuffled past, their footsteps barely making a sound. At the double door to the east wing, a workman on a stepladder was mounting a bracket to the molding.

"I have one just like that. I love my stepladder," Tommy told Dani. "But it makes me sad to think I never knew my real ladder."

The headmaster, Dr. John Adams Wharton, approached from the door where they'd heard someone typing. He looked like what Dani thought a headmaster should look like, distinguished and wise and well-mannered and pretty much the last person you'd want to have dinner with. His smile was perfunctory and curt, and he gave the air of someone who was both relaxed and enormously busy at all times. He looked about sixty, with thinning white hair, tortoise-shell reading glasses on a chain around his neck, and a double-breasted gray suit with black buttons. His tie was striped in the school colors, red and purple.

Phil made the introductions.

"You'll be meeting with Amos and Dr. Ghieri in Dr. Ghieri's office. Dr. Ghieri is the head guidance counselor, but he's also a practicing clinical psychologist, which I say to alert you to the fact that the things that he and Amos have exchanged in their private sessions are protected by doctor-patient privilege. But he'll tell you what's off-limits and what is not," Wharton said. "Can I arrange for any refreshments before you begin?"

"We're good," Tommy said.

They were led by a secretary down a corridor past two sets of double doors that opened into a massive library. They turned down a hall where a sign marked Guidance Counseling and an arrow brought them to the counseling office. The secretary showed them to an oak-paneled waiting room. The carpet was Persian, Dani noted. The window was Tiffany glass and not an imitation, as far as she could tell. The grandfather clock was German. One of the doors off the waiting room had a brass nameplate that read Dr. Adolf Ghieri. There was no receptionist.

"You don't meet a lot of guys named Adolf anymore," Phil commented.

They waited less than a minute before a man opened the door. He was heavyset and bald, with a goatee that covered the better part of a double chin. He wore a blue shirt with the sleeves rolled up over his elbows, black shoes, black pants, and a school necktie, loosened at the collar. He looked, Dani thought, more like an aggravated supermarket manager than a psychologist. He introduced himself and invited them to come in. Dani saw a desk with two chairs on one side, one for the doctor and one for the boy, and two chairs opposite. Ghieri looked at Tommy, then at Detective Casey.

"I was told there would only be two of you," Dr. Ghieri said, not as in, *Our mistake—let me get you a chair.*

"This is my assistant," Dani said, gesturing to Tommy.

The doctor only waited.

"I'll wait out here," Tommy said, backing away and apologizing to Dani with a glance. "Not a problem."

Dani chided herself for not calling ahead for permission. Another rookie mistake. She'd have to make the best of it.

29.

Tommy was checking messages on his phone in the waiting room outside Dr. Ghieri's office when a boy entered, a book bag slung over his shoulder. Must be Amos. He wore the school uniform, khaki pants, blue shirt and school tie, black shoes. He had fair hair, short on the sides and longer on top, parted on the left and neatly combed. His eyes were set widely apart, separated by an aquiline nose and thin lips. He looked like he probably didn't need to shave more than once every two weeks. His complexion was pale, his cheeks lightly freckled. He had big hands.

The boy did a double take when he saw Tommy. Tommy pretended he was still checking his e-mail and turned on the camcorder in his phone, pointing the camera at the boy surreptitiously, then smiled.

"Yup. I'm that football guy," Tommy confirmed. "You a fan?"

"Yeah," the boy said. "What are you doing here?"

"Waiting for friends," he said. "You ever go to any NFL games?"

"My dad took me to a Giants game last year," the boy said.

Tommy ordinarily minimized his celebrity status. Today it was a card he could play.

"Gotta love the Giants," he agreed. "I hated their old stadium though. The visitors' locker room smelled like fish. Our equipment guy had to spray it with air freshener before we could use it. And that didn't help much."

Amos smiled, but in a way that seemed to Tommy more self-conscious

227

than natural, the way a robot might listen to a joke and process the appropriate programmed response: *If humorous, then go to: laughter/moderate; duration/ volume level two.*

"Are you in trouble?" Tommy asked. "That why you're here? Dr. Ghieri call you in?"

Amos nodded. "Are you?" he asked.

"Am I what?" Tommy said.

"In trouble," the boy said. "For killing that guy."

"No," Tommy answered.

In the three years since the Dwight Sykes incident, most people had known better than to ask such a direct question.

"Did that make you feel bad when it happened?" the boy asked.

Tommy might ordinarily have presumed a degree of innocence behind the question. Kids Amos's age often had a fascination with death. Tommy tried but had difficulty finding the innocence behind Amos's question.

"What do you think?" Tommy said.

Amos shrugged. "It was just an accident," he said.

"It was," Tommy agreed. "But even if you kill somebody in a car accident that isn't your fault, you still feel bad."

"I wouldn't know," Amos said. "I've never had a car accident."

"You like cars?" Tommy asked.

"I like Mustangs," Amos said.

Tommy tried to conceal how startled he felt.

"Have you ever watched the video of the play where you killed the receiver? It's on YouTube."

"I haven't seen it," Tommy said. "Have you?"

Amos nodded. "It's pretty cool," he said.

Tommy felt something rising in him, a feeling he'd once cultivated, the strong desire to hit someone just to see them fall. Carl Thorstein had taught him how to forgive himself for it.

"*We're aggressors by nature, because we need to protect ourselves and our families,*" Carl had said. "*You were one of the smallest middle linebackers in football—if you hadn't trained yourself to be more aggressive than everybody else, you would have died. The instinct is good.*"

"I'm supposed to meet with Dr. Ghieri," Amos said. "Can I ask you a question?"

"Sure," Tommy said.

"When you hit that guy," he said, "just for a split second, wasn't there a part of you that felt glad?"

Tommy felt his heart race. Amos had zeroed in on the worst of it, the way he'd crowed and strutted after the hit, filled with the glory of himself, suffused with the joy of combat, while another man was dying. That was something Tommy could never live down.

"No," Tommy said. "That's not what I felt."

The door to Dr. Ghieri's office opened. The doctor nodded to Amos to come in.

Tommy made a V with two fingers.

"*Mir*," he said to Amos, using the Russian word for peace—a word he knew only because it was also the name of the orbiting international space station, a collaboration between the United States and Russian space programs.

Amos made a similar gesture.

"*Igun*," he said.

Rather than wait outside Dr. Ghieri's office while Phil and Dani questioned the boy, Tommy decided to go for a walk, partly to clear his head but mainly because he knew there was absolutely nothing he could learn about anything sitting in the waiting room.

He found a back door that opened out onto a green expanse, with a path leading around the edge of a pond. In the distance he saw the science building and the athletic facilities opposite it. He walked toward the pond, where he saw a poem by Robert Frost, "The Road Not Taken," on a brass plaque mounted at eye level on the trunk of a large oak tree. He decided, if he understood the poem correctly, that the plaque gave him permission to stroll down to the edge of the pond to have a look.

It was a lovely body of water, with an island in the middle where a variety of marigolds still bloomed. Then he noticed, in the shallow water where the pond met the grass, a small frog, green with dark brown spots and stripes.

He bent low and approached with as much stealth as he could manage, reaching his hand out until it hovered just above the frog. He'd caught more frogs than he could remember as a boy, playing around the vernal pools with his buddies. The trick was to get as close as you could, then make a sudden lunge.

This frog allowed him to get closer than any ever had before.

Odd.

He held out a finger and laid it lightly on the frog's back.

It didn't jump, or even blink.

He picked it up and looked at it, his hand open and flat.

"Are you sick?" he asked the frog.

It was then that he heard a voice behind him say, "Sir, please step away from the pond."

30.

In the doctor's office, Dani envied the man's library. She recognized tomes on child psychology and cognitive development by Piaget and Bettelheim and Kochanska, even one entitled *Faith in Medieval Europe* written by Tommy's friend Carl Thorstein (unless there was more than one Carl Thorstein). She noted a shelf full of hardbound collected volumes of scholarly journals, and popular magazines like *Wondertime* and *Parenting*, and books on education. In one section she saw books listing Ghieri as the author or coauthor. In another, books that were more historically than currently relevant, biographies of Fröebel and Rousseau and Dewey and Montessori, and the works of Freud, Adler, Jung, Malinowski, and others, in what Dani guessed were original leather-bound first editions.

The framed diplomas and citations and awards on the wall behind Dr. Ghieri's desk indicated an extensive education, with PhDs from the Sorbonne in psychology and Princeton in sociology. Framed photographs below the diplomas told her Dr. Ghieri was an accomplished hunter and a successful lacrosse coach, also attested to by a display of trophies on a shelf. He had, on his desk, several framed photographs of what Dani assumed were family members. Also on his desk, she saw a closed laptop, a tobacco humidor, and an ashtray in which lay a meerschaum pipe carved in the shape of a bearded man's head. The room smelled of tobacco, not a stale or sour smell but aromatic and sweet, more like baking bread. She finally noted, mounted high above a bookshelf where no one could reach it, a ceremonial Chinese sword. Its purpose was decorative, but she nevertheless found it odd to see a weapon on display in a child psychologist's office.

"Amos will be here momentarily," Ghieri said, glancing at the clock on the wall. "Punctuality is one of the first things we teach."

Dani sat up in her chair when Amos entered. He looked like a clean-cut all-American boy, his fair hair neatly combed, his eyes a light hazel, his fair skin with just a faint spray of freckles across his cheeks, his school uniform hanging loosely on his gangly frame. When she shook his hand, it was surprisingly large and felt clammy and cold.

Dr. Ghieri explained the ground rules to Amos. Amos would talk only about the party he'd attended and the people who were there on the night that Julie Leonard was killed. He should not feel compelled to discuss his own personal or medical history.

Irene had told Dani she didn't think she'd have any trouble getting a grand jury to subpoena the school for Amos's psychiatric medical records if necessary. Compliance was another matter.

"Do you understand?" Dr. Ghieri asked.

"I think so," Amos said.

"Just tell the police the same story you've told me," Ghieri said.

"If you don't mind, doctor," Phil said, "it works better if we ask questions and take it one step at a time."

"Of course," the doctor said.

"How ya doin', Amos?" Phil said. "You all right?"

The boy shrugged.

"You know why we're here?"

"I think so."

"We're trying to figure out what went on at that party," Phil said. "We understand that you were there, but that you left early. Who invited you?"

"Logan Gansevoort," Amos said.

"How? How did he invite you?"

"On Facebook. He sent me a message."

"And you knew him from grade school? It was where—East Salem Elementary?"

"Yes, sir."

"Were any of the other kids at the party from East Salem Elementary?"

"Yes, sir."

"People you knew?"

Amos nodded.

"Who?"

"I knew Liam from town camp. And Rayne and Khetzel, I think. But not the others."

"Liam didn't remember you," Phil said. "The girls didn't seem to know who you were either."

"I was pretty quiet in grade school," Amos said. "I didn't know much English at first."

"How was that for you?" Dani said. "Trying to fit in. It must have been pretty hard to make friends if you didn't speak English."

"This is getting into Amos's personal history," Dr. Ghieri cautioned.

"It's okay," Amos said. "I don't mind."

Ghieri gave Amos a withering gaze that said, *I will decide what you can talk about.*

"Just the kids at the party," Phil said. "You didn't really have a relationship with any of them except Logan, is that right?"

"Yes, sir."

"You knew him from Cub Scouts? Pinewood Derby? You made a car together? What'd it look like?"

"It was silver," Amos said. "It looked like metal, but it was wood."

"Don't most kids build their cars with their dads?" Phil said. "It's unusual for two kids to do it with each other."

"Logan's dad was too busy," Amos said. "My dad thought it would be better if I did it all on my own."

"Did you do half and Logan half?" Phil asked.

"I did most of it," Amos said.

"You and Logan won first prize?"

"Yes, sir."

"Except that the local paper always runs a picture on the front page of the winners," Phil said. "Did you see the story they ran after you won?"

"I don't remember," Amos said.

"Help me understand exactly how this might be relevant," Dr. Ghieri said.

"Just that we found the newspaper," Phil said, "and according to the newspaper, only Logan Gansevoort won. It doesn't mention Amos at all. It looks to me like Amos did all the work and Logan took all the credit. Somebody did that to me, I'd be ticked off at him for a long time. I don't think I'd ever forget it."

"I didn't care," Amos said. "I just thought it was fun to win."

Phil looked skeptical.

"You lost touch with Logan, but you got back in touch via Facebook," Dani said. "Did he friend you or did you friend him?"

"I don't remember," Amos said. "I mean, you plug in what schools you went to and stuff and then people just show up on a list of suggested people and you click on whether or not you want to be their friends again."

"Did you know Julie Leonard before the party?" Phil asked Amos.

"No, sir."

"You never instant-messaged her in some anonymous chat room?"

"What part of anonymous don't you understand?" Amos said.

"Amos," Ghieri cautioned.

"It's all right," Phil said. "I phrased that poorly. Pardon my public education. So you had no contact with Julie Leonard, that you know of, prior to the party."

"No, sir," Amos said.

"You did have contact?" Phil appeared confused again.

"I was agreeing with the negative statement you made by echoing it," Amos said.

"So, yes, you agree that you had no contact?"

"Yes," Amos said.

Dani watched Amos closely, the way his eyes narrowed. His fingers became slightly arched instead of relaxed. His shoulders rose a quarter of an inch higher than they needed to be, and then he touched his nose, often a sign that someone was lying or about to lie. Phil was getting to him. Amos was clearly growing angry, frustrated by the stupid questions from the stupid man in the stupid sport coat who, for reasons Amos could not understand, had authority over him.

Dani knew the detective was anything but stupid. There was a method to his presentation, and possibly to his wardrobe choices.

"So Logan hits you up on Facebook about the party," Phil repeated. "Did you save the message?"

"Our system automatically deletes e-mails and social network content after three days," Ghieri said. "Students may, of course, print out or copy and paste anything they want to save."

"You didn't happen to print out Logan's message, by chance?"

Amos shook his head.

"So the night of the party. Walk me through it. What happened?"

"I was at Starbucks," Amos said. "It's kind of a hangout. I'd earned a midnight pass."

"Part of our system of rewards and reinforcements is to grant off-campus passes to students who've demonstrated consistency in various targeted behaviors," Ghieri explained.

"Go on," Phil urged Amos.

"I knew that was the night of the party. I was at Starbucks . . ."

"You drive there?"

"I took the shuttle," Amos said. "My car is being repaired."

"What's wrong with it?"

"I don't know," Amos said. "It's really loud."

"Where'd you take it?"

"I took it to the Shell station in Ridgefield," Amos said.

Dani had observed the student parking lot, a virtual fleet of Mercedes Benzes and Audis and BMWs. She'd also seen the St. Adrian's shuttle around town, a white van that took students into town and back. Tinted windows had always given the van a sinister aspect, she thought.

"You were meeting Logan at Starbucks?" Phil asked.

Amos nodded.

"So he picks you up and then what?"

"We drove to his house."

"Was anybody else in the car with you?"

"Terence and Parker," Amos said.

"But you didn't know them very well."

"No."

"What were they doing?"

"Smoking marijuana," Amos said. "And drinking."

"Did you have any?"

"I had a beer," Amos admitted, looking shamefully at Dr. Ghieri. "But I don't do drugs."

"So why were you going to this party?" Phil asked. "What kind of a party did you think it was going to be?"

"I wasn't really sure," Amos said. "Kind of wild."

"Wild in what way?"

"Well," Amos said, struggling. "Logan said there would be girls there."

"There usually are at parties," Phil said. "So it was a mixer?"

Amos squinted. Dani couldn't remember the last time she'd heard anybody call a party a *mixer*.

"Did Logan say there was going to be anything different about this particular party?" Dani asked.

"Yes," Amos said. He looked at Dr. Ghieri, who nodded. "He said he thought there would probably be some skinny-dipping in the pool."

"Swimming naked?" Phil said.

"Yes," Amos said. "That's generally what people mean when they say skinny-dipping."

"That's what you meant by wild?" Phil asked. "Things were going to get a little crazy?"

"Yes, sir," Amos replied.

"Why were things going to get crazy?" Dani asked. "Did you have the impression that Logan was going to put something in the punch? Maybe GHB or roofies?"

"I don't know what that is," Amos said.

"Gamma-hydroxybutyric acid and Rohypnol," she told him. "Date rape drugs."

"No, ma'am," Amos said. "I mean, Logan didn't tell me what he was putting in the punch. But I knew it had something in it. That's why I didn't drink any."

"So he was going to drug these girls," Dani said. "And you went to the party to take advantage of them."

"No," Amos said.

"Then why?" Dani asked.

"Just to see what happened," Amos said.

"So you weren't going to participate," Dani said. "You just wanted to watch. Did you stop to think that might be wrong?"

"That's why I left," Amos said. "At first I thought maybe it was just going to be sort of harmless."

"When did you realize it wasn't?"

"I'm not sure," Amos said. "Maybe it was the music."

"What were they listening to?" Phil asked, leaning closer to the boy.

"Fanisk," Amos said. "Panzerfaust. Stuff like that."

"I'm not familiar with those bands," Phil said.

"Pro-white," Dani said. "Neo-Nazi hate music. Who was listening to that music?"

"Everybody," Amos said. "But it wasn't like they agreed with it. They were making fun of it. The music itself was pretty good. It was just the words that were idiotic."

"Too hard-core for you?" Phil asked.

"Yes, sir."

"Have you heard of something called a passage party?" Dani asked him.

"No," Amos said.

"Was anybody talking about that at the party?"

"Not to me," Amos told her.

She couldn't be sure, but if she had to guess, she'd say he was telling the truth.

"Did you talk to Julie at the party? How did she seem?"

"We talked a little," Amos said. "She seemed to be having a good time. I think she was pretty wasted by the time I left."

"And when was that?"

"Around twelve thirty."

"Weren't you supposed to be back on campus before midnight?" Phil asked.

"Yes, sir."

"So why didn't you leave sooner?"

"I was trying to get somebody to give me a ride," Amos said. "People said they would give me a ride but then they didn't, so I decided I'd better walk back."

"Has this been called to your attention?" Phil asked Ghieri.

"Amos's off-campus privileges have been suspended," Ghieri said. "Which is one reason why he was unable to meet with you elsewhere. We do not make exceptions to our rules. Many of our students come from situations where they have . . . high levels of autonomy. From wealth or power or privilege. Some, for whatever reason, feel that rules don't apply to them, or that everything is fungible. Part of what we offer here is a very firm, very clear structure."

"I get that impression," Phil said. "I know what you mean. I'd tell my kids when to go to bed and they'd always wait until two minutes before bedtime to do something they absolutely had to do that took half an hour."

"That kind of behavior is not tolerated at St. Adrian's," Ghieri said. "Those who compare us to a boot camp are not misinformed. Many of the same principles apply."

"Dani?" Phil said. "Do you have any other questions?"

"Just one," Dani said, returning to Amos. "And this may be something you couldn't possibly answer, but did you have any sense that any of the people at the party had any reason to dislike Julie? Any reason why somebody might want to hurt her?"

Amos thought.

"Not really," he said. "I think Logan thought she was sort of . . . weak."

"What do you mean, weak?"

"She kept telling him how much she liked his house and all his stuff," Amos said. "Like she'd never seen any of it before. Logan would make stuff up, like that his golf clubs used to belong to Tiger Woods, and Julie believed him. She was pretty gullible."

"So he thought she was lower class?" Dani said. "And sort of held her in contempt?"

"Something like that," Amos replied. "But like you said, it's not really something I can answer. It was just an impression."

"I think we're done here," Phil said. "You've been very helpful. Thank you for speaking with us, Amos."

When he offered his hand, Amos shook it without changing his expression.

Dani expected to find Tommy in the waiting room, but the room was vacant. Dr. Ghieri asked them to wait there while he found out where Tommy had gone. Phil asked Ghieri for directions to the men's room. It left Dani, momentarily, alone with Amos, who seemed to hesitate, unsure if Ghieri had told him to stay or if he was free to go. Dani saw it for the opportunity it was, a chance to befriend him.

"So you do your studying at Starbucks?" she asked.

"Sometimes," he said.

"I'm not sure if I've seen you there," Dani said. "I go there in the morning, usually. When it's mostly real estate agents and mommy bloggers."

"I've seen you before," Amos said, looking Dani squarely in the eye and holding her gaze. "Next time I see you, I'll buy you a venti vanilla soy latte and we can commiserate about what it's like to be orphans."

Dani felt a sudden falling sensation, as if she were sinking and spinning, spiraling downward, weak in the knees. She tried not to show how stunned she was. How did he know these things about her? He was smirking, but his eyes revealed no mirth. She saw instead a cold malevolence that made her take a step back.

He turned and walked slowly down the hall without looking back.

Dani's legs felt heavy, as if she could hardly move. Time seemed frozen, and when she tried to take a breath, there was no air to breathe, until she was able to unblock her throat and inhale. By then, Amos was gone.

31.

Tommy was in the campus security office when Dani and Phil found him. He was glad to see her, though she looked slightly paler than usual. The detective looked about as annoyed as he always looked. Tommy explained briefly that the groundskeeper who'd asked to see his pass had detained him when he couldn't produce one. Tommy had apologized profusely and said he was unaware of the restrictions, other than to keep off the grass. In the car, headed back down the long drive to the main gate, they passed a pair of groundskeepers trimming a hedge.

"They don't call them guards, but that's what they are," Tommy told the others.

"I leave you alone for five minutes . . . ," Dani said. "What were you doing, anyway?"

"Actually, I was trying to get arrested," Tommy said. "I wanted to see the security office, but I didn't think they were going to show it to me if I asked. This whole place is lousy with hidden cameras. I think I saw at least thirty simultaneous feeds on the monitors."

"Why?" Dani asked as Phil braked to allow the wrought iron gates to swing open.

"I wanted to see what system they were using," Tommy explained. "Campus wireless is Avanti, but the security program is Eyeline Pro with all Dell servers hardwired and firewalled against the outside, but not internally."

A security camera followed them as they passed through the gate.

"For example," Tommy said, pointing at it.

"And you learned all this how?" Dani asked.

"The head of security was a football fan," Tommy said. "I told him I needed to install some sort of surveillance system at my house. Which I don't, because the investment banker I bought the house from had one installed after he figured out he was laundering money for a Mexican drug lord."

"What was your impression?" Phil asked Dani. "Normal kid? Abnormal?"

"Amos seems to have a fairly high opinion of himself," Dani said. "Narcissistic. Probably to overcompensate for a reciprocally low shame-based sense of self. People with traumatic childhoods often grow up thinking that deep down inside, they really are the bad person their parents told them they were, the kid who deserved to be hit."

"You got that from just now?" Phil asked.

"I got a pretty clear sense of internal conflict," Dani said.

Tommy handed her his phone with a set of earbuds plugged in and showed her the video he'd made of Amos. When she got to the part where Amos asked Tommy if he'd felt glad after the fatal hit, her mouth dropped open.

The look she gave him told him she agreed—something was very strange about Amos.

Very strange and very wrong.

"The ME says he's going to have the labs back from Quantico tomorrow afternoon," Phil said before dropping Tommy off. "Let's get together tomorrow and see where the FA is at."

"Forensic analysis," Dani explained to Tommy.

"Am I invited?" he asked.

"I'd like you there," she said.

"I'm going to go talk to Carl," Tommy told Dani. "You feel like meeting me at The Pub later to reconnoiter?"

"I don't know," Dani said. "Probably. I have to meet with Willis Danes. Old friend of my parents. Call me."

"You okay?" he asked her.

"No," she said. "*Unraveled* might be a better word."

He would tell her about the frog that didn't jump another time.

32.

When she used her phone to log onto the Friends of Julie Leonard Facebook page, Dani found she wasn't the only one who was scared. On one post, at one thirty in the morning, a fourteen-year-old girl had said: *I'm too scared to get to sleep. Is anybody out there?*

Three other kids had answered her, kids who also should have been sound asleep.

Dani scanned down the list of people who'd joined the group.

"Where are you?" she said out loud. "I know you're enjoying this. It must make you feel very important to scare little girls."

She wasn't surprised when she couldn't find any of the kids from the party on the list. If the killer was lurking on the Facebook page, he—or she—probably would have created an avatar.

She sent an e-mail to Stuart Metz:

Stuart,

Have you checked to see if all of the 3,183 people who've joined Friends of Julie Leonard are real people? The killer may be using a fake name. Just a thought.

Dani

Will do. P.S. Davis Fish called to say we need to reschedule with Logan. No explanation offered.

Stuart

Her appointment with Willis Danes was for four thirty. She got to her office on Main Street at four and spent the half hour of downtime playing

242

with a paper clip. Her brain had been racing nonstop for what seemed an eternity. She knew, clinically and scientifically, what her brain was doing as she batted the paper clip back and forth. She could describe in considerable detail the electrochemical parameters of mindless activity and the subsequent sense of respite, but to do so now would have defeated the purpose. Soldiers called it "the thousand-yard stare." Her daydreaming ceased when she saw a car pull up out front.

The caregiver opened the passenger side door for Willis and escorted the blind man by the elbow. Dani met them on the porch, where his caregiver told Dani she had some errands to run and that she'd be back in an hour.

"Sorry I didn't have time to straighten up," Dani said. Then she caught herself, remembering that her guest was quite unaware of the piles of papers and stacks of unshelved books sitting on the floor.

"I was just going to say, this place looks like a hurricane blew through," the old man joked.

Dani smiled, recalling how as a girl, operating on the perimeters of her parents' dinner parties, she'd been impressed by his sense of humor and sheer joy of living, the smile he always had on his face despite the adversities he'd had to overcome. That and the fact that he was always more stylishly dressed than he needed to be, given that he couldn't know what he looked like in the mirror. He was fond of vests and bow ties and a coffee-colored fedora that he always removed with two hands and never one, explaining to Dani that grasping the crown with one hand would inevitably cause the dents to become asymmetrical, canted toward the thumb side, while distempering the pitch of the brim. What also impressed her was the way he took his hat off when he tuned pianos but never forgot where he put it.

She led him to the wingback chair and asked if she could get him anything.

He smiled and said no. "How's that Steinway your dad had?" he asked. "I hope you play it once in a while. Pianos are like pets. They don't like to be neglected. I'd be happy to come by and tune it if you'd like."

"I hardly have time to play these days," Dani apologized, trying to recall the last time she'd sat down at it.

"So many people have electronic pianos these days," Willis said. "It makes sense, I know. They don't sound as good, but they're a lot easier to move."

"How can I help you?" she asked him, moving her office chair around to the other side of her desk to sit opposite him. She realized that most of what she'd learned about the therapist's proper demeanor and body language was inapplicable. She hoped sitting a little closer might make up for the usual intimacy-enhancing tools and tricks. "What's going on?"

"Well," he said, his smile weaker now, "I guess if I knew what was going on, I wouldn't need to talk to you. You know that line from *Macbeth*, in Act II, when he talks about the 'sleep that knits the raveled sleeve of care'?"

"The balm of hurt minds," Dani quoted, surprised that she could remember a play she hadn't read since college. *Unraveled*, she'd told Tommy that very day.

"That's the one," Willis said. "I guess I could use a little more balm."

"You're having trouble sleeping?" Dani asked. "You know, there are a lot of new medications these days that could help you."

"Well," Willis said, "I suppose we could do that. You're the doctor. It's not so much the lack of sleep, I guess. I've been having some fairly troubling dreams."

Dani recalled the section she'd taken in abnormal psychology covering sensory impairment, but it was hardly something she felt expert in. The mind of a blind person started out the same as everybody else's, but then what happened to it as it developed?

"What sort of dreams?" she asked him.

"Well," he said. He paused, thinking. "I wish I knew. It's something I have trouble putting into words. If my wife . . . Anyway, I can't quite express it. Have you heard of neural plasticity?"

She had. The term referred to the way the brain adapted to injury and reorganized its functions by reassigning tasks to new neural networks. One example was how paralyzed stroke victims regained motor functions by training new parts of their brains to control voluntary muscle activity.

"What about neural plasticity?" she asked him.

"You know, when blind people dream . . . ," he began. "They've done experiments with MRIs or CAT scans, I forget . . . that show that when blind people dream, the visual cortex lights up, just as it does in sighted people. Lights up when we read Braille too. Did you know that?"

"I remember reading something about that," she said. Braille readers experienced touch as a kind of sight, her ab psych professor had said.

"They used to think it was use it or lose it," Willis continued. "That it atrophied. Now they know that sometimes the other senses take over the part that isn't being used. My doctor told me that's why I have perfect pitch. And what he calls a phonographic memory."

Dani knew that Willis had been a musician who'd played piano in jazz bands his whole life, even though he was unable to read sheet music. She knew blind people often possessed remarkable aural memory, able to recite long conversations word for word.

"Are you remembering things in your dreams?"

"Am I?" he asked. "Well . . . I just don't know. That's a good question, Dani. I knew you'd be good at this. You know, there are sounds animals can hear that we can't hear, like those high-pitched dog whistles. And there are colors animals can see that we can't see. Infrared and ultraviolet and even beyond that. You wonder what else we're surrounded by that we can't see or don't know. So I was thinking, what if, suddenly, you could?"

"It would probably be very disturbing," Dani said.

"So I guess," Willis said, "maybe I'm seeing things, in my dreams. I mean, *seeing* things. Maybe it's totally normal for people like you, but it's new to me. For you, maybe it would be like discovering a sense you didn't know you had, if you can imagine that."

"It's very difficult for me to imagine what that must be like," Dani said.

"I had sight until I was eighteen months old, you know," Willis told her. "Childhood retinoblastoma. So maybe . . . maybe it's actually a memory. I take it most people can't remember anything much before the age of three, right?"

"Isolated images," Dani said. "But intact complete memories are rare."

"Uh-huh," Willis said.

"Can you describe what you see in your dreams?"

"It's hard to put into words," Willis said. "I mean, sometimes I'll sit on a couch, and I'll think, *This couch is orange.* But it's not orange to people who can see. Just to me. So I can use words, but they mean different things to me and to you."

"Is it one dream or several different dreams?" she asked.

"Just one," he said. "But I've had it more than once."

He reached down with his right hand to where he'd set his briefcase on the floor beside him and picked it up. He held it in his lap as he undid the straps that closed it. "I've got something for you," he said. "I hope you don't mind. I tried . . . not sure if this will help." He took out an object wrapped in bubble wrap.

"Blind people hate bubble wrap," he told Dani, smiling as he felt with his fingertips to find the Scotch tape holding the package closed. "It's like reading a book where the words explode." He unwrapped the object. "You remember that my wife, Bette, is a potter?" he said.

"I do," Dani said. "I have a platter she made for my parents' wedding anniversary."

"Well, I was going to try to draw you a picture of what I saw," Willis said, "but I thought maybe this would work better. Except that what I saw in my dream wasn't solid. But if it was solid, it would have looked something like this. Best I can do." He handed her a figurine about ten inches high.

She examined it. "You say it wasn't solid," she told him. "What was it made out of?"

"Heat," he said. "It was warm. So maybe it was made out of light. I want to say the light was white or golden. But it's like I was saying about the orange couch. What's orange to me isn't necessarily orange to you. I know that."

The figure she held was a human form. Human, except for what appeared to be wings sprouting from his back. Or her back. The gender was not defined, but the image was familiar.

"What did this . . ." She paused. "Was it male or female—can you say?"

"I can't," Willis said. "I'm sorry. You'd think I should be able to remember because it spoke to me. But the voice wasn't . . . I couldn't tell."

"What did the voice say to you?"

"Well, that's just it," Willis said. "That's why I wanted to talk to you. To warn you."

"Warn me about what?"

"It said, 'Tell Dani I'm coming.' Though I don't know if that's good or bad."

33.

"Tommy—Frank DeGidio," Tommy heard when he checked his voice mail. "You asked me to call you if anybody found a dead dog. Some kids called one in today. It's down at the station if you want to look at it. I'm here late tonight."

His second message was from Carl: "I'm home if you need me—come by for dinner if you'd like. I'm making beef stew."

Tommy had called Carl with a question. He jumped on his bike and rode the three miles to his friend's house. He found the older man by his woodshed, chopping firewood, and helped him stack the last quarter cord. Carl reiterated his invitation to dinner, and while he set the table, Tommy lit a fire in the fireplace.

"Have you ever seen a bay tree?" Carl said, fishing a bay leaf out of the stew and holding it up for examination. "It's actually from the laurel family. Unbelievably aromatic. The Greeks made wreathes from them to give away as prizes at athletic events, in honor of Apollo. Hence the phrase 'resting on one's laurels.' In the Bible, the laurel symbolizes the triumphant resurrection of Christ. It's also on the dollar bill, on either side of George Washington."

"It's also the name of a girl I knew in college," Tommy replied. "Hence the phrase 'Hi, this is Laurel—why don't you call me?'"

"So you said you wanted to know who St. Adrian was," Carl said.

"Just curious," Tommy said. "The place gives me the creeps. I've never known exactly who it's named for."

"There were actually two St. Adrians," Carl said. "Or 'Hadrians.'

247

Hadrian of Nicomedia was a Roman guard who converted to Christianity and was martyred in AD 306. They chopped his arms and legs and head off, but when the Romans tried to burn his body, a thunderstorm put the fire out and the executioners were killed by lightning bolts."

"Let that be a lesson to you," Tommy said. "What about the other one?"

"The other one was a Berber from Greek-speaking North Africa who became the abbot of the monastery at Canterbury, in England. Pope Gregory I actually offered him the archbishopric, but he declined, so Gregory Uno gave it to Theodore of Tarsus. Both Theodore and Adrian were highly educated men who spoke Greek and Latin. Adrian did a lot toward making education available to the common man. I suspect that's why they named the school after him. He made the monastery's library available to lay scholars and tried to teach the peasants to read, that sort of thing. One source credits him with wiping out paganism in England."

"By doing what?" Tommy asked.

"By offering them something better," Carl said. "I'm not sure we can appreciate today the kind of raw hope and peace that the message of Christ offered to people in the Dark Ages. These were people who'd never heard of a God who loved them. They spent most of their time propitiating gods who plagued them constantly with diseases and misfortunes. The pagan gods they knew were filled with wrath, and they were everywhere. So when they got the real deal, it was revolutionary. Transformative. Imagine you've never tasted sugar before, and then somebody hands you a chocolate ice cream cone. Maybe not the best analogy."

"I hear what you're saying."

"But on the other hand," Carl continued, "not everybody got it. The pagan leaders felt challenged and fought back, in which case they had to deal with Adrian's holy warrior, Dark Charles. Some sources call him Black Charles. I sort of like Dark Charles. Sounds like a dessert—like Bananas Foster. Anyway, Charles of Gaul led a militia of monks on raids into pagan camps and waged a campaign against them, not unlike how we're fighting insurgents today in . . . well, everywhere. Holy warriors. He succeeded, but he was pretty ruthless. No one seems to know where the pagans went, so either he got them all or they had to swim for it."

"Who were they?" Tommy asked. "The pagans?"

"Druids," Carl said. "Which is slightly ironic, because before the Romans, the druids were considered the learned scholars. The Romans had already driven them out of Europe by the end of the second century, but they fled to England and Ireland. Probably no more than a few hundred of them left by Adrian's time, meeting and living in caves."

Tommy broke off another piece of sourdough bread and buttered it while Carl served him a second helping of stew.

"So Adrian got rid of the druids?" Tommy said.

"Dark Charles did," Carl said, opening his second beer. "One scholar said Adrian didn't know what Charles was up to. As long as he got results, Adrian probably looked the other way, would be my guess. As far as they were concerned, this was war. Holy war. Not on a par with the Crusades, but not dissimilar."

"Didn't the druids practice human sacrifice?" Tommy asked.

"They did," Carl said. "Are you trying to connect this to the killing on Bull's Rock Hill?"

"I don't know if it connects at all," Tommy said. "But the evidence suggests the murder was ritualistic. And nobody can figure out what the ritual was."

"So you think we're dealing with druids?" Carl said, smiling.

Tommy laughed. "No," he said, "but I wouldn't put it past a bunch of kids to Google 'druid rituals' and come up with something they think looks authentic. Isn't there a saying about a little knowledge being a dangerous thing?"

He thought again of the music the kids at the party had been listening to, loud and driving and filled with hate. He could imagine how kids might be drawn to the power of symbols like swastikas or skulls and crossbones, ignoring the evil they signified.

"I don't know what they'd find on Google," Carl said. "Certainly nothing authentic. The druids left no written records. The histories we have are Roman. Caesar and Suetonius, Cicero, I believe. Nobody really knows what the druids believed because the tradition was entirely oral. We think they were animists and possibly sun worshippers. And definitely necromancers."

"Black magic?"

"I took a class in primitive religions at seminary," Carl said. "Ordinarily, they sacrificed animals and saved human sacrifice for special occasions."

"You mean like Super Bowl parties," Tommy joked.

"Uh . . . no," Carl said skeptically. "The Aztecs practiced human sacrifice as a way of telling the future. To answer the really big questions, they'd plunge a dagger into the heart of the victim and then watch how she thrashed about as she died. How that could predict the future, I have no idea. But predicting the future has always been a big part of black magic. Ever hear of alecromancy? It's predicting the future by throwing corn to chickens and watching what order they peck the corn in."

"It makes about as much sense as predicting the future using frog guts," Tommy said.

"Or astrology," Carl said. "Needing to predict the future is the opposite of true faith. True faith means believing in a future you can't predict. Bear in mind, the people being sacrificed didn't always object. The idea was that one person would sacrifice themselves so that the others could prevail. In a lot of cultures that practiced human sacrifice, including the Aztecs and certain Polynesian cultures, the victims went willingly. It was an honor to be chosen. You'd think we'd be more evolved today, but we had kamikaze pilots in World War II sacrificing themselves for the Emperor. I doubt any of this has anything to do with . . ."

"Julie Leonard," Tommy said.

"I doubt any of this applies to her," Carl said. "Do the police think she was sacrificed?"

"I don't think they've used the word, but I don't know," Tommy said. "Thanks, Carl. You've been a big help. As usual."

He called Dani, got her voice mail, and asked her to meet him at The Pub in an hour. He had one more stop to make first.

The East Salem police station was a house where Main Street met Route 35, next to the fire station and the highway department. There was a large parking lot next to the station where commuters with permits could park to catch the shuttle to the train station in Katonah.

When Frank DeGidio called him back to say the blood he'd found in the hollow stump was canine, Tommy had asked Frank to let him know if anybody found the missing dog he'd seen on the poster at the foot of the trail leading to Bull's Rock Hill. At the police station, Frank led Tommy around back, explaining that two teenage boys were fishing and saw what they'd thought at first was a dead raccoon floating in Lake Atticus. They'd called animal control when they realized it was either a coyote or a dog.

"It's a little hard to tell," Frank said. "This thing is a mess."

The carcass had been placed on the lid of the Dumpster. Tommy shooed away the flies and lifted the plastic garbage bag covering the remains. The animal had what appeared to be brown fur with threads of black in it. The fur was coarse and wiry, consistent with a coyote, or maybe a terrier. He tried to remember the poster he'd seen. He closed his eyes to quiet the visual noise.

"Any idea how long it was in the water?"

"You're asking me?" DeGidio said. "People gas up and float anywhere from a few days to a few weeks depending on the water temperature and what was in their stomachs when they died. Dogs, who knows?"

"Ballpark guess?"

"Two weeks?" DeGidio said.

Tommy retrieved his evidence kit from the back of the Jeep, donned a headlamp and a pair of latex gloves, and then reached into the guts of the animal, feeling around. Frank wrinkled his nose in disgust. Tommy examined the skull and the teeth and what was left of the lower jaw, which came off in his hand.

"Arf, arf!" he said, jabbing the jaw at his friend.

"Very funny," DeGidio said, flinching nevertheless.

"Can you grab the metal detector from the back of the Jeep?" Tommy asked.

"Why?" DeGidio asked. "You think this thing ate somebody's watch?"

Tommy told DeGidio how to turn the detector on and then had him pass the dish over the mangled corpse while Tommy held it. The detector beeped as the dish passed over what Tommy assumed had to be the dog's hip bone. He dug his fingers into the soft flesh, felt a lump, took out his Boy Scout knife, made an incision, and removed a small plastic vial about an inch long, capped at either end with a metal plug.

"What the heck is that?" DeGidio asked.

"It's a microchip," Tommy said, backing away from the corpse and shining his flashlight on the plastic vial. "They inject them under the skin when they're puppies so that if they ever get lost or stolen, you can identify them if somebody turns them in. The vet or the animal control officer will have a scanner that can read the identification code. This dog's name is Molly. The vet will be able to get you the owner's phone number. When you call, just tell them she died of natural causes."

"So what did she really die of?" Frank asked.

"See how the chip is melted?" Tommy said, shining the light on it, then on the carcass. "And this blackened tissue here. I think somebody lit her on fire. From the inside."

He handed the microchip to DeGidio, who put it in his shirt pocket.

"Oh, man," Frank said. He looked like he might be sick. "I swear, Tommy, the hardest part of this job is seeing what people do to animals."

"If it makes you feel better, she was probably dead before he burned her," Tommy said.

"It doesn't."

"Thanks, Frank," Tommy said, pulling off his latex gloves and throwing them in the Dumpster with the carcass before getting back in the Jeep. "I owe you one."

"You guys have any idea who did that?" DeGidio said, glancing toward the Dumpster.

"No," Tommy said. "But we might be getting closer."

34.

Dani was waiting for Tommy in The Pub, staring at the fire blazing in the large stone fireplace, when her phone rang. She'd just ended a long call with Stuart and thought he was calling her back. Davis Fish had filed a petition stating that Logan would be unable to give testimony due to a medical condition. Dani had wondered out loud if "guilty conscience" qualified as a medical condition.

She glanced at her caller ID; it said "Unknown Caller."

"Danielle Harris," she said.

"Ed Stanley," the man said. "I'm a friend of your grandfather's."

"Oh yes, sure," she said. "From the State Department. Thank you for getting back to me."

"You had a matter you asked me to look into," Ed Stanley said. "You e-mailed me about an orphanage in Moscow."

"Yes, I did," Dani said.

"Well, I'm happy to help," he said, then paused.

"If it would be easier for you to e-mail me . . . ," Dani offered.

"No, no," the man said. "It's just that . . . well, you work for the government in Russia for over thirty years, you think you've seen everything. But this is a little disturbing."

"What did you find out?"

He told her he'd contacted a Russian politician he'd known who still wielded enough influence to get answers other people might not be able to get.

"You can waste a lot of money in Russia if you don't know the right people to bribe," Mr. Stanley told her. "I gave him the names and the identification numbers you gave me, and he made some inquiries. He said it wasn't easy. Tell me—do the people who adopted the boy you mentioned know anything about his story?"

"Just what I told you. They haven't tried contacting the orphanage. I think Amos's adoptive parents were afraid his birth parents might try to get in touch with him if they knew where he was."

"Well," Mr. Stanley said, "you can tell them they don't have anything to worry about. Do you have something to write with?"

"I've got it," Dani said, finding a pen and a small notebook in her bag. "Go ahead."

"Amos was born Alex Kalenninov," Mr. Stanley said. "His father, Sergei, was a low-level KGB goon. State files had him as an alcoholic. He lost his job because of it, and believe me, if you lose your job in Russia because you drink too much, you *really* drink too much. The mother, Sonya, was a drug addict. Or still is, if she's still alive, but my source thinks she's not."

"And the father? Is he alive?"

"No."

"But?"

"The father abused his children," Mr. Stanley said. "In pretty much every way you can imagine. 'Horrible' only scratches the surface. Alex had three older brothers. One was murdered a few years ago, one committed suicide shortly after that, and the third is currently a guest of the state, for carrying on the family tradition. I'm not about to defend the Soviet penal system, but for every innocent Alexander Solzhenitsyn or Mikhail Trepashkin in the Gulag, there're ten others you wouldn't want anywhere else."

"What happened to the father?" Dani asked.

"Alex killed his father, Dani," Mr. Stanley said. "When he was five. The KGB element in the government, and that goes all the way up to the Kremlin, buried the details to protect one of their own and farmed the brothers out to separate orphanages."

"May I ask how he killed his father?"

"He hit him with an ax. Repeatedly. While he was sleeping. And when he was done . . ."

It was clear that the man did not wish to continue. Dani recalled an old nursery rhyme about Lizzie Borden.

"It's all right," she said. "I don't think the details are important."

Ed Stanley explained that the KGB never revealed why they left five-year-old Alex Kalenninov on the orphanage's doorstep. At the time, the number of people waiting to adopt children from the Soviet Union was far greater than the number of available children. Placing Alex in a home in America was easily accomplished. The adoption agency didn't know Alex's history when the Kasdens chose him.

As the older man spoke, Dani saw Tommy in the doorway and waved to him. When he sat down, Dani put her thumb over the microphone of her BlackBerry and whispered that she was talking to the man from the State Department. Tommy asked if he could have a word with him when she was done.

"You've been very helpful," Dani said finally. "This is useful information."

"May I ask," Mr. Stanley said, "is Alex in trouble?"

"We're not sure," Dani said. "He may be connected to something. I have a friend who wants a word with you." She handed her phone to Tommy.

"Real quick," Tommy said, "I just wondered if you knew what the Russian word *igun* means? Uh-huh. Uh-huh. Thanks." He hung up and gave her back her cell. "Tell you later. You eat already?"

"Not hungry," she said. "Are you?"

"A little."

The Pub was just off the square in an old mill building next to a man-made waterfall. It was as fancy as the Miss Salem Diner was plain, but at the same time, it was a gathering spot where horse people and CEOs and celebrities could find a dark corner of their own or mingle with the auto mechanics and soccer moms. The decorations were equestrian, saddles and bridles and riding crops and carriage traces and whippletrees on the walls, mixed with framed engravings of horses and horsemen in hunt clothes.

When the waitress approached, Dani ordered tea. Tommy asked for a cup of coffee with cream and two Sweet'N Lows and a slice of pecan pie.

"Two forks?" he asked Dani.

"Why not?"

She filled him in as to what Ed Stanley had just told her, how Amos had been abused, how he'd killed his own father with an ax, and how the adoption agency appeared to have either covered up his origins or else were ignorant of the facts of Amos's early childhood. When she'd finished, Tommy leaned back in his chair to make room for the waitress to set down their drinks and dessert.

"Remember that woman in the newspapers who adopted a kid from Russia and put him on a plane to Moscow when she couldn't deal with all his psychological problems?" Tommy said.

"Terrible," Dani said. "But not uncommon. Amos's father was KGB."

"So how does it factor in?" Tommy asked.

"When we started this case," she told him, "they asked me how a group of kids could do such a thing, and I told them I suspected one person leading the rest. I said it was unlikely that you could find more than one person capable of doing what the killer did to Julie's body."

"And Logan is obviously the leader of this crowd," Tommy said. "With Rayne Kepplinger as his accomplice."

"He is," Dani said. "I'm not ruling him out. But now it's pretty clear there's more going on with Amos than we've known."

"Agreed," Tommy said.

"Have you ever heard of something called DID?" she asked him.

He shook his head.

"Dissociative Identity Disorder. I worked with kids in Africa who'd been forced to become soldiers," Dani said. "They were taken from their parents and isolated and forced to accept a substitute authority figure who told them they were somebody else. They were assigned new identities, and they lived with these false names for so long that some of them forgot who they were to begin with. Which is almost a technique with some cults, because the new identity has to do things the old identity never could. The new identity dissociates."

"I don't understand," Tommy said.

"We were trying to teach these boys how to reintegrate. When you've been exposed to the kinds of things they were exposed to, at minimum you develop a hypersensitivity to anything resembling a threat. That's post-traumatic stress disorder. They'd magnify simple misunderstandings, things other kids wouldn't even notice."

"So," Tommy said, "with Amos, if kids at school giggled at the way he pronounced something, he'd take it as a threat?"

"Possibly," Dani said. "Or find refuge in revenge fantasies. DID is more than just identity confusion. It's how the mind copes with torture or abuse that repeats itself. Sometimes people who experience something so awful they can't bear it—torture or extreme physical or emotional abuse—find a way to leave their bodies," she continued. "It's a way to survive. Especially kids who are highly intelligent or creative. Animals have a fight/flight response, where they either run away as fast as they can or stand and fight. Trauma happens to humans when they can't do either. When something so severe happens, beyond what they can process, they disengage from what's going on, say to themselves, 'That's happening to my body, but it's not happening to me.' So one part is under attack, but the other part is safe and doesn't feel anything. And with enough repetition . . ."

"It becomes permanent?"

"It can," Dani said. "In some instances it leads to multiple personalities. My boss, Sam, had a woman come in once and when he asked her what was wrong, she said she felt like she was already dead. Nothing seemed real to her. She asked him, 'Am I a ghost?' Part of being human is being able to empathize with the world around us and feel connected to it. And she didn't feel connected. That's why some girls cut themselves with razors, just to feel something real. The cutting reconnects them."

"Or why people torture animals?" he said. He told her about the dog carcass they'd found and the burn indications.

"Why did you want to talk to Ed Stanley?" Dani asked.

"I needed to talk to somebody who speaks Russian," Tommy said. "You saw the video I made. Amos asked me if I felt glad when Dwight Sykes . . . went down. I said no. But the truth is, for a second . . . before I knew how bad it was . . ."

"Tommy, it's okay."

"I know. So when we said good-bye," he continued, "I said, '*Mir*,' which means peace, and he said, '*Igun*'."

"Which means?"

"Liar."

"Tommy," Dani said, "you have to know something. There are patients psychiatrists talk to who can be crazy as the proverbial loon, but they figure out how to read people and how to push their doctors' buttons. Their madness gives them some sort of special insight . . ." She reached across the table, took his hand, and squeezed it.

"Being a private detective isn't exactly the barrel of monkeys I thought it was going to be," he said, squeezing back. "Maybe Amos is psychic?"

"Psychic-schmychic," Dani said. "Don't confuse astrology for astronomy. We still can't place him at the scene."

"You don't believe in the supernatural?" Tommy said.

"Tommy . . ."

"That's okay," he said. "You don't have to."

"Science—"

"Can explain a lot," Tommy said. "But not everything. Science can only take you so far."

She paused, thinking. What Willis Danes had told her was, of course, protected by patient-doctor privilege. She couldn't say anything about it. The figurine he had given her was in her purse. She wanted to show it to Tommy, to see what he made of it. The message was clear. *The blind can see. Open your eyes.*

"Do you believe in angels?" she asked Tommy.

"Absolutely," Tommy said. "Why do you ask?"

She hesitated.

"Nothing," she told him. "Just something somebody said to me."

"Dani," Tommy began. He was interrupted when her phone beeped.

She didn't recognize the number, but sat up when she read the text. She showed it to Tommy.

I WANT 2 TALK 2 U BT DAD WN'T LET ME.

"Logan?"

"I think so," she said. She texted back.

LOGAN?

YES.

Dani typed with her thumbs as fast as she could.

WHERE'S YOUR FATHER NOW?

FRNT SEAT. LIMO. IF HE TURNS ARND, IAM DEAD. DO NOT CALL.

OK. I WON'T.

She waited. Had Logan's father caught him texting?

I THINK I KLLD JULIE.

Dani showed the text to Tommy, who moved around to sit next to her in the booth so that he could read her screen too.

WHY?

IT WAS SUPPOSED TO BE A PRANK TO MAKE EVBODY THINK WE KILLED JULIE & THN VIDEO REACTIONS.

"That's what the dog blood was all about," Tommy said. "They needed blood to make the prank convincing."

"Then why pour it into the tree stump?" Dani asked.

"I don't know," Tommy said. "Change of plans?"

WHY A PRANK?

$$$. FEAR WEBSITE WWW.SCREAMSCHEMES.COM—$10,000 4 BEST SCARE PRANK VID. SMTHING WNT WRONG.

WHAT?

D-KNOW. D-RMBER ANYTHING.

"Ask him who he means by *we*," Tommy said, but Dani was already sending a different message.

WHERE ARE YOU GOING?

ARPORT. WSTCHSTR.

"They're flying him out of the country," she told Tommy.

They raced to the parking lot. Tommy drove while Dani tried to reach Detective Casey on her phone, frustrated once again by the poor cell coverage between East Salem and the freeway. They were on 684, tearing south at speeds topping a hundred mph, before Dani was able to get through to the dispatcher.

It took a minute for the dispatcher to reach Phil. It took another minute to learn there were no more flights out of Westchester, and another to learn the location of Andrew Gansevoort's private jet, a black Gulfstream G650 that he kept in a corporate hangar at the end of Tower Road.

Tommy took the airport exit and followed the signs to Tower Road, navigating the corners as fast as he dared in the Jeep, not the car he would have chosen had he known he'd be driving at high speeds. He reached the end of Tower Road just in time to see a black Gulfstream G650 lift from the ground and soar into the night sky.

"I can call Irene," Dani said as the lights on the plane disappeared from view, "but I'm guessing hiring a plane to follow it isn't in the budget."

"Not a G650," Tommy said. "The owner of my old football team had one. He told me I could use it if I came back to play. That thing doesn't have to stop until it hits Dubai. Will a text message confession stand up in court?"

"He didn't confess," Dani said. "He said, 'I *think* I killed her.' That's not the same thing as saying, 'I killed her.'"

35.

Tommy followed her home, saying he wanted to check to make sure the cat hadn't locked himself in the basement again. Irene had reassigned the officer she'd tasked to keep an eye on Dani after the threatening message on Dani's voice mail proved to be a hoax, but Tommy still felt protective. When they reached Dani's house, she paused at the end of the driveway. Tommy pulled up next to her and waited for her to roll down her window.

"I think I'm going to go to a hotel," she said. "I'll see you tomorrow."

"Don't," Tommy said.

She waited.

"What hotel?"

"Maybe the Peter Keeler," she said. "I don't want to stay in my house tonight."

"Because?"

"Because it's a mess," she said. "That's a lie. I'm just feeling a little iffy."

"Why don't you stay in my guest room?" Tommy said, knowing what she was afraid to say. "It's totally private, and you'll be completely safe there. Seriously."

"Are you sure?" she said.

"Positive."

She thought a minute, then nodded and followed him.

At the wrought iron gates, Tommy punched a code into a keypad and the gates swung open. She followed him and paused when he hit the garage door opener. Six garage doors opened. He parked the Jeep next to his Jaguar XKR convertible, botanical green. His camper van occupied the next bay, and beyond that, a silver ten-year-old Ford Focus station wagon. He also owned three motorcycles, two bicycles, and a go-cart. Dani parked her BMW in the empty bay next to the Jeep that the Mustang had occupied. She regarded his vehicle collection.

"I get why you might want all the other toys," she asked, "but why a Ford Focus station wagon?"

"You kidding me?" he said. "That thing is a chick magnet."

"Which end of the magnet?" Dani asked.

"It's for surveillance," he said. "My other cars sort of stick out. This one is inconspicuous."

"You're right," she said. "I'm standing right next to it and I can hardly see it."

"That's the idea."

It was a short walk across the courtyard to the main house. Dani paused a moment.

"I like your house," she said. "Lots of stone. Doesn't the ivy hurt the mortar?"

"They took that into consideration when they built the place," he said. "You probably read about the guy who owned it before me. The Ponzi mutual fund guy? He had to sell this to repay his investors. It's a bit of a fort, but I like it."

He led her to the kitchen door and opened it for her. At his kitchen table, an African-American man the size of a refrigerator was eating a sandwich.

"Dani Harris, this is Lucius Mills. He takes care of my dad when I have to go out," Tommy said, turning to the man. "How's Pops?"

"Fell asleep while I was reading him a story," Mills said. "I can carry him to bed if you want, but he's pretty comfortable, so I thought I'd leave him be."

Mills looked at Dani, then back at Tommy.

"You want me to go somewhere?" he asked Tommy.

"No, no," Tommy said, realizing that Mills assumed they needed privacy. "Actually I was hoping you could stay the night. Did you bring the girls?"

Mills called out, "Beyonce! Aretha!"

A pair of massive black rottweilers trotted in from the television room, cropped tails wagging. Dani took a step back, then held out a hand for the beasts to sniff.

"They're friendly," Tommy said. "Unless you don't belong here, and then they're not. That's what I meant about being safe. Plus . . ."

He crossed the kitchen to a panel by the door, where he pressed a sequence of buttons on another keypad.

"The Ponzi guy I was telling you about was paranoid," Tommy said. "With good reason. Anyway, the security system he put in is state of the art. Watch."

He showed her the video feeds on his computer monitor. One revealed a pair of bright orange shapes moving along the side of his garage.

"Tommy!" Dani said, pointing at the screen in alarm.

"Relax. That's infrared," Tommy said. "Heat vision. Those are raccoons trying to get into my garbage. The cans are sealed, but they won't give up."

"I thought you said the security system was state of the art," Dani said. "You can't even keep raccoons out of your garbage?"

"Nothing can keep raccoons away from the garbage," Tommy said.

He led her upstairs. He'd done most of the decorating himself, choosing the furniture and the carpets and the art on the walls. The house was masculine, but not in a way that made women uncomfortable—no deer heads mounted on the walls or beer can pyramids to step over. He'd picked up a house's worth of mission furniture at an estate sale. They turned right at the top of the stairs. At the end of the hall, he opened the door to Dani's room.

"I have two more guest rooms for guys, when my friends come by to hang out," he told her. "The bathroom has shampoos and creams and body lotions and whatever. I just told the girl at the spa shop to give me a bunch of stuff women like. The bathtub has bubble jets, so if you want a bubble bath, don't use too much or you'll fill the room with suds. There's a terry cloth bathrobe in the closet, and just use the intercom if you need anything." He pointed to a panel and speaker set into the wall by the door. "My room is #1. Press All Call if you want to reach every room in the house."

"I think I'm good," Dani said. "Can I just ask you—did Cassandra Morton ever live here?"

"Nope," Tommy said. "I bought this place after the whole Tom-Sandra thing blew up. I was living in Laurel Canyon when we . . . dated."

"Just curious," Dani said.

"I'm at the other end of the house," Tommy said, "but I'll leave the intercom open. Lucius's room is off the kitchen. The dogs will stay downstairs."

He suddenly remembered something. "Oh, man . . ."

"What?"

"We ran out of The Pub without paying the tab," he said.

"Without eating too," Dani said.

"I'm hungry," Tommy said.

They returned to the kitchen, where Tommy told her he could make a pasta alfredo with fresh prosciutto, whip up a quick chicken pad Thai, throw together an omelet with fresh eggs from his French Marans, or she could choose from a variety of breakfast cereals. She said cereal sounded fine.

He set two bowls on the table and filled two glasses with orange juice, grabbed a twelve-pack of single-serving cereals from the cupboard and a gallon of milk from the refrigerator, set them on the table, and retrieved a pair of spoons from the silverware drawer. He tore two sheets of paper towels from a roll suspended on a rack above the sink and handed one to Dani. He watched as she tore open a box of Corn Flakes, a box of Raisin Bran, and a box of Froot Loops, emptying all three into her bowl before adding milk.

"What are you doing?" he asked.

"What?"

"You can't do that."

"Do what?"

"Mix different cereals in the same bowl," he said. "General Mills would have you court-martialed."

"Why?"

"Who does that?"

"Lots of people."

"Name one."

She had to think. "Angela Merkel," she said. "Former president of Germany."

"You're bluffing," he challenged. "How do you know that's true?"

"How do you know it isn't?" she argued. "The Germans are surprisingly creative where breakfast cereals are concerned."

For a moment Tommy felt as if they were an old married couple, comfortable with each other in a way he hadn't known before. He'd known plenty of women who were impressed by the things about him that didn't matter, his looks or his money or his celebrity. With Dani, none of that made the slightest difference.

He had to ask.

"Do you ever think about what happened?" Tommy said. "Something happened in high school. At the homecoming dance. You felt it too, right?"

"I did."

"Have you thought about it?"

"I hadn't for a while," she said. "But I have since running into you again."

"So what do you think it was?"

She hesitated.

"We were eighteen," she said.

"I was nineteen," he reminded her. "You were like . . . I don't know, thirty."

"That's a good thing?" she said. "I certainly wouldn't have thought so then."

"That came out wrong," he said. "I just mean, you've always been so . . . functional."

"You sure know how to turn a girl's head," she said, smiling. "First you yell at me for the way I eat cereal, and then you tell me I'm old but functional."

"I didn't mean it that way," he said. "You've just always been this person who gets things done and gives 110 percent. You always knew what you wanted, way before the rest of us did."

"I overfunction," she said. "I'm overcompensating. Because I'm constantly thinking I'm not good enough. It's childhood trauma–related."

"What childhood trauma?" he asked. He wanted to know everything about her, but he didn't want her to think he was prying. "Unless you don't want to tell me."

"My parents left me at a highway rest stop." Dani laughed. "No, seriously. They did. We were on vacation when I was seven and Beth was five, and we flew to Las Vegas and rented an RV, but my mother wanted to have a car too. We were in Monument Valley somewhere, and I had to go to the bathroom, but the bathroom in the RV didn't work, so we stopped at a tourist trap. I went to the bathroom while my parents were bickering. When they left, my mom thought I was in the RV, but my dad thought I was with my mom. This was before cell phones. So it took almost an hour for them to realize I was missing. I was certain they'd left me behind because I'd caused all the trouble in the first place."

"That must have been terrifying," Tommy said.

She yawned and finished the last of her orange juice. He took the dishes to the sink, then walked her to the bottom of the stairs. He thought to offer to walk her to her room, but didn't. He asked her to remind him in the morning to go back to The Pub and pay their tab.

"Sweet dreams," he said. "Or at least meaningful ones."

"Let's hope," she said. "I was thinking tonight I'm going to intentionally try to dream about my folks. Just to see what they have to tell me. And by the way, don't think the irony is lost on me. They abandoned me at the tourist trap, so I abandoned them at the airport in Africa. Subconscious payback. That's the guilty secret I have to live with."

"I wasn't going to say anything," Tommy said. "Aren't dreams the way we work through the stuff we can't talk about when we're awake?"

"Something like that," Dani said. "Do you realize how smart you are?"

"Smarter than the average bear," he said.

"Good night," she said.

The next morning she told Tommy that she was disappointed. She didn't dream about her parents. She'd hoped they'd have something to tell her. Instead, her dreams had been empty, vague, useless, devoid of meaning.

"I wouldn't be so sure," Tommy said, offering her a cup of coffee.

"Why?"

"Maybe the dreams didn't mean anything," Tommy said. "But look at what you're feeling right now. You're angry, right?"

"A little," she said. "Which is pretty stupid."

"I don't think so," he said. "You're angry because your parents let you down. You wanted them to help you in a dream, and they didn't."

"And?"

"Just like you're angry with them in real life," Tommy said. "You don't feel guilty because you abandoned them. You're angry because they abandoned you. They died. They left you behind. You're mad at them."

She nodded in agreement. As obvious as it was, it was something she hadn't thought of before. Kara Leonard had been angry at her sister. It was one of the predictable stages of grieving.

"Physician, heal thyself," she said. "Now you know why I went into psychiatry. You never stop learning. Particularly from your mistakes."

She told him she had a big day ahead of her, one that included a briefing that afternoon from Baldev Banerjee, the medical examiner. Tommy walked her to her car and watched as she drove away, but after she was gone, he thought about what she'd said about learning from one's mistakes.

Acting on the premise that that was true, he went to his computer and navigated to YouTube, where he searched for "Gunderson" + "Sykes," which brought him to the video clip of the accident, which he had never viewed until now. It all came flooding back. He saw the offense break from the huddle, approach the line and set, and he watched the defense react. He watched the opposing quarterback call an audible, and he could remember precisely what the quarterback had said. He saw himself gesticulating as he called out a defensive audible. He saw the play take shape. He saw Dwight Sykes slicing across the middle. He saw the ball leave the quarterback's hand. He saw himself make contact, just as the ball reached the receiver . . .

He clicked on the Pause icon to freeze the frame.

He studied the picture, the other players in the frame, their expressions, the referee positioning himself to make the call. What was there to learn from his mistake? He decided to search the frame the way one might search a crime scene, dividing it into grids and taking it apart one grid at a time. Even then, he almost missed it.

He noticed a digital readout of the time left on the clock in the upper right-hand corner, not part of the action on the field at all.

The clock read 2:13.

⎯⎯⎯⎯⎯⎯⎯

Tommy wondered, as he stripped the bed she'd slept on to change the sheets, what Dani would have to say about the time left on the game clock.

What he found under her pillow was equally inexplicable—a twelve-inch carving knife from his kitchen. Apparently she'd sleepwalked again, though when he replayed the interior events log from his security system, none of the motion sensors had triggered.

When he ran the troubleshooter program on his security system, he was informed that both his hardware and his software were in perfect working order. That ruled out any temporary technological failure.

To be thorough, even though the doors and windows to the house had been locked and secured, he decided to check his outside cameras as well. His exterior motion sensors would have tripped the floodlights had anything approached the house. A quick scan of his exterior events log was negative as well, as was a quick scan of his thermal imaging files.

Something had moved the knife. What?

Or maybe the more appropriate question to ask was when?

He clicked on the Begin Scan box and typed in 2:10 AM and then watched his thermal images. He saw nothing. When the chronograph in the lower right-hand corner reached 2:12:30, he rolled forward in his desk chair and paid closer attention, his pulse quickening noticeably as he counted down, waiting to see the telltale bright red or orange image that would tell him he'd had an intruder. He watched straight through to 2:15.

Nothing.

Nothing was not a good enough answer.

He rewound to 2:12:55 and directed the computer to scan the file at 2X slow motion.

This time, exactly as the clock turned to 2:13, he saw a flicker.

Rerunning it at 10X slow motion, the flicker appeared more like a blur.

The slowest he could scan at was 30X. He began at 2:12:59 and watched. Now he saw a shape approaching the house, about the size and shape of a human, but not defined enough to say for certain that the nebulous image was of a person. More terrifying, Tommy realized, was that rather than presenting a yellow, orange, or red silhouette, signifying heat, what he observed was something deep blue, verging on purple and beyond purple into the ultraviolet spectrum, indicating cold.

He watched as, at two hours, thirteen minutes, and 2.09746 seconds after midnight, the blue form approached his house and passed through the wall of his living room. At two hours, thirteen minutes, and 3.00176 seconds after midnight, less than a tenth of a second later, the same vaguely defined cold blue shape passed back through the wall, exited his house, crossed the yard, and disappeared into the darkness.

Tommy stood up and pushed away from the desk, almost knocking over his chair as he felt behind him for the wall. His heart was pounding. What was that? He took as many deep, slow breaths as he could to calm himself.

Of one thing he was certain: it was not a technical glitch or digital aberration.

He watched the sequence three more times to make sure he'd seen what he thought he'd seen, still astonished but less startled with each viewing. The temptation, one he knew better than to concede to, was to erase the file and pretend he hadn't seen it. Instead, he marked and cropped the segment, then made two safety copies on separate SD cards, saved a third copy to the cloud on his backup service, and e-mailed a fourth safety copy to Carl. He put one of the SD cards in his safe, even though whatever had passed through the wall of his house to move the knife could probably pass into the safe, and put the second SD card in his pocket.

He didn't know exactly what he had, but whatever it was was physical, verifiable proof of something. Without going so far as to say what it proved, though he had a theory, it was the kind of thing Dani would want to see.

THURSDAY,
OCTOBER 21

36.

Dani had sat in on briefings by the medical examiner for Westchester County before, but always as John Foley's assistant. Today she was on her own. The office was housed in an annex to the New York Medical College's expansive Valhalla Campus (Stuart had dubbed the campus "a symphony in cement"), in a flat-roofed two-story building on Dana Road across from the police academy. The building always reminded Dani of an elementary school. In a field across from where she parked, a flock of geese rooted in the grass. The sky was overcast. She heard, in the distance, traffic on the Sprain Parkway. A gust of wind blew the door closed behind her as she entered the building.

Dr. Baldev Banerjee was a British expatriate of Indian descent whom Dani had had the pleasure of sitting next to at a dinner party at Stuart's house. Banerjee had originally come to America to be a dentist after realizing he'd never make much money if he stayed in England. He'd changed his mind about being a dentist and trained himself in forensic pathology from a need to be of public service. He had polished British manners and a sense of humor verging on black, which perhaps came with the territory. But he was also good at what he did and aware of how good he was.

He was in his late forties, tall, with dark skin, heavy eyebrows, and penetratingly brown eyes. He was wearing khaki pants and a blue button-down oxford shirt with a black silk tie. The reading glasses he wore on a chain around his neck made him seem older than he was. The wedding ring on his left hand glowed brightly against his black skin.

273

His office was large, with a wall of windows looking out at the overcast sky, and felt like a classroom, with workstations and empty tabletops. Banerjee's computer was connected to a projector on the ceiling that projected an HD image against the blank white wall behind his desk.

He closed the curtains to darken the room before beginning his presentation. In four office chairs forming the front row of the classroom sat Dani, Phil, Stuart, and then Irene. The ME sat behind his desk, facing them.

"All right then, let us begin," Banerjee said, clicking on a photograph of the victim's face, or what was left of it. His accent was 90 percent British and 10 percent Hindi, his speech and mannerisms gentle and refined. "Julie Rene Leonard. Age seventeen. Time of death, 0200 hours, plus or minus fifteen minutes in either direction."

Dani quickly calculated that 2:13 fell within those parameters.

"Cause of death," Banerjee continued, "exsanguination due to the severing of the right common carotid artery, the superior thyroidal, lingual, occipital, et cetera, by a wound inflicted by a sharp and heavy instrument. Instrument as yet unidentified."

"A hatchet?" Dani asked. She recalled what Ed Stanley had told her about Amos. "Or an ax?"

"Thinner, sharper blade," Banerjee said. "I think probably one of those big Chinese meat cleavers. Though I can't really say it was Chinese. The action was either a series of right-handed blows coming from someone on her left, by the angle of attack, or by a left-handed person sitting to her right. She was in a prone position, lying down, when she was killed."

"On the location where she was found?" Irene asked.

"Nothing suggests otherwise. Now as to her secondary wounds," Banerjee continued, "we have third-degree burns in the superior orbital fissures, supraorbital and infraorbital foramens . . ."

You could know the names of everything in a person, right down to the subcellular level, Dani thought, and still not know what could make a person do what had been done to Julie Leonard.

"My opinion," Banerjee said, "is that the heart was not beating at the time she suffered her burns. Also that the wounds were exit rather than entry burns, as might be accomplished by something like a blowtorch or a hot iron or something like that, because . . ."

He clicked to the next screen and continued.

"You can see here that we also find scorching in the esophagus, the stomach lining, a bit on the liver, and the duodenum."

"And this is possible how?" Phil asked.

"I believe it was something she ate," Banerjee said. "But to explain it better for you, I've prepared a demonstration."

He placed on the table a stainless steel pan, two shot glasses, three packets of table salt from McDonald's, a bottle of Poland Springs water, and a pair of test tubes, each containing some kind of white powder.

"Most of these materials you're already familiar with," he said, tearing open the salt packets and dumping the contents into one of the shot glasses. He opened the bottle of water and filled the second shot glass halfway. "Over here, sodium chloride, or common salt, NaCl, and here, water. Plain water. H2O. This"—he held up one of the test tubes—"is ammonium nitrate. NH4NO3."

"Used in fertilizer bombs," Phil said.

"Correct." Banerjee dumped some of the white powder into the first shot glass with the salt. "And finally, this is the common element zinc. Atomic number 30. The twenty-fourth most common element on earth. Most of it comes from Australia. Also relatively easy to obtain."

He mixed a measure of zinc with the salt and the ammonium nitrate.

"Now watch what happens when this is combined with water."

Dani looked on as he put the second shot glass into the stainless steel pan, then poured the powder mixture into it, causing it to burst into flames. Banerjee allowed it to burn, then placed the empty shot glass upside down atop of the flames to smother the reaction.

"Fire from water," he said. "Though you also need oxygen. I found traces of zinc and ammonium nitrate in the girl's eyes and in her chest and stomach wounds. The scorch pattern indicates that the killer poured the compound into her eyes, where it reacted with the water from her tears to create combustion.

"As for the thoracic wounds," the ME continued, "I believe the girl swallowed some sort of container filled with the mixture of compounds, and then the killer pierced the chest cavity with something, maybe an ice pick or a filleting knife, something long and thin and sharp, to let the air in to create combustion and to pierce the container."

"But Julie was gone before any of this occurred?" Dani asked.

"I can say with a high degree of certainty that the poor child was gone well before any of this happened and did not feel a thing," Banerjee said softly.

"What about serology?" Irene asked. "You said complicated?"

"Quite," the ME said. "Because we had blood from eight different people. Type A, type B, type O, all sorts of conflicting markers. I'm speaking only of the blood used to draw the symbol on the victim's stomach. Separating the DNA took time. The symbol was drawn in blood from eight people, all four of the girls, including Julie, and all of the boys except the one who I gather had gone home early . . ."

"Amos," Dani said.

"Yes," Banerjee said, "though we've yet to obtain a DNA sample from him, correct?"

"Correct," Phil said.

"And we don't have one from Logan Gansevoort because he's fled the country. Do we know where he went?" Dani asked.

"Not yet," Irene said. "My guess is Nevis/St. Kitts, where the Gansevoorts have a home and dual citizenship. Unfortunately, we can't extradite because the treaty Nevis/St. Kitts signed protects its citizens."

"Actually, we do have a sample from Mr. Gansevoort," Banerjee said. "Don't we? I'm confused."

"I got one off the seat of his car," Phil said. "I sent it in yesterday."

Dani looked at him inquisitively.

"He picks his nose," Phil explained.

"Thank you, detective," Irene said. "Unpleasant, but good work."

"Cars," Dani exclaimed. "We can get DNA from Amos. During the interview with Amos in the school psychologist's office, he said his car was at the Shell station in Ridgefield."

"Thank you, Dani," Irene said. "Stuart?"

"Sending someone to the Shell station in Ridgefield ASAP," Stuart said.

"What about toxicology?" Irene asked Banerjee.

"Now this is interesting," the ME said, clicking to a new screen and showing a chemical molecular diagram. "We found all the predictable cannabinoid and SSRI remnants one might expect to discover in the blood of any random sampling of America's youth, but also three other elements. It was not possible to tease it out from the several blood samples on Julie's body to tell who had done what drug, but we got traces in the same proportion as traces in the blood samples collected from the kids at the party on the day they were deposed. Though Mr. Dorsett's sample showed only trace elements."

"He said he didn't drink any 'zombie juice,'" Dani said.

"I would agree," Banerjee said. "I don't think he did. In the others, we found gamma-hydroxybutyric acid, or GHB, and flunitrazepam, sold commercially as Rohypnol. Euphorics, which, as you all already know, render the user compliant and suggestible. However, I also found metaboloids for the drug midazolam, trade name Versed."

"Which does what?" Scotto asked.

"Midazolam is a potent amnesiac," Banerjee said, "which explains why none of the people at the party can remember anything. It's commonly used in surgical sedation. Sometimes doctors give what's called a kiddie cocktail containing Versed to small children who are terrified of pain or shots. Also used for in-chair anesthesia by—"

"Dentists," Dani interrupted. "Amos Kasden's father is a dentist."

Irene was about to speak when Phil anticipated what she was going to say.

"I'll have someone find out if Amos's father is missing a bottle of Versed from his supplies," Phil said. "Soon as we're done here."

"The problem is putting Amos at the scene," Irene said. "We have nothing."

"The blood on Liam's shirt matches the victim's, by the way," Banerjee said. "And the mud on the bottoms of everybody's shoes matches the crime scene. Also traces where people stepped in the blood that was spilled at the scene."

"Have we challenged the video that puts Amos in the dorm?" Irene asked.

"We did," Stuart said. "Successfully. Thanks to Dani's assistant, Mr. Gunderson, who so kindly obliged us with the specifications for the St. Adrian's security system."

"He did?" Irene asked.

"He did," Dani said.

"How?" Irene asked, turning to the assistant DA. "Never mind. I don't care. What did you learn?"

"I took what Tommy told me about the security system at St. Adrian's and then I went online to get the system specs. The footage of Amos entering his dorm and walking from his room to the bathroom and back again is 760 pixels. It's not hi-def, but it's pretty good. However, the cameras used by the school's security system only deliver 300 pixels. If they recorded everything at 760 pixels, they'd use up the storage capacity of their servers in no time. Which means the footage we saw of Amos was taken with a different camera. Maybe a Flip or one of the older pocket cams. The new ones are all higher resolution."

"Taken by whom?" Irene asked.

"Probably by Amos," Stuart said. "He could have shot the fake footage, not sure when but at approximately the same time to get the light right, with the camcorder mounted somewhere at the same angle, edited it, and then hacked the server and either deleted the real footage and pasted in what he shot, or just left a flag that would open the new .avi file he made instead of opening the real file whenever anybody wanted to review what happened that night. The system is firewalled from external attacks but not from attacks inside the firewall. He's conversant with the technologies. It's not out of the question."

"Okay," Irene said. "So we need blood samples from Amos." She turned to Banerjee. "Would it still have traces we can match?"

Banerjee shrugged.

She turned to Dani.

"Doubtful. The metaboloids would have passed through his system by now," Dani said.

"So what are we looking at?" Irene asked. "Logan said they were playing a prank. So now Logan and Amos—"

"Old buddies from Cub Scouts," Phil reminded everyone.

"So Logan and Amos hatch a scheme to win $10,000 from a website—what was it called?" Irene asked.

"Something like screamschemes dot com or dot net, I think it was," Stuart said.

"And this is a site where people can post their scary prank videos," Irene summed up. "So their plan is to scare their friends into thinking they killed Julie, so presumably they video the whole thing. Do we know where the video is?"

"It could be anywhere," Phil said.

"But then something goes wrong," Irene said. "Plan A misfires. What happened? Logan confesses and leaves the country . . ."

"He didn't confess," Dani said. "He said, 'I *think* I killed her.' He doesn't know what happened. He's got the whole cocktail of hypnotics and amnesiacs in his blood like everyone else. But only he knows what Plan A is. The prank."

"Who else knows?" Scotto said. "Liam?"

"I don't think so," Dani said. "If he knew they were going to play a mean trick on Julie, he would have warned her."

"But they weren't playing a trick on Julie," Phil said. "They were playing a trick *with* Julie. She had to be in on it."

Dani thought about it. It made sense, to a point.

"Except that in the end, the joke turned on her," Dani said. She thought of the difference between Logan and Amos. Logan was self-centered, entitled, and narcissistic enough to play a mean joke on a girl without regard to her feelings, but was he psychotic enough to be a killer? She estimated the odds for someone with his background as one in ten. Did Amos have the precursors and psychological predictors for depravity or violence? He had all of them. The odds that he could become a killer were nine in ten.

"Maybe that was the real plan all along," Dani said. "Julie thinks she's going to get even with the girls who played a prank on her at a slumber party in seventh grade. She pictured them all laughing about it afterward.

Maybe even growing closer friends when it was all over. 'Ha ha—I got you guys.' Peer acceptance in teens is a powerful motivator."

"Logan says to her, 'Here, swallow this,'" Irene speculated. "'It will look like fire is coming out of your mouth.' Something like that? She believes him?"

"She does if he's drugged her," Phil said. "If she's suggestible."

"So Julie thinks they're going to play an elaborate prank," Dani said. "She's going to pretend they're killing her, and yell and scream, and she's covered with blood."

"Dog blood," Stuart added.

"Dog blood," Irene echoed, "except that whoever is bringing it dumps it along the way. Why?"

"Because he knows he's not going to need it. Or they know," Phil said. "Is it Logan and Amos, or just Logan, or just Amos? Do we know Amos is capable? He seems kind of wimpy."

"Let me tell you what I learned about Amos Kasden," Dani said.

For the next five minutes, she related what she'd learned from her conversation with Ed Stanley. She described the impaired emotional and cognitive development of severely abused children. She explained how the fantasies abused children create to help them survive can develop into adult psychopathologies. She described dissociative identity disorder and how, in her opinion, it was likely that Amos suffered from it.

When she finished, the room was silent for a moment as everyone took in what she'd said.

"Wow," Irene said. "Excellent work, Dani. John will be proud of you. So are you thinking Amos is leading Logan?"

"He knows how to push people's buttons," Dani said. "Tommy and I both found that out. I think it's an aspect of the survival instinct, exaggerated to the extreme. An abused child needs to know what other people are thinking or feeling. He has to be hypersensitive to the mood swings and the psychological dynamics that threaten him and change from moment to moment."

"How does he push Logan's buttons?" Irene asked.

"By impressing him with how outrageous he can be. Logan self-identifies as one wild and crazy guy. Amos is the only guy he knows who is wilder and crazier than he is," Phil said. "But he doesn't know the half of it."

"What I can't figure out is how they got to Bull's Rock Hill," Irene said. "We know they're drinking whiskey and beer and then this 'zombie juice' at Logan's house. So they need at least two cars. Is somebody the designated driver? How do they get from Logan's house to Bull's Rock Hill?"

The room fell silent.

"Actually," Dani said, "they wouldn't have to."

"Because?"

"We don't know that *they* were there," Dani said. "We just know that their *shoes* were there. And their blood."

"Talk to me," Irene said.

"Suppose it goes like this. Amos drugs everybody," Dani said, feeling the picture become clearer and clearer, "maybe not Julie, or not as much, because she has to be able to walk. He thinks he's drugged Liam, but actually, Liam has just had too much hard liquor and passes out. After everybody is sedated, Amos takes their shoes. And he gets a blood sample from all of them with a syringe. He draws it somewhere where it won't leave a mark, and they're feeling no pain so they're not going to notice or remember. Maybe under the tongue."

"I can see this," Phil said.

"So he and Julie go to Bull's Rock Hill," Dani continued, "just the two of them. He doesn't need Logan. He puts on the other kids' shoes, one pair at a time, and walks around to make sure they get blood on them and leave footprints. He mixes the blood together and uses it to draw the symbol on Julie's stomach, to make it look like some sort of satanic ritual."

"What do you mean, make it *look*?" Phil said. "That's like the line, 'I can't tell if my wife is pretty or if she just *looks* pretty.' Does it *look* like a satanic ritual, or *is* it one?"

"Good point," Dani said. "Because if you think about it, there's no reason for the fire. Why call attention? Somebody might have seen it. Amos has something in mind, satanic or maybe something he just made up." She turned to Baldev Banerjee. "How long do these chemicals burn?"

"No more than a minute or two, I should think, but quite hot," Banerjee said.

"What's his point?" Dani tried to think. "It might have impressed somebody, like the way a magician impresses an audience with a big flourish of fire or doves flying out of a hat, but if there's no one there but Amos and the girl, who's he trying to impress?"

"Who indeed?" Irene said.

"Whoever sees the video," Stuart said.

"And just to make sure the cops know where to look," Dani said, "Amos takes Liam's cell phone from his pocket, after he passed out at Logan's house, and leaves it in the bushes at the crime scene. Then after he kills Julie, he goes back to the party, puts everybody's shoes back on their feet, smears a little of Julie's blood on Liam's shirt, and goes home. And before all this happens, he practices on a dog named Molly to make sure it all works, and when he's done with Molly, he throws the carcass in the lake."

"So why does Logan flee the country?" Irene asked.

"Logan didn't flee the country," Dani said. "His father put him on a plane to keep him out of trouble."

"We've got enough to go after both," Irene said. "Let's bring Amos in. And get an arrest warrant for Logan Gansevoort. We'll sort it out once they're in custody."

37.

Tommy spent the afternoon at the library hoping to find out more about the history of St. Adrian's Academy in the town records. He found a reference to the school as a stop on the Underground Railroad during the years preceding the American Civil War, and another mentioning it as a place General Washington used temporarily as headquarters during the Revolutionary War, but no record of the actual founding of the school. Nor had anyone, to Tommy's surprise, written the school's official history. It was a place that had long strived for privacy and discretion.

He'd gotten a text from Dani that sounded like she'd made more progress than he had.

Good news. Arrest warrants for Amos and Logan. Call me.

Tommy was in the library men's room washing his hands when he realized he wasn't alone. He turned to see a familiar face.

"Hey, Tommy," the man said.

"Vito Cipriano," Tommy said. "What are you doing here?"

"I'm working," Vito said.

"You're a men's room attendant?" Tommy said. "That's a step up."

"Very funny. It's a public library, isn't it?"

"It is," Tommy said. "Stick around, because in half an hour my aunt'll read *Green Eggs and Ham* to you and the other children."

"Don't tell me you're still mad at me," Vito said. "C'mon, Tommy—

everybody was taking shots at you after you dumped Cassandra. That's what we do."

Tommy considered his options. He'd had a fair amount of practice dealing with tabloid reporters. Vito Cipriano, a pudgy bald-headed creep with a goatee and a pseudo–New York hipster stink to him, was no smarter than any of the others, though he certainly thought he was.

"Actually, I think I got a lot more coverage from you guys after I dumped Cassandra than I would have if I'd married her," Tommy said. "I probably made an extra ten or fifteen million because of you."

"So where's my cut?" Vito said. "It's good to see you again, really. I thought you'd dropped off the face of the earth. So listen—the *Star* has me working this Westchester Ripper thing, but I'm wondering—what are you doing, working for the DA's office?"

"What am I doing?" Tommy said. "That, my friend, is a very interesting story, which would include a lot of very interesting facts and names about the case that nobody else knows. You might even call it an exclusive."

He wanted to bait the tabloid reporter and feared he was being too obvious, though he recalled what his father used to say when they'd go fishing together: *"Don't overthink it. Hungry fish don't care if the hook is showing."*

"I might know somebody willing to pay for information like that," Vito said.

"I might know somebody too," Tommy said.

"How much do you want?" Vito said. "Don't make this an auction."

"How high can you go?"

"Five thousand," Vito said.

"See you later," Tommy said, walking away.

"Ten," Vito said, "but no higher. That's all my editor would clear me for."

"Call him," Tommy said, walking away again.

"All right, all right," Cipriano said. "I can do twenty, if it's good, but seriously, that's it. I gotta have all the names."

"Oh, it's good all right," Tommy said, glancing around furtively. "But not here. You remember my house out in Montauk? The one where I shook you out of the tree? Meet me there tonight at midnight and bring an SD card with plenty of memory. And the money."

"Long Island?" Vito Cipriano said. "Tommy, that's four hours . . ."

"Do you want the story or not?"

"See you at midnight, pal," Cipriano said, washing his hands.

When the reporter was gone, Tommy waited a moment, then called Dani. She told him what they'd learned from the medical examiner. He told her whom he'd just encountered in the men's room at the library.

"What did he want?"

"Information," Tommy said. "I told him I'd give him the full story and to meet me at my summer house in Montauk tonight at midnight."

"You have a summer house in Montauk?"

"No," Tommy said. "Not anymore. But he doesn't know that."

"Phil just got off the phone with the head of security at St. Adrian's," Dani said. "They're holding Amos for us. We sent a car to pick him up. I have to be back in the morning for the initial intake. We'll probably have to talk to Amos's parents then."

"They're going to be heartbroken," Tommy said.

"Yeah, they are," Dani said. "I'm feeling the same way. When I see a child as damaged as Amos, it just makes me sad. Sadder than I can say."

"Maybe you can help him."

"Don't hold your breath," Dani said. "When kids that young get abused . . . one in a million is resilient enough to recover."

"You got any plans for tonight?" Tommy asked her.

"I have a strong desire to do something completely brainless like read magazines and watch something idiotic on television," she said.

"Good luck finding something idiotic on television."

"What are you going to do?"

"I'm going to go home and hug my dad," Tommy said. "And thank him for raising me right. And tell him how lucky I feel and how much I love him."

"Give him a big kiss from me," Dani said.

Tommy did exactly what he'd told Dani he was going to do. Arnie was listening to classical music on the radio with his eyes closed. Tommy sat next to him and put his arm around the old man.

"Is this Beethoven?" Tommy asked.

His father nodded. "'Moonlight Sonata.'"

"What would you think if I told you I'm going to be a private investigator?" Tommy asked.

"That's a good job," Arnie said. "You'd be good at it."

Tommy looked at his father, surprised to get such a lucid answer.

"Thanks, Papa," he said.

But his father was gone again, lost in the light of the cathode tube in front of him.

Tommy ended the night with a half-hour sweat in the sauna and was getting ready for bed when his phone rang. He wondered who could be calling so late at night. He hoped it was Dani. Instead, he heard Detective Casey's voice.

"Tommy, Phil Casey. Listen," the detective said, "I just wanted to give you a heads-up. We sent a car over to the school. They said they don't have Amos and don't know where he went. My guess is he's a thousand miles away by now, but you never know. I'm sending a squad car over to Dani's house, just to sit in the drive. No big deal, just be aware. Amos is loose."

Tommy immediately called Lucius Mills and apologized because he'd given Lucius the night off. Given the short notice, he told Lucius he'd pay him double if he could come back and sit with Arnie.

"Bring the girls," Tommy added.

He hung up and went to his dresser. He found his Boy Scout knife, for luck, and his .45 Taurus 1911SS automatic, just in case his luck ran out.

Faith is good, he thought, *but faith and a gun is better.*

He went to his closet, stripped down to his T-shirt, tucked the gold cross necklace his father had given him as a confirmation present inside the shirt, donned his own military-grade Kevlar vest, and threw a sweatshirt over it.

Faith and a gun is better, but faith and a gun and a Kevlar vest is best, he thought.

If all went well, Dani would never know that Tommy had come to her house to watch over her. Perhaps it was unnecessary. He hoped it was, but that didn't mean he had a choice.

He reheated a cup of that morning's coffee in the microwave while he waited for Lucius, who lived ten minutes away. While he watched out the window for headlights at the gate, he had just enough time to log onto his laptop, click to his favorite tech-gear website, and order a handheld infrared thermal imaging camera, though it was obviously too late to be of any use tonight.

When his security system notified him that Lucius had keyed in the entry code at the gate, Tommy ran for his Harley and told Lucius, in the courtyard, that he wasn't sure when he'd be back.

38.

Across town, Dani needed a night to unplug. She shut off her BlackBerry, disconnected her landline, took a bath, found her favorite sweatpants and cozy red hooded sweatshirt, and curled up in the den with a pile of magazines.

It was a good night to light the first fire of the season. The woodbox had been empty all summer so she went to the side porch where she kept her firewood, half a cord left from the previous winter's last delivery. She filled her arms with wood and carried the load into the den, dropping it on the bricks of the outer hearth. She moved the fire screen aside and built a fire, adding kindling first and then larger logs stacked crisscrossed to the back wall of the firebox. She checked to make sure the flue was open, then struck a wooden kitchen match and was about to light the newspapers she'd crumpled beneath the andirons when she sensed the presence of somebody else in the room.

She turned to see Amos standing behind her.

When she looked to grab the poker, it was missing from the rack of fire irons.

"Are you looking for this?" he asked her, holding the poker in his left hand. In his right he held a large meat cleaver with Chinese characters on the handle.

She blew out the match.

"*Vy gorazdo krasivyee, chem moya mat.' Moi otets mog by zarabotat' mnogo deneg, prodavaya vas na ulitsah Moskvy*," Amos said.

"I don't speak Russian," Dani said, her heart pounding.

"I said you're pretty," Amos said. "My father would have liked you."

"What are you doing here?"

She reminded herself that above all else, she needed to stay calm.

What were her options?

Think, Dani, think.

Amos was a healthy young man of above average size, not athletic, according to what she'd learned about him, but no doubt faster than she was and probably stronger. She gauged the distance to the closest door. She looked for anything she could use to defend herself.

Widen your focus, Dani. You have more than those two options.

"What are *we* doing here, don't you mean?" he said. "Why has destiny brought us together?"

Where was the safest place? There were no weapons in the house. Her father's golf clubs were in the basement, along with all his tools. Hammers. Screwdrivers. Saws. What else could she use? The basement was too far away.

Where was the safest place?

The kitchen is the safest place.

"I don't know," Dani said. "We're free to choose our own destinies, aren't we?"

Take deep, slow breaths.

Calm your mind.

"Are we?" Amos said. "You can't stop what's going to happen, can you? None of us can. That's why they call it destiny."

She saw his knuckles whiten where he gripped the poker.

The kitchen is the safest place.

There are knives there.

Cayenne pepper in the cupboard.

A can of oven cleaner under the sink, and ammonia, and bleach—chemicals she could throw in his eyes . . .

Widen your focus.

"I was about to put water on for tea," she said.

"You were about to build a fire in the fireplace," Amos said.

"You're right," she said. "But after that, I was going to make tea. Would you like some?"

He was blocking her way to the kitchen. She didn't dare move any closer to him. Closing the distance might prompt him to act. She needed to get to the kitchen.

"If you don't want tea, do you mind if I make myself a cup?"

He smiled. "By all means," he said, moving aside.

39.

As Tommy waited for the gate to open, he noticed that he'd forgotten to take his mail in. Something struck him all at once.

The mail.

Snail mail.

The PDF Dani had sent him had been a scan of the letter Amos had sent her.

A scan of a paper letter, not an e-mail, printed on St. Adrian's Academy stationery, mailed to her house, her home address, even though Dani had told Tommy she'd removed her home number and address from the available databases.

Somehow, Amos knew where Dani lived.

He throttled up, his rear tire fishtailing and kicking back gravel as he sped away. The blacktop flew beneath his wheels and the deep growl of the Harley's engine revved to a shrill scream as he rapidly closed the distance between his house and Dani's, a single line looping in his head: *Yea, though I walk through the valley of the shadow . . .*

40.

In the kitchen Dani filled a cast iron teakettle with hot water. It was something she could use to defend herself, but if she knew it, Amos knew it too. She put the water on the stove and turned the dial to ignite the gas. The fire was another weapon. She tried to think if she had any cleaning products under the sink she could use in combination. She had a large can of wasp spray. The spray itself might sting his eyes. If the aerosol propellant was flammable, it gave her a flamethrower with a range of fifteen feet.

Think, Dani. You do this for a living. Talk him out of it.

If her diagnosis was correct, her best chance would be to convince him that she was a human being and not an object. She needed to make him feel something. Everybody wanted to talk and be understood and feel seen and valuable. Was it possible to find some small part within Amos that could feel connected to another human being?

People wanted credit for the things they'd done, wanted to feel validated. If she showed empathy, could she receive it in return? Perhaps that was her way in.

"So was killing Julie Leonard Logan's idea or yours?" she said. "Or were you a team, like those two kids at Columbine?"

Amos didn't answer.

"Did you know he's fled the country?" Dani said. "It's looking like he's going to get away with it. With his father's money, he'll be able to stay hidden for years. I don't think we'll ever find him."

"Logan Gansevoort never had an original idea in his life," Amos said.

"That's what I thought," Dani said. "This took a higher intelligence than anything Logan could come up with, but the police think it was all him."

"Who cares?" Amos said.

"It's not fair though," Dani said. "After the way he took credit for the Pinewood Derby car in Cub Scouts, when you did all the work . . ."

"Who cares?" Amos said.

"Or was that planned too? You knew one day you were going to need him?"

Keep him talking.

"Let bygones be begonias," Amos said with a smirk.

He thought he was clever, Dani realized. She smiled, to acknowledge how clever he was.

"He thought you were playing a prank on the others," she said. "But he didn't know you were going to kill Julie for real and then make the others think they'd done it, did he?"

"*Kogo eto volnuet?*" Amos said. "That means 'who cares'?"

"How is it that you've remained fluent in Russian?" she asked him. "Most kids who learn a second language so young forget the first one if they don't have anybody to practice with."

"*Vy skoro umryete,*" he said.

"Please translate," she said. "I want to understand you."

"I said, 'You will soon be dead,'" he replied calmly. "*Kogo eto volnuet?* Who cares about anything?"

"It seems to me you must have cared," Dani said. "I can imagine why you didn't like the kids at the party. I'm sure they all must have made fun of you or hurt you in some way or another. Why didn't you just kill all of them when you had the chance? That's what I don't understand."

And then, suddenly, she did. Her own words looped back at her. "*Peer acceptance is a powerful force among teens.*"

"But you didn't want to kill them," she said. "You wanted to put them in the same hell that you're in. You wanted them to know what it feels like to kill somebody. Because if they did, then they'd know how you feel. And then you wouldn't be so lonely."

The way that Amos paused told her she'd made some kind of sense to him.

"Who cares?" he said.

Amos set the fireplace poker on the kitchen table and the cleaver next to it, out of Dani's reach but close enough that he could reach them. Then he reached into the pouch of his hooded St. Adrian's sweatshirt and withdrew a small black nylon zippered bag, from which he removed a syringe and a bottle of white powder. The syringe was filled with a liquid.

Amos set the bottle and the syringe on the table.

"Is that what you used on Julie?" Dani asked. She heard the water boiling behind her. Throwing boiling water in Amos's face might work . . .

She heard a meow from beneath the table.

Before she could stop him, Arlo jumped up into Amos's lap. Amos caught the cat. Dani hesitated. Another opportunity to catch him off guard had come and gone. She couldn't allow it to happen again.

Be ready.

Amos smiled, then picked up the cleaver and waved it in front of the cat's face. The cat thought Amos was playing and tried to paw the blade of the cleaver.

"Do you want me to shave you, kitty?" Amos said, scraping the blade against the cat's coarse whiskers.

"How'd you come up with the drug cocktail?" Dani asked. "Did you inject Julie because she wouldn't drink the punch? You put the drugs in the punch, right? The zombie juice. But why Julie?"

"Why not?" Amos said. "She was stupid. She'd do anything I told her to do."

He gestured that she should make them both tea. She considered her options. The teakettle was heavy. She could knock him out, maybe even kill him, if she hit him with a clean blow, but her odds of hitting him with a clean blow were slim. Talking him down from any sense of urgency was still her best option.

"Was Julie in love with you?" Dani asked. "And you couldn't trust that?"

He laughed out loud. "Who cares? Really," he said, sliding the syringe across the table to her and gesturing, with a lift of his chin, that he wanted her to inject the drugs into her vein. "If you use that, you won't feel a thing. If you don't, you'll feel everything."

Dani looked at the syringe.

"It's up to you," Amos said, placing the blade of the cleaver against the throat of the cat. "You can't stop what's going to happen."

Dani looked at the hypodermic syringe. She wondered how fast the drugs acted. Even if she managed to jab Amos with it, it probably wouldn't act fast enough to slow an attack.

"I want you to understand something," Dani said, hoping to buy more time. "It's not too late. I can testify that you don't know the nature of what you're doing. You don't know it's wrong. Or that your conduct is the product of a mental disease or defect. There are court rules that may apply. The Durham rule is one."

"The McNaughton rule would be another," he replied. "A disease of the mind. It's amazing what you can learn online."

"So you know," she said. "There might be a way out of this for you."

"Innocent by reason of insanity? 'Delusional thinking,'" Amos said. "*Diagnostic and Statistical Manual of Mental Disorders-IV*, page 814, I believe. If you can prove I entertain false beliefs, you can diagnose schizophrenia and say I can't appreciate the criminality of my actions."

"Do you?" Dani asked.

"Do I what?"

"Entertain false beliefs?"

"How can a belief be true or false?" he said. "I believe in the flag, Mom, and apple pie."

He moved the cat to the floor, lifted the cleaver, pulled it back as if aiming to throw it at Dani, then brought his arm slowly forward, stopping at the point of release. She slid his mug of tea across the table to him.

"Was that the idea? To make it look crazy?" Dani asked him. "Why the ritual? Did you want to maximize the terror? Or the humiliation? What were you going to do with the video you made? Who were you going to show it to?"

He gave an exaggerated shrug. "YouTube maybe?" he mocked. "Think how *famous* I'd be." He looked at his tea.

"Do you have any milk?" he asked. "Don't get up. You've done so much already. I'll get it." He switched the cleaver to his left hand and held the blade to Dani's throat while he opened the refrigerator with his right hand.

"One percent?" he said. "You don't have any whole milk?"

"I must have used it up," Dani said, feeling the sharpness of the blade against her skin.

Amos took a half gallon of milk and poured some into his mug. For a moment, he took his eyes off Dani to focus on what he was doing, but he still held the weapon. He put the milk back in the refrigerator and sat down again, gently tapping the glass tabletop with the cleaver.

The noise startled Dani. She jumped in her chair. She took a deep breath.

"The medical examiner said Julie was already dead when you burned her," she said. "Why disfigure her? For whose benefit? Who were you sending a message to?"

Amos smirked. "Your medical examiner may have been wrong. It's too bad you weren't my therapist," he said. "We could have had so much fun figuring me out. You could write a book about me."

"I'd like to," Dani said. Perhaps this was what he wanted. "I could make you world famous. Seriously. Would you like that?"

"You're pretty," he said. "Like my mother."

"She should have helped you, shouldn't she?" Dani said. "She should have done something to protect you from your father."

Amos said nothing.

"You were so helpless," Dani said. "Drugging Julie was a way to make her helpless. Is that why you want to drug me? To make me understand what it was like? Because if your mother had understood, she would have done something. But you did what you had to do and killed your father."

Amos appeared to freeze at the mention of his father. Dani knew now that she'd touched a nerve, but she needed to be careful not to push Amos any further. He needed to feel understood, not antagonized.

"Or your brothers. They should have done something about it," she said. "They were bigger than you. They were stronger than you. They should have protected you, but they didn't lift a finger. You had to be the one to do something about it. Were they the ones you made the video for? To show them what their helpless little brother Alexei was capable of?"

"Shut up," Amos said.

"I'm not blaming you," Dani said. "If you'd killed your father in this country, it might even have been ruled a justifiable homicide. You would have gotten help. You can still get help. I could help you. I know you don't think you need to be helped, because what you did to your father was righteous, wasn't it? It was righteous and holy, so why repent?

"I'm not judging you for what you did, Amos. But things aren't really working out for you right now, are they? I can help you get your life back on track."

"This would be more interesting if you were as smart as you think you are," Amos said, finishing his tea with a slurp.

"I'm not your mother, Amos," Dani said. "Neither was Julie. Your mother's the one who should have protected you. She's the one who abandoned you."

"Stop talking," Amos commanded.

Suddenly Dani understood the real reason for the way Amos killed Julie.

"Have you ever heard the saying 'The eyes are the window to the soul'? That's what you were trying to do to Julie, wasn't it? To your mother?"

She watched his hands. The left gripped the handle of the cleaver. The right held the fireplace poker.

"You were trying to destroy her soul," Dani said. "The soul resides within the heart. Or the eyes. So you burned them out. Was that it? To send it to hell? You wanted to send your mother's soul to hell?"

Amos didn't answer.

"It's okay, Amos," she said. "I understand you. You don't have to feel alone anymore."

"Shut up!" he said, raising the poker over his head.

41.

Tommy saw the squad car idling at the end of Dani's driveway. The officer was a state trooper, not a local cop, which was why Tommy didn't recognize him as he pulled up to the opened window. He turned off the motorcycle and leaned in to have a word with the trooper, and only then saw that the man's throat had been cut, the blood soaking his shirt and pants.

He tried to call for help on the squad car's two-way radio, but it had been disabled. He searched his pockets, but in his haste to get to Dani's house, he'd forgotten his cell phone.

He left the motorcycle by the squad car and moved to the house on foot, keeping away from the drive where he might be seen, moving instead through the trees.

He saw lights shining from the kitchen windows.

As he approached, he saw two people. Dani was one of them. The other had his back to Tommy, but Tommy knew who it was.

He was grateful that all the lights were on in the kitchen. It meant that no one inside the kitchen would be able to see out into the yard.

He stepped quietly onto Dani's back porch and drew his gun. From where he stood, Tommy couldn't get a clear shot at Amos without Dani being in the line of fire. He wished he'd found time to practice with it, given that he'd never fired it before. He realized, upon closer examination of the weapon, that it also would have been a good idea to put the bullets

he'd unloaded when he'd slept on the floor of Dani's bedroom back in the gun before he left his house.

When he saw Amos raise the poker, he was out of options.

Tommy flipped the switch.

He charged full speed, striking the lock stiles above the midrail with the top of his head, his forearms taking the rest of the blow, the doors splintering inward as glass flew across the kitchen.

Dani screamed.

Amos turned and brought his arm down, cracking the brass fireplace poker against the padded right shoulder of Tommy's leather motorcycle jacket, his Kevlar absorbing the rest of the blow.

Tommy felt a tongue of fire in his right shoulder but ignored the pain and kept his head low, his powerful legs driving him into Amos as he speared the boy, the top of his skull connecting with Amos's sternum, a move that would have been illegal on the football field, but Tommy didn't hear any whistles.

Something cracked.

His momentum drove the chairs aside and tipped the table over. He kept driving with his legs, grabbing Amos by the wrist as Amos tried to slam the cleaver into Tommy's head. Amos crashed against the stove. Tommy heard the air press out of the boy's lungs, and then the two of them fell to the floor. He grabbed Amos by the sweatshirt to throw him into the cupboards.

But Amos had a strange look on his face, not quite a smile, as he stopped resisting and went limp.

Tommy let go of the boy, threw him down and moved back, rising from his knees and struggling for solid footing amid the debris.

Dani took a step closer, then stopped when Tommy held up his hand.

Amos opened his mouth, and a stream of blood poured from it. He made a gurgling noise as his eyes turned glassy and began to deaden. He looked up at Dani, then at Tommy, then again at Dani.

Tommy lowered his gaze and noticed a broken shard from the half-inch-thick glass kitchen tabletop piercing Amos's torso, the point of the glass spear sharp and coated in liquid red as blood pulsed from the wound and flowed across the floor.

Tommy moved to Dani's side.

"Are you hurt?" he asked her.

She shook her head, then picked something up from the floor.

He saw a syringe in her hand.

He watched as she pulled the sleeve up on Amos's limp arm and injected him.

"What's that for?" he asked.

"The pain," she told him.

Dani knelt beside the boy. *"Mir,"* she said softly. *"Mir. Mir."*

As Amos died, Tommy hoped to see an expression of peace on the boy's face, some kind of final resolution or recognition. Instead, Amos's eyes opened wide, as if he saw something terrifying.

FRIDAY,
OCTOBER 22

42.

Detective Phillip Casey had moved quickly after dispatch put out the code when the officer posted at the end of Dani's driveway failed to respond to his radio. Dani told Phil as much as she could remember from the night, and he took notes.

She'd been grateful when Tommy handed her her overnight bag, packed with pajamas, toothbrush, toothpaste, an assortment of skin care and hair products, and a few books to read in case she had trouble sleeping. She declined his offer of the guest room for a second night. He told her, as he drove her to the Peter Keeler Inn, that by tomorrow afternoon the cleanup crew he'd contacted would have her house looking as if nothing had happened.

"Maybe when you feel ready, we can make a trip to IKEA and get you a new kitchen table," he said.

"How is it that you seem to know exactly what to do and say?" she asked him.

"I'm just making it up," he told her when they reached her room. "I think I'm going to talk to Carl tomorrow. Irene asked us if we could come in tomorrow morning. You think you'll feel up to it?"

"Hard to know," she said.

"I'll pick you up at eight."

"Thank you," she told him. "You've been . . . kind of amazing."

"Have room service bring you some warm milk," he said. "It's over."

The next morning in Irene Scotto's office, the DA asked Dani and Tommy how they were managing. Dani admitted that she'd been unable to fall asleep the night before.

"If you need to take a week or two to clear your head, do," Irene told her. "There's a clinic in Maryland that specializes in treating PTSD in first responders. We learned that after 9/11. Nobody can walk around scooping up body parts and think they're going to come out of it unchanged. You do what you have to do. I need you."

Phil and Stuart arrived and then Irene debriefed the case, making sure they had all the evidence in place. They had proof that Amos had altered his school's security system video files. They found bottles of ammonium nitrate and zinc in his room, as well as traces of GHB and Rohypnol in his dresser drawer. Amos had borrowed a classmate's computer to send incriminating e-mails to Julie, in which he'd explained the elaborate prank he wanted to play. One of the e-mails talked about how they were going to split the $10,000 and how they were going to spend their shares. Julie was going to save hers for college. The clothes the teenagers had worn the night of the party showed blood and DNA only on their shoes, but none anywhere else, consistent with Dani's redaction of events. There was no evidence to suggest that Amos had acted in concert with anyone else. Logan was in on the prank but not the murder. Amos had planned and executed both the crime and the cover-up.

And Amos was dead.

Case closed.

"So next," Irene said, "I've got the kids from the party and their lawyers and their families waiting in the conference room down the hall. I asked Stuart to make me a list of any further charges we might file. Aiding and abetting. Obstruction. Thoughts?"

Dani felt the need to speak up. She pointed out to the DA and everyone else that none of the kids had any recollection of what happened the night Julie was killed. She hoped they could leave it that way.

"Amos wanted them to feel haunted," Dani said. "He wanted them to feel stigmatized. He wanted to ruin their lives. If we release the names, we're going to be carrying out Amos's plan. Even if they're innocent, they'll always be associated with this. I don't see the need."

"Agree?" Irene said. "Disagree?"

"Agreed," Phil and Stuart said in unison.

"All right then," Irene said, rising from her chair. "It stays where it is, with one exception Stuart and I discussed. Dani, would you care to join me?"

Dani accompanied Irene into the conference room, where the DA told the parents that all pending charges against their children had been dropped. Davis Fish barely acknowledged Dani's presence. He told Irene that Andrew Gansevoort Sr. would be most grateful to hear the news about his son and would show his gratitude the next time Irene was holding a fund-raiser.

"I appreciate that," she said, handing Fish a letter-sized envelope. "When Logan gets back, tell him he's been served for obstruction."

The next day the newspapers talked about "the Preppy Murderer." Amos Kasden died while trying to escape police custody, according to the official report. Dani read an account in the *New York Star*, under the byline for Vito Cipriano, saying that part of the evidence, a strange occult symbol found on the victim's body, had to be thrown out of court because of the bungling of young forensic psychiatrist Danielle Harris, who'd been assigned the case after her boss resigned.

"It's not fair," Tommy told her, calling her on the telephone the next day after he'd read the article. "It's my fault. I oughtta lock that fat bucket of lard in the sauna and leave him there until he melts into a puddle of grease and polyester."

"Let it go," Dani told Tommy. "As long as it's me and not the kids they're looking at, I don't care."

"I had a long workout with Liam this morning," Tommy said. "I told him to take it out on the weights. He's still pretty freaked out."

"He should talk to someone," Dani said. "Or to me, if he wants to. But I'd think it would feel a little weird to have your old babysitter for a therapist."

"I already suggested Carl," Tommy said. "Just as a friend. He has a way of saying really smart things and making you think you thought of them yourself. Liam started to cry when we were working out. I told him God gave us tears the same way he gave us laughter. All part of the same system."

"You're a good trainer," Dani said.

"He needs to know he's got people on his side," Tommy said. "He also asked me if he could come to church with me on Sunday. I gather his mom and dad don't see eye to eye on that subject."

"Claire hasn't mentioned it to me," Dani said.

"How about you?" Tommy said. "You busy Sunday morning? I'll buy you a nice new bonnet to wear."

"I'll take a rain check," Dani said. "I'm flying down to Maryland to talk to those PTSD specialists for first-responders Irene mentioned. I just can't get to sleep. I keep seeing Amos's face . . ."

"When will you be back?" Tommy asked.

"I don't know," she told him. "My reservation is for a week. It might not take that long . . . I just don't know."

"You can always talk to me," Tommy said.

"I know I can," Dani said, realizing that she'd never felt that way about a man before . . . a complete sense of trust, and the knowledge that someone saw her for who she really was. Even when she'd fallen in love with the brilliant chemist in Africa, she'd realized in hindsight that he'd loved talking about himself. She'd loved it too, loved how his mind worked, but he'd never shown as much interest in her as she'd shown in him. It occurred to her that Tommy was someone she could fall in love with, and perhaps she already was, except that falling in love was something she could not possibly think about until she straightened out everything else in her head. One thing at a time.

"I'm counting on it," she told him. "But right now I think I need somebody totally neutral. Somebody I can start from scratch with and see where it goes."

"I gotcha," he said. "I'll take care of everything while you're gone. Call me when you get back."

She drove to the clinic the next day, where she talked about what had happened until she was tired of talking about it, and in doing so created her own narrative, which she could revisit or avoid according to her own free will. The counselors explained to her how it was common for policemen and firefighters and first responders to feel they were immune to the things normal people would be traumatized by, that part of their job was to suppress their feelings and do the difficult work and not let it get to them. One of her counselors had been one of the first American military personnel to visit the compound in Jonestown, Guyana, where 918 members of The People's Temple had committed mass suicide at the behest of a madman named Jim Jones.

"My job was to collect the remains," the counselor said, "bodies of men and women and children, bloated by the sun . . . and I told myself I'd been trained for it, but nobody can be trained to handle something like that. Nobody's that tough, so don't try to be tough, Danielle, because tough doesn't work."

She explored the supernatural elements of the case with her counselors, who told her that survivors of trauma often feel superstitious, pawns in a larger game, or blessed with extremely good luck. "People think, *Why me? Why did I survive?* Some think, *I've been blessed—nothing can hurt me—I'm charmed.* It's completely normal to feel the way you do."

They were good, Dani thought. They helped her. She talked, and she listened, and she talked about her parents, and about Tommy, and then one night she was able to sleep. She slept the next night too. She felt back on track.

She'd decided not to return any e-mails while she was in Maryland, but did respond to a text message from Tommy, who asked her how she was doing and when she'd be back.

I WILL CALL YOU ON FRIDAY — FLYING INTO WHITE PLAINS MIDMORNING.

FRIDAY,
OCTOBER 29

43.

Dani had called and agreed to meet him for lunch, driving straight from the airport. In the week that she had been gone, a windstorm had blown all the leaves from the trees; their branches were bare and stark against a dark gray sky. While he waited for Dani at the Miss Salem Diner, Tommy stared out the window at the pouring rain, the kind of hard, steady autumn rain that knocked the leaves to the ground and beat them to pieces where they lay.

The old cook was at the grill with his spatula and tongs, his apron tied behind his back. His daughter was at the cash register, trying to read a number in the phone book by holding it at arm's length.

Tommy had once considered buying the diner and putting a sign in the window that said Now Clean. Business would triple overnight.

He wondered if Halloween was going to be rained out. The diner was decorated with artificial cobwebs and masks and pumpkins. Kids enjoyed being scared. If they only knew what there was to be frightened of, he was pretty sure they wouldn't enjoy it quite so much.

He saw Dani park her black BMW in the lot. She was wearing an orange North Face waterproof shell over an Irish cable sweater, jeans, and a pair of red rubber rain boots. Her hair was in a ponytail that stuck out the back of her Mets cap. She walked quickly from her car with her head down, splashing in the puddles. The waitress arrived at the booth the same time she did.

Dani ordered a cheeseburger, a chocolate shake, and a side salad as she hung her coat from a hook at the end of the booth. Tommy ordered a bacon cheeseburger, onion rings, and a Diet Coke. They both ordered coffee.

"It's good that you're watching what you eat," Tommy said. "You've got the empty calories from the shake, and then the salad—balanced diet. Something healthy, something not. You look great, by the way."

"Great? I don't think so," she said. She sounded subdued, or maybe just tired. "But thank you. You'll be pleased to know I started running again when I was in Maryland. I won't be able to keep up with you, but it's a start."

"If you want to go running together, I don't mind a slow pace," Tommy said.

"We go off daylight savings next weekend, right?" she asked. "Spring forward, fall back. I never liked 'fall back.' It gets dark so early."

"I think of the song 'What a Wonderful World,'" Tommy said. "Bright precious day, dark sacred night . . .'"

"That's a good way to look at it," Dani agreed.

"So this is check-in," Tommy said. "How're you doing?"

"Better," she said, stirring her coffee slowly. "I'm glad I took the time off."

"What did you talk about? I mean, I know what you talked about, but how did you talk about it?" he asked. "And tell me if I'm being too nosy."

She smiled. "They help you define your narrative until you take possession of it," she told him. "Sorry if that sounds like psychobabble. It's interesting how far we've come. Soldiers coming home from World War I with what the army called 'shell shock' were told not to think about the things that traumatized them, not to ever talk about it. They sent them to nursing homes and told them to paint pretty pictures of flowers. Now it's the opposite. You talk about it until you can't stand to talk about it anymore, and when you're done you have a narrative that contains the trauma. A story you can choose to either tell or not tell. That oversimplifies it a little, but that's the gist. How about you? Have you thought about it?"

"I have," Tommy said. "I met with Carl a couple of times. I know what you're saying. But for me, it's not like it was with Dwight Sykes."

"How is it different?" Dani asked.

That had been the first question Carl had asked him. He'd given it a great deal of thought. He'd felt guilty, beyond terrible, for the macho posturing he'd done on the field after knocking the life out of Dwight Sykes. He'd been at a loss to explain why it had happened.

"How do you feel about killing Amos?" Carl had asked.

"Not good," Tommy said. "But not terrible, frankly. He was going to kill Dani. He had to be stopped."

Carl had agreed.

"With Dwight, I wondered why it happened," Tommy told Dani. "It didn't make any sense. But with Amos, I don't have any doubts. I don't feel any remorse. And I don't think I should. Actually, the thing with Dwight helped me understand Amos. Did I ever tell you what happened? After the accident?"

"How you walked away?" she said.

"No," Tommy said. "After that. I went to Dwight Sykes's funeral in Oakland. His mom and dad invited me to their home afterward. I was afraid they'd hate me, but they told me they knew it was an accident. That I was just playing the game as hard as I could, which was the same way Dwight played. But his mother said, 'Tommy Gunderson, I want you to do good. Because Dwight wanted to do good things with his life. So now you have to do all the good things he would have done.' I wasn't sure what that meant, but now I think this is what it meant. This is why I was the one who got up and walked away. Because I was meant to do this. I know it was the right thing to do. Amos was going to hurt you. He was evil. I don't know how you feel about evil, but that's the way I saw it."

"For the record," Dani said, "I'm totally against evil."

"Great minds think alike," Tommy said. "You don't feel so bad when you know you did the right thing."

Dani sipped her shake.

"In a way, I don't think of Amos as evil," she said. "I mean, he became evil. He chose evil. He allowed evil in. After the things I saw in Africa, I started really questioning the things I'd been taught about faith. But the Amos you . . . stopped was evil. I know that. I guess I can't help thinking about who Amos was before he turned evil. The evil that was done to him. I think about the scared little boy in Russia, running from his father . . ."

"I know," Tommy said.

"Did you know," Dani said, "there was a second syringe in his kit? The first one had the same cocktail he gave Julie. The second one was full of pentobarbital."

"Isn't that what they use to euthanize pets?"

"Yup."

"Maybe that's what he was going to use to kill you," Tommy suggested.

"Instead of the meat cleaver?" she asked.

"Then why—"

"To kill himself," Dani said. "He was on a suicide mission. He wasn't trying to hide his fingerprints or cover his tracks with a fake surveillance video. He knew he wasn't going to get away with it. Pentobarbital is fast-acting. Almost instantaneous. He must have figured he had one last thing to do and then he was going to take himself out."

"We don't have to talk about it if you don't want to," Tommy said. "Case closed, right?"

"Is it?" Dani asked.

"Meaning what?"

"I don't know," she said. "There's a part that just doesn't fit. Why was Julie Leonard chosen to be the victim? It wasn't just because she was available. When serial killers choose victims, it's almost never entirely random. They may be sitting on a park bench, waiting for someone to come along, but they're not waiting for just anybody to come along. They're waiting for the first person who fits their fantasy. If the mother who abused them was a redhead and wore a blue hat, they're waiting for the first redhead wearing a blue hat to walk by to trigger them, even if they don't consciously know that's what they're waiting for. So how did Julie fit Amos's fantasy?"

"I thought you said she reminded him of his mother," Tommy said.

"I was wrong. Julie was a peer," Dani said. "If Amos was looking for mother figures, he would have fixated on older women. The other pieces of the puzzle fit together perfectly. Here's the crime, here's who did it, here's the story about his poor life in an orphanage that explains it, case closed, wrapped up in a bow. But why did he pick Julie? I can't quite see the logic."

"Maybe looking for a logical answer is looking in the wrong place," Tommy said.

"What are you saying?" Dani asked. "You're still thinking it has something to do with the death of the firstborn?"

"Maybe," Tommy said. "But I was also thinking—what do we know about Julie? What's unusual about her? Or illogical?"

"Her medical history," Dani said. "Or lack thereof. What are you getting at?"

"It's just too odd not to mean something," Tommy said. "And in case you haven't noticed, there's a 900-pound gorilla sitting in the booth with us. The dreams. The signs. You're looking for logical answers—"

"Tommy," Dani said. "That's what psychiatrists do. That's what doctors do. Cause and effect. You assess the situation, note the symptoms, perform the tests you think are necessary, eliminate what you can, make a diagnosis, and arrive at a logical treatment."

"But what if the answer is beyond logical?" Tommy asked her. "When have logical answers ever explained things that are paranormal or supernatural? They can't. By definition. This isn't logical. What qualifies as supernatural about this case?"

"Amos's psychic abilities?"

"Possibly," Tommy said. "But that could just be cheap parlor tricks. Set that aside. What else?"

"Willis Danes," Dani said.

"What about Willis Danes?"

"I can't tell you without violating doctor-patient confidentiality. But trust me."

"Okay," Tommy said. "What else?"

"The deer in the wires?"

"The deer in the wires was just a deer in the wires," Tommy said. "Think."

"Abbie Gardener," Dani said.

"Abbie's elevator doesn't go all the way to the top floor anymore," Tommy said. "I'm not even sure it can get out of the basement. But suppose for a second she wasn't raving. What was she trying to warn us about?"

"Satan?"

"Yes," Tommy said. "So let's assume for one second that Abigail Gardener isn't completely off her rocker. What's Satan's chief distinguishing characteristic? Satan, the great . . . ?"

"Deceiver," Dani said.

"Right," Tommy said. "And it's not like he's some Las Vegas lounge magician pulling quarters out of people's ears. He's not in it just to fool people. He wants to destroy God's work. To destroy souls. To destroy everything. God gives us free will, but Satan actively tricks and lies and manipulates. He wants us to destroy ourselves. So suppose we've been deceived by the master of all deceivers, who wants us to destroy ourselves. We think the case is closed. Amos did it. Here's how he did it. Here's why he did it. Pretty convincing, don't you think?"

"Amos didn't do it?"

"No," Tommy said. "He did it. But he didn't do it alone."

"The evidence says no one was with him," Dani reminded him.

"No one was there," Tommy said. "But somebody was guiding him. While you were in Maryland, I read the deposition you gave Phil. You said, 'Amos, you don't have to do this.' And his reply was what?"

"'You can't stop what's going to happen.'"

"Like he didn't have a choice," Tommy said. "Why kill you? Why bother? He wasn't mad at you. It wasn't going to change anything. Why did he go to your house? Why not just run?"

"He didn't want to run," Dani said.

"I think he thought he had to kill you because he'd be in big trouble if he didn't," Tommy said. "Like someone ordered him to do it. Someone sent him. So who sent him? The same person who sent him to kill Julie. So we have two questions. Who sent him, and why Julie? And he killed Julie, but it wasn't for any reason of his own. It was somebody else's reason. Which opens up the range of possibilities."

"By the way," Dani told him, "I thought about Julie's lack of a medical history. I searched my father's medical records when I got home. Kara was his patient too. Same story. Normal checkups, but no office visits. The odds of having two kids with perfect health have to be astronomical. And it wasn't because her mom couldn't afford insurance. She had full coverage."

"So why kill someone who never gets sick?" Tommy asked. "Maybe Julie has some kind of genetic . . . thingy?"

"Genetic thingy?"

"You know what I mean."

"No, I don't," Dani said. "Do you think she's some sort of genetic carrier for a disease? Why kill somebody for that?"

"I didn't say it made sense," Tommy said. "Yet."

"Yet," Dani said.

"Here's something else that doesn't make sense," Tommy said, taking an SD card from his pocket. He found his briefcase on the floor where he'd put it, took out his laptop, turned it on, and once it had booted, popped the SD card into the card reader. When his media player appeared, he played the file he'd saved from his security program.

"This is from the night you stayed at my house, two seconds in real time."

He clicked Play.

"At regular speed, you can't see anything. Now watch when I slow it down four times."

He clicked Play again.

"See that flicker? Okay, here's the same two-second interval, slowed down thirty times normal speed." He clicked Play and narrated, pointing at the screen with his finger. "Watch here. If something registers heat, you see a signature ranging from green to yellow to orange to red. But this—this shape here ranges from blue to ultraviolet, almost like a hole in the image. Now watch. Just after 2:13 in the morning, it enters the house, right through the wall . . ."

Dani gasped, placing a hand on her chest.

"And then nine-tenths of a second later," Tommy said, "it exits. You said you were the kind of person who needed scientific proof. There you have some. I don't know what it means, but feel free to have that analyzed by whoever you think could do it right."

He popped the SD card out and handed it to her. "That's yours. I have copies."

"That's terrifying," she said.

"What is it?" Tommy asked, sensing there was something more that she wasn't telling him.

"I had another dream," she said. "When I was in Maryland. Wanna hear it?"

"Only if you wanna tell it."

"I was at the top of a cliff, climbing around on the rocks with my parents," Dani said. "And far below, way, way down, there was a pool of clear blue water, and my parents said, 'Oh look—that looks like fun,' and then they dived before I could stop them. I was terrified, certain the fall would kill them. I watched them splash, and then I saw them climb out onto a sunny rock. I felt so relieved. Then they smiled and waved to me and wanted me to follow them. But I couldn't jump because I was afraid. I was frozen. And then they were gone."

"Then what happened?" Tommy said.

"Then I dreamed of an angel." She thought of the figurine Willis Danes had made for her.

"Did the angel say anything?" Tommy asked her.

"He said, 'Go ahead and jump—I'm here to catch you if you need me.'"

"Did you jump?"

"I did," Dani said. "But that's where I can't remember anything more. I don't know if that was the end of the dream, but that's all I could remember. So what do you think it means? You be the psychiatrist."

"I don't think the answer is psychological," Tommy said. "It's theological. You need to make a leap. Of faith. And there's a risk. That's what jumping off a cliff meant. You have to take your logical, rational, scientific self and set it aside and do something entirely counterintuitive. And you're going to be all right, but you have to follow where this goes."

"Okay," Dani said.

"Was the angel in your dream dressed like a biker? With tattoos and a jean jacket vest?"

Dani was too startled to say anything in reply and could only nod.

"I met him," Tommy said. "The night Abbie first wandered into my yard."

"Tommy—we can't tell anyone. If we tell Irene or Phil, they're going to think . . . They'd tell me I need a psychiatrist."

"I think I know what needing a psychiatrist feels like," Tommy said, taking her hand and squeezing it. She squeezed back.

"His name is Charlie, by the way," Dani said.

"Charlie?" Tommy said. "Okay. Charlie it is."

"That's exactly what I said."

"What do we do first?" Tommy asked.

"Well," Dani said. "I don't know. I feel like my medical training isn't going to be of much use."

"No," Tommy said. "Stop right there. You have a lot of gifts and talents. God wants you to use them all. If I may speak on his behalf, this is something I know. Something I've said to athletes who question themselves. God wants you to be you. So strictly as a forensic psychiatrist, what do you want to do next?"

"I was thinking I want to see Julie's body."

"Let's start there," Tommy said.

Dani dialed a number on her BlackBerry. Tommy listened to her half of the conversation as she spoke with the medical examiner, and heard enough to know it was bad news.

"Julie's body was cremated three days ago," she reported. "He has tissue samples preserved as evidence, but that's it. Amos's body went out this morning. It's at the Whitney Funeral Home. He's not sure if it's cremated already or not. It depends on how backed up they are."

"If we hurry, we might be able to catch it," Tommy said. "My car or yours?"

44.

Tommy drove, slinging the sleek green Jaguar around the corners on the wet roads strewn with leaves. Dani dialed the funeral home on the way but got an automated voice message informing her that the mortuary was closed and to call back during normal business hours. She wasn't sure what she hoped to find, but she decided to trust her instincts.

At the mortuary, Tommy parked in the rear, explaining to Dani that in high school, working for his father, he'd made countless flower deliveries to the loading dock. The crematorium was in the basement, down a flight of stairs next to the dock.

Through the thick steel door, Dani heard loud rock-and-roll music. Tommy rapped on the door with a flat hand. Finally a man in his late twenties answered.

"Is Gerry here?" Tommy shouted over the music. "I tried to call, but you must not have heard the phone."

"Wait a sec," the man shouted. He stepped into the office and turned the music off.

Dani heard only a steady muffled roar. It was hot inside the crematorium.

"Sorry," the man said, offering Tommy his hand. "I'm Dennis. I have to turn the music way up because the furnaces are pretty loud and we had 'em both cooking tonight. How can I help you?"

Dani explained who she was and who Tommy was, and that she was with the district attorney's office, and told the mortician's assistant that she wanted to see the body of Amos Kasden. Dennis asked her to wait a moment and went back to the office to check a list on his clipboard. When he returned, he shrugged apologetically.

"Sorry," he said. "He's cooling down in number two. I was just about to rake him in."

"Can we see the remains anyway?" Dani said.

"Sure," Dennis said, a puzzled expression on his face. "But there's really not much to see. Can I ask why?"

"We're not sure why," Dani told him.

"We just want to be sure," Tommy said.

"Okay," he said. "Good enough for me."

He led them down the hall and opened the door to the crematorium. It was even hotter there. Dani saw a pair of ovens into which bodies could be conveyed via racks of steel rollers. She could hear the gas jets roaring in oven number one. Oven number two was quiet. Exhaust hoods above the ovens vented the fumes.

Dennis explained the process. He'd leave the body in the fire for an hour, slide out the tray holding the body, stir the pieces around to make sure everything was burning evenly, break the larger chunks into smaller pieces, and then slide the tray and the body back in for another hour at 5,000 degrees. Once the ashes cooled, he'd rake what was left into metal bins marked with the name and identification number of the deceased, and then he'd fill the urns provided by the funeral home or by the family.

Dennis donned a pair of thick asbestos gloves, opened the door to furnace number two, and withdrew the tray containing the ashes of Amos Kasden.

"Well, that's odd," he said.

He stepped aside so that Dani could see.

In the middle of the tray, as if someone had drawn in the ashes with a finger, Dani saw a familiar symbol:

(j)

45.

Tommy drove Dani home, neither of them saying much. When she opened the door to her kitchen, Arlo came running to her and meowed happily, weaving between her legs. She picked him up and stroked his fur, then set him down. She surveyed the kitchen.

"They did a good job cleaning," she said. "What do I owe you?"

"Nothing," Tommy said. "We can shop for a new kitchen table tomorrow. It's on me."

"Okay," she said. "Is that what we do? Just go about our business as if nothing's changed?"

"For now," Tommy said. "Get some sleep and we can regroup in the morning. And pray for guidance in the meantime. That's my plan, anyway."

"Sounds like a good one," Dani said. "See you tomorrow."

But her eyes said she didn't want him to leave.

He crossed the kitchen floor, took her face in his hands, and kissed her gently. She kissed him back.

He broke it off. "I've wanted to do that for a very long time," he said, gazing into her eyes. "I'm going home now, but I want to tell you something. I know you're scared. I can't say there's nothing to be afraid of. But wherever this is going—I'm with you. We're in this together. Okay?"

"Okay," she said.

He drove through town, past the diner and The Pub, both closed now, and headed out Gardener Street to where it met Atticus Road. The rain had stopped. Moonlight shone down through the spaces between the clouds to dapple the landscape with its impartial light. It was cold enough that Tommy guessed there would be ground frost in the morning. He turned left past the country club and took the turn on Keeler Street to Bull's Rock Hill. He parked at the end of the gravel road and walked the rest of the way to the top.

There was no police tape, no evidence that anything evil had taken place here, just the sky and the moon and the lake below and the town asleep.

"Put yourself in the victim's shoes," one of his criminology professors at John Jay College had advised. *"Try to see what the victim might have seen. Feel what the victim felt."*

He decided to take the advice literally and lay down atop the rock shaped like a sleeping bull where Julie Leonard had lain on her last night in this world. It had been two weeks since the murder. The stars shone brightly in the moon's absence.

He spread his legs and his arms. He imagined looking up to see someone with a sharpened cleaver.

But Julie wouldn't have looked up.

She would have closed her eyes.

Perhaps she'd rested her hands on her chest, like so . . . or on her stomach, like this . . .

He tried to picture the symbol they'd found on her body. Then he tried to trace it with his fingers. To better trace it, he took off his gloves and unzipped his jacket. He used one hand, then two.

Two!

The symbol was perfectly symmetrical, and perfectly simple to draw, using two hands.

And then it was obvious.

She'd drawn it *herself.*

He sat up and tried to picture it. Amos had poured the blood he'd taken from the other kids at the party on Julie, but Julie had drawn the symbol herself. She was trying to leave whoever found her a message. Had she started at the top of the curves and ended at the horizontals, or was it the other way around? Did it matter? Was she drawing a map?

What was she trying to say?

Omega.

The end.

The final chapter.

"Closing the book," someone behind him said.

Tommy turned and saw a man standing ten feet away, wearing jeans, Harley boots with a buckle at the ankle, a black shirt with a blue jean vest over it, tattoos, a silver chain around his neck, with long hair and a beard.

"Closing the book?" Tommy asked.

"Tommy," the man said. "Think, man—what book? The insight you just had—wouldn't you call it something of a . . ."

Tommy thought.

"Revelation," he said.

"Religion for two hundred, Alex. Revelation 2, verse 13," the man said, touching a finger to the end of his nose. "Chapter and verse, dude—look it up."

"Charlie—wait," Tommy said.

But the man dissolved, absorbed by the night.

When he got home, Tommy opened his Bible to the final book, Revelation. He turned to chapter 2, verse 13. After he'd read it twice, to make sure he understood it, he knew he needed to call Dani, even though it was late. He looked at the clock and was not surprised to see the digits turn from twelve minutes after two in the morning to—

His phone rang.

"Dani?" he said.

"I have some news," she said.

"So do I," he said. "I figured out why you've been waking up at 2:13. And what the symbol on Julie's stomach meant."

"Tommy—"

"Just hear me out," Tommy said. "I saw Charlie. He told me where to look. The symbol is for omega. The end. In the beginning was the word, so what's the word at the end? The final book? It means the book of Revelation."

"Tommy, I really need to—"

"Revelation, chapter 2, verse 13," he said. "'I know where you dwell, where Satan's throne is; you hold fast my name and you did not deny my faith even in the days of Antipas my witness, my faithful one, who was killed among you, where Satan dwells.'"

There was a pause on the other end of the line.

"You hold fast," Tommy said. "That's what Charlie said the night Abbie came to my house."

"What does 'the days of Antipas' mean?" Dani asked.

"John the Apostle made Antipas bishop of Pergamon, a town in what's now Turkey," Tommy said. "He was killed and martyred in AD 92, which is why they made him a saint. Guess how he was killed?"

"How?"

"Burned on a bull-shaped altar," Tommy said. "Which was used for casting out demons. So guess what demon they worshipped in Pergamon?"

"What?" Dani said. "Or whom?"

"Baal," Tommy said. "Satan's number-two guy. The Duke of Hell. Whose power, by the way, is strongest in October. Commonly depicted as a bull."

"How do you know all this?" Dani asked.

"Wikipedia," Tommy said. "Also my Bible. I think I know what your parents were trying to tell you. You remember when we talked about the ten plagues of Egypt?"

"Lice and locusts and all that," Dani said.

"Yeah, except I miscounted," Tommy said. "I left one out."

"Which one?"

"Water turning into blood," Tommy said. "Exodus 7, verses 17 and 18. 'I will strike the water of the Nile, and it will be changed into blood. The fish in the Nile will die, and the river will stink; the Egyptians will not be able to drink its water.'"

"Okay," Dani said. "But how is that a sign? The other things you've mentioned actually happened. Water only turned into blood in my dreams. It didn't actually happen."

"Right," Tommy said. "I think God is trying to warn us about something by talking to us in our dreams. Or to you, anyway. The one that didn't happen is a prophecy. Just because it didn't happen yet doesn't mean it won't. Abbie Gardener handed me a frog and said, 'This is going to happen to you.' And then the frog dissolved."

"Are you saying God is going to put something in the water?" Dani asked.

"Not God," Tommy said. "But if Satan is the great deceiver, it would make sense for him to try and destroy the world and make it look like God did it. I'm not going to try to guess what God or Satan is up to right now. All I know is, it has something to do with water. And blood. Which is mostly water. I think that's interesting."

"It's more than interesting," Dani agreed. "What about the stone my father was trying to show me?"

"It could be a lot of things," Tommy said. "But right now I'm thinking that Satan's throne is made of stone. *I know where you dwell, where Satan's throne is.* That's what your father was trying to tell you. Where Satan's throne is."

"Which is where?"

"Here," Tommy said. "Where we dwell. In East Salem."

"Where in East Salem?"

"Excellent question," Tommy said. "Do you realize what it means if we're right, Dani? How serious this is?"

"The end of days," Dani said. "The end of the world."

"It doesn't get more serious. And Julie Leonard's murder is just the beginning. She was trying to warn us."

There was a long pause on the other end of the connection.

"Dani?" Tommy said.

"I'm here," she said. "I'm not disagreeing with you. I'm glad you called."

"I didn't call," Tommy said. "You called me."

"Oh yeah," Dani remembered.

"You said you had some news."

"I did," she replied. "I got a text message from Phil. Connie and Kara Leonard were killed tonight in a house fire. Apparently a leak in the propane tank outside their house. The bodies were not recoverable. They think it was an accident."

Tommy paused. "Right," he said. "And pigs fly."

ACKNOWLEDGMENTS

If you are reading this now, then thank you for taking a look at *Waking Hours*. Thank you to Dr. Dale Archer, for his advice on all things psychological. Thank you, O'Reilly, from Wiehl. And Roger Ailes, who always told me "love what you do." And to Dianne Brandi. And Deirdre Imus.

Thanks to my mom for reading all the drafts and giving support and constructive criticism. Now, finally, I really do appreciate your correcting my grammar.

Thank you to Pete's lovely wife, Jen, and son, Jack, for all their patience.

Thank you to the amazing team at Thomas Nelson, including Allen Arnold, Senior Vice President and Publisher (a man with amazing vision and spirit); Ami McConnell (Senior Acquisitions Editor and friend); L.B. Norton (with an amazing eye); Amanda Bostic, Acquisitions Editor; Natalie Hanemann, Senior Editor; Becky Monds, Associate Editor; Jodi Hughes, Editorial Assistant. In Marketing, thank you, Eric Mullett, Marketing Director; Ashley Schneider, Marketing Specialist; Ruthie Harper, Publicity Coordinator; Katie Bond, Publicity Manager (with whom I've shared more frantic emails than just about anyone, and that's saying a lot); and Kristin Vasgaard, Packaging Manager (who is a creative genius). Your spirit and enthusiasm is inspiring and humbling.

Thank you to our book agents, Todd Shuster and Lane Zachary of the Zachary, Shuster, and Harmsworth Literary Agency. We couldn't have done this without you!

All of the mistakes are ours. All the credit is theirs. Thank you!

READING GROUP GUIDE

1. Each of the kids attending the "passage party" has a different reason for wanting to obtain a brief glimpse into heaven by using a drug to produce what modern medicine refers to as a "near death" or "out of body" experience. If such a thing were possible, would you do it, and if you did, what would your reason be?

2. Dani and Tommy experienced a moment on the dance floor at prom that both thrilled and frightened them. What do you think that moment meant, and why do you think it was frightening? Have you ever experienced a moment like that with another person, the overwhelming feeling that something huge was about to happen?

3. Why does Dani feel guilty about her parents' death? What would you say to her if you were trying to counsel or help her? What does it say about her personality, that she feels this way?

4. Tommy has not let his fame go to his head. Why do you think he managed to avoid the pitfalls of fame that other famous athletes sometimes fall into?

5. Do you agree with his decision to quit football? What do you think you'd do in his position?

6. In what sense might athletes qualify as "heroes?" Compare them, as heroes, to policemen, firemen, or soldiers.

7. Dani's function as a forensic psychiatrist includes, among other responsibilities, evaluating or assessing the mental states of criminal suspects who might be declared "innocent by reason of insanity." Men of great evil are often called "mad men"—where do you think the line might be drawn, on a scale of criminality or depravity, between sane and insane?

8. Do you think it's possible to dream of something you've never perceived while awake? Can a blind man dream in color? Have you ever had the kind of dream Dani and Tommy have, a dream that might be described as apocalyptic? Dani comments that in Freud's day, dream analysis held a much higher place in psycho-analysis than it does today—how meaningful do you think dreams are?

9. Have you ever gone through extended periods of little sleep, and if you have, how did it effect you?

10. Can you find any clues in the seemingly crazy things Abbie Gardener says?

11. If you could somehow interact with the fictional characters of Tommy and Dani and send them a message via Twitter to warn them or advise them, what would you say, in 144 characters or less?

"Crime novels don't come any better!"
– BILL O'REILLY, ANCHOR, FOX NEWS